LUMINIFEROS
THE OMEN OF LIGHT

11 37
PRESS

YANA METRO

LUMINIFEROS
THE OMEN OF LIGHT

SOMETIMES TO FIND MEANING
YOU MUST GO TO A PARALLEL WORLD

11 37
PRESS

1137 PRESS

First published in print in Great Britain in 2023
1

A CIP catalogue record for this book
is available from the British Library.

ISBN 978-1-7392-6261-7

Printed and bound in Great Britain by Clays Ltd, Elcograf S.p.A.

Papers used by 1137 PRESS are from well-managed forests
and other responsible sources.

www.yanametro.com

To my mother.

Even after physical death, she – my holy guardian
angel – has never stopped protecting me.

CONTENTS

CHAPTER 1
MADNESS
1

CHAPTER 2
RAVEN
17

CHAPTER 3
OMNIA
33

CHAPTER 4
WARRIOR
50

CHAPTER 5
VOICE
66

CHAPTER 6
SAVIOUR
85

CHAPTER 7
SHAMAN
104

CHAPTER 8   121
TÊTE-À-TÊTE

CHAPTER 9   140
ENGAGEMENT

CHAPTER 10   153
WALTZ

CHAPTER 11   168
REVELATION

CHAPTER 12   183
LUMINIFEROS

CHAPTER 13   201
OFFER

CHAPTER 14   222
MISSION

CHAPTER 15   242
PEACE

CHAPTER 16   262
INFATUATION

CHAPTER 17   281
CALATHEA

CHAPTER 18   299
SACRIFICE

CHAPTER 19   316
FAITH

CHAPTER 20   336
FAMILY

CHAPTER 21   351
GARGOYLE

'Who in the world am I? Ah, that's the great puzzle.'

LEWIS CARROLL
Alice's Adventures in Wonderland

CHAPTER 1

MADNESS

I DIDN'T KNOW who I was anymore.

People around me were growing up, filling in available slots of identities: a friend, lover, daughter, son, mother, father – you name it. They were contributing somehow and fitting into the fabric of this society, while I was an outcast even among outcasts. I'd tried to be normal. I really had. But the burning desire to find *that world* never let me go.

Back at the orphanage, Dr Blake struggled to convince me that my dreams of having been born in another world were a mere fiction my subconscious had made up to replace real, most likely extremely tragic, memories. She was scared of me... and now I was scared of myself. How many more years of fruitless searching did I need to finally admit that she was right? It was time to move on.

But if it was the right thing to do, why did it feel so wrong?

Something cracked in the crown of a gnarled oak I passed by on my way home. Just a dull snap that thundered in my restless mind, skittering a shudder down my spine. I peered through sunbeams twinkling against the background of yellowing leaves. They swayed as if an invisible bird had just fluttered away. How strange…

A moment passed and the tree stilled, teasing my mind into thinking it didn't happen at all.

Hallucinations? I wouldn't be surprised. Things kept going from bad to worse.

I closed my eyes, waiting for the flashes of sunbeams to stop bursting behind my closed eyelids. When I opened them, I still squinted like a mole. The morning freshness had given way to the heat of yet another cloudless, sweltering September day.

Continuing on my way, I kept looking back over my shoulder. Certainly, there was a bird in that tree. I'd just missed it in the beams of light…

Willing myself to stop thinking about it, I arrived home and, when I walked into the foyer, a humongous black poodle jumped up on me, licking my face.

'Lukshi, enough!'

Against my will, I smiled, trying to dodge her kisses. I might have even let her continue, but the intoxicating stench of her matted fur made me feel dizzy. So many times I wanted to wash her but didn't know how to suggest it to Madame DuPont – my landlord. Lukshi's scent, mixed with dust and stale cigarette smoke, was the constant atmosphere of the once glorious house. It had given me a blinding headache my first few days here, but at the time, I'd been searching for a place to live for months. I had no job and no proper paperwork, so most landlords wanted to steer clear.

But despite the stench, I grew to like this house. Nested close to a vast forest just twenty minutes away from Paris, it was an austere building – two floors and an attic under a gable roof – but inside there were thousands of books and bizarre, oil-painted pictures covering almost all the walls. Although this treasure trove lay under a thick layer of dust, it still made up for the smell.

Among the thrillers, classics, and textbooks on music and art, I found shelves of books on myths and legends, various philosophies, science and nature. The myths and legends didn't interest me anymore. I'd been in an orphanage until I was sixteen, then I'd worked in a library for two years and read every book on the subject I could lay my hands on, trying to find answers to my questions about the world I had seen in my dreams for as long as I could remember. Most authors were sceptics, considering the worlds of fairies, sirens and other fantastic creatures to be fables written to express some psychological truth or maintain the spirit. Others, assuming that myths were rooted in history, offered rather speculative ideas that could be neither confirmed nor refuted.

Recently I'd been spending more time reading philosophy and science, trying to find at least some theoretical basis that could explain the existence of an invisible parallel world. My feeble attempt to grasp the nature of reality had led me into Plato's cave and through various Eastern philosophies to quantum theory and Kabbalah. I'd filled my head with different thinking on the question but still never found an answer – where is that world and how do I get into it?

I climbed the creaking wooden stairs to the attic where my tiny room was, opened the door and, without changing my clothes, flopped down on my bed with such force that the squeak of the old springs echoed through the house. Someone being swallowed by a fish head with legs looked down at me from the picture hanging on the wall – Hieronymus Bosch's take on parallel worlds.

I sighed.

3

The blazing sun heated my room to greenhouse temperatures, but still it was better than sleeping on the street. I had tried both. And unlike the orphanage, here I had privacy and autonomy – this place was entirely mine. And the price was—

The rent!

I grabbed my phone to check the date. The second of September.

Damn!

I forgot to pay my rent again.

Feeling a drop of sweat running down my spine, I recalled Madame DuPont's twitching face when I was late paying her last time, her telling me to pack my stuff and clear out. There was no chance she'd let me stay.

My room turned into a scalding furnace. I was breathing stuffy air in abrupt quick gulps, my empty stomach twisted into knots.

'Stop it!' I ordered myself, taking a deep breath. In through the nose, out through the mouth.

Maybe it was the right time to give up entirely on that world and return to England. After all, I had come to France six months ago because... because my mother had summoned me in a dream. I'd followed a delusion, thinking it was a sign. I'd always been drawn to this country and studied French for a few years at the orphanage. But now it seemed just stupid. I had to give it up and start living. I wasn't going to find a portal to the parallel world here. Six months had passed. Everything remained ordinary, calm, dead.

Maybe the library in London would hire me back and I could spend my life escaping into fictional worlds far more interesting than my own. I could join imaginary heroes on their perilous journeys, replacing my sorrows with their victories, my emptiness with the audacity of their brave hearts.

4

Taking the money from my wallet, I went to Madame DuPont's room, but she had already left. I returned to my attic and, worn out by the sun and worry, soon plunged into the world of dreams.

I WAS RUSHING through the deep woods, pushing through branches of fir and cypress. Their soft young needles didn't hurt me. In fact, they seemed to give me part of their energy, and I used it to run faster towards the house I'd been searching for all my life.

I couldn't believe I'd found my family and was moments away from meeting them.

I stopped in front of an arch bridge that spanned a foamy mountain river, rumbling in a narrow rocky gorge. A little house with one conical, vaguely Victorian tower covered in a dense net of crimson ivy nestled on the other side. A few moments passed and I found myself on the doorstep of the house – our house – listening to loud childish laughter from inside. My hands were shaking, but I reached for the doorknob and opened the door.

A dark spiral staircase led to the top of the mysterious tower, but the children's laughter came from further along the hallway. I walked into the stone-walled living room with the coffered wood ceiling and majestic granite fireplace carved with ivy and roses. A fire crackled inside it, filling the room with comfort and warmth. Antique lanterns mounted on the stone walls held tiny golden lights, like hundreds of will-o'-the-wisps floating around them instead of candles. They scattered the gloom of the autumn twilight falling over the forest outside.

A brown hooked rug lay next to the fireplace with rocking chairs on either side of it. I remembered my mother sitting in one of them, humming some tune and knitting a scarf or maybe a pair of socks. Her velvety voice was an angel's lullaby to my ears, and I often lay down on this thick carpet, falling asleep at her feet like a faithful dog.

Now a young boy was sitting there – close to the hearth, protecting a young girl from the fire and watching her try to walk. Unsteady on her tiny feet, she fell over but got up again as determined as ever, and the boy was there to give her a helping hand. I glanced into the bright green eyes of the cheerful girl and gasped.

Another dream. The baby girl was me.

So carefree, so happy. She didn't know loneliness, loss or grief. She'd been loved unconditionally all of her life and lived in security and peace. Remembering this, how could I settle for anything less? How could I forget my past and move forward?

I left the children behind and went down the hall to the kitchen, where a tall man was standing by a stained-glass window of a blooming white lotus, deep in thought. A red-bearded household spirit entered, passing next to me, holding the hand of baby me who beamed at the sight of her – my – father. Smiling, he picked her up and held her above his head. She giggled and spread her arms as if they were wings – as if she was flying like a bird. I gulped...

'Goodbye, Father.'

Holding my breath, I glided into the master bedroom. There was my mother feeding baby me on the four-poster bed with carved mahogany columns, half-covered by emerald folds of velvet canopy. The golden lamplight lit up her glowing skin and made her green eyes shine even brighter. Just for a moment, I dissolved into the memory of her warm embrace, and it torched my plan of forgetting about my family the way napalm burned through a thin bush of dry grass. I walked over to her—

Suddenly, baby me disappeared from her arms.

'My sweetheart,' she whispered, her eyes meeting mine.

I froze a moment, then threw myself into her arms. 'I'm so sorry.'

She held me close, stroking my back, and I felt as if I was being embraced by a radiant, merciful, unattainable goddess. If I could, I would stop time just to live in this moment, just to be with her forever.

'Lilly, you have nothing to apologise for.'

'I can't do this anymore. The search is killing me. If only you could tell me where you are and how I can get there. Tell me the name of that forest I was born in. Tell me anything I could use to return home.'

'Soon, my dear, very soon. Your fate is waiting for you just around the corner.'

'Why can't you just tell me? I mean... this is my dream, right? It's supposed to be wish fulfilment, but it never fulfils my deepest wish. Maybe I'm imagining all this. You're just a figment of my imagination.'

Her lips tugged up at the corners. 'Have faith, my sweet child.'

'I'd give anything to find you, to come back home. But... thirteen years have passed. I mean, you couldn't just... I was five. Why did you leave me in the Human World? Is there something wrong with me? Did something happen to you?'

She just gently kissed my hand. 'All in due time.'

I held my breath, taking everything in. The softness of her voice. The kindness of her eyes. Her warmth. She was too good to be real. It seemed all the sun's energy gathered together would be nothing comparing to the light that filled my soul next to her.

'Mum...' I breathed, clasping her in my arms. 'If my dreams are the only way to be with you, I don't want to wake up.'

'You must, I'm afraid. The future of both worlds relies on your awakening.'

I pulled away from her. 'What?'

'You're a clever girl, the kindest girl in the world, the person for whom I and many others live, even if they don't know it yet. I love you so much, my angel. You will always be strong. No matter what obstacles come your way, you'll overcome them all, because you are wise, because you are a gift from the Universe.'

'Strong?' I snorted. 'I think of giving up every single day.'

'But you haven't,' was her calm response.

'Not yet.'

'You have everything you need inside you. Just have faith.'

Suddenly, the room went dark, as if a giant comet had obscured the setting sun. Its shadow fell over the world, like a funeral veil, plunging everything into cold and darkness. A silver lacework of frost spread across the window panes. My breath became mere whisps of steam. I suddenly remembered something – something that had been long forgotten. This growing shadow... it wasn't just a falling star. It was alive; it reeked of death and it came to Earth to harvest.

My mother got up and headed for the door, as if hypnotised.

'Where are you going?'

She paused. 'My time has come, Lilly. But never forget, I'll always be here for you.'

Her gentle murmur resonated like a thunderclap in my mind, sending a shock wave through my body. Her soul and mine seemed lashed together with an anchor chain, and now something was tearing that bond apart – ripping it out of my chest along with half of my frantically beating heart. I ran after her, but she opened the door, and a blinding silver light leaked in from the hallway, filling all the space around her.

'Mum!'

My cry faded into the void, but its muffled echo came back. Louder. Louder. At once the darkness swallowed the light. When my eyes adjusted to the gloom, I broke into a cold sweat. I was still standing in my family house, if you could call these roofless ruins a house. Sparkling snowflakes fell from the sky, dotting the smoked walls covered with ash. I traced my fingers across them. 'What's happened here?'

The calming crackle of burning logs and the creaking of the rocking chair reached my ears from the living room.

'Mum?'

I ran to the fireplace but stopped mid stride. A man in a black cloak sat in my mother's chair. My very essence, my every cell cringed, shuddering and bellowing at me to run away. His body looked human, but he was a demon... I didn't know how, but I felt there was no soul inside. Only darkness. Utter lethal darkness... It was overfilling his body, even slipping through his skin in a shape of tattoos slithering – actually moving – across his neck and cheeks like hellish serpents. The tongues of flame danced madly in his coal-black eyes, and as much as I wanted, I couldn't look away. My mind was chained.

Just a dream... No need to worry. Just a dream.

He smirked without raising his eyes from the fire. 'I regret to inform you that your mother is dead.' Not one but thousands

9

of devilish voices rang from his mouth, stinging my ears and even my soul.

Panic writhed in my gut, but I pushed it away, not giving in to feelings. This was exactly what he wanted...

She was alive. He was lying. It was just a dream.

Those deadly onyx eyes drifted to me. 'Sit.' The voices reverberated from his mouth.

It was painful to stay in the same room with him, let alone sit next to him. But my legs took a step, a second, a third. I had no more control over my body. Invisible hands slammed me into the chair.

Wake up... Wake up!

He took a sip out of a silver cup encrusted with seven jewels, gazing into the fire and rocking gently back and forth. I felt nauseous watching him but couldn't look away.

Suddenly the chair ceased moving. 'Better?'

Could he read my mind?

'Yes, indeed, I can. But one thing remains a mystery to me. I have been on your planet for over a hundred years, and I still cannot understand why humans are so dead set against darkness. It is an integral part of them, is it not? Hatred gives them strength. Separation precedes the joy of reunion. Sadness is a herald of happiness. War is the key to peace. Death makes life more meaningful...' He smiled. 'Extinction is just another word for rebirth.'

My head was spinning, my limbs turned leaden, but I gathered my strength to mutter, 'Who are you?'

'I am the darkness. I am the omen of light.'

It wasn't just a dream – his darkness was real; I felt it, and I knew once it touched me, I would never wake up again.

Trembling from head to toe, I struggled to get up, to run away, but I couldn't even move a finger. I wanted to scream, but my lips were glued.

Leisurely, he came over and grabbed me by the throat, lifting me up like I weighed nothing.

Wake up!

Thick darkness crawled out of his other palm in the shape of oily tentacles. They slithered into my chest, storming into my veins like a tsunami, devouring my soul and dissolving my body into atoms.

Wake up...

I tried to scream, but only a muffled grunt echoed in my foggy mind. He threw me onto the stone floor. My head was pounding as if with squawks of a many rooks breaking from a tree to assault me. Through this buzz, I heard a dull crack.

Wake...

The floor itself opened. Dozens of oily hands came out, like a giant centipede, pulling me down. Falling ever faster, sinking ever deeper, I heard his thousand voices pierce the murk. 'Awaken the darkness within you. Become the omen of light...'

I JOLTED AWAKE, panting. The images were so vivid, it was as if it had actually happened. I jumped off the bed and began to pace back and forth across the attic.

It couldn't be. She couldn't leave me.

I took off my clothes and rushed into my tiny shower stall, switched the temperature to cold, then turned the tap. The water should have been frigid, so why couldn't I feel it?

She was still alive. She couldn't die.

It was just a dream.

I told myself that, but I couldn't believe it, and any plans of abandoning my search for the parallel world were forgotten.

'I *will* find you, Mum...'

Turning off the water, I stepped out of the shower, and trudged to the sink. I filled myself a glass of water and drained it, then another, and peered at the sketch taped to the compact square mirror. How could I remember my family house with such precision but not the faces or even names of my parents and my brother?

Have faith, my mother had said.

My eyes fell on the cash on my nightstand.

Madame DuPont!

I checked the time: half past ten in the evening. It was late, but I had to try my luck anyway. If I was going to take up the search again, it had to be here, in France.

Clattering down the stairs, I turned towards her room but—

I backed into a wall, almost crying out at the sight of an onyx creature that was sitting on the newel in the gloom.

A huge winged... cat?

It fixed its big yellow eyes on me, and I quivered at its sharp, predatory gaze.

Not a cat.

Deep black, featherless wings adorned a body that was covered with glossy black fur. It might have been batlike but it had dragon-like leathery legs, matching the wings, and its head, vaguely catlike but with a short, stubby horn set between its large pointed ears, was enormous but at the same time proportional to the massive body.

And it was not of this world.

I took another step towards the horned catbird and stared into its yellow eyes. It was studying me, analysing me, swishing its long tale from side to side. A faint spark kindled in my heart, trying to reignite the fire of hope.

'Hello.' I smiled at the creature, and it nodded in response. 'Are you from a parallel world?'

'Ah, there you are!' Tiny, wizened Madame DuPont rounded the corner. 'Mademoiselle White, this is the third overdue rent in the short period you have lived here. You know what this means?'

The creature vanished.

'Are you deaf?' She glared at me.

I should have pulled myself together and focused on Madame DuPont, but I just couldn't. This creature was the first concrete hint that the parallel world actually existed. My parents could have sent it to me.

'I'm sorry,' I drawled, 'but did you see—'

'What?'

'A... cat.' I pointed to the railing. 'It was sitting here when you came in.'

'A cat? Never have I had cats and never will I. Do you think this will help you avoid talking about the rent? You promised me it wouldn't happen again.' She was waiting for an answer, but my mind was elsewhere.

The animal had still been sitting on the railing when Madame DuPont came round the corner. Yes, it was dark in here but light enough to spot a humongous black thing... My knees grew weak and my whole world boiled down to one question: what if I'd imagined it?

'Spoiled girl! Who do you think you are?' she snapped, her patience gone.

'I'm – I'm sorry.'

'Is that all you have to say?'

'No. I – I—'

Real. I saw it… It happened; it was *real*.

'That's it! Even my kindness has a limit. Pack your things and leave. Now!'

'Madame DuPont, I'm so sorry. I just feel lost recently. I should have kept track of the time. I have all the money here.'

She ignored my outstretched hand with the cash. 'You've fed me enough of your promises.'

'I have no right to ask you for another favour. You've been too good to me already, and yet I am asking. Please give me one more chance, and I'll live up to your expectations. I'll pay on time in the future.'

'I let you in here without a reference, taking your word for it. I forgave you two delays. You know, I also have bills to pay.'

'I understand, Madame DuPont—'

'As much as I'd like to help you, I need a responsible tenant who pays on time. Don't hold it against me, but I need you to leave tonight. You can use this money to get a room in some hostel.'

I drew a breath, ready to justify myself, but released it. She wouldn't have listened anyway. 'Okay. I'll pack my things.'

I returned to my room, shuffled over to the chest to collect my few belongings and, without delay, shouldered my battered backpack and set off.

It was dark and late, but still warm outside. The scorching sun had set, leaving the gentle remains of its heat in the air. The reasonable thing to do would be to find a hostel, as Madame DuPont had suggested, but what was the point in following reason now?

My legs carried me on while my mind floated in space, until I reached the small lake on the edge of the forest and came to a standstill. A string of small cosy houses ran along one bank, warm light shining from their windows. On the other side, a row of weeping willows hung their long branches into the vastness of the lake. The ghostly radiance of the moon scattered the forest darkness, and I imagined myself taking off my shoes and walking along the shimmering moon path that stretched out onto the surface of the water, straight into the parallel world.

Delusions... I had spent my life on delusions.

Finding a little jetty that was almost hidden by the trees, I dropped my backpack on the ground, took off my shoes and sat on the edge, dabbling my feet in the dark water.

I glanced at myself in the mirror-like surface. The only thing I liked about myself were my mother's light-green eyes, but now their expression seemed just hopeless. My overgrown choppy bob stood out in all directions, making me resemble Medusa, while my eyebrows were drawn together, shrinking my forehead and forming pained creases on my transparent skin. Even my naturally upturned lips couldn't soften this expression. And further weight loss during my stay in France had made my ribs protrude, adding to the overall sickly, tired look.

Pathetic.

My heart felt as depraved as my body looked, and ghostly memories of the past flashed in my mind as if I was trying to prove something to myself. I remembered being a five-year-old girl... I remembered falling asleep in the warm embrace of my mother and waking the next morning in an unfamiliar room with yellowed wallpaper and six single bunks. Back then I'd talked to Dr Blake without hesitation about the lush evergreen world I had previously lived in.

But had I actually lived there? I couldn't say anymore. The years of fruitless searching had dissolved my spirit, transforming me into a pitiful creature with no future and no past.

A sudden gust of wind set the gloomy forest on the other side of the lake in motion. It was warm, but the hair on my skin stood on end.

Our forest is enchanted – it is alive. The memory of my mother's words rang in my head. *It has a soul... and every tree has its own spirit. Hear the leaves rustling in the wind? It's the language of the trees, Lilly, and one day you will learn it. You'll understand what they say.*

Was it just my imagination?

I wrapped my arms around my knees. A lump was filling my throat, depriving me of breath, but I didn't let my swelling tears roll down my cheeks. If even one of them fell, it could wreck my courage and shatter what was left of my spirit.

A loud crack snapped behind me, making me leap to my feet. Something was moving in the tree.

A dark shadow jumped from the branch to the ground, crawling towards me. I staggered back and almost fell into the water but recovered my balance at the last moment, teetering precariously on the edge of the pier.

The winged creature stepped into the moonlight and my shoulders sagged.

Real. Every bit of it was real.

CHAPTER 2
RAVEN

But maybe I was still hallucinating. If so, why weren't my hallucinations about my mother, father or brother, or tree spirits, or those demons that haunted my dreams? If I'd gone mad, it would be logical to assume my visions had to be based on my conscious or subconscious cravings. I had no idea what this creature meant.

The moonlight reflected from the silk fur on the creature's back; I studied its little horn, broad ears, golden eyes. I'd never seen anything like it in reality or in my dreams. It had to be true. This creature had to be from that world. What if, after so many years of searching, I had finally found some clue? I wanted to touch the creature, just to make absolutely sure my mind wasn't tricking me.

'Are you real?'

It nodded, scanning me up and down.

'And you understand me?'

It nodded again. It was communicating with me, understanding me, so why couldn't I believe my eyes? Maybe I'd spent too much time in the Human World to see the silver lining in an endless veil of leaden clouds.

The creature crawled up to me like a giant lizard, its gaze fixed on mine. Its anteater claws could tear my flesh in the blink of an eye. It occurred to me to ask where my sense of self-preservation had gone. But this creature, despite looking threatening, hadn't come to harm me. I couldn't say why, but I just knew it.

It stopped in front of my backpack, sniffing something, as if catching a pleasant scent. Then it opened my bag with its skinny paws as easily as a monkey could, plunged its nose in and came out with a packet of oatmeal strawberry cookies – the only food I had with me. It opened the packet and picked up the sweet treat, bringing it to its mouth.

I let out a low chuckle. 'Cookies? Seriously?'

The creature nibbled a small bite, chewing as cautiously as if it was a piece of dynamite that could explode at any moment, but soon enough it purred, chomping the treat down. It glanced up at me as if asking for permission to take another cookie, and its large pleading eyes made me smile.

'Go on. They're all yours.'

The catbird gulped the second one in a heartbeat. Then another one, and another, and one more and so on until a single cookie was left in the packet. The creature took it and stretched its paw with the treat to me.

I smiled. In front of me was something that looked like a mixture of a bird, a cat, a bat and a baby dragon, but at the same time it acted paradoxically human.

'Thank you, but I'm not hungry. You can have it.'

I waited until the catbird finished chewing and asked, 'Are you from... a parallel world?'

The creature seemed to frown, shaking its head.

'You're *not*?'

It shook its head again.

'Is—' I swallowed to release the dryness of my mouth. 'Is there another world?'

The creature was almost penetrating me with its large golden eyes, as if trying to see through me. What was it thinking about? Why was it hesitating?

'Please,' I breathed.

The creature nodded slightly.

'It exists?'

It nodded again.

'The lush evergreen world, where nature is alive and forests have souls? The world where trees have spirits? The world parallel to this one? Does it exist?'

It nodded, but I still wasn't ready to let my guard down and jump for joy. Fate was not in the habit of rewarding me with such strokes of luck.

'Do you know how I can get there?'

The creature glanced away.

'Please?'

It still wouldn't meet my eyes; it just crouched as if trying to become as small as possible.

'Look, I was born in that world. I need to find a way to get back there. If you know anything, please tell me.'

Please, please, please, I begged the creature inwardly, as if I could influence it with my brainwaves. Why was it sitting so motionless, so calm, as if thinking about eternity, while my whole gut was frozen waiting for its answer? How much time had passed? A minute? Ten? An hour?

As slowly as possible, it lifted one of its wings, taking a small object from under it and handing it to me.

A golden tube?

I picked it up and turned it over in my hands. The words *Lilly White* were engraved on one side in exquisite calligraphy. I ran my hand over delicate carvings of blooming roses and climbing ivy that reflected in the bleak light of the moon and turned the tube again. The side opposite my name had a peculiar crest of two crossed hammers. One was normal-shaped, and the other had a pointed end. They reminded me of mining tools.

I unscrewed the lid, taking out a fragile sheet of scorched black parchment that engulfed my hands with a fine coal powder. The creature inhaled the dust, sneezed and jumped onto the tree branch behind me. There were markings on the letter, but I couldn't read them through the thick ash; I shook it off and found a letter scrawled untidily in brilliant gold ink.

Dear Miss White,

I, the official representative of the guardians of the portal keys, hereby decree that, in connection with loss of residence, you are given permission to live in the enchanted forest of Faivendei, located in the Spirit World, until your situation improves or until the end of your days (at your discretion). We have already notified representatives of Faivendei of your arrival. They will meet you tomorrow at 1 p.m. at the bank of the Pont aux Chats river in the Forest of Coëtquen. Please provide this letter to Omnia as a confirmation of our permission.

Best regards
Conrad,
Lead Dwarf of the Black Forest
Keeper of the Portal Keys

P.S. You are allowed to take the gargoyle with you.

I peered at the letter absentmindedly for quite some time.

'Where did you get this from?' I asked the catbird after coming back to my senses, but it just swished its tail. 'Why didn't you give it to me right away?'

I returned to the letter and read it again. And again. I stared at the parchment for a while, trying to comprehend the message, but it was difficult to make much sense of it. I started to analyse it word by word, line by line.

The guardians of the portal keys. That was an easy one – they obviously had the keys for the portals to the parallel world.

The enchanted forest. My memory didn't fail me – there were enchanted forests.

Spirit World. That was the tough one.

I lifted my gaze from the letter and found the creature's eyes already on me. 'Is the Spirit World the same as the parallel world?'

It nodded.

I swallowed hard. 'So... the Spirit World. Is it the world where people go after death?'

The catbird shook its head. Was it smiling?

'Why is it called the Spirit World then?' I asked, but it was silent. 'It would be handy if you could talk,' I teased.

The catbird gave a small flap of its wings that I would swear was a shrug.

Pont aux Chats. Coëtquen. I wasn't even sure how to pronounce Coëtquen correctly, but if that forest was in this world, it would be easy to find online.

Omnia.

'Do you know who Omnia is?'

The catbird nodded.

I returned to the parchment again. 'What gargoyle?'

The catbird grunted in response, leaping up and down on the branch and pointing its long clawed fingers at itself.

'You?' I couldn't hold my smile back. 'You can't possibly be a gargoyle!'

The catbird stared at me as if failing to understand why I thought it was funny. It *did* look menacing, and it would have looked at home perching on the gutter of a medieval cathedral. But for some reason I couldn't believe it was an actual gargoyle. Maybe it was its sweet tooth.

'I'm sorry,' I said. 'But you're... cute.'

Suddenly there was a change in the expression of the creature's muzzle. Before, I'd sensed it was harmless. Now I wasn't so sure. I couldn't shake the feeling it was glaring at me like a starving feline at a field mouse. It rose on its hind legs, its body expanded, its enormous claws grew even larger. Piercing me with its predatory glare, it straightened up and hissed at me, revealing a double row of long shark teeth.

I reeled back. 'Okay, I'm sorry. I didn't mean to offend you—'

I was so focused on the gargoyle that a sudden crack from the willow behind me almost made me squeal. The gargoyle stopped posturing and pricked up its ears, as if struggling to focus on the source of the noise. I stepped back, peering into the darkness and putting the letter and the tube in my backpack to protect it.

The crackling grew louder; the tree trunk moved through the twilight. I blinked. Were my eyes deceiving me?

I edged closer to the tree, took out my phone and turned on the flashlight. The weeping willow was actually moving: its trunk was opening up. A shiver ran down my spine, and I held my breath to keep quiet.

Inside the tree stood a humanoid creature – a tall girl with green skin, a long, thin neck and a sinewy, drawn face with an unnaturally sharp chin.

The gargoyle screeched, shaking its head as if trying to warn me. I turned back to the green-skinned girl. Her ebony eyes were now fixed on me. I stood motionless, as if the murk of those eyes had benumbed my mind and fettered my soul.

The green girl extricated herself from the willow, shaking like a resurrected mummy escaping its tomb, and I recoiled, watching her every move as if hypnotised. Only the gargoyle's shriek brought me back to reality.

I snatched my backpack and darted away. She raced after us but inhumanly quick – I could never have outrun her in a straight line. My choice was simple: to sprint to the houses or head into the dark woods growing up the hill. I bolted towards the houses.

'Lilly White!' an eerie voice hissed behind me, sending a shiver down my spine.

How did this thing know my name?

I dashed even faster. My backpack was so heavy I would have thrown it away if not for the treasured letter inside. She was getting closer by the second.

The gargoyle screeched, calling me into the woods. Going in there was insane, but that girl-thing was catching up with us, so I followed the gargoyle – only one of us had sharp teeth and long claws.

Gasping for air, exhausted, I climbed up the hill when the gargoyle disappeared behind one of the trees. I looked in all direction and to my relief spotted it sitting on a tree with long grey roots that covered a massive boulder like the tentacles of a giant squid. I reached it, and the gargoyle leaped off to sit on my back. I almost fell under the additional weight. A purple-black light emanated from the gargoyle's horn, surrounding us both with a faint glow.

'Wha-What are you doing?' I blurted, panting.

The gargoyle put a finger to its lips.

I struggled for air, trying to catch my breath, but when I heard this thing approaching us, I covered my mouth with my hands. My heart was jackhammering so loud I was afraid the green girl could hear it. She was a couple of feet away from us, scanning the forest, when her ebony eyes stopped, fixed on mine. I froze motionless like ice bounding the surface of the winter river, but under this frozen, immobile shell raged the unbridled current of my horror. My whole gut ached to rush away, for she noticed me, but I fought the instinct with everything I had.

I could swear she was looking at me, but a moment passed, and she turned away. She couldn't see us.

Why was she stalking me? Why was it I hadn't en-countered anything out of the ordinary for thirteen years, and today I'd met an actual gargoyle and this... What could she be? She was abnormally tall, and her body, arms and legs seemed disproportionately long and thin. A cross between a human and a stick insect. Fairies were the first thing that came to mind, but I rejected the idea. I could believe they were not as pretty as Tinker Bell, but I didn't think they'd look quite so creepy. She must had been a tree spirit. A dryad? Dryads were always depic-ted as ethereal forest creatures – maidens with a dangerous beauty. I remembered how vindictive they could be to people who harmed trees, but I'd done nothing of the kind. I always treated them as living and thinking beings. I thought of nymphs, but that also seemed impossible.

Wait. The tricky evil spirit of the woods... Of course! It must had been a spriggan.

'Damn gargoyle!' the monster's wild cry rang out, dragging me back to the present. 'I know you're here! Give her to me!'

What did she want from me? I tried to recall if I'd read anything about how to defeat a spriggan, but nothing came to mind.

Soon I had another problem: my legs were turning numb. I looked at the gargoyle, but it shook its head, putting a finger to its lips again. Its weight on my shoulders wasn't making things any easier. I wanted to lift each leg – it would help to get the blood flowing. But just as I was about to do so, the gargoyle gripped my forearm with its claws. I clenched my teeth, trying not to scream. The gargoyle shook its head again before pointing first at its own ears, and then at the green-skinned girl. I realised the spriggan's hearing was very sharp. But if I didn't stretch my legs, I'd fall backwards.

I was biting my lip, trying to keep my shaking body still, when the green-skinned girl cursed, went over to the nearest beech and dissolved into it. I exhaled, shifted from one foot to another and looked up, but the gargoyle placed a finger to its lips for a third time. Then it pointed at its eyes, and at the tree where the spriggan had dissolved.

'So what do we do?' I whispered.

The gargoyle folded its paws together and put them behind its head. We had to spend the night here? I doubted I'd be able to fall asleep.

I placed my backpack on the ground and sat down on it. The gargoyle wasn't sleeping either – it kept the purple-black dome up, protecting us. I sat motionless for quite some time, not sure how much the spriggan could hear or see from the tree.

Slowly my pulse was returning to normal. Being under the gargoyle's protective dome was like floating in the heart of a miniature galaxy. It seemed to consist of a billion tiny glistening stars that danced in the air, joining and spreading and emitting a mesmerising rainbow glow. I felt calmer, safer. For just one short moment this light broke the shackles of my soul, and I was free and incredibly happy.

Yes, I'd been chased by this spriggan and an actual gargoyle had come to me, but I couldn't remember ever feeling as alive as I did now. A haze no longer clouded my vision. My hearing was sharp. It seemed I had awakened from a thirteen-year-long nightmare. Tomorrow I would be in the parallel world.

I took the letter from the golden tube and read it again, lighting the page with my phone. I found the Forest of Coëtquen and the river online. It was located out in the wilds of Brittany, and the nearest place with a train station was a little town called Dinan. Time dragged on as I waited for the morning, but a few hours later fatigue took over and I fell asleep.

A STAB OF adrenaline opened my eyes before the alarm clock. I checked the time; it was only seven. The gargoyle was awake. I wasn't sure if it slept, ever.

The rays of the morning sun penetrated the tree canopy, warming my skin, but I was shivering after spending a night on the ground. I took my yellow raincoat out of the backpack and put it on.

'Can we go now?' I asked the gargoyle, and it nodded.

I got up but too quickly. The world swirled around me. I put my hand on a tree trunk to steady myself. The gargoyle whimpered, its ears flat against its head.

'It's all right,' I said, smiling. 'Let's go.'

On the way to the train station, I scanned the faces of sleepy strangers trudging to work, hoping the gargoyle's magic would prevent them from seeing it. I was right – no one even looked at the two-foot-tall horned catbird walking by my side.

At the station, I bought a ticket and boarded the train. The moment I sat down, I fell into a dreamless slumber, waking up only in Rennes – the capital of Brittany. There was no one in the coach, and I hurried to catch the second train to Dinan.

The two-hour nap didn't help. My body was whining like an exhausted child, begging for more sleep and food, and the voices of passers-by merged into an eerie cacophony. I went to a coffee shop and bought a strong espresso with two almond croissants: one for me, one for the gargoyle. Despite enjoying the cookies, it turned its nose up at the pastry, so I had both. The caffeine and sugar quickly dispelled the haze in my mind, and I boarded the train to Dinan.

Wide awake now, I was entertaining various scenarios of how 'the representatives of Faivendei' might meet me. I didn't know why, but today I was no longer tormented by chilling premonitions. A glimmer of hope overshadowed the doubts born of sound logic. I indulged in sweet memories that played like a worn film strip in my mind.

I remembered walking with my mother through the woods, her showing me the trees and telling me how to identify them by the type of bark and shape of the leaves. I believed she knew the name of every bird, every tree, every blade of grass – she loved the world she lived in absolutely, unconditionally. I remembered my temperamental but joyful, brave but sometimes reckless father, who would pick me up, calling for water horses that lived at the bottom of the river. A white mustang with a shimmering silver mane would leap out of the water towards us, and we would ride it across the surface of the river while sirens with their iridescent tails would race us, jumping high as dolphins from the water. I remembered how our household spirit stayed always invisible, trying to hide from my brother's tricks. He was a real troublemaker but not a cruel one – he had a noble soul even as a child.

Would I meet them today? I didn't know how many enchanted forests existed in that world, or whether Faivendei was the only one. For a brief moment, I recalled yesterday's nightmare, in which a demon had told me my mother was dead, and that moment was enough to leave a taste of poison in my soul.

No. I would find my mother. I would find my family no matter what.

The gargoyle was sitting in front of me on the table, watching me intently. Its penetrating yellow eyes made me forget everything and smile. They were innocent and completely at odds with the creature's overall alarming appearance. Besides, no matter how hard it tried to prove it could be menacing, I just wasn't scared at all. Especially now, when it sat there akin to a potbellied kitten, its hind legs stretched out like the three-toed claws of a small dragon. There was a thin, slightly crooked silver ring hidden behind the short hairs on the knuckle of one of its toes. I stretched my hand towards it, but the gargoyle yanked its claw back, as if unwilling to show the ring, or perhaps embarrassed about the hair. I wouldn't be surprised.

I let out an amused huff. 'You have only one hairy toe.'

The gargoyle shrugged.

'Hairy toe...' For some peculiar reason I liked the sound of it. 'Hairytoe... Hairito!' I said a bit louder and looked around to make sure nobody had heard me. 'I'll call you Hairito, okay?'

It shrugged again and nodded.

'Lilly. Hairito. Nice to meet you, Hairito.' I held out my hand to the gargoyle, who shook it as if it knew perfectly well what it was doing.

'Hairito, are you a boy?'

28

The gargoyle shook her head.

'A girl then.'

She nodded and I smiled to myself. I'd met this creature only yesterday, but I was glad she was with me. For a change, I wasn't alone.

We reached Dinan. The air here was much cooler than in Paris and felt lighter and noticeably cleaner. Lifting my head to the sky, I greeted the stormy curtain of clouds with a smile. A chilly wind was blowing through the narrow streets, whistling and sneaking treacherously under my raincoat.

As I walked along the wet time-worn cobbled hills, covered by the half-timbered houses with crooked walls leaning against one another, I couldn't wipe a beatific smile off my face. This medieval town, surrounded by ramparts, carried me several hundred years back into the past, and only the distant cars' noise pulled me back to reality.

After some time, however, I found it difficult to focus on the architecture when the mouth-watering scent of freshly cooked Breton crêpes wafted from everywhere. My mouth watered; I was swallowing and breathing in deeply, as if the smell alone could satiate my appetite.

But when I passed by a Gothic cathedral, I forgot about crêpes. An organ melody floated to my ears, and I slowed down before I realised it. It seemed these sounds, like invisible strings, drew my mind and body, as if the performer, fingering the chords, had quite accidentally created a melody that reson-ated with my soul.

I retraced my steps to the cathedral. A statue carved in the tympanum above the entrance seemed to look straight at me, warning me to keep out. How strange. I wanted to come in al-most as much as I wanted to run away.

Hairito grabbed me by the trouser leg, pulling me back.

'What are you doing?'

She shook her head.

'What's wrong? I just want to go inside for a second.'

She shook her head again, looking towards the entrance.

'Can you enter a church?'

A nod.

'So why not?'

Her eyes drifted away, as if she wasn't sure of the reason.

'Okay, wait for me here. I just want to take a quick look.'

I opened the massive wooden door and stepped inside the cathedral. It was empty apart from the performer and the organ tune that reverberated in my ears, possessing my mind and enslaving my heart. How could a melody – a simple combination of notes and sounds – have such power over me?

I ambled to the centre of the nave, not really seeing anything, not really feeling anything, just lost in the music. For a fraction of a second, a golden altar under the dome caught my attention, but I spun back to the front facade, where the gleaming instrument stood in the mahogany loft.

It seemed the keys absorbed the performer's soul and transformed it into the tune that filled the air of the shrine with universal sadness. *The Aria of Death* – the words rang in my mind. Every cell of my body was responding with a shudder to the elegiac lilts of this melody. I resisted it but in vain – the memories of yesterday's nightmare came flooding back, drowning me in the sense that my mother wasn't among the living anymore. Why? Why were these thoughts coming to me now?

I gulped, struggling to stop the growing tightness in my throat when a raven flew from the loft, sat on the rail and cawed, looking imperiously down at me.

The music stopped.

All went quiet. Only the echo of the interrupted melody sounded in the walls of the cathedral. Slow and heavy footsteps approached the edge of the loft. My blood rushed in my veins in hot waves, making everything pulse. Was it the effect of the melody? Or of the raven emerging out of the dim light in the Gothic shrine?

A man in his thirties came into view, looking down at me. His eyes shone with arrogance, as if he were a Roman centurion and I were a mere slave who'd dared to interrupt his peace and solitude. He was tall... very tall but didn't slouch or fidget, standing straight and bold. He had dark hair without a hint of a wave and thick eyebrows above light eyes... green or possibly blue. His nose seemed straight and as perfect as his full lips and stubbled, chiselled chin. I must admit... if he wasn't scowling at me like I was a pathetic stray mongrel, he could make quite an impression. *Flawless*, came to my mind.

But no, he wasn't flawless. His beauty was cold as steel, and his gaze though captivating lacked any signs of kindness or compassion.

I opened my mouth to say something, but nothing came out. What was going on with me?

The wooden door creaked and Hairito walked in, coming my way.

The man switched his gaze to Hairito, going deathly pale. Suddenly, the raven soared, circling above the head of its master and showering him with jet-black feathers that turned into a twisting funnel. The bird dissolved, transforming into huge wings on the man. He took a black feather from a pendant that hung around his neck, and it turned into an inky sword. There was no more man. In a flash he transformed into a demon from hell that leaped from the loft, charging at Hairito.

Her ears flattened, her back arched and her tail dropped between her legs. She whimpered but glanced at me and suddenly reared up on her hind legs, preparing her claws for a blow. She was trying to protect me.

I scooped her up, curling myself around her and turning my back to the man. He landed next to me. A stiff wind wafted from his deathly wings.

'What the hell are you doing?' he gritted out.

CHAPTER 3
OMNIA

HAIRITO TRIED TO pull away from my iron grip, but I held her tightly. She peeked out above my shoulder and hissed at the stranger. His cold aquamarine eyes glowered at her.

'Put the beast down. Now!' Not a request – an order.

'No!'

Her heart was galloping – its every beat echoed on my chest; I was afraid it could stop, unable to withstand the tension.

The man seemed to struggle to believe what he was seeing and lowered his sword. 'Lilly? Lilly White?'

I straightened up, my sanity returning. 'How do you know my name?'

He ignored my question, scrutinising Hairito again.

'Are you from Faivendei?' I asked.

His frosty eyes slid to me. 'Where did you find an animated gargoyle?'

'Animated?'

'You didn't answer my question.' The ominous warning seeped through his calm tone.

'Well, you've ignored three of mine, so I'm still ahead of the game.'

He didn't respond, keeping his lethal focus on me, making me feel minuscule and insignificant. In an instant his sword became a feather again, and his wings split into thousands of feathers, transforming back into the raven. I shuddered. He didn't even flinch, putting the feather back into his pendant. His losing the sword reassured me a little. If he had attacked me, the outcome of this short battle would have been obvious and deplorable. He was tall and broad-shouldered. An enraged grizzly… but no – not quite so. His build was more of an indomitable mustang that wasn't born to kill, yet could trample to death if crossed.

'The gargoyle. Where did you find it?' I could still hear a threat in his deep voice.

' "It" is a she.'

His jaw muscles clenched; now he seemed ready to strangle me with his bare hands.

Hairito slipped through my tired arms, and I stepped between her and the stranger. 'I didn't find her – she came to me yesterday. She saved me last night from that girl – a spriggan, I think. I'm sure she's harmless, and there's nothing to worry about.'

'A spriggan?' He scowled at me. 'In the Human World?'

'I think so. Super thin, tall, green skin, sharp chin—'

'That was a dryad, not a spriggan.' He rolled his eyes. 'What did you do to her?'

I let out an irritated huff. 'Nothing. It appeared out of nowhere, and if it wasn't for this gargoyle, I probably wouldn't be here now.'

'There is no such thing as a benign gargoyle. Don't even think of passing through the portal with her.'

'Why? You can see for yourself she's benign.' I'd raised my voice without intending to.

His lip curled in disdain. 'Seriously? Do you know anything about spirits and the world you're going to live in?'

'How could I?'

'What do you mean how? Didn't your parents tell you anything?'

Parents? What did he think I was, a child? 'I haven't seen them since I was five.'

'Relatives?'

'None.'

'How did you learn about the Spirit World then?'

'The gargoyle that you hate so much brought me a golden tube with a letter from someone called Conrad.'

He seemed to know the name and it made him ponder. 'Are you saying you have no idea where you're going?'

'You could say that.'

His jaw dropped slightly. 'You must be kidding me.'

The door creaked and an elderly couple entered the church. They didn't pay attention to the bird – apparently the raven was as invisible to other people as Hairito.

He watched them pass by and, almost snarling, whispered to me, 'I don't know what you've imagined in your little head, but… just stay away from the rabbit hole. There is no Wonderland.'

I returned his death stare. 'I wasn't looking for one.'

It wasn't easy to set me off – for all its flaws, my life had taught me patience. But for some reason his condescension was like fuel spilling onto the wick of my soul and turning it to hellfire.

'In any case, this' – he pointed at Hairito – 'is not allowed. Its kind were once evil spirits imprisoned in stone by the strongest shamans. Now they are unconscious, soulless beings that exist to protect shrines and come to life only if there's extreme danger. And then only for one purpose – to destroy the source of it.'

I blinked.

'This gargoyle animated in order to kill somebody, and if she came to you, then you're her target.'

I couldn't help but laugh. 'She saved me from the dryad last night. She tried to save me now from you. Look at her! She's a sweetheart!'

He came down on me, looming over my head like a thundercloud. I suddenly became aware of every breath I took. Beneath his gaze, my composure was shattering, instinct trying to force me to retreat to a safe distance, but I wasn't ready to let this brute see me intimidated.

'Gargoyles never come to life for good reasons,' he growled.

I tilted back my head to look into his eyes – like two lasers, they were incinerating my self-control. I thought I was forgiving, but he, somehow, had got under my skin in the matter of a few minutes, setting me completely off.

'Okay. Look, the letter says I can take her with me.' I stepped away from him and handed him the tube from my backpack.

He snatched it, took out the letter and read it. 'They've lost their minds! An animated gargoyle in Faivendei? Will they send invitations to *noxes* too?'

Noxes? I didn't care.

'I'm not going anywhere without her.'

He glanced at me, and his lips broke into a sarcastic smirk. 'Oh, that's great. Good luck then!' He handed the letter back and strode out of the cathedral.

I froze. During the last twenty-four hours I had been kicked out of my room, met an animated gargoyle, had an actual dryad try to kill me, and just now I'd seen a man who could transform his raven into a pair of wings and a feather into a sword. My mind was reeling and couldn't think as fast as I'd been able to talk. Moment passed, then it struck me.

'Wait!' I shouted, running after him.

He had vanished.

What had I done?

I'd dreamed about this all my life and now was acting as if access to the parallel world was something I could take for granted.

Stupid!

My pulse was racing as if I'd run a marathon, but I wasn't ready to give up. The letter said I was to be met at the riverbank in that Forest of Coët— whatever it was. If not him, maybe somebody else could meet me. I had to try at least.

I headed to the forest. Perhaps if my mind wasn't so occupied by the idea of crossing the border of two worlds, I'd pay more attention to the tiny French villages, fragrant meadows, and endless yellow sunflower seas that met my eyes on the way. Although, when I reached the woods, the picturesque views and fresh air of the countryside gave way to the thick mist and moist, earthy scent of the forest. I hesitated before diving into the boundless smoky depths. Who knew what was lurking in there?

Opening the maps app on my phone, I plotted my route and set off.

The deeper I plunged into the forest, the shorter and slower my steps became. The fog thickened, and it seemed I was already crossing the border between two worlds.

I glanced at the trees, trying to see if any of them harboured anything unusual, but the forest remained the same. Slender ash trees stood in a sea of coppiced hazels, hornbeams and chestnuts. The golden blanket of fallen leaves had already begun to cover their mossy roots. But there was something dark in the air – this deep haze kept me in tension. From afar floated the whistle of the howling wind. The tree branches swayed; their leaves rustled. It seemed I heard them whispering, 'Run... Run away...'

The screen on my phone went to black; my battery had died. Standing amidst the grey darkness, I tried to make out something, anything – but I wasn't even sure where I'd come from.

I put my phone away and plodded ahead, relying on my intuition alone.

Stepping quietly as a cat and trying to look in all directions at once, I wondered if goblins were real and if they could sleep somewhere here – in the abyss of ominous silence under the cover of ashen haze. All my senses were on alert when the sudden creak of a broken branch echoed like an explosion through the forest. I spun around. The mist was moving as if alive, and a tall bony figure emerged from the twirling smoke.

'Lilly White!' the dryad's voice cut through the obscurity.

I pelted away wherever my eyes led me, just to get away from this dryad.

How had she found me?

My legs carried me quicker than ever before, but she was faster.

I turned around to see how close she was but tripped over something and fell, hitting my head on a decaying log. My pulse raced as if all the resources of my body had been thrown into keeping me conscious, yet the darkness pulling me into the abyss was stronger. The trees and the sky were spinning like a baby mobile, and my eyes drifted involuntarily shut.

Something shook me. I half-opened my heavy eyelids – Hairito was trying to bring me back to consciousness. The dryad's long, green, match-like legs were at arm's length from mine. A new wave of adrenaline surged through my veins, and I shot to my feet.

A heavy flapping of wings came from deep within the forest. The dryad halted, focusing her laser gaze at the onyx bird that glided into sight then flapped in her face, forcing her to back away.

The raven made a circle and landed on the shoulder of the organist from the church, who appeared out of nowhere behind me.

'Got lost, I suppose?' he said to the dryad, his dense velvet voice threateningly low. 'You should probably go. Now.'

She scanned him, then glanced between Hairito and me and simply faded, dissolving into the mist, as if she were a mere ghost.

I turned to the man. 'Thank you—'

'What is wrong with you?' He scowled at me.

I opened my mouth, but he didn't let me say a word.

'You're a walking disaster! First a gargoyle takes up with you, something which never, *ever* happens. Now this dryad! I can't believe she'd follow you for no reason. What have you done to her?'

A gust of searing flame burned my chest, but the voice of reason extinguished it in an instant. *Be wise, Lilly. Be wise.*

'Are you going to answer my question?'

'I didn't do anything to that dryad.' I willed my voice to sound even. 'I'd never seen her until yesterday. And Hairito –

the gargoyle... Well, I don't know why she came to me, but you can see for yourself she's benevolent.'

His eyes slid to Hairito as if for a heartbeat my calm voice had broken through his wall.

'I can't take you to Faivendei with a gargoyle.' His tone was uncompromising. 'It's too great a risk. You come with me alone or you stay here. That's my final offer.'

Hairito glanced at me with flattened ears as if she understood what choice I should make. But if not for her, I'd never have received that letter and I'd probably be lying dead in a Parisian suburb. She had protected me from the dryad; she was ready to protect me from this winged man. It seemed she was willing to sacrifice her life to save mine. So how could I leave her behind? There had to be another option.

I took out the letter and handed it to him. 'Read it again please. I have an official invitation, which says I can live in Faivendei and the gargoyle can stay with me. I don't know much about your world, but something tells me you should respect this lead dwarf's decision.'

He ignored my outstretched hand, darkness filling his aquamarine eyes. 'I'm not letting you pass with the gargoyle.'

Damned bastard!

'If you won't let me through, I'll find Conrad, and I'll make you answer to the law. I'm sure it exists in your world. Tell me your name!'

He smirked, scowling at me like a Great Dane at a yapping chihuahua. 'William C.J. Raven. Good luck finding the dwarves.' He turned his back to me and headed towards the river that was becoming visible now that the fog had started to break.

'William!' I shouted but a second later came to my senses and watched my tone. 'I've been looking for that world for thirteen years. I need to get there. Please – let me see Omnia. Let me talk to her, and if she agrees with you, Hairito and I will leave and you'll never hear from us again. I give you my word.'

'What do you hope to find there?'

I fell silent, but he kept waiting.

'My family,' I finally said.

He looked me straight in the eyes, as if trying to subdue me with his will and force me to tell the truth. But I had nothing to hide, and eventually he seemed to sense it.

He sighed, shaking his head. 'All right. You'll see Omnia.'

I sagged, but it was too early to celebrate – I had yet to set a single foot out of the Human World.

As he left the bank of the lake, his black boots sank into the water, and I spotted two vertical slits on the back of his leather jacket. It brought me memories of his wings and how he'd jumped from the cathedral tribune, trying to attack Hairito.

Brute! Arrogant brute!

Half of me already loathed him. But another half still remembered the melody he'd played. It wasn't just about the masterful technical skill. That tune had been imbued with the richness of the performer's spirit and the vastness of his heart. Maybe it wasn't him who'd been playing?

He rolled up the right sleeve of his jacket, baring his wrist, which was tattooed with three wavy parallel lines – the first being the longest and the third the shortest. Dipping his big masculine hand into the water, he whispered in what might have been Latin, '*Verteriteretro.*' The middle line of his tattoo slithered into the pool like a tiny snake. Air rose from the bottom, and the water seemed to boil.

' "Curiouser and curiouser",' I whispered.

'What?' he snapped at me.

'Nothing.'

'Hide the gargoyle.'

I took off my raincoat, wrapped it around Hairito and picked her up.

He glanced over his shoulder, letting out an angry sigh. 'Hide the tail!'

Suddenly, an ivory boat, built in Ancient Egyptian style, emerged from the dark water. I almost dropped Hairito. It seemed the owner of this boat had looted a pirate stash: shells and starfishes, pearls and jewels densely covered the bow, which was carved out of wood in the shape of a seahorse looking proudly ahead. The whole thing was so surreal I was ready to believe I was in slumberland. The water splashed next to the boat, as if a giant catfish were surfacing. I stepped closer, blinking.

Was that...?

William turned to me. 'For fairy's sake, hide her!'

The moment I pulled my raincoat over the curious black muzzle, a green-haired maiden emerged from the water – a beautiful doll with bluish skin; thin, bare shoulders; and a pair of scallop shells set with pearls and precious stones that covered her breasts. She leered at William, her feline eyes twinkling, her small lips smiling.

It couldn't be.

I peered in the water: light flickered from her iridescent tail.

A siren. A real siren.

'Who is this girl?' she drawled, keeping eye contact with him.

'A new one.' William's dense voice suddenly rang as smooth as silk upon the wind. 'Could you please let her into Faivendei?'

She gave me an appraising look and scoffed, 'I don't like her. Let's leave her in the Human World.'

'Oh, trust me, I would be more than happy to leave her here, but she has permission from Conrad. And that gives us little—'

'Dwarves! They're only the keepers of the keys!' she spat, diving into the depths.

'Nairin, don't hide from me,' he called. 'I have a gift for you.'

A gift... What the hell was going on?

The curious face of the siren immediately reappeared from under the water, her eyes sparkling. 'Gift? What kind of gift?'

He reached into his jacket and pulled out a silver pocket mirror enveloped in a halo of ultramarine stones. The siren swam in an ecstatic circle at the sight of this little gift. Of course the mirror was exquisite, but she acted as if it were the Elixir of Life.

In the blink of an eye, a white ladder extended from the deck of the ship to settle at William's feet. He beckoned me over. Did he want me to walk along this precarious thing?

'Go, before she changes her mind,' he whispered.

I stepped on the ladder, and to my relief it was as stable as the ground. Upon reaching the boat, I stepped in, but the vessel swayed from side to side; I lost my balance, fell over and a frightened Hairito jumped out of my raincoat.

'What was that?' The siren dashed to the boat and gaped at the two large yellow eyes staring back at her.

A shriek broke in twain the silence of the woods; I pressed my palms to my ears. Even after she stopped screaming, her cry was still ringing in my head. No human could ever reproduce that razor-sharp howl – it could cut through flesh.

William ran up the rapidly disappearing ladder to the ship and jumped in at the last moment.

'You couldn't follow one simple order?' he shouted at me. 'Idiot!'

The water was stirring; the boat spun around, gaining speed as if caught in a maelstrom.

'Hold on to the side!' he snapped.

I clutched at the sides with both hands; Hairito did the same.

William sat on the boat rail and opened the mirror; a white mist poured out of it, thickening to form a three-dimensional image of himself in a tuxedo at a grand piano. His miniature version went to the instrument, opened the lid and played a melody. Gradually, the volume increased – it was the Prelude in C major from *The Well-Tempered Clavier* by Bach.

The difference between this tune and the one he'd played in the cathedral was as great as the difference between a summer breeze blowing through the young leaves of a slender aspen and the thunder of storm waves breaking on sheer cliffs. Every mellifluous note seemed to calm the raging water and slow down the boat.

The siren emerged, gazing at the miniature image of William playing the piano. Her eyes were shining, as if she was a cat who'd spotted a treat. Nothing but that mirror and that melody existed for her.

'Nairin, I know you don't want to let a gargoyle into Faivendei, but Conrad gave his permission.' William held out his hand to me.

I fumbled through my backpack, pulled out the golden tube and handed him the letter. With his other hand, he gave the mirror to the siren. Nairin took it gently, as if it were as

44

fragile as butterfly wings. He unfolded the letter and showed it to the siren.

'All right...' she drawled, without even looking at it.

She sank under the water, and the melody grew fainter. William gave me back the letter and sat down in the middle of the boat, gripping both sides. 'Now, hold on tight.'

Suddenly, the water underneath us disappeared, and the boat plunged downwards. The free fall forged my insides, and I wanted to scream but couldn't even breathe. Water surrounded us, closing in above, and pitch darkness swallowed the world.

Finally, a faint light penetrated my closed eyelids; I opened them, and my shoulders drooped. Our boat was still floating in the middle of that river. The dense fog pressed against my eyes whilst heavy rain crashed upon us. My stomach churned as if I'd just bungee jumped off a cliff.

I leaned over the side, hanging my head above the water, dry heaving. When there was nothing left in my stomach, I sat back, trying to steady myself. Breathing puffs of warmth into the cool air, I glanced around one more time – and froze.

This was *not* the same place.

It was colder, for one thing. The mist here was much thicker, and there was no downpour at the river near Dinan. The shadows of the trees filtering through the fog were thicker here, and while our boat moved, inching into the unknown, I noticed on the right side an earthen path, lined on both sides with glass candleholders, running alongside the lake.

No, it was running through the middle of the lake. And instead of candles, the holders were filled with tiny floating golden lights. And the earthen path – I blinked a few times to make sure my eyes weren't deceiving me – actually hovered above the water's surface. Vibrant shawls of moss hung from its edges like seaweed.

'Bloody hell! I'm here!'

'Indeed. Welcome to bloody hell.'

A sprawling majestic tree, growing in the middle of the lake, appeared before my eyes. It resembled a willow, but the whiplike branches hanging down to the water were covered with blush flowers among emerging narrow leaves. Some kind of a cross between a weeping willow and a Japanese cherry? I'd never seen anything like that before – not in real life, not in books. The boat floated right up to the tree, and its drooping branches parted before us like the curtains of a theatrical stage.

'Don't say a word until Omnia speaks to you,' he said.

I nodded.

The tree was growing on an island just big enough to hold it. Once there, we got out of the boat and stood in front of the wide trunk. The ground was surprisingly dry – not a single drop of rain had penetrated the foliage.

Flowers and leaves flew from the tree branches, gathering before me and taking on a human shape. I stood motionless, holding my breath, until William bowed, and I figured I should do the same. The flowers transformed into radiance, from which a translucent spirit manifested: a slender female body, shining with a pale glow. She was dressed in brilliant white silk, like the chiton of an ancient Greek goddess. Her long, wavy hair floated in the air as if in water, and her serene sapphire eyes emanated uncompromising power and benevolent vigour. Maybe I was supposed to look down, but I couldn't take my eyes off her.

She walked around me, smiling, studying, and submerging me in the scent of briars, lilacs and mimosa – so refreshing and dense. I breathed in the moist sweet air in big gulps. So pure…

It seemed I'd only now discovered what it was like to actually breathe, as if before I'd been inhaling poisonous gases that were slowly dissolving my body from within.

She stopped in front of me, reaching out her thin, shimmering hand towards my face. I instinctively backed away.

'Do not be afraid.' Her voice was mellow and full of echoes. 'I will not hurt you.'

She touched my forehead. I didn't feel it physically, but the soothing warmth of her hand somehow filled my mind with ever greater peace. I closed my eyes, enjoying the long-awaited silence, when suddenly a shiver passed through my body, shaking me from head to toe. I opened my eyes.

Omnia's serene expression was gone. Her brows were drawn together, her chin was trembling, and shining tears were streaming from her eyes like two tiny rills of diamonds. She pulled her hand away and broke into thousands of flowers that were carried away by the wind.

I stared at the space where she had been standing. 'What just happened?'

William glared at me as if I was a messenger from the devil himself. 'I should never have listened to you.' He charged back to the water, rolling up his sleeve.

'What are you doing?'

'You're going back to the Human World.'

'Why?'

He got up and charged at me. I had to step back.

'I've only seen her cry once before, on a day when hundreds of lives were lost in this forest. Her touch can sense your true self, your past and your future. I don't know which of these are so messed up to make her cry, but you're going back, and you'll never pass through the portal again.'

Trembling all over, I stared into nothingness. There was something wrong with me, something that had forced my parents to leave me in the Human World, something that made those demons haunt my dreams, something that had made this pure spirit, Omnia, cry.

Awaken the darkness within you. Become the omen of light.

For thirteen years I'd hoped this world would be a place where I could feel at home, where I'd be welcomed. But there was no such place in either world.

My tears rolled down – I couldn't hold them anymore. I was so... tired. Yes, I was tired, but it was exactly the wrong time to let myself loose. Had Omnia said she saw darkness within me? Had she told me to go away? No. I had no idea what had made her cry, but I wouldn't leave until I'd figured it out. I swiped the tears from my cheeks.

The blush flowers and leaves gathered together again, taking human form. Omnia was back, and her face was calm, as if nothing had happened. She walked over to me and smiled.

'Thousands of years have not made me any wiser. I do not know what to do, thus I leave the choice to you, Lilly White. I advise you to return to the Human World. There your life will be long, calm and sometimes even happy.'

'Why? I just – I thought—' A lump was growing in my throat, but I steeled myself. 'Was I born here?'

'Not in my land, but yes, you were born in the Spirit World.'

'Then why can't I stay?'

'You can, but I am trying to give you a chance to live... like other people. However, you will still find a way to fulfil your destiny. Fate has too much power over you. Hmm...' She fell silent for a moment. 'Here you will find what you are looking for, but it will not be what you think. You might change the future, but the price you pay will be high.'

Changing the future? What was she talking about? It didn't matter. I had to finish what I'd begun – I had to find my parents and understand what happened. I had to stay true to my plan to finally get rid of these constant doubts that crawled through my mind like maggots in rotting flesh.

'I was born here,' I said. 'My place is here.'

'The choice is yours, Lilly White. But if you cross the line now, there is no going back. Many times you will blame yourself for such a hasty decision, but it will be too late. Believe me, you will be better off if you go back to the Human World.'

Hairito whimpered softly, her ears low.

'If I can choose, then I choose to stay in your world.'

'So be it.'

William tried to say something, but she cut him off. 'It is decided. Lilly will stay here, and, yes, the gargoyle will stay with her.'

She broke up into a thousand flowers and dispersed into the air.

CHAPTER 4
WARRIOR

THE TREE BRANCHES parted in front of us, and we walked along the earthen path that floated above the water's surface. Icy droplets of pouring rain stung my skin. The new information and the questions it raised swirled in my mind like the colours in a kaleidoscope, but I walked in silence and didn't disturb William. That I'd made it here after so many years of searching was already a miracle. I didn't want to ruin it.

We approached roughly shaped granite steps that led to an immense Gothic castle nestled at the foot of a wooded hill whose top was hidden in a misty cloud. Its many rectangular towers, armed with arrow slits and parapets, seemed to be built on top of each other. They all were dark grey in the downpour.

William marched across a vast marble square that lay between the steps and the castle towards the door. It brought me back to the moment, and I followed him with Hairito. The massive arched door swung open for us, and we stepped inside.

I couldn't see much in the gloom of the entrance hall, but I did notice the clean odours of furniture wax and fresh field flowers mixed with the scents of shoe polish and old books.

We walked into a room next to the entrance. A sylphlike girl sat there at the desk, writing something in a large leather-bound book of parchment. A fluffy aureole of long, fiery red hair surrounded her freckled heart-shaped face. Her bright olive eyes, set under impeccably shaped ginger eyebrows, looked up at us, and she smiled.

'Here you are!' She got up but went still at the sight of the onyx creature by my side. 'Is that... an animated gargoyle?'

'Aisha, you're a Fera, aren't you?' William asked. 'Can you read the gargoyle's mind?'

'Gargoyles aren't animals. But how? What—'

'Apparently it's a benign gargoyle,' he said, as if he were describing a square circle.

'A benign gargoyle? Now isn't that cool!' She grinned, then her eyes shifted to me. 'I hope she ate something in front of you?'

'Yes, she did. Why?'

'The first thing a gargoyle eats after coming alive becomes its sole diet, and given the reasons they animate, most often they eat human flesh,' she stated nonchalantly. 'What exactly did she eat?'

'Erm... strawberry cookies.'

'A benign gargoyle who eats strawberry cookies. Ophelia will be over the moon!'

Apparently she noticed my confusion. 'Ophelia is my little sister. I'm sorry, I never introduced myself. You're Lilly, right? My name is Aisha.' She shook my hand, the smile never leaving her face. 'Nice to meet you! Have a seat. I'll need to take down your details for the archive.'

'When you're done, bring her to the leaders' meeting.' Again, a cold order. Did he know any other way to communicate? I wondered what exactly his role was in here.

She blinked at him.

After a moment, he added, 'Please.'

It did surprise me that he knew that word.

'Of course, Will.'

Letting out a barely perceptible sigh, he left the room.

She turned her attention back to me. 'Is it your first time here?'

I nodded, lacking the strength to explain the whole situation.

'You must have a lot of questions, but I'd ask you to save them for later. I'm your mentor, Lilly. You'll live in my house for the time being. Normally, Omnia allocates a house to each of the residents of Faivendei, but something went wrong and... It isn't a big deal. I'm sure she'll give you a house after your initiation.'

'Initiation?'

'It's a rite of passage. You recite a vow and become an official member of our family. I'm sure after that you'll get your own house. But in the meantime, you're welcome to live with me.'

'I hope this doesn't cause you a lot of problems.'

'Not at all! Ophelia was thrilled to find out we're having guests.'

Slowly her smile faded as she studied my face. 'Are you feeling all right? You're so pale.'

'I'm fine.' I smiled at her, trying to sound convincing.

'Look, your coming today isn't the best timing. Sometimes Will can be blunt, and he's not in the best mood right now, but he has a noble spirit. Also, Faivendei is drowning in rain, but I'm sure tomorrow everything will calm down. You'll see how beautiful and welcoming the forest can be. So don't worry about the damp, lukewarm reception.'

'No, it's all right.' I still felt it was a miracle I could be here at all. The sun not shining didn't seem like a problem.

'Look, Lilly, you can tell me anything. I'm your mentor, but first and foremost, I want to be your friend. I see in your eyes you're a kind person. I can also see you're afraid. But that's absolutely normal. You're in a world where everything is new, with no family or friends. I promise I'll support you and help you adapt.'

I was trying to figure out what I'd done to deserve such friendliness. At first, the voice of cold logic made me look for a trick, but I couldn't find even a shadow of hidden guile or pretence in her olive eyes. Besides, I wanted to believe her.

'Thank you, Aisha,' I said and meant it with all my heart.

'Welcome then. Let's get you registered in the archive. If I don't bring you to the leaders' meeting on time, Will will go ballistic, and it's better not to anger him today.'

She sat down at the massive wooden desk, picked up a quill, dipped it in emerald ink and added the date in the upper-right corner – 3 September. 'Your full name?'

'Lilly White.'

'What an interesting name!' she said, writing *Lily White* in a looping, extravagant hand.

'Actually, it's Lilly with two Ls.'

She narrowed her eyes. 'Are you sure?'

I let out an amused huff. 'Certain. And they gave me the surname White because my hair was blond when I was a child. With age it got a little darker.'

'What do you mean, they gave you a surname? Who?'

'I was raised in an orphanage.'

'Oh, I see.' She drew a breath, scanning my face, but released it. 'Okay. Date of birth?'

Interesting. I half expected her to ask about my parents. She obviously wanted to know but restrained herself. And I was grateful for that.

'Fifth of November 2005.'

'We're almost the same age: I'm just a year older than you. Height?'

I blinked. 'Height?'

'Yes, it's for the size of your coffin.' Her face is a calm mask.

I fell mute for a heartbeat, making sure I'd heard her right. 'My what?'

'Don't worry, it's just a formality.'

I swallowed. 'Five feet five inches.'

'Place of birth?'

If only I knew…

'Just tell me what's written in your passport,' she said.

'Dorking, England.'

She wrote it down. 'Are you a witch or a shaman?'

I raised my eyebrows. 'I don't really—'

'Aisha!' A young boy rushed into the room, panting. 'Ophelia's lost Tarry near Vandorfort!'

She jumped up from the table. 'Where is she now?'

'She's getting closer to the ruins!'

Aisha muttered something under her breath and rushed for the exit but suddenly stopped and glanced back at me. 'Lilly, go upstairs and find the Leaders' Council. Ask someone the way. I'll be back when your meeting is over. Sorry.'

She rushed away.

I walked towards the main stairs. What was Vandorfort and why did it scare her so much? Hopefully her sister would be all right.

Aisha's kindness and openness had been like a sip of life-giving water in a sweltering desert. I was eager to pass through all the necessary formalities so I could meet her again as soon as possible to delve into discussion about the Spirit World. The thought of a friend with whom I could talk openly about what had for so long just been a distant fantasy lifted my spirit a little.

Will came around the corner.

'Where's Aisha?' he snapped as if I were a criminal who wasn't allowed to walk around the castle without an escort.

'She had to leave. She told me to find the Council.'

He shook his head. 'Follow me.'

As we climbed a marble staircase, my feet sank into a thick burgundy carpet. This passage had no windows and would have been submerged into obscurity, but the darkness was dispelled by the amber glow of a peculiar chandelier, hanging from the ornamental ceiling. It was made of many glass spirals, growing out in all directions. Hundreds of tiny lights hovered at the heart of this structure like bees around a hive.

Statues of golden ravens sat proudly on the newels, as if preserving peace and order in the castle. The solemn silence was broken only by the slow tickling of an ancient pendulum clock.

I glanced at two massive murals painted in airy pastel colours surrounded by the stone walls. One of them depicted a charming maiden, dancing in the depths of a midnight forest with tiny fairies flitting around her. The second one showed sirens playing harps on moonlit rocks bathed by the frothy ocean.

We reached the top of the stairs. Will started down a hallway, but I stopped. Flickering firelight, filtering through the glass panes of a heavy wooden door on the left, caught my eye. I crept up to it and peered inside. A golden radiance from several table lamps and a lit fireplace set under a massive mirror cast soft shadows on the ruby leather furniture and chestnut shelves that were filled from floor to ceiling with books.

I stretched my hand to the door handle before I realised what I was doing. This library could contain so much information about this world. And then I stopped.

I was actually in the parallel world... The thought made me dizzy. In fact I felt more fear than joy, as if everything here was ephemeral. What if it was just another dream and soon I would have to wake up?

No, it was real.

Or so said the weak whisper of euphoria that struggled to break through the doubt that shackled my spirit, like a tiny ray of sunlight breaking through winter clouds. But the leaden sky swallowed up that faint glow in the blink of an eye. Even if it were real, I didn't know what to expect from the Leaders' Council, so I shouldn't have rushed to lose myself in exultation.

'What are you doing? Quick!' Will came back and hurried me along.

I rolled my eyes but followed him.

Soon we were standing in front of a slightly open mahogany door. A female voice rang from inside. 'How long can you keep asking this question? We only have the diamond caves because we live in strict compliance with the law and order of the Spirit World. Those rats deserting the ship won't get a penny from us!'

Will started to listen, but when he spotted me doing it too, he closed the door with us outside it. He seemed to be drawn as tight as a bowstring, and I decided to stand quietly on the sidelines.

But there was no way to hold my curiosity back. 'Diamond caves?'

'It's none of your business. And if you think your gargoyle can help you get to the diamonds without being noticed, then forget it. Her protective dome only works in the Human World.'

I shook my head. 'All my life, I've been dreaming about coming here – literally. Do you really think I'm after your diamonds? I'm just wondering where we are. Are we underground?'

'No.'

'So there are diamond caves on the surface here?'

'Oh for fairy's sake! Can you just keep quiet?'

I said nothing.

'Hallelujah.'

I scowled at him, any number of retorts bubbling just under the surface. But then I remembered what Aisha had said. This was apparently a very bad day for him, for some reason. And... oh, well, I had thrown some fuel on the fire. First, I'd come with a gargoyle that in normal circumstances could kill not only me but also other people here. Then I'd been paralysed when the siren had appeared. She could have drowned us if Will hadn't had that mirror. I might be frustrated too, if I were him.

'Thank you,' I said.

'For what?'

'For saving me from the dryad. And from the siren. For getting me here.'

He stared at me in silence. 'Don't make me regret it.'

'I'll do my best.' I smiled, and suddenly my head began spinning as if the world itself was turning upside down. I had to lean against the wall. Hairito whimpered, looking up at me.

'What's wrong?' Not concern. A snarl.

'Just a little tired. I'm fine.'

He clenched his jaw as if my weakness were a personal af-
front. I needed to pull myself together. I had to make a good
impression on the Leaders' Council.

But I still couldn't leave it alone. 'Will?'

He inclined his head slightly to me, his eyes watching me
with irritation and a question: *What now?*

'Have you been to other lands in the par— Spirit World?'

A slight nod. 'Why?'

I took the drawing of my family's house out of my pocket.
'Have you ever seen this house, by any chance?'

He glanced at the picture and shook his head.

'All right.'

I glanced away and slipped the sketch back in my pocket.
He kept his eyes on me. What was he thinking about? Perhaps
he thought I was a pathetic weakling who searched for her parents out of a need to be protected and loved. But... I just
wanted to understand who I was. Anyway, why did I even care
what he was thinking? It shouldn't have concerned me at all.

He checked the time on the wall clock and knocked on the
door. That female voice we'd heard before rang out. 'Come in!'

We entered a conference room decorated in royal scarlet. It
was the only detail I noticed because all my attention was focused on the five people sitting around a large round table – two
women and three men. Will joined them. I wasn't invited, and
I was glad of it. They all went still, staring at me and Hairito.
All except the woman in the centre, who was too busy writing
something in a journal. Nobody talked, and the scratch of her
black quill, breaking through the drumming of the rain outside,
seemed eerily loud.

She wore a smart black dress, her posture was perfect and
even though she was sitting down, I could see that she was very
tall and slender. Her black hair was immaculate, shining like

silk in the light, and her lean face, despite being aged and cold, had fine features.

To her right sat a man in a formal, perfectly tailored suit. He had radiant, smooth skin, and his light-brown hair was impeccably coiffed. The soft but masculine features of his slightly aged but unwrinkled face spoke of a good nature, yet there was something disconcerting about him. When we entered the room, his eyes widened, as if he'd seen a ghost. It would have been understandable if he was peering at Hairito. But his startled gaze was focused on me.

Next to him was a withered old man with ashen hair and a neatly trimmed beard. He didn't care about me. All his attention was focused on Hairito.

To the left of the leader sat another woman with mature but lively eyes, long, straight silver hair and sunken cheeks. And beside her half reclined... well, less a man and more a beast with pale savage eyes that shone with the shadows of all his victims. A deep scar ran across his reptilian face. His massive arms were crossed over his chest, and the skin beneath his nails was stained red. It didn't look like paint.

Hairito crouched, growling at him.

I stood in front of them like a defendant before a jury. It seemed that a single wrong word would be a death sentence. And that beast with blood under his fingernails would certainly be happy to execute it at short notice.

'Is that a gargoyle?' asked the woman with white hair.

The quill ceased to scratch. Their leader examined me and Hairito without raising her head.

Her eyes shifted to William.

'This gargoyle is benign. Conrad and Omnia have already cleared it,' he stated leisurely as a matter of fact. Not a trace of his concern was visible, as if he was trying to... help me? It didn't add up.

'Can I read the letter?' she asked me.

'Sure.' I took it out of my backpack and handed it to her.

She scanned the letter, rolled it up and put it back in the tube, her every movement sharp and edgy. 'Well then. What do you know about the Spirit World?'

'I know I was born here.'

She kept scrutinising me as if waiting for the rest. 'Anything else?'

I shook my head.

She exchanged a meaningful glance with Will. 'Aisha Fera will teach you the laws of our world, but let me briefly explain our mission. My name is Gabrielle Raven. I'm the leader of the Ravens and supreme leader of Faivendei. This is Azrael Blumstein – the leader of the shamans.' She pointed to the bearded old man who was still staring at Hairito. 'Christopher Raven – the ambassador of Faivendei and my deputy.' She indicated the well-dressed man sitting on her right. 'Felicia Viridis – the leader of the witches.' She pointed to the woman with long silver hair. 'And General Fairfax – the leader of the warriors.' She nodded towards the beast.

'Nice to meet you. I'm Lilly White, and this is Hairito.'

She gave me a chilly, indifferent look. 'Our mission is to protect the people of the Human World from evil spirits and other dangers. Every day, Ravens, shamans, witches and warriors fight for the well-being of people like you. Faivendei is not just a forest. It has its soul and heart, whom you've already met. Omnia. This place protects us, feeds us, shelters us and will continue to do so as long as we do our duty. Every member of Faivendei must contribute to the protection of the planet and humanity, or Omnia will deprive us of her guardianship. If you received this letter, you must have a special gift. What is it?'

'I… have no idea.'

'Have you ever heard the thoughts of animals or smelled disease?' the witch Felicia Viridis asked. 'Controlled air, water, earth or fire?'

I shook my head.

'Have you seen ghosts in the Human World?' asked the shaman, Azrael Blumstein.

'No.'

'She is clearly not one of the Simtri clan. This means she is a warrior.' Gabrielle Raven glanced at the beast, General Fairfax. 'One of yours, General.'

I had to make a great effort not to betray my true reaction to this statement. But my memory – that obliging fellow – reminded me how out of breath I'd been running away from the dryad and how I'd almost fainted three times so far today. I was anything but a warrior.

General Fairfax agreed. 'You must be kidding. A gust of wind would knock her off her feet.'

'If she got this letter, then she's one of us,' Christopher Raven said. 'Dwarves don't make mistakes.'

Despite his peculiar gaze, I was glad he was taking my side.

'If she had the gift of a witch or a shaman, it would have shown up from childhood. You have no choice but to train her,' he continued.

'However,' Gabrielle said, 'if she fails, she will leave Faivendei immediately.'

'That's ridiculous!' spat General Fairfax. 'Just think. This is the first time Omnia hasn't created a home for a new guardian. Does that mean nothing to you? She doesn't belong here!' He glared at me. 'Go back to the Human World and stop wasting my time.'

His stare made me shiver. But I had no choice.

'I'll be happy to join the warriors,' I said in a calm, confident voice I barely recognised.

'Then the matter is closed,' Christopher Raven said.

The beast heaved a sigh. 'Don't expect any favours. Be in Belator tomorrow at the crack of dawn.'

I nodded.

'All right,' Gabrielle said. 'Off you go.'

I left the room, perhaps a bit too quickly.

A warrior, was I?

I descended the stairs. Were my parents warriors too? It didn't surprise me that witches and shamans existed – I'd have been more surprised if they didn't. I still didn't know who Simtri and the Ravens were, but I was sure I'd find out. I was afraid I might overwhelm poor Aisha with my questions.

She was supposed to be waiting for me at the exit, but there was no one there. I went to the room where she'd registered me, She wasn't there either, so I returned to the entrance hall, sat on a navy leather chair and waited for at least half an hour. She didn't come. The last thing I wanted was to bother the Leaders' Council, but I had to ask where Aisha lived.

I was walking up the stairs when I heard Will's voice in the second-floor hallway. 'I think there's something you should know about the new girl.'

I froze.

'What do you mean?' It was Gabrielle Raven.

'In my eighty-eight years, this is only the second time I've seen Omnia cry. I think she saw something in the girl's future that scared her.'

My jaw dropped. Eighty-eight years? How could Will look so young and be so old?

'Omnia cried?' Gabrielle asked. 'That is odd.'

'Indeed.'

'Watch her closely. If you notice anything strange, let me know right away. Omnia's reaction has to be a bad omen. We must get rid of the girl.'

A short silence was followed by him saying, 'Yes, Mother.'

Mother? How had I failed to realise that? Of course she was his mother. They had the same haughty look, imperious tone and aristocratic manners. They were both important people in Faivendei, and I'd angered each of them already. But I'd done nothing criminal and didn't intend to. I'd only come here to find my parents.

My chest tightened, but it quickly passed. I never expected much from people, so it was easier to cast aside resentment.

I walked out of the castle into the downpour outside. Hairito walked next to me, arching her back and flattening her tail between her legs. She glanced at me as if the rain were my fault.

'I'm sorry about that,' I said and couldn't help but smile.

Walking along the shore of the lake, I hoped I would meet somebody to ask the way to Aisha's house. But I couldn't see anything or anybody through the rain and swirling fog.

Soaking wet and shivering, I was about to go back to the castle when I caught a glimpse of light percolating through the mist. I ran towards it but suddenly crashed into something so hard I almost fell over.

A stocky, blond man with narrow eyes and very thin, almost invisible lips looked me up and down.

He took me by the elbow. 'I'm so sorry! Did I hurt you?'

I stepped back. 'No, I'm fine.'

He moved closer and held his umbrella over both of us. 'I haven't seen you before…'

'I'm new here. Actually, I'm looking for Aisha Fera's house. She's my mentor.'

'I know where she lives. Want me to walk you there?'

'That would be great.'

'I'm Thomas, by the way.'

'Lilly. And this is Hairito.'

The gargoyle flew up and snuggled into my chest, apparently glad to be out of the rain as well.

'Wow!' Thomas drew back. 'What's that?'

'She's a gargoyle. Don't worry though, she doesn't want to kill anyone. She's benign.' I wrapped my arms around the wet, shaking creature.

His lips curled into what looked a lot like a smirk. 'I never heard of anything like that.'

'So, which way should we go?'

'This way.' He started walking, and I followed him.

'Did you arrive today?'

'Yes.'

'Not the best day to come, but tomorrow Omnia should calm down.' He smiled coldly, his eyes hostile.

There was something off-putting about him, something alert and watchful. I couldn't explain why, but I felt it with my gut. Along the way, he asked many questions, but I had no energy left for chatting. What's more, I got the feeling he was showing more than an idle interest in me. At some point, I even began to wonder if he was leading me to Aisha's or somewhere else, but maybe I was just tired and imagining things. Nevertheless, I answered all his questions politely and concisely. And then he asked me about my gift.

'I don't really know, but apparently I'm a warrior.'

He guffawed. 'You can't be a warrior.'

I was looking down at my feet. I agreed with him, but it still wasn't pleasant to hear.

'No, it's not because you're a girl. There are plenty of girls among us. You just don't look like a warrior. I'd say you're a witch or a shaman.'

'Are you a warrior?'

He nodded. 'You can't be more than sixteen.'

'I'm eighteen.'

'My point stands. Warriors protect the guardians, and sometimes we have no choice but to kill noxes.' He stopped in front of a spiral staircase that wound around a gigantic redwood trunk, rising so high into the fog it was impossible to see the top. 'Are you ready to kill?'

'Who are these noxes?'

'Oh, Lilly, you're here!' Aisha ran down the spiral staircase.

'Hi! She got lost, and I helped her find you,' Thomas said.

'Thank you so much! Do you want to come in for some tea?'

'No thanks. I have to go to Belator. See you, Lilly.' He winked at me and left.

My shoulders sagged. I had no idea why, but I hoped we wouldn't meet again.

CHAPTER 5

VOICE

Aisha held an umbrella over both of us. 'Lilly, I'm sorry. I just walked my sister home and was about to go to Sodalitas to get you.'

I guessed Sodalitas was the castle I'd just left. 'No worries. I hope Ophelia is all right?'

'Thank the Universe, she is. Let's go home. Just be careful – the stairs are very slippery.' She headed up the spiral staircase.

I tilted my head back. The giant red trunk disappeared into the grey cloud above us. Not even a shadow of the house could be seen through it. I gulped. Treehouses were nothing new to me, but I'd never heard of anyone living quite so high up.

'Are you coming?'

I returned to reality and followed her. The chestnut stair treads levitated in the air a few inches away from the mahogany trunk. Soaking wet, their red was so vibrant, as if somebody had stained them just the night before. They were solid under my feet though, and I kept an iron grip on the amber handrail. However I doubted it would save me if this whole construction failed – like the stair treads, the handrail hovered in the air just above the balustrade, which was made of dried tree roots covered with moss and miniature ferns.

I really was in the parallel world.

It was getting through to me. As if the gust of joy had pushed away the menacing clouds, and for a moment the sun appeared, turning its cheerful gaze on me.

I was in the parallel world!

The excitement, though pleasant, was also problematic. My pulse was racing, and I still couldn't see the house. I stopped and bent over the stair treads, panting. Thank goodness nobody from the Leaders' Council could see me right now. They'd have a good laugh at their new 'warrior'.

Aisha glanced back at me, a half-smile lingering on her face. 'Are you okay?'

'Fine... I'm fine.' I smiled and kept climbing.

'Normally our house isn't this high up. Today, everything is upside down in the forest.'

'What? Your house moves?'

'That's right. When I'm in a hurry, it's close to the roots of the redwood. Otherwise it's further up – to keep me in shape, you know.'

We chuckled.

When the scent of damp earth was replaced by the smoky fragrance of pine resin, at last I saw the base of the house. It seemed as if we were floating in the clouds – the ground had completely disappeared into the mist. The stairway emerged onto a wide terrace that encircled a wooden bungalow. The thin planks of the floor creaked underneath us. Hairito walked cautiously, looking down at her feet, growling, and she had wings.

My wary face seemed to amuse Aisha. 'Don't be afraid. Our house has been standing for more than a hundred years and will last at least twice that.'

I tried to smile. I didn't suffer from acrophobia, but this house built around the redwood trunk and floating in the air was pushing my limits.

We reached the front door. Aisha opened it but suddenly closed it again and turned to me. 'I forgot to ask. You're not afraid of spiders, are you?'

'No, why?'

'I hope your gargoyle isn't either. I have a tarantula friend. Tarry can seem frightening with his hairy black legs, but he's harmless. Honestly.'

I bit my lip. Not being afraid of spiders was one thing, but living under the same roof as a tarantula was quite another. 'It's okay.'

'Don't worry. I'm sure you'll like him once you get to know him.' She opened the door.

I scanned the honeywood floor, making sure there was no tarantula, and stepped inside. It was warm. Not only the air, but also the aroma – soothingly soft and comforting. The herbal redolence of chamomile, liquorice and rosemary greeted me at the entrance, and I took a full breath. That alone seemed to calm my mind.

Despite having no windows, the corridor was very well lit thanks to the numerous vintage brass sconces holding tiny golden lights of the kind I'd seen before.

'What are they?'

Aisha walked over to them, lifting her hand and playing with the whisps. 'Without them we wouldn't be able to survive in Faivendei. Fern-flower seeds. They're really miraculous in medicines, and they give us light.'

It seemed that both my eyes and my soul were drawn to their golden glow. 'I didn't know ferns bloomed.'

Aisha smiled. 'In the Human World they don't.'

We walked down the corridor. The wooden walls were covered with family photographs. In between them hung a gilded dagger, its handle set with three stones the colour of blood.

'That's my mother's dagger,' Aisha said, noticing my stare.

'Is she here?'

'No. Noxes killed her and the rest of my family five years ago.'

The tranquillity and quiet with which she said this burned me with cold. But she clenched her jaw, and her eyes drifted to some distant place. I knew that expression. Many children in the orphanage had lost their parents in tragic circumstances. And I'd watched their anger and denial transform into unavoidable acceptance. But ask them about their parents and they would have the same expression. Despite accepting the loss, the deep lasting wound in their hearts had never vanished – it gaped open at every agonising flash of memory, bleeding over and over again.

'I'm so sorry, Aisha...'

She cracked a smile. 'Come on.'

We went into the living room. Here the herbal and coniferous aromas mixed together, making the air even sweeter. The mahogany trunk of the majestic tree passed through holes in the floor and ceiling without touching them. The building was levitating without any support, though that should not have surprised me. I shook my head, still having a hard time believing my own eyes.

In front of the trunk stood a sofa with two old-fashioned floral armchairs. In one of them sat a tiny girl with round cheeks and wet red hair. She was reading a book that was only a little smaller than her, with the title *The Basics of Arbolinguistics* printed on its green cover. She was so absorbed in it that she didn't hear us entering the room. But when we drew closer, she closed the book with a loud clap and leaned forward, gaping at Hairito.

'This is my sister, Ophelia.' Aisha gestured to her. 'Ophelia, this is Lilly and her gargoyle.'

'An animated gargoyle?' Ophelia exclaimed as if Hairito was a piece of creamy cake and not a lethal creature. She jumped to the floor and focused all her attention on the gargoyle, who started to groom herself.

I smiled at Ophelia. 'Her name is Hairito.'

She glanced up at me as if she had just noticed I was there.

'Oh, sorry! Nice to meet you. Please, feel at home. Can I pet her?'

'If she'll let you.'

'Hi, Hairito!' Ophelia touched her flank carefully.

Hairito raised her head and gazed at Ophelia with her large yellow eyes. There was a beat as I waited for her reaction – then she stuck out her pink tongue and licked the little girl's face. Ophelia laughed; Aisha and I loosed a breath.

'Are you sure she isn't dangerous?' Aisha's eyes drifted to mine, and I nodded. I hadn't known how Hairito would react to strangers, but I was sure she wouldn't harm the innocent.

Aisha studied Hairito one more time as if still adjusting to the idea of her only little sister playing with an evil spirit in her house.

'Ophelia, take a towel and dry her. The poor thing is soaking wet.'

'Okay,' Ophelia replied absentmindedly, and I was certain she didn't even hear what her elder sister had said. 'But what's she thinking about?'

'I can't read her. Although, I bet she'll be happy if you dry her off. Chop, chop!'

Ophelia ran to a large wardrobe with carved floral motifs on the doors, opened it and searched for a towel.

'Lilly, come here. I'll show you where the shower is,' Aisha called.

Shower. That sounded heavenly.

I followed her back down the corridor. She opened the door to the left of the main entrance, and we entered the bathroom.

'I warn you right away: sometimes the hot water in the shower disappears. If that happens, just smile and ask politely for it to come back. If you start shouting or swearing, you'll never get hot water again.'

I let out an amused huff, but then I saw that Aisha's face was as serious as ever.

'Who should I ask?'

'The lutins,' she simply said.

'Of course. The who?'

'The lutins. You know, household spirits.'

'So they exist?'

'Thank the Universe, they do. I can't imagine how we'd manage without them. Here are your towels, bathrobe and slippers. You can take anything you want – toothpaste, make-up, perfume. Make yourself at home.'

'Thank you, Aisha. But...' I hesitated, not wanting to sound stupid. 'Where does the water come from and where does it go, at this height?'

'A lot of newcomers from the Human World ask things like that! How were houses built up here? Where does the water go? Why is the house warm when there are no heaters? And so on. The answer is Omnia. She protects us and gives us shelter. Call it magic if you want, but in my opinion it's about balance. We do our duty to the Universe, and it takes care of us.'

That was what I'd thought, but I needed the confirmation. This was a new world to me. I was in the parallel world! I thought I'd never get used to the idea.

'Come on. I'll take you to your room. You need to change and take a shower, or you'll catch a cold.' She said this like a stern but caring mother.

On the right side of the main entrance was a staircase leading to the second floor, and when we reached the top, I saw two doors. We went into one of them, and the first thing I noticed was a small balcony outside.

'It's not a royal chamber of Sodalitas, but this room has everything you need.' Aisha's eyes seized mine as if she was genuinely concerned about how much I liked it. 'And tomorrow hopefully the fog will be gone. I promise you'll love the view!'

I agreed – here was everything I needed and more. In the corner stood a wide bed with a wooden nightstand, next to a small wardrobe, a chair and a desk, on which lay a stack of books, plus a notebook and stationery.

'Compared to where I used to live, it's a mansion.'

'Good.' She gave me a satisfied smile. 'So change your clothes, take a shower and I'll be waiting for you in the living room.'

'Wait. It might sound stupid, but… I don't see any sockets here. My phone is dead, and I was wondering if I can charge it somehow.'

'Oh. You can forget about phones and other electronic devices. There's no electricity here.'

I'd suspected as much, but my eyebrows rose anyway. 'How do you call each other and… and what about the internet?'

She laughed loudly, revealing those beautiful even white teeth.

'It's always amusing to see this look on newbies' faces when they find out there's no electricity. Some even return to the Human World because of it.'

'So you're completely isolated from the rest of the world?'

'No, of course not. From childhood we learn the language of trees and communicate that way. All the trees on our planet are connected to each other, transmitting and receiving information. It's faster, easier and safer than mobile service.'

'Arbolinguistics...' I drawled, remembering the title of the book Ophelia was reading. 'Will I be learning that?'

'Of course, but it'll take some time. Communication with trees requires two things. First, you have to speak Albor – the language people can pronounce and trees can understand. Second, you must learn how to interpret tree songs and gesticulations – rustling of leaves, dancing of the twigs and all this stuff. It's tough. But arbolinguistics will help you with that. Listen, it's all very exciting, but you have to change and take a shower. I'll be waiting in the living room.'

And with that, Aisha left me alone before I could ask her any more questions.

I went to the bathroom. Staring at spotless enamel, glass and wooden surfaces that were as shiny as everything else in the house, I couldn't help thinking about lutins – the household spirits who took care of it. The snow-white towels were stacked so neatly in a straw box with linen lining that I was afraid to touch them. Three straw laundry boxes stood next to one wall with labels written in perfect calligraphy: colour, black and white. Beside them stood a storage cabinet with Aisha's creams and make-up, impeccably arranged. Everything here was clean and modest... Just perfect.

After showering, I went into the living room, where an enticing smell of fried potatoes, mushrooms and melted cheese filled the air.

'Feeling better?' Aisha asked.

'You have no idea.'

She smiled back. 'I hope you're hungry.'

'I am. Thank you.' I sat down at the wooden table next to the sofa.

There were two plates on the table, one filled with fried potatoes and stewed vegetables, while the other had oatmeal cookies. I could have sworn they looked exactly like the cookies I'd given to Hairito last night.

I lifted my gaze from the food only to find her curious inspecting eyes on me. 'Won't you have lunch with us?'

'No, we ate earlier,' she explained. 'Please – eat. And the cookies are for the gargoyle, I suppose. Ophelia begged me to let her feed Hairito, but I didn't want to risk it.'

'Let's do it together.'

I took the plate of cookies and walked over to the little girl, who was still playing with the inky creature. Hairito caught a familiar smell, stretched out her nose towards the plate and purred, prancing around like a pony. I gave the plate to Ophelia, and she held it out to Hairito, who immediately wolfed down its entire contents, her toothy maw gaping wide. She chewed, swallowed too quick and belched.

Aisha laughed. 'She's hilarious. All right. You need to eat too, otherwise it will get cold.'

I sat down at the table and ate slowly, respecting the rules of propriety. But actually I wanted to throw the utensils aside and dump the entire contents of the plate into my mouth, just as Hairito had done with her cookies. It was one of the simplest yet most delicious dishes I'd ever eaten.

'Aisha, you're an incredible cook.'

'Oh no, I didn't cook it. Thank the lutins.'

'I do. It's a pity there are no lutins in the world of people. Life would be so much easier.'

'They used to live in the Human World...' She studied me thoughtfully. 'What do you know about spirits?'

'Not much.'

'Well... To sum it up now, people aren't the most developed species on Earth. Spirits are much wiser and more powerful than us. Lutins are also spirits of a semi-ethereal type.'

'Semi-ethereal?'

'Yes. There are two types of spirits: ethereal, like ghosts, and semi-ethereal, like lutins, sirens, dryads and so on. Ethereal spirits don't have a physical body. Semi-ethereal can take on physical form at any time. We used to coexist with spirits in the Human World, lived in harmony with each other in the time before time. The spirits shared their wisdom with us and taught us the laws of the Universe. Thanks to them, people were able to create many of the greatest architectural monuments. Thanks to them, people mastered healing and lived for several centuries. But, despite all their advantages, spirits lack artistic talent. For them, writing something like Beethoven's *Moonlight Sonata* or painting Aivazovsky's *The Ninth Wave* are as hard as building an interstellar spaceship for us.'

'That's why Nairin was mesmerised by that mirror,' I said.

'A musical mirror? Yes, Will has a real talent for crafting them. Spirits are hypnotised by the works of art we create.'

'So... it all sounds pretty harmonious. What happened to make the spirits leave?'

'People decided chaos was more profitable and banished the spirits from their world. But Earth has always been home to both humans and spirits, so the Universe created a new world still connected to our planet where spirits can live in safety. That's how the Spirit World came to be.'

Somehow, the history of spirits and humans made it sink in that I was here, that it was real. I wanted to know everything, every single detail about this world. I wanted to know which parts of my dreams were true and which weren't. My body was still tired and wanted to sleep, but my mind couldn't let this go.

'Aisha,' I said, 'I'm warning you: I'm going to ask you a lot of stupid questions.'

'There is no such thing as a stupid question. Go on.'

'When I was searching for a parallel world, I tried to wrap my head around it... I mean how is it possible to have a world visible to some people and invisible to others?'

'Well... how to put it simply... Are you familiar with the concept of the world as a sea of energy operating in terms of vibrations and frequencies?'

'A bit.'

'That will make it simpler. People's senses – touch, sight, smell, hearing and taste – only work on a limited frequency range. Their brains are built to limit the infinite information of the Universe down to understandable proportions. So when you say "a parallel world" it's not quite correct. The Spirit World isn't parallel to the Human World. It exists within it, just on higher frequencies invisible to ordinary humans.'

'So it's not a parallel world. It's an invisible world. But how is it visible to us?'

'We're guardians. Our brains are sensitive to a wider range of frequencies. Although our abilities are limited compared to those of spirits – no dematerialising or shape shifting. So we're not ordinary people but not spirits either. Something in between, if you will.'

'But... why are you different from other people?'

'*We*, Lilly, not *you*. You're one of us. You can see this world, right? Ordinary humans couldn't even pass through a portal, let alone see the Spirit World. We're different because we were born to protect people and the planet as a whole.'

'From what?'

'Witches protect from physical harm, mental illnesses and natural disasters. Shamans protect people from evil spirits.'

'You and Ophelia are witches, aren't you?'

'Right.' Aisha let out a low chuckle. 'And, no, we don't have black hats and warts on our noses. There are different kinds of witches. We're all in harmony with the flora, fauna and the elements of the Earth but in different proportions. Viridis witches, like Ophelia, have a fantastic sense of smell. They're in absolute harmony with the flora of the Earth. They're able to smell human diseases and find herbs with the necessary qualities for healing from a few miles away. They balance human physical resources with the help of the Earth's flora.

'When you showered, Ophelia said you smelled like the musk of fear. She went to the kitchen and mixed dozens of different oils in proportions only a Viridis witch can understand. Your room is already saturated with a perfume tailored to your needs. One hour in there and you'll become a different person. She was born with this gift, which is why she's Ophelia *Viridis*. She can learn to communicate with animals or control the elements, but only through decades of practice and great effort.' Her eyes slid to Ophelia, who blushed immediately as if embarrassed at being caught not studying as she had been told.

'But you can read animals' minds, can't you?' I remembered Will and Ophelia asking her if she could read Hairito's mind.

'Yes. I'm a Fera – a witch in harmony with fauna. We can hear the thoughts of animals and see through their eyes. If animals nearby are being abused or in pain, we feel it, find them and help them heal. We can also ask them for favours. But it's impossible to manipulate their minds. For example, I can see through the eyes of a mosquito, but I can't make it bite someone. For me, the eyes of all existing animals are like hidden cameras I can tap into at any time. With their help, I watch people and can detect danger.

'Then there are Initia witches. They're probably the most exciting. Being in harmony with the elements, they can control one or more elements at the same time. Initia are rare but very powerful. They protect our planet from global cataclysms.'

'I'd love to see them in action,' I said, and she smiled at my enthusiasm. 'So, Felicia Viridis is your leader?'

'Yes. Did you meet her at the Leaders' Council?'

I nodded.

'How did she react to Hairito?'

'Oh, she was shocked. As was Azrael, the leader of the shamans. How do shamans protect people, by the way?'

'Well... shamans deal with the world of energy beings and spirits. Every human action, every thought, leads to the formation of positive or negative energies that affect people's lives and emotional state. For example, a violent household can actually form negative energy beings. They aren't independently conscious, but they have a vector of movement aimed at chaos and destruction. The more violence in the house, the stronger the energy being becomes, until eventually it transforms into an evil spirit that actually is conscious. This is when it gets dangerous. Shamans transform negative energy beings into positive ones and destroy evil spirits.'

'Okay, back up just a little. What is an energy being, and what does it look like?'

'It doesn't have a specific shape; it's more like an invisible cloud. When you enter it, your mood might change abruptly.

For example, if you're sad and enter a positive energy being, you might start to feel better.'

'I think you have a very positive cloud in your house.'

'We try our best to keep it so. But in the Human World, there are so many negative energy beings. You'd be terrified if you could see some of the clouds hanging like domes over the biggest cities. I don't know how people manage to stay positive in such an environment... They're real heroes in my eyes. But when the density of the negative energy cloud increases, it can transform into a living, thinking being – an evil spirit that can harm and even kill. So shamans protect people from negative energy beings and evil spirits.'

'Okay, I get it now. Is this why you don't live in the Human World? Because of the evil spirits?'

I started to feel guilty for badgering Aisha, but I just couldn't contain myself.

'No, not really. Long ago, we just lived among people and helped them. But some witches and shamans came to believe that because the Universe had given them a gift, then they were the chosen ones – better than the rest. This worldview justified cruelty in their eyes. People began to fear us and soon rebelled against us. The bloody reign of the Spanish Inquisition had begun. Benevolent witches and shamans stopped using their gifts, fearing for their lives. Soon strange people accompanied by ravens, wolfs or lynxes appeared. They promised their patronage and protection to witches and shamans in exchange for an oath to work for the benefit of all living beings, to use their gifts to bring good to people and the planet as a whole. They called themselves the Simtri clan. It included three families: the Ravens, the Wolves and the Lynxes. They were sent by the Universe to bring justice and keep order among shamans and witches. Sharing their soul with their assigned animal spirit, they can see through its eyes and, in times of danger, unite with it, acquiring superhuman strength. Will is one of the Ravens.'

At the mention of his name, I lost the thread of thought, remembering him uniting with his raven. I shook my head, trying to shake off those thoughts. 'Besides witches and shamans, are there other people with supernatural powers? Like wizards?'

Maybe there was a chance I could study and become a witch or a shaman, but those seemed to be things you were born into or not. I wasn't a warrior, but I wanted to become one of those people, and I was hoping for something else I could train at.

'There are prodigies who are often called wizards. These people can create matter from light, shrink to the size of an atom and return to their initial state, teleport, read minds, move at the speed of sound and so on, but they don't need spells to do it. Their abilities are close to those of spirits. I've never met anyone like that. Only a few are born every century.'

'Maybe it's a silly question, but... can I become a... prodigy, a witch or a shaman?'

Aisha blinked. 'What do you mean by "become"? You already have a gift, don't you?'

I couldn't tell her that I was a warrior, but I didn't want to lie. 'I don't have a gift. The Leaders' Council decided I'm a warrior.'

Her mouth dropped open. 'A warrior? You?'

'That was my reaction.'

She fell mute.

I made it easy for her. 'I know I don't look like a warrior—'

Suddenly the plates disappeared from the table. I jumped.

'Don't worry, a lutin took them. They rarely show up in front of people. Lilly, we need warriors, unfortunately, but you don't have to become one. Many of us leave Faivendei. It's no longer safe here. Maybe you should, I don't know, go back to the Human World too.'

Her words brought me down to reality with a bump. Did no one want me to stay here?

'I'm not going back. I've been looking for this place all my life. And… why do you say it isn't safe here?'

'Faivendei is an enchanted forest, literally, but life here is far from a fairy tale, Lilly. Why do you think I asked about your height for a coffin? We don't really need this information. It's a warning to every newbie: if you want to live here, be ready to die.'

'I'm not looking for a fairy tale. I'm looking for my parents.'

I told my story, and Aisha, Ophelia and even Hairito listened intently. For the first time in my life, I could speak freely on the subject without sounding mad. I trusted that Aisha wouldn't look at me as if I were a freak.

I was to be disappointed.

'Wait a minute.' Aisha narrowed her eyes. 'So you've spent your entire life searching for this world, trying to find your parents, whom you never properly knew? Without any actual evidence beyond dreams?'

I nodded.

'But why?'

'I don't know. I guess I was trying to find out who I am.'

'And that's it?'

She was waiting for an answer, but I didn't say anything. It was a big enough reason for me.

'I just want to make sure you realise what you'll be risking your life for,' she said after a moment. 'Becoming a warrior is like signing your own death sentence. And if you really decide to go for it, then admit why. To yourself at least.'

'Aisha, I don't think I'll ever become a warrior. But it's my only chance of staying here and finding my family.'

She kept her gaze on me in silence. 'This is bad news for me, as you're my first mentee and I always wanted to teach newcomers. My future depends on your progress here.'

I hung my head.

'Nevertheless, I understand you, and I'll do anything I can to help. But! On one condition.'

'Anything.'

'You'll have three months of mentoring, and I need you to put your nose to the grindstone. You'll work hard and you'll study a lot. After that, you can do whatever you want. Deal?'

'Deal.' I inched forward on my seat. 'Aisha, thank you so much.'

'Don't mention it. Look, I know what it is to lose parents. If you have a chance to find them, do it. Just not at the cost of your own life.'

Ophelia's laughter rang out, and we turned to see Hairito tickling the girl with long, clawed paws.

Aisha's wary eyes lingered on Hairito. 'I've never met a gargoyle before, but I know for a fact this behaviour isn't typical. Tarry's unusual for a spider too, but he's never behaved so... in such a human way.'

I instinctively lifted my feet from the floor. 'Where is Tarry, by the way?'

'He's too shy to show up today.' She glanced at her watch. 'Holy fairy dust, I'm so late. Lilly, I'm sorry, but I have to leave you again. If you want, you can rest in your room for a while. You must be tired. Ophelia will be quiet. Won't you?'

She nodded, and Aisha hurried away. I headed off to my room, leaving Ophelia to play with Hairito.

When I entered it, the fragrance of rosehip, orange zest and milk chocolate filled my lungs. Smiling, I inhaled as deeply as I could. *Thank you, Ophelia.*

I plopped down in the soft bed and my strange thoughts merged with odd fantasies, carrying me into the world of dreams.

Lilly... MY MOTHER'S VOICE echoed in my mind.

'Please – say my name again...'

Lilly...

'I hear you! Where are you? Call my name...'

Lilly!

Her ringing cry snapped me out of my dream.

What the hell? Where was I?

I cast an eye over the lampshades filled with glowing fern-flower seeds, and everything came rushing back to me. The wall clock showed it was three in the morning. Suddenly Hairito jumped off the wardrobe onto the bed, stretching and yawning widely.

'You scared me to death!' I softly hissed at her.

Lilly, my mother's voice echoed again.

But this time I was awake.

I froze. It couldn't be. The voice was coming from outside.

I rushed to the balcony, opened the curtains and peered out. Impenetrable night enveloped the forest. I wanted to plunge into the darkness, swim in it like in a soothing ocean.

Concentrate!

The world spun. Ocean... warm as fresh milk... viscous as glue... bottomless abyss...

I shook my head.

Lilly, the voice came again.

I put on my raincoat and sneaked out of the house into the night. I had to follow it. I had to follow...

CHAPTER 6

SAVIOUR

I RAN OUT ONTO the terrace and stood there, peering into the dark. Every cell in my body was trembling. The light of the pale moon reflected off the slippery steps. They twisted around the trunk and disappeared in the misty ocean just a few feet ahead of me. I started to descend, but the celestial lantern hid behind a thick veil of clouds, plunging the world back into utter gloom.

I halted. What was going on with me?

I was about to turn around and head back into the house, when two glass nightlights lit up on each side of the nearest step.

Lilly, came the soft voice again, and I continued down the stairs. All my doubts vanished. One by one, each step was lit up by the golden glow of fern-flower seeds.

'Mum!' I called into the night.

Hairito whimpered. I hadn't realised she was beside me.

Lilly, the voice rang. I rushed towards it.

Lilly. It came from the opposite direction. I changed course.

A weak whisper fell from my lips. 'I'm coming.'

Lilly... It had moved again.

I froze and listened.

Lilly! Lilly! Lilly! Lilly! Lilly! Lilly! Dozens of voices screamed at me from all sides.

I spun around, struggling to find the source of the shouts, but they were coming from everywhere. 'Where are you?'

Just as suddenly as this cacophony started, it stopped. I gasped for air. Where had it gone?

Hairito whimpered again. In front of me, the nightlights lit one after another, as if showing the way. I followed them.

Lilly, the voice reached me, definitely coming from ahead. I ran towards it.

Soon I was in front of a crumbled stone staircase leading upwards. Lanterns flickered on either side of it, casting pale rings into the fog and making it difficult to see what was beyond. It didn't matter. All that mattered was the voice... my mother's voice...

Lilly...

I started to follow it until Hairito bit my trouser leg and tugged me backwards.

'Let go!' I kicked my leg, pulling loose of her grip.

She wailed and flew away. It didn't matter. I needed to find the voice... *her* voice.

I trod on something and glanced down at the stairs beneath my feet – they were covered in cracked limestone pebbles. I kept walking, trying to keep from slipping. The moon peeked out from under the clouds, lighting up a cadaverous archway in the middle of a broken, weather-worn wall stained by mildew. The wind howled through the holes in the dilapidated building, bringing the stench of death and mouldy stone with it.

The moon hid. The dim golden light faded. I stood on the threshold, peering into the obsidian void beyond.

What was I doing?

Lilly... Her voice was as clear as if she was within arm's reach. *Come here, sweetheart.*

I crossed the threshold.

What the—

Inhuman screeches and ear-piercing wails surrounded me from all sides. Hundreds of glowing ghosts with decaying flesh and bulging, scarlet eyes flew at me at once. I drew back but fell to my knees as they passed one by one through my body like lightning. Like a hooked fish that had spent hours fighting for its life, I was exhausted. I opened my mouth to let out my last breath.

They hollowed me out, robbing me of my own feelings and poisoning my mind with their memories. A broken heart can't kill, but shattered into pieces, smashed in formless liquid mass, it could hurt more than anything else. I moaned, breaking down in tears. My wretched mind scanned the unfamiliar memories like a damaged old film.

Help...

Loss, rage, pain, remorse, powerlessness, despair...

Help...

My chest was burning. I moaned, rubbing my solar plexus. It was inside me! The darkness, swirling and crawling through my chest like a million mad tiny black snakes.

Help!

'Please stop it... please...' I collapsed on the wet ground and curled up around the pain.

The ghosts flew towards me, ready to attack again. I closed my eyes, ready to die.

Something grabbed me. I squeezed myself tightly into a ball. Was I floating? I heard the heavy flapping of wings. Somebody was holding me. The snakes... they were going to kill me...

'Stop them!'

An echo came to me from far away. 'Lilly... Lilly... listen to my voice, stay with me... you're safe... you'll be okay.'

His voice. The dense velvet voice.

Another voice, a female one, sounded nearby. 'What happened?'

'She was in Vandorfort,' the velvet voice explained. 'I had to pull her out.'

Pull me out? No... They were still inside me...

'Snakes. Please... Get rid of them—'

'Put her on the bed. Who is she?'

'Lilly White, the new one.'

'Holy Universe! What's that?'

'It's a gargoyle. She's benign, long story. If it wasn't for her, the girl would already be dead.'

'Snakes!' I cried.

'Oh dear! The poor thing's delirious!'

'No... please.'

'Could you stay with her for a moment?' the female voice said. 'I'll be back shortly.'

'Sure,' he drawled as if against his own will.

'Snakes... Will, please... get rid of them.' I scrubbed at my chest. 'Pull them out.'

'It'll be all right. The nurse will help you.' Wrath simmered through his words. 'Why the hell did you go in there?'

A snake pierced my stomach, and I curled up, sobbing.

He dwarfed my hand in his own big warm one. 'Lilly, focus on my voice. The pain is just an illusion. You're safe – everything is fine.'

Tears rolled down my cheeks. What did he know about this pain? It was real. It was dissolving me from within. I squeezed his hand tightly, grinding my teeth.

'Okay, everything's ready, William,' the female voice said. 'You can go.'

I heard him stand up, but his voice was the only thing keeping the snakes from killing me. If he left, I'd die. I clung stubbornly to his hand.

Silence. Nobody moved.

'Maybe I'd better stay here for a while.' It seemed he tried to fill his words with a bite but failed.

'Of course. It's no problem,' the female voice replied.

He sat back down on my bed. I wanted to say thank you, but the tightness in my throat wouldn't let me.

My eyes were still shut. I smelled herbs burning, an intense rosemary evergreen scent wafting up my nose. With every breath I took, one snake died. I leaned towards the source of the aroma and breathed as quickly as I could, killing them all.

Soon, there were none. I was clean. And hollow.

My mind was drifting off when I heard a female voice saying, 'Drink it, Lilly.' I opened my mouth, and a bitter taste burned my tongue. I drank it all, and soon fell into a dreamless slumber.

I STARTLED AWAKE. Will was sleeping next to me, our hands still entwined. My pulse quickened, making my vision sharp. In the dim glow of fern-flower seeds he seemed different. His forehead, which had always been tense, expressing sternness, irritation and sometimes hauteur, was now calm and clear without a single wrinkle. His Cupid's-bow lips, slightly uneven, were open, which made them even more plump. Their pink was so delicate it was hard to look away. My fingers ached with the need to touch them. He had shaved off his stubble, and now, sleeping so calmly, with his smooth, glowing skin, high cheekbones and full lips, he no longer looked like a Roman centurion. He looked like an angel who had just descended from heaven itself.

He opened his aquamarine eyes, as if sensing my gaze.

I jumped out of bed. Hairito, who had been sleeping on the floor, woke up at once.

'Feeling better, I see?' he snapped. The centurion had returned.

I nodded, feeling warmth tingling my cheeks. 'What happened to me?'

He sat up in a fluid motion. 'That's what I'd like to ask *you*.'

I lowered my gaze, searching my mind, trying to make sense of the dreamlike images. 'I heard my mother calling me. It was… like a dream, but it wasn't. I followed her voice. I know it's weird. But back then I couldn't help following it. My body seemed to be moving on its own.'

'Didn't Aisha warn you about Vandorfort?'

'Vandorfort? She mentioned it, but—'

'The ruined castle full of subits. Do you remember what happened there?'

I shivered at the memory of the snakes inside my body and pressed my palm to my chest.

'I'd rather not,' I admitted. 'What are… subits?'

'So, Aisha didn't warn you. I'm afraid we were too hasty in appointing her as a mentor.'

'It isn't her fault. I went to bed very early yesterday, and I'd monopolised her with questions before then. She didn't have time to warn me. Will… what is that place?'

'I have to go. I've already been here longer than I should have.' He strode towards the door.

'Please just explain this one thing, and I won't bother you anymore. I mean... when those subits attacked me, I felt... I already knew the feeling from my dreams. The demons with tentacles coming out of their palms, draining my energy. But in reality, it was a thousand times worse. I don't understand. What did I see in my dreams? What were those subits? Do they have anything to do with noxes?'

He glanced out at the nocturnal mist still enveloping the forest. 'Well... if you're determined to pretend to be a warrior, you need to know who you'll be fighting at least.'

'Thank you.'

His cold eyes drifted to mine. 'In your dreams you saw noxes – our biggest enemy in the Human World. As a warrior you're supposed to fight and kill them.'

'Okay. But what are the subits? Why did they attack me?'

'They attacked you because you're an easy target. They can't influence the locals. So when they sensed new flesh in Faivendei, they got inside your head and found your weakness.'

'Why?'

'To kill you. You were incredibly lucky to survive.'

'But I didn't do anything wrong. Why did they want to kill me?'

He closed his eyes, took a deep breath and a few seconds later opened them again. 'I hope you know at least what a ghost is. Ghosts are created when there's a strong surge of human energy before a natural death, for whatever reason. It's essentially harmless. But a subit is formed when a person dies violently. Subits can harm, they can kill, but fortunately, unlike ghosts, they're tied to the scene of the crime.'

I remembered the shattered pebbles and the half-crumbled castle. 'What happened there?'

'Noxohit happened.'

'What's Noxohit?'

'Not what. Who. The dark spirit – creator of those demons you saw in your dreams. More than a century ago, one of the strongest shamans in history, Solomon Ratanten, led by his greed, disturbed the forbidden part of the Universe. He awakened the darkness, which took the form of a spirit and followed the shaman to our planet. After killing Solomon, the spirit looked into the souls of other people and decided to stay on Earth until he had purified it.'

'Purified it of what?'

'Humans.'

I stared at him blankly, trying to process what I'd just heard. But no, it wasn't making sense.

'Noxohit possessed thousands of people. But that wasn't enough. Then he found us – the guardians. Having supernatural power, we could destroy far more humans more quickly. Noxes are guardians infected by Noxohit's poison.'

'What? Why? Why does he do that to the guardians?'

'He sees the world in the form of vibrations and frequencies. All your worries, hopes and fears are just wavelengths to him. What are you afraid of, Lilly? Losing your mother? So he won't have to say anything. He'll just affect you with wavelengths that you won't see, hear or feel, but every cell in your body will shudder, knowing that your mother is dying and there's nothing you can do. He can read any person like an open book. You can't hide a thing from him.

'But the irony is that, though he despises people, to influence them he needs a physical vessel – a body. So he uses guardians to create noxes. They find dark places in the human mind,

92

like oil floating on the surface of milk, and expand them to such a size that they fill all the bright areas. Under his power, all your fears, longings and negative thoughts will escalate until you destroy yourself. He acts as litmus paper, just revealing the darkness of humans' minds. He doesn't actually kill. Why get your hands dirty when people can do all the dirty work themselves?'

'I don't understand. You say he's been here over a century, but our civilisation is still alive.'

'*Barely* alive. People are exhausted, anxious, unstable. The percentage of them suffering from mental disorders grows every day. Their sense of belonging, of compassion for all living things, is dissolving while their hunger in the material world increases as they try to fill the inner void. Look at how the flora and fauna of the Human World have been depleted over the past hundred years. Their polluted world is suffocating in chaos, corruption, terrorism, wars. Look at how global warming is destroying the planet and no one seems to care enough to stop it. Noxohit is worse than the asteroid that destroyed the dinosaurs. Under his yoke, people are destroying their own world, dooming themselves to imminent extinction.'

My whole body was shaking. Of course, when I was in the Human World, I heard about the deplorable state of things. But I never could have guessed the demons from my dreams were behind it. And that these demons were once guardians, possessed by a dark spirit from a forbidden part of the Universe.

'I can't believe it...'

'The Human World's days are numbered. The sixth extinction is just a matter of time.'

I shook my head. 'No. There are people who strive for prosperity out of love and not fear. There are people who are fighting for the future of humanity and the planet as a whole.'

'Indeed there are. But they're muted by the other ninety-nine per cent of the population, who contribute to the annihilation process or simply look away from the dying world.'

'But you're guardians. Surely you can use your powers to defeat Noxohit.'

'Our power is a leaky bucket of water against a wildfire. That's why we live here in the Spirit World. Some spirits pitied us and granted us access to their world.'

'You aren't here just to hide from him, are you?'

'No. There are many forests with guardians in the Spirit World. We created LEEF – the League of Enchanted Forests – to fight him. But it's useless. When we kill a nox, the body of the guardian dies, but the dark energy stays intact. We're making literally no difference.'

'Can't shamans transform this dark energy? Or destroy it?'

'No. Even the strongest shamans can't do that.'

'There should be something. There should be a way to defeat him. Nothing is indestructible.'

'We had a chance once. In the late 1920s, the spirit of the prophet Taliesin foretold that the vandors would come, and with their help, Noxohit would be overthrown.'

'Vandors?'

'Soul-healers. They extract the darkness from people and transform it into light.'

'So… where are they now?'

'Noxohit started to hunt them, and some spirits helped him get into the Spirit World. For years he ransacked the enchanted forests, one by one, and soon all the vandors were transformed into noxes. The most dangerous kind of noxes, because they can destroy a person physically, mentally and spiritually: feeding on human energy, sowing doubt in their minds and hardening their souls.'

I suddenly realised. 'Vandorfort... Is that where the vandors lived?'

'Yes.' His distant gaze focused on nothingness. 'Fourth of June 1946. Hundreds of guardians died trying to protect them. The subits were formed there, and it's still a black hole in the heart of Faivendei. Day and night, it's shrouded in mist, so Omnia isn't constantly reminded of the tragedy.'

'Can't Omnia destroy it? Or doesn't she have enough power?'

'Vandorfort can't be destroyed because the subits are still there.'

'What about shamans? Subits are evil spirits, right? So shamans should know how to lay them to rest?'

'If there was a way to fix this, don't you think we'd have done it already?'

'I'm sorry, I just – I can't believe there's no hope. There's always hope. There has to be.'

'There is none.' He broke off. 'Shamans aren't able to lay those subits to rest, because the bodies that once hosted them are alive and moving around the Earth in the form of noxes. So shamans can only pray to the Universe to calm them down a little.'

'Hold on. He didn't kill all the guardians back in 1946, right? So you managed to defeat him somehow?'

'No. He simply decided to leave some of us alive. He says that *unfortunately* he needs some guardians' bodies to purify the Human World... that all he wants is to leave the whole planet for the Spirit World. For people who live at higher frequencies and spirits, who would never harm the Earth.'

'Is that true?'

'Of course not. He's just lying to ensure spirits won't interfere with his process of extermination. And they, like gullible sheep, believe him. But the moment he finishes with us and the Human World, he will cast his gaze upon the spirits.'

'So why can't you just reason with the spirits?'

Darkness filled his aquamarine eyes. 'Imagine you're living happily on the equator. One day, an enemy comes and banishes you to the North Pole, where you're forced to hide for millennia. Then a long-awaited saviour appears. He tells you he'll kill your enemy and let you return back home. Would you resist him?'

'Of course! If it was obvious that he's lying.'

'Bullshit. You wouldn't know he's lying. He would make you believe in what he wants.'

'No. There has to be a way.' A chill passed through my body. Subits... Vandorfort... a black hole in the heart of Faivendei... tragedy... All my life, the world of my dreams was a warm, welcoming place where I could be my true self. Now it turned out to be an occupied territory fighting a hopeless war.

Suddenly, I remembered Will's true age. 'That day – 4 June 1946. Was that the day you saw Omnia crying for the first time?'

'That's right. And the second time was when you came. I have no idea what she saw in your future, but it can't bode well for any of us.'

I lowered my gaze. What could Omnia see that might be comparable to such a tragedy?

'Lilly, I know you don't want to be a warrior. I hope you'll leave today. You've already made a big mess here.'

I kept my eyes on the ground, trying not to let the words sting.

'Listen, the end of the guardians and human civilisation is just a matter of time. As a warrior, you'll be killed on your first mission, or even worse, transformed into a nox. Remember how those snakes were eating your body from the inside out? Multiply that by a thousand and you'll understand what guardians feel all the time if they get infected with Noxohit's darkness. So go back to the Human World. Enjoy your life while you can.'

'But I must—'

'Must what? Find your parents? If you don't have a gift, they were warriors. I bet they left you in the orphanage to protect you. Staying here would disrespect their wishes.'

'Why do you stay here then, if it's so hopeless? Why don't you give up and go live to the Human World?'

'Because I was born to protect guardians.'

'So was I – born among the guardians. And even if my parents thought I'd be better off in the Human World, I don't have to follow the path they've chosen for me. You don't know me. If you think all this talk will scare me, you're wrong. I didn't want to be a warrior because I had nothing to fight for. Now, thanks to you, that's changed.' I stopped to catch my breath. 'I have nothing to lose, Will. If I'm killed on my first mission, nobody will care. But at least I'll die fighting for a good cause rather than living comfortably knowing the world will collapse around me at any minute.'

He glared at me murderously and left the room, slamming the door behind him.

I was trembling, but I'd meant every word I'd said. I couldn't believe people had been living under the yoke of the dark spirit all this time. I couldn't believe the Human World might soon be destroyed. I just couldn't accept it. And I knew I would fight to stop it.

I walked out of that building, ready to fight Noxohit to the death. However, as soon as I looked up, my inner storm began to cease. The early morning calm was still everywhere. The birds were chirping in the trees. A faint haze – all that was left of the dense fog – scattered the rays of the rising sun into a soft, warm light. It lay like a weightless blanket over the ancient hemlock grove. Impossibly tall and draped with shawls of moss, the trees seemed as old as time, their roots hidden in the emerald carpet of ferns. Not a single shade of russet could be seen in the lush green bushes, as if every fern leaf was immortal and ever young. They were each crowned by a flower, surrounded with unfurling spirals of pale green. The closed petals of these flowers reached up for the sky like six criss-crossed tongues of writhing flame. Each of them was coloured yellow at the base and crimson at the tips.

As slowly as possible, like a cat stretching after a soothing sleep, they opened before my eyes. Their hearts were shining gold, and one by one, small sparkling lights rose from their core, floating up. The fern-flower seeds.

Fronds swished against my knees as I walked carefully through the field towards the flowers, avoiding stepping on the leaves. The warm breeze in the air was so gentle it couldn't make the fern leaves dance. But the petals of their flowers were swaying under every light wind like ethereal fire. I thought I could hear them sing.

Hairito began to chase the lights. They flew around her, teasing, but not giving in. I kneeled in front of one flower and it suddenly closed.

I gently stroked the soft amber fur of its spirals. 'I would never harm you.'

It opened to me again, casting a warm golden glow on my face. The fern-flower seeds flew from its core and hovered around me appraisingly. I stretched my hand out and they landed on it, releasing all my tension and calming my mind.

Tears welled up in my eyes. 'So beautiful.' This was the world of my dreams.

The conversation with Will had answered many of my questions. But it had also left an unpleasant aftertaste. I didn't know if he really believed we were all doomed or if he was just trying to scare me. Probably both. I still remembered, and would never forget, the heartrending sorrow of the tune he'd played in that church. His heart was broken. By whom or by what, I didn't know. I felt sorry for him.

But I couldn't share his grim fatalism. I wasn't a warrior, but I was ready to fight. I loved this world too much to let it die.

Maybe I should have listened to him, Omnia, the leaders of Faivendei and even Aisha. But following common sense had never been my strong suit. I decided to train day and night to turn my weak limbs into a warrior's body. It was already dawn, and I ran to Aisha to ask directions to Belator. With no mist in my way, I could easily see the majestic redwoods with wooden cabins at their tops nearby, and Hairito remembered where Aisha's home was.

When we approached the redwood, the cabin hovered close to the roots, as if waiting for us. We entered, and Aisha ran from the kitchen to me, hugging me tightly.

'Oh, Lilly! Thank the Universe you're alive! I went to the Equilibrium after I heard the subits screaming. But you were asleep so I came back here and waited for you.'

'Equilibrium?'

'The place where Will took you. Oh, I should have warned you. I'm so stupid!'

'Don't worry, Aisha. Everything's fine.'

'I'm so, so sorry. I really am. If I'd warned you, they wouldn't have been able to get into your head.'

'It's okay.'

'How do you feel?'

'I'm fine, honestly.'

'Thank the Universe Will got there in time. I can't imagine what would have happened if he hadn't saved you.' She shivered. 'Okay, let's go to the kitchen. You need to have breakfast before your training at Belator.'

'I'm afraid I don't have time for breakfast. I'm already late.'

'You're my mentee. I'm taking one hundred per cent responsibility for you. After your adventures in Vandorfort, you must have something to eat. I'll go with you to General Fairfax to explain everything.'

'Aisha, I really don't—'

'We're doing this my way. The longer you argue, the more time you waste. You must ease off a little after Vandorfort. It's a miracle you're alive!'

I nodded, feeling there was no use fighting.

We headed towards the table. A pitch-black tarantula, the size of my palm, scurried underneath the sofa as we approached. Hairito followed him with a dazed look. He didn't seem scary at all.

'Tarry is still shy,' Aisha explained.

When we entered the living room, I stopped as if rooted to the spot. I hadn't felt it, but the house had already lifted itself up to the canopy.

'You have the same view from your room.' Aisha stood beside me, smiling.

I strolled closer to the full-length window and gazed at the layers of landscape: a ghostly haze curled on the surface of the lake; a verdant valley stretched over the hill mounting to the sky; low clouds skimmed the canopy of the forest with the sun breaking through them. Its face peeked at us from between the hilltops, casting its rays on the glorious pines and painting the sky in warm peach shades. Hairito stood next to me, also admiring the view.

Aisha came by my side. 'The Vita River flows through Faivendei. It passes through three lakes. Domus is the largest.' She pointed at the lake in front of us. It had three floating paths joining at a huge spreading willow with cherry blossoms growing on it. Omnia.

'There's another lake – Opus – but you can't see it from here. Do you see that grey building over there, with a square tower that looks like a crematorium? That's Belator. It's on the bank of Opus. The village of warriors is there too.'

I glanced to the right at a Gothic castle. 'That's Sodalitas, right?'

'Yes. See the marble square? We organise seasonal balls there. Council meetings are held in the castle, but it's open to all residents of Faivendei as well. However, I wouldn't advise you to venture any further than the library and study rooms.'

'Why?'

'Because the Ravens live there. It's not nice to have strangers walking around your house.'

So that was where Will lived...

I shook my head and looked at the opposite side of Sodalitas. There was an area covered in dark-grey cloud. 'Is that—'

'Vandorfort. Did Will tell you about it?'

I nodded.

'It gives me the creeps to think of you being in there.'

I dived into my memories of the glowing, red-eyed ghosts, the snakes crawling in my chest...

'And those are our school and nursery.' It seemed she was trying to distract me from my thoughts and pointed down at two little gingerbread houses on the bank of Lake Domus, between Sodalitas and Vandorfort. One of the floating paths led directly to them. 'Come on. I'll show you what's on the other side of the house.'

We went out onto the terrace. Hairito hopped up onto the rail, peering into the distance. Dozens of cabins hovering in the crowns of mighty redwoods surrounded us. The coniferous forest rose up ahead, gradually transforming into craggy cliffs and scree slopes dotted with boulders. The air here was so fresh and pure.

'The Dormont Mountains,' Aisha said. 'There are diamond caves there, but the Ravens don't let anybody take the gems. They're responsible for resource control. Many guardians have tried to steal diamonds and run away, but there's no fooling Omnia.'

A raven flew overhead, glancing down at us. I averted my gaze, blushing.

'Over there is Amedas – the village of shamans.' Aisha pointed to the right, where dozens of cylindrical basalt towers with conical roofs were arranged in a spiral. 'It's located near the third lake, Amicus.'

The towers were built on what seemed to be the only large flat field in Faivendei. There were no trees, only some flowering bushes growing between the towers.

'Why are they built in a spiral?'

'Erm… shamans spend most of their time in prayers and meditation. I think the arrangement and shape of the towers helps them amplify one another's energy waves and broadcast them more easily. Well, at least that's how I understand it.'

My attention was drawn to a small single-storey white building near the shaman village. 'Is that the hospital?'

'Equilibrium. They don't just cure symptoms there but balance physical and mental health. The human body is one of the most perfect systems, but sometimes it gets out of balance. At Equilibrium, it's restored to normal.'

'I see. And we live in—'

'Exilis.'

'Exilis. I like the name. By the way, are there other places I should avoid besides Vandorfort?'

'No. Vandorfort and the subits are quite enough... Oh, I'm so stupid! I almost forgot. There's a wall of trees around Faivendei. You can't mistake it for anything else if you see it. Don't cross it, otherwise you'll end up in another part of the Spirit or the Human World. If you end up in the land of spirits, watch out. They don't like us. They think Noxohit is a blessing, not a curse. And you'll only be able to get back here with a guide.'

'A guide?'

'Yes. They're trusted people with portal keys. Like Will, for example. Did you see the wavy tattoo on his arm? That's his key. You can't go back to Faivendei without one, and if you go beyond the wall of trees, no one can help you.'

She glanced at her watch. 'Okay, Lilly, let's go inside. I know you had a crazy night, but your initiation at Belator might be even worse.'

CHAPTER 7
SHAMAN

COULD MY FIRST training in Belator be worse than being attacked by subits? I was ready to go through fire and water to contribute whatever I could to the guardians' fight with Noxohit, but I'd never been particularly strong. My memory drew from its dusty attic pictures of how my sharp tongue sometimes clenched the fists of other children in the orphanage. I couldn't remember a single time when I'd won those fights. Even when I had a chance to win, I'd held back for fear of hurting my opponent. How could I kill noxes, who were just guardians infected by Noxohit's poison?

And then, of course, I was scared. It seemed in the centre of my chest was an industrial magnet that drew all my stiff-as-iron organs to itself. I hunched and couldn't straighten up.

Until we descended from the treehouse and I lifted my eyes.

Strewn with thousands of shimmering flowers, a verdant carpet of ferns lay on the ground between the gigantic trunks of redwoods. Tiny lights hovered around them like drowsy, just awakened fireflies. Their golden radiance infused me with healing warmth, and for a moment all the tension left my body.

'This is unbelievable.'

'Fern flowers.' Aisha was smiling, also taking in their beauty. 'Kind of pretty, aren't they?'

'But how did I miss them yesterday?'

'They weren't here. Yesterday Faivendei was in mourning.'

'Mourning?'

Her smile faded. 'The day before, General Fairfax killed a nox. Omnia doesn't like bloodshed.'

I remembered his hands – the dried red stains under his fingernails – and shuddered. My instincts had been right about him. If only I could choose another way to become a guardian...

We crossed the lake, bowing to Omnia as we passed by, and continued through the woods, when suddenly a loud cawing pierced the air. I swung around. A raven perched on a spruce branch just a few feet from us. My pulse quickened, but I turned away from the bird at once.

Soon we were in front of Belator. I tilted back my head to cast an eye over the 'crematorium' tower. Grey, cold, lustreless. A Soviet tractor factory dropped into the middle of Fairyland. Several dozen warriors were training on a wide green field in front of it. Not running or doing push-ups or squats, but swinging very real swords and nunchaku, batons and knives at one another. Steel rang, creating an eerie symphony of death.

'Are you sure you want to go in there alone?' Aisha asked me for the third time.

'Yes. He doesn't take me seriously already. Showing up with a minder would only make things worse.'

'Okay, maybe you're right. Go through the main entrance, then turn left, and at the end of the corridor you'll find his office. Good luck, Lilly.'

'Thanks.' I forced a smile and headed to the entrance along the central path that bisected the field. Inside, the place was deserted. I headed to the left, found his office and knocked.

'Come in!' a deep, rough voice grunted from inside.

I turned to Hairito. 'Wait here, okay?'

She nodded.

I opened the door. 'Good morning, sir.'

'You...'

His savage glare sent goosebumps down my back.

'I thought after your visit to Vandorfort you'd already run back to the Human World with your tail between your legs.'

'Sir, I'm here and ready for training.'

'Ready, are you?' He bared his teeth. A growl? A smile? 'Find Constance the Bull on the second floor. She'll be your coach. Tell her to break you in. Now get out of my office.'

I closed the door behind me.

The Bull... What a weird surname. I tried not to dwell on those thoughts, for I had doubts it wasn't a surname.

I found her office and knocked on the door.

'Yes!' A raspy, smoky voice.

I walked in. A broad-shouldered woman with hyena's eyes, big disproportional face and thin lips curved in natural disdain glowered at me. I gulped. No... the Bull was definitely not a surname.

'Who are you?' She wrinkled her nose, then her eyes drifted to Hairito. 'Ah, the new one. What do you need?'

This was going to be fun. 'General Fairfax told me you're to... break me in? You're to be my coach.'

She looked me up and down, as if unable to find the qualities that would make me worth wasting time on. 'Is this a joke?'

'I'm pretty sure it's not.'

'No, it's crossing the line, even for me. Go and tell him to assign you another *coach*.' She let out a crow's laugh at some joke only she could understand.

'He was quite clear about it. I assume we both have to follow his orders.'

Her mouth dropped open, making her resemble an attacking triggerfish. But in a heartbeat her expression changed and she smiled. 'Well, if you insist.'

It was the most threatening smile I'd ever seen in my life.

We marched down the hall into one of the training rooms, where people were paired off practising various martial arts, landing blows that gave off meaty *thwacks*. Against my own will, my knees started to shake. I wasn't ready for this.

'Whatever happens, the gargoyle can't help you, or you're both out of here. Fabian, Jack!' she called two men who were training nearby. 'Make sure the gargoyle doesn't intervene.'

'The gargoyle?' they mused in unison.

Constance approached me so close, I could feel her stale breath on my forehead. My elbows instinctively pressed into my sides.

'Last chance. Are you sure you want me to be your coach?'

The clanging and clutter and all the moves ceased. I felt myself like a frail lion cub challenging the alpha while the rest of the pride froze, staring at us. The situation wasn't new to me.

'Well, it doesn't matter what I or you want, does it? An order is an order. Coach.'

Giggles and whispers reached us from the crowd. Now they were definitely waiting for the show.

'Indeed, well then...'

Without warning, she backhanded me, swinging at my head like a batter at a pitched ball. Sharp pain stabbed through my skull, and I staggered back, gritting my teeth.

She didn't give me even a second before she hit me again with a fist like a hammer. I was on the floor. Starbursts shimmered before my eyes, and drops of blood trickled down my lips. I swallowed the blood that had ended up in my mouth and tried to stand but fell to my knees.

'Get up and defend yourself!'

Startled faces watching my humiliation doubled, multiplied and whirled in a psychedelic kaleidoscope. I glanced away, staring at the crimson drops on the floor and feeling my consciousness drifting away.

'What were you thinking when you decided to become a warrior, huh? You think we're playing games here? Look at yourself! If I were a nox, you'd already be dead!'

If she fails, she will leave Faivendei immediately. Gabrielle's words rang in my blurry mind. I couldn't fail... not after what the subits had shown me, not after what I'd learned about Noxohit. The world was spinning, the blood was dripping from my nose, but I wiped it away and pulled myself to my feet.

'Oh, come on! Just give up. Go back to the Human World. You'll never be able to fight noxes!'

'No,' I barked.

She swung again.

Somehow, I blocked her, but she slammed her other hand into my belly, hammering the breath out of me. I crumpled to the floor again.

'Do you think I enjoy this? I want you to understand what you're signing up for. Being a warrior is a death sentence for you.'

Through a thick haze I saw Hairito, trying to break free from the two warriors who held her back. I struggled to my feet. No matter how hard I tried, the nausea and the lack of oxygen were pushing me deeper into bottomless darkness.

'These are love taps compared to what you'd face in the field, do you understand? Noxes will attack not just your body but also your mind. You're not a warrior and never will become one!'

'Anybody… can become a warrior… when there's something… worth fighting for.'

She raised a fist again. I struggled to stay upright but stared her in the eye.

'Enough!'

She lowered her fist. 'It's none of your business, Raven.'

I turned to see Will, and this slight move drained the rest of my energy. I fell but not to the floor – into his hands. The last things echoing in my diving-into-the-darkness mind were a desperate sigh and his dense velvet voice purring, 'You're a walking disaster, Lilly White.'

I WOKE WITH a start. Where was I?

White walls, two simple beds. Hairito draped across my legs, snoozing. I was in the Equilibrium. Again. The rays of the setting sun flowed through two narrow casement windows behind white translucent curtains, painting in warm hues a black piano and a porcelain vase with a fresh bouquet of field flowers on it.

The piano was playing… by itself.

I got up from the bed and tiptoed to the instrument, trying to make sure my eyes weren't fooling me. One after another the keys were sinking and rising again, creating a quiet and sooth-ing melody. I gently passed my hand through the air over the piano stool but felt nothing.

'A lutin is playing.'

I swung around. By the door stood Christopher Raven – the ambassador of Faivendei. Elegant and classy, he was dressed in a three-piece tweed grey suit and white shirt with an impeccably knotted, deep-blue tie.

'They help us here,' he continued. 'Classical music calms the mind, relieves physical tension and speeds recovery.'

Hairito woke up; her wary eyes focused on him.

'I heard about your encounter with Constance.'

The flash of memory passed through my mind. I touched my cheeks, nose and lips, but they were just fine.

He smiled softly. 'Fern-flower seeds are miraculous heal-ers.'

'Mr Raven—'

'Please – call me Christopher.'

'Christopher. Why are you here?'

'Don't worry, nobody will exile you because you lost your first battle.'

He was, indeed, very intuitive.

'But I can't help noticing how resilient you were with Con-stance. Not many people get back up after her first punch. Even fewer after the second. You lost some blood there but gained some respect.'

'You were there?'

'No. Will told me the details.'

I blushed. So he'd witnessed my humiliation too.

'However, it's not your adventures in Belator that brought me here today. I came to ask you about your parents. What do you remember about them?'

I hadn't expect that. Why was he interested in my parents? Had Gabrielle sent him? But it didn't matter – I had nothing to hide.

'I haven't seen them since I was five, but I know they lived in the Spirit World. I was raised in an orphanage in England.'

'What year were you born?'

'Two thousand five.'

He smiled, looking at the floor as if he'd found there something only he could see. 'Eighteen...' His mind returned from faraway lands, and his soft eyes drifted back to me. 'Please forgive my sentimentality. I'm one hundred and forty-six years old. Eighteen's a rather distant memory.'

I tried to contain my surprise, but my jaw dropped. He looked no older than fifty, even forty-five. 'One hundred and forty-six?'

He let out an amused chuckle. 'And just past the bloom of youth. Ravens live up to three hundred years, Lilly.'

'That's why Will looks so young,' I blurted before I could think better of it.

And of course, he grinned slyly at my comment.

'So why are you interested in my parents?'

'It might shed some light on who you are. Don't you know anything about them?'

'Not from memory. But I often see them in my dreams – my parents and my brother.'

'Older or younger brother?'

'Older.'

'Do you remember what they looked like?'

'No, their faces are always a blur. I see them, but when I wake up, I can't remember a thing.'

'Do you remember anything about the place where you were born?'

His simple interest was turning into an interrogation.

'We lived in a stone house, like a small castle on the riverbank. I even drew a picture of it. There were water-horses living at the bottom of the river—'

His healthy complexion turned deathly pale. He looked away and nodded, forcing a smile. I waited for him to say something, but he was lost in the gloom of his thoughts. What was wrong with him?

'Yesterday,' I said, 'when I walked in, you looked at me like you'd seen a ghost, like you… recognised me.'

He was silent, as if sorting out what he could say to me and what he could not. 'You remind me of somebody.' His murmur barely reached my ears.

'Do—' I cleared my throat. 'Do you know my parents?'

'I hope I don't. Because if I do, you're in trouble.'

'What? Why?'

'For you own sake, I won't tell you anything else right now. Let's make a deal. Give me the picture of your house, and I'll contact my friends who live in the woods with water-horses. If they confirm what I'm thinking, I'll tell you everything, all right?'

'Sure, but why can't you tell me right now?'

'Because if I'm right, it will destroy your life once and forever. Pray that I'm wrong. And whatever happens, don't tell anyone about our conversation. Otherwise, my hands will be tied, and I won't be able to help you. Do we understand each other?'

I just nodded, still trying to process what I'd heard.

'Good. I won't bother you any longer. You still need to rest. See you later, Lilly.'

He left. What was that supposed to mean? Had my parents sided with Noxohit? I shook my head, unable to believe it.

I was ready to run after him, but just as I got up, the door handle turned and a girl entered the room. I stood rooted to the spot. She walked graciously, holding her head up like a black galleon floating slowly through the fog. But there was something about her gait that betrayed the weight of the whole world she carried on her shoulders. She was as skinny as I was but tall, which made her look lanky. Her pale lips and grey, almost white eyes contrasted sharply with her umber skin and thick inky hair, which streamed down to her lower back in a flawless waterfall. Her gaze was blank and distant, and she didn't notice us until she approached one of the beds Hairito had leaped onto.

Her eyes widened, showing the whites, and a vein stood out against her golden forehead, as if one gust of wind had transformed this graceful gall⸻ into a pirate ship that had spread its menacing black sails.

'Gargoyle!'

She waved her hand, opening her long, thin fingers, and bright silver energy poured out of them like a thousand tiny lightning bolts. They joined together to form a long whip. Hairito leaped towards me, but the girl swung her weapon and wrapped it around her neck, crashing her on the floor in front of me.

Wailing and twitching, Hairito tried to get rid of the shackle, which seemed to be burning her.

'Let her go! She's not like other gargoyles! Let her go!'

The girl seemed to be hypnotised, ignoring my pleas. I grabbed the whip with both hands, then yanked my burned hands away. It was as hot as a branding iron.

Hairito's eyes rolled back. Life was leaving her body.

I ran to the girl and slapped her face as hard as I could. 'Wake up! You're killing an innocent!'

It worked. The girl's eyes cleared, and the whip disappeared. Hairito crawled under my bed, coughing. I ran to her and crouched down. She was trembling all over, her hair standing on end, but her neck looked surprisingly unharmed. I glared at the girl.

She watched Hairito and just shook her head, then pulled the top cover off the bed, lay down under the duvet and closed her eyes.

What the hell was that?

The nurses came in with a portable table and stopped by her bed, fluttering around her as if she were a precious, fragile flower.

'Vesta, are you asleep?' one of them murmured in a half-whisper, as if to an innocent child.

The girl opened her eyes. Gradually, my pulse was returning to more or less normal. And I was becoming aware I was in pain. I glanced at the white blisters striking through the crimson skin of my throbbing palms.

'Have a cup of tea please,' the second woman said, holding a mug in her hands.

The girl rose from the bed, picked up her mug and drank the tea in one gulp. 'Stop the music, or I'll throw the lutins out of the window.'

The music cut off. She closed her eyes, and a moment later her breathing became deep and rhythmic as she drifted off to sleep.

'Play, but keep it quiet,' one nurse whispered, and the music started again. 'Her wounded soul needs music.'

'It feels like she's trying to work herself into the grave,' another nurse said. 'She must rest.'

'Yes, but she won't listen to anyone. And who else can do her job?'

'That's true. But I wouldn't want to be in her shoes.'

They lit some candles, placed them on either side of her bed and were about to leave when they noticed me.

'Lilly, you can go home,' one of them said.

I reached for my shoes and winced.

'What's this?' She took my hands in her own. 'Holy Universe! How did that happen?'

My eyes slid to the girl. 'She tried to kill my gargoyle,'

'Oh dear. You'll have to stay here a little longer. Sit down and I'll get you what you need.'

'I'd rather go home, thank you.'

'Do you want to get an infection? Don't argue please.' The nurse left the room.

I sat on the bed, not sure what scared me most: my inflamed hands or being in the same room with this crazy girl. At least she was asleep.

Soon the nurse returned, holding a copper bowl. She placed it on the table next to my bed, took my hands and spread a brown-green paste over the burns. I flinched.

'There, there. It stings, but it'll help.'

She bandaged me up, told me to stay in the Equilibrium for a bit longer and left the room. Hairito crawled up onto my bed, sniffed at the burns and sneezed. Startled, she covered her mouth with her dragon-like paws and glanced at the girl. But she was still sleeping, and Hairito breathed a sigh of relief.

'Are you okay?' I whispered.

Hairito nodded, looking apologetically at my palms.

'I'll be fine.' I smiled. Seeing her alive and unhurt calmed me a little.

Sitting on the bed, I watched the sun set, gradually plunging the forest into twilight and darkness. It was nearing midnight when my patience finally ran out. I got up to leave, but the girl opened her eyes. I stopped dead. Hairito hid behind me.

The girl looked at me – her flat gaze seemed to come to life. 'You've got to understand, the last gargoyle I met left three deep scars on my back.'

I said nothing.

'I've never heard of, or read about, or met a friendly gargoyle. When I saw her, my reflexes kicked in.'

She was completely different now, talking like a sane person. But my shock was too fresh to let my guard down.

'I'm sorry,' she went on. 'I didn't mean to scare you.'

'So you don't want to kill her anymore?'

'No. She's different from other gargoyles. It's very strange. She radiates positive energy.'

'I'm glad you can see it now.'

'I'm Vesta. What's your name?'

'Lilly.'

'Wait, Lilly White? So it was you who made the subits scream last night.'

I nodded, frowning.

'They could kill you in the blink of an eye, you know. How did you survive?'

'I don't know.' The memory of the snakes was returning, and I suddenly recalled the voices screaming at me. *Help! Help! Help!* 'They... asked me for help.'

'You must have been hallucinating. Subits don't ask for help.'

'I'm sure they did though. They showed me their memories. I couldn't imagine all those horrors, and faces, and...' I shook my head, trying to rid it of the agonising images.

She propped herself up on her elbows. 'What's your gift?'

'I don't have one. I'm a warrior, kind of by default.'

She smirked. 'No you're not. Warriors need some aggression. You don't have it at all. Even when I was about to kill the gargoyle, you felt sorry for slapping me.'

'I definitely didn't. How can you know what I felt?'

'I'm a shaman. I can read your aura. And from it I can derive the feelings you have.'

'Look, I got a letter from some high-up dwarf that says I belong here. I've got no power. So I must be a warrior.'

Her penetrating grey eyes lingered long enough on me to wobble my composure. 'Why do you want to become a warrior?'

'I want to fight Noxohit, just like you do.'

'Why?'

What was she getting at? 'Noxohit sucks energy from people. He's destroying the Human World. Do I need more reasons?'

She let out a venomous huff. 'And what if humanity is draining energy from the Universe? What if humanity is destroying all life on our planet? The Universe operates on the principles of harmony, and humans must follow these principles, but they're too power-hungry and cruel. They don't care about the world. They don't thank the Universe for giving it to them. No. They just take... more and more and more.'

'They do that only because they live in ignorance under Noxohit's yoke.'

'He reveals humans' filth, yes, but he doesn't create their vices. They were like that before he came, and without him they would still destroy their world, just not as quickly. You'd have to be a complete idiot not to see: people are a cancer on the Universe, and Noxohit... he isn't a curse. He's a cure.'

I eased into a sitting position, trying to process what I'd just heard. She believed that Noxohit might be medicine sent to Earth to destroy a deadly illness: humans. And she was one of the good guys?

'Look,' I said eventually, 'not everything is perfect in the Human World, but it's not all bad. What makes you think that?'

She grinned, shaking her head. 'See now, a warrior would have told me to go to hell and reported my words to the Leaders' Council without trying to figure out the reasons behind them. They're almost devoid of empathy. You have too much of it. Unhealthily so. You're no warrior, Lilly.'

'Maybe. But after what the subits showed me, I can't sit by and do nothing. I want to help.'

'You can't help.'

'I can try.'

Her eyes drifted to the ceiling. 'Shamans can't transform spirits – only energy beings. But I can transform a Cruelty Spirit into a Spirit of Compassion. I inherited this sort of "anomality" from my parents. Who were murdered, *not* by Noxohit but by the people they were trying to protect.'

'But... that's helping, isn't it?'

'It's an unending job.' Her lethal eyes slid to me again. 'Cruelty Spirits gather in places where people commit atrocities then hover over Earth, sowing discord as they go. If shamans didn't continually purify the energy of our planet, humanity would have destroyed itself long ago. But we're finding it harder and harder to keep up.'

'Vesta, I lived there for many years, and I know for sure there are lots of good people too.'

'Really? You should have seen the *good people* I met last night. Even without Noxohit, human civilisation would destroy itself. We're supposed to believe the Universe created the guardians so we could protect humanity, serve them. Nonsense!

Spirits used to live among people too. They believed we could coexist, and eventually they had to flee to a hidden world to save themselves. We can't defeat Noxohit for one simple reason: he *mustn't* be defeated.'

'Then why are you here? Why are you still protecting people?'

She turned away and stared at the ceiling. 'I ask myself these questions every day.'

Neither of us said anything more. Her parents had been murdered by people, and she was still protecting them from spirits that were made of their own cruelty. I was beginning to understand why she saw Noxohit as an answer.

Somebody knocked on the door. I glanced at Vesta.

'I doubt it's for me. I'm not exactly a social butterfly.'

'Come in,' I called out.

It was Thomas who entered the room. What was he doing here?

'Hi, Lilly. I hoped you were still awake. Hi, Vesta.'

She ignored him boldly.

He seemed unsurprised, looking back at me. 'I heard Constance gave you a good thrashing this morning. I wanted to make sure you're all right.'

I cringed at the thought that all Faivendei was aware of my failure in Belator. 'I'm fine. The fern-flower seeds are good healers.'

'Good. I talked to Bogdan – General Fairfax – and persuaded him to make me your coach.'

Did Thomas notice how I flinched inside? 'But... I thought Constance was my coach.'

'No. The Bull never trains anybody. Bogdan often asks her to teach the newcomers a lesson. Last guy had broken ribs after a fight with her. He ran from Faivendei the next day.' He chuckled as if broken ribs were endlessly entertaining.

I stared at him – there was no hint of a smile. 'Are you going to teach me a lesson too?'

'No, but you'll have to train a lot. We have just three months to make you a competent fighter. I think I'll teach you fencing – it's more appropriate for your build. Speed and finesse rather than brute force.'

'Fencing these days? Wouldn't firearms be more effective?'

'Depends what for. Guardians and noxes don't want to kill each other. They need us to create new noxes, and their bodies belong to the guardians we hope to save. Hope dies last, right?' He made this sound like a sneer.

'I see. Thomas, that's very... kind. But won't I be an extra burden for you?'

He winked at me. 'I'll be happy to help.'

'I really don't want to bother you.'

'We'll find a way for you to thank me. Be in Belator tomorrow at seven.'

He closed the door behind him before I could say anything else.

Vesta turned to me. 'Don't mess with Thomas. He's a tricky guy.'

CHAPTER 8
TÊTE-À-TÊTE

IT WAS ALREADY 6 a.m., but the memory of yesterday still haunted me, and I couldn't bring myself to get out of bed. We had been training for almost two months, and Thomas had been more and more flagrantly flirting with me for that time. Tired of my daily indifference, he had decided to pass from fruitless flirting to direct attack. He'd tried to kiss me against my will, but I already knew enough self-defence skills to protect myself.

That had been a big surprise for him, since he hadn't put any effort into my training. Fortunately, there were many warriors who didn't have the same level of aggression as Thomas or Constance or General Fairfax. Thanks to them, I knew something about the art of fighting after two months in Faivendei.

But his attempted assault wasn't what bothered me.

Since my first day here, a raven had been following me everywhere, and I was sure it was Will's bird. However, we hadn't spoken to each other since that incident in Vandorfort. Except for one time when I'd fallen asleep in Sodalitas reading the *Encyclopaedia of Forest Spirits*. He'd woken me up nonchalantly, telling me to go home.

Every Sunday there was a general meeting in Sodalitas Square where Will, Gabrielle and Christopher would take stock of the past week. Only on these Sundays could I observe Will without being noticed, because many other eyes were fixed on him as well. My first days here, he'd looked stern and sullen. There had been so much arrogance in his bearing it had made him look like a statue carved out of granite. But a few weeks later, I'd seen him smile and couldn't help but smile myself. He'd been talking to Christopher at that moment, his eyes shining and the tightness gone from his body. After that, I'd seen him smile more often. Yet, sometimes the black veil would fall over his face again.

But yesterday my thoughts hadn't been about him. They'd been about the consequences of the incident with Thomas. I'd been so absorbed in it that when I'd glanced up and caught Will looking at me, a cold wave had passed through my body. An ordinary person would have averted their gaze at being noticed, but Will continued to look at me. And... there had been so much warmth and tenderness in his eyes. It'd seemed his temper had raised a white flag and exposed a sensual heart for a moment. But suddenly tension had gripped his jaw, and he'd glanced away as if some dark thoughts had won his invisible inner battle.

This gaze had rippled through my mind like a shock wave, and the fantasies I had previously held back had come crashing down, rushing past the steep slopes of my cold logic. I dreamed of him holding me tightly against his broad chest, wrapping me in his arms. I saw him lifting my chin and pulling it closer to his face. I imagined him tracing the shape of my lips with his fingertips. I wondered how his lips would taste...

I tried to appeal to my pride, reminding myself how rude he'd been in the beginning. But it was in vain. My inner voice, crying that his external sharpness hid a gentle nature and a wounded soul, was way too loud.

But still... what did I know about him? He was a local prosecutor ensuring law and order in Faivendei. Known to be impatient and intense, he had a low tolerance for procrastination and many other human flaws. However there was nothing more important to him than the safety of the guardians, whether physical or mental. With his highly developed intuition, he knew when to push people and when to let them rest and recover. Some considered him harsh and demanding; others just and compassionate. But no one was indifferent to him. A bright character, with his appearance, power and authority, couldn't help but attract attention.

And I'd fallen for it too. Shallow and pathetic. I'd tried to fight my fantasies, I really had. But he possessed my mind. I forgot everything except his aquamarine eyes, his lips and his dense velvet voice.

I got up and read aloud the Guardians' Oath, forcing myself to stop this pointless reverie. I repeated it over and over again as a mantra, and it worked – my mind calmed down. When I finished, Hairito woke up, yawning.

'Good morning, sunshine.'

She purred back.

'Let's go. It's time for breakfast.'

She jumped towards the door, eagerly lifting her long tail. We went downstairs to find Aisha, Ophelia and Tarry already at the table. As always, Hairito sat beside Ophelia. She gobbled up her humongous portion of strawberry oatmeal cookies before I really started on my porridge.

'Tarry, could you pass the salt please?' I asked the tarantula, who was sitting on the table, watching our meal. He and I had become fast friends in the last two months. He picked up the white shaker with his front legs and hurried over to me.

'Thank you.' I smiled, and he rustled his pincers.

'He said, *Always a pleasure*,' Aisha translated, patting his belly. 'So, what are you planning to do today? Have you finished *The History of Spirits*?'

'I'm on the chapter about daoshee and their conflict with the sirens.'

'Very good. Are you going to practise with Thomas today?'

'No. I'll go to Vesta's.'

She lowered her spoon, scowling at me. 'Lilly, what do you see in that rude creature?'

'Please... not again. She has a gentle soul behind that rough exterior. And... she helps me study.'

'I can help you with that. Not for nothing, no one in Faivendei is friends with that crazy girl. The only reason she hasn't been kicked out is because she's a powerful shaman. All this talk of Noxohit being a saviour? If it were up to me, I'd have thrown her out of here by now. And don't look at me like that. I know her parents were murdered, but grief doesn't excuse her behaviour. She's selfish and inhuman.'

'She talks a lot, but she doesn't believe half of it herself. Just think: people killed her parents. She could have joined Noxohit in her grief, but she didn't. She stayed true to her mission. I don't know if I would...'

'I would.'

'Don't listen to what she says – watch what she does. I'm pretty sure if you got to know her better, you'd change your mind.'

'I don't want to get infected with her pessimism, thank you very much.'

I sighed, giving up, and returned to my porridge.

'Well, it's your choice,' she said. 'Don't stay with her long. You need to practise the waltz. You still dance like a donkey on ice.'

'Aisha. I don't have time for this ball, and I have nothing to wear,' I repeated for the thousandth time.

'Nonsense. The dress isn't a problem, and you have to take a break, even if you think you don't have time. A lot of guardians from other lands will be there. It's a tremendous event, and you *will* go. I won't take no for an answer.'

I drew a breath but released it. One thing I'd realised after living with Aisha for two months: if she set her mind on something, she'd get it at any cost.

'We'll practise waltzing tonight, all right?' Not a question. Almost an order. 'I'll try to get away early.'

I nodded, counting on finding a last-minute excuse to escape. She would be busy tomorrow and maybe she'd just forget about me.

After breakfast, I left the house with Hairito. It was warm and sunny outside, but morning dew still lay on the surface of the steps. Descending, I was cautious, but when the raven cawed, I slipped on the last step and fell to the ground.

The loud, intermittent cawing echoed through the wood again. I jumped to my feet and glanced at the bird perched on a nearby pine branch. I could have sworn he was laughing at me. I dusted off my jeans and smiled, imagining Will watching me through the eyes of his raven and once again calling me a walking disaster.

Hiking through the forest, I couldn't wipe that smile off my face. The golden carpet of spruce needles deadened my footsteps as I made my way through my favourite stretch – the most ancient part of the woods that lay at the foot of a majestic mountain valley. Huge evergreens towered over the forest floor, among fallen hollow logs and moss and algae and lichens and ferns. I still couldn't get used to the size of these titanic tree trunks that made me feel like Alice after the 'Drink Me' potion that left her the size of a ladybird. And the fern flowers, shining like tiny red torches in the midst of the lush green only added to the feeling. I inhaled deeply the refreshing scent of coniferous resin mixed with the sweet musk of decaying wood and continued to Vesta's.

'Lilly!' Thomas's bark yanked me back to reality at once.

He stalked towards me, his movements sharp, his body visibly stiffened with wrath. I gulped, looking around. I was in the woods between two villages, Exilis and Amedas, and nobody was in sight. How the hell had he found me?

Hairito stepped next to me, growling.

'Hi, Thomas.' I tried to sound casual.

'Hi?' He almost spat the word. 'That's all you have to say?'

'What do you want me to say?'

'You could start by explaining why you aren't in Belator. What's going on?'

'I—'

He grabbed my face with both of his hands, his nostrils flaring. 'Why do you run away from me? Why do you make me worry?'

I reeled back, my pulse throbbing in my ears.

'Oh come on, sweetheart, don't start this again. I thought I made myself clear yesterday.'

'Yes, you did. That's why I stopped training with you. You don't seem to understand that I am not your sweetheart and never will be.'

His reddish skin flushed brighter, his nostrils flared, his fists clenched. Hairito hissed and growled, straightening up on her hind paws. The raven cawed on a pine branch nearby. Thomas glared at the bird, then at Hairito and released his fists, smirking venomously at me.

'I'll wait.' He blew me a kiss and walked away.

I continued on my way, just barely restraining myself from pulling out my folding sword and challenging Thomas to an actual duel. How dare he threaten me? Could he...? A chill ran through my body, but the fire of fury surged back at once. Let him try, and I would cut his throat.

I closed my eyes and took a deep breath, remembering Vesta's words about emotional balance, energy flows and the consequences of strong negative outbursts. I glanced around at the blooming ferns, at Hairito who was always there for me. I thought of Aisha, who'd taken me in, of Vesta, who trusted me, of Christopher, who was looking for my parents. Of Will... I couldn't let this incident with Thomas cloud my mind.

I crossed the arched bridge that spanned the Vita River to Amedas – the village of shamans. It rested in the middle of a broad circular meadow with no trees close by but many wild briars that blossomed in between the cylindrical stone towers arranged in a spiral. The strongest shamans lived in the centre, and to get to Vesta's house, I walked a long spiral path until I reached the familiar carved wooden door. I raised my hand, but before I could knock, Vesta opened the door.

'What are you doing here?'

I smiled. 'It's good to see you too.'

Vesta stepped aside, and I came in.

The rays of the morning sun were filtering through tall, narrow, arched windows lined up in three rows along impossibly high walls that were covered by ivy crawling around brass scones. As always, it was sombre but warm inside.

'Why aren't you training?'

I dropped into a chair. 'Thomas and I had a misunderstanding.'

She scanned me from head to toe, as if making sure I wasn't harmed. 'I did warn you about him.'

'And you were right.'

She sat down in front of me. 'What happened?'

'Erm… nothing, yet.'

'Yet?'

'I knew you were right from the beginning about Thomas. But I thought if I acted properly, he'd do the same. I never flirted. I did everything to show him he's just my trainer, nothing else—'

'Lilly, you're scaring me. Please tell me he didn't—'

'He didn't,' I reassured her. 'But he tried to kiss me yesterday and said I belonged to him, that it was just a matter of time. Today he found me somehow on my way to you.'

Vesta sat motionless, electric sparks flying from her fingers.

'Well, he didn't hurt me or anything—'

'Yet. You've been playing with fire for far too long. His dark side won't let him stop until he gets what he wants. You must leave Faivendei and move somewhere he can't find you.'

I shook my head. 'I'm not leaving.'

'In that case, during his next trip to the Human World, a Cruelty Spirit can *accidentally* push him down the stairs. People trip every day. People die every day.'

It took me a few seconds to realise what she meant. 'No. That's not an option.'

'Lilly, while he's here, you're in danger.'

'Maybe I can report him to the Leaders' Council?'

'And what do you think they'll do? If they expelled guardians for what they say, nobody would be left in Faivendei. And, remember, I'd be the first one out. Besides, being expelled would only increase his thirst for revenge. He'll stop at nothing, and you'll be dead. So either we kill him or you leave Faivendei – there is no other option.'

'Leaving Faivendei would be worse than death to me. Vesta, I know how to defend myself. Maybe he's stronger, but I have Hairito and—' I wanted to mention Will's raven, but I didn't.

She was silent, as if considering what I'd said. 'You're taking a huge risk.'

'Oh come on, I already did that when I agreed to become a warrior. I'm training to fight noxes and you seriously want me to run away from him?'

'Noxes don't kill for pleasure. Please listen to me. You can't see the world the way I do. I feel the cruelty creeping through his veins, spreading throughout his body and corrupting his soul. He's losing control. You must leave Faivendei.'

'I can't leave now. What's meant to be will be.'

She shook her head and looked at Hairito. 'Never leave her alone, even for a moment. And you, Lilly, try to be with other people all the time. Then he won't dare attack you.' She glanced thoughtfully down. 'I'll try to convince Azrael to make you my partner. But I hunt Cruelty Spirits, and I don't know whether it's worse for you to be attacked by them or by Thomas.'

'I can defend myself.'

She sighed. 'I have to leave now. Go to Aisha's, stay there, study. I'll be back tomorrow night, and we'll decide what to do, okay?'

I nodded and left her house with Hairito. Vesta always expected the worst, but I didn't think Omnia, who saw everything in this forest, would allow Thomas to hurt me. What's more, I had Hairito... and my sword. I wasn't afraid of Thomas, but the last twenty-four hours had been so eventful that I was almost shaking. I definitely couldn't concentrate on reading now.

So I decided to go to one special place near the base of the mountain I'd found about a month ago. No paths led there, and the only way was through a thick forest. It was a small patch of relatively flat land next to a dilapidated arched bridge that lay over the Vita River.

A long walk helped to burn some of the adrenaline in my blood, and the sea of maples and birches, dogwoods and oaks dressed in bright autumn gowns calmed me a little. Ferns didn't grow here, but even if their seeds floated in the air, they would hardly be visible against the background of a thousand warm shades of fall.

The noise of the river was growing insistent enough to erase other sounds. I was almost there and hiked the last bit, keeping my eyes on my feet. But when I glanced up, I froze at the sight of a man by the shore.

Will.

I couldn't believe my eyes. He was standing with his back to me, and he wouldn't have noticed how I came here or how I left. *Easy, Lilly, easy.* It was just a coincidence that we were in the same place at the same time. Just a coincidence...

I stepped into the open and cleared my throat.

He was watching the rumbling river. 'Do you really think it's a wise idea to wander alone in the woods after what happened between you and Thomas?'

I didn't even bother to ask how he knew. 'I'm not afraid of him.'

'You should be. There's something… twisted about that bastard. Anyway. I gave him my first warning. The second will be his last.'

I listened to my inner voice, trying to figure out how I felt about that, but my mind was benumbed by his presence.

'Thank you,' was all I said.

'No need to thank me. It's my duty. I won't allow anybody to act like that in Faivendei.'

It seemed I could physically feel the flame of rage he was radiating now. But those beautiful aquamarine eyes drifted to me and his ardour suddenly faded.

'Why do you always come back here? What's so special about this place?'

'Is this an interrogation? Did I do something wrong?'

His eyes flicked with joy. 'No, I'm just curious.'

'Erm… it reminds me of the place where I was born.'

And here it was. I hadn't told a soul about that, but under the spell of his charm I opened my heart so simply – effortlessly almost.

He nodded, looking at the forest dancing serenely under the breath of a warm breeze. 'I thought so.'

And again: silence. It didn't bother him. He seemed to have forgotten about me, diving into his own thoughts. How could one exude so much power, just standing so silently, so calmly? It wasn't just his incredible height and build. It seemed every cell in his body was made of granite. An invincible majestic cliff. I couldn't take my eyes off him, and despite my own will, my attention was magnetically drawn to his lips.

Suddenly he came back to reality and smirked at me like a cat. 'You feel too loud, Lilly.'

Arrogant prick!

'Thanks again for Thomas,' I snapped and turned away.

He grabbed my hand. As if electrocuted, I snatched it back, scowling at him.

'I'm sorry. I didn't mean to hurt your feelings.' A half-smile still lingered on his face.

'You might have thought about that before you had your raven follow me everywhere like a warden.'

'After Omnia's reaction to your arrival, my mother asked me to keep an eye on you.'

'I think you've got enough proof to tell Mrs Raven that I'm an ordinary girl. No need to waste your time on me.'

He smiled foxily at some thoughts he didn't choose to share.

'Fancy a walk?' he suddenly asked.

'What?'

'I want to show you a part of the forest that you haven't seen yet.'

'Why?'

'Why not?'

I was still mad at his arrogance, and even his clear aquamarine eyes couldn't melt the ice. I stood still and silent.

'Please?'

This word was so alien to his vocabulary that when it left his lips, it sounded as if he was speaking a foreign language. I fought a smile but couldn't help it.

'Whatever.'

He let out a low chuckle.

'What's so funny?'

He didn't answer my question but gestured uphill. 'We can walk or we can fly there.'

Walk. Definitely walk.

I strode ahead. He fell in beside me.

'I noticed you like running up the hills. But not in the southern or western part of Faivendei.'

It was a question, but I ignored it. It took a few minutes to cool myself down. He wisely remained silent and abstained from teasing me again. I couldn't imagine a single person who could stay indifferent to his overwhelming handsomeness, but it didn't give him the right to blabber whatever he wanted.

'The southern part reminds me of my adventure in Vandorfort, and Belator is on the western side. I get enough of it during my training,' I said when my blood finally stopped simmering in my veins.

'So you were serious about becoming a warrior.'

'I just want to be one of you.'

'And your youthful stubbornness tells you that's a good idea.'

Youthful? Did he think I was a child who he could tease on a whim?

'But I must admit your progress in fencing is quite impressive. You're quick and have a good sense of balance. I didn't expect that. And running up the mountain? Honestly, I don't know if I could do that. I *am* impressed.'

No. Don't smile. Don't let his flattery cloud your mind.

I bit my lips but grinned anyway. 'So I'm not completely hopeless?'

'No, not completely.'

His smile reached not only his lips but also his eyes. And I wondered how... how on Earth was it possible to stay collected next to him? Did those ravens have some sort of pheromone that blew the minds of ordinary people like me? Why did only *he* have this effect on me?

'Have you guessed where I'm taking you?'

'I have no idea. I still hardly understand what's going on.'

'Me neither.' He leaned a little closer to me and our hands accidentally touched.

I snatched my hand away. Silence.

It was Will who spoke first. 'So, where did you learn so much about trees?'

I blushed, remembering how my unbridled enthusiasm had energised my words when I'd been telling Hairito (who had never asked for it) about every tree we saw. I studied his eyes, trying to understand if this question was another way to mock me, but his mesmerising gaze expressed only a genuine interest.

'From my mother and books,' I said dryly.

'It's actually charming to see somebody so passionate about trees. I don't think anyone has ever touched them or talked to them with so much affection.'

'What else do you know about me?'

And again, that teasing smirk.

'Tell me or our walk stops here.'

'Threats? Really? How well do you think those will work on me?'

I stopped mid-stride. 'I'm willing to find out.'

He let out a chuckle. He was definitely in a taunting mood today.

'Fine. You were born in the Spirit World. At the age of five you ended up in an English orphanage, where you stayed until age sixteen. Then you worked for two years in a local library before you moved to France. All your life you were looking to get back to the Spirit World.'

He glanced at me as if to see whether I was satisfied with the answer. I wasn't. 'Go ahead. I have a right to know the truth.'

'The truth?' He grinned. 'Okay, what else do I know about you... You work hard, but when you have free time, you spend it with Vesta or Aisha, but mostly reading in Sodalitas or wandering in the woods. You search for wild animals, who are amazingly calm around you. You talk to the trees in human language, praising their beauty – they don't really understand you but appreciate the tone of your voice. You dance with fernflower seeds, first making sure that Ray – my raven – doesn't see you.' He smiled to himself. 'He always does.'

'Fine. What else?'

'You're kind with people but never let your guard down, except for in nature. You love this forest... every tree, every fern, every fallen log and broken branch. Not to mention the wild animals. And the forest loves you back. You never notice, but as you walk, the trees move their branches to hide your sensitive eyes when the sun is out. It feels like you give yourself to this world and it gives itself back.'

His smile started to fade, the black veil again falling over his face at some gloomy thoughts. I suddenly realised that his uplifted mood could change with the snap of a finger and the centurion could return.

'You know what?' I said. '*I'm* going to ask you a lot of questions about yourself. To make us even for you stalking me.'

I leaned closer to him and our hands touched again. I didn't flinch this time.

'Fair enough.' His face had been slowly transforming into a mask of granite, but a hint of a smile dissolved the grim look.

'Okay, William C.J. Raven, my first question is... what do the C and J stand for?'

'My great-grandfather Christopher and his son James. They fought in a war against the dark elves in France.'

'Wait, what? Christopher and James Raven? I read about them in the History of Spirits. But I never imagined they were your grandparents. You have quite a lineage.'

He gave me his crooked smile. *Better. Much better.*

'Okay, next question. Imagine yourself an ordinary man, raised in the Human World. You're sixteen and you have to choose a subject to study at university. What would you choose?'

'Neuroscience. Particularly memory retention and retrieval.'

'Why?'

'To find a way to erase certain memories.'

His frankness took me by surprise. Maybe it was his way of making up for that previous boldness. Neither of us spoke, and only birds chirping broke the silence as heavy grey clouds hid the sun. He frowned, looking away from me, that granite mask returning. What memories did he want to erase? If only I could read his mind...

A wild desire to draw him close and dissolve his sorrow in my embrace stirred up in me.

And I did it.

I slipped my fingers in his hard calloused hand, squeezing it slightly before the flurry of senses could knock me off my feet.

His eyes flicked at my hand... at me. And he squeezed it softly back. It was as if an adult was holding the hand of a child.

Come on. Ask me something.

'And what about you?' It was as if he'd heard my silent plea. 'Which science field do you enjoy most? If any?'

'I think quantum theory or astrophysics,' I answered, desperately trying to act normal.

A chuckle. 'You never cease to amaze me. Why these two?'

'They explore infinity.' I raised my other hand, lifting my head to the sky. The triumphant thickening clouds plunged the forest into gloom, and a small drop of rain fell onto my forehead. 'Will? I think it's going to rain.'

'We're almost there – come on.'

We ran up the hill, but the quicker we moved, the heavier the rain grew. Soon it was stinging our skin.

Then the heavens opened. I laughed loudly. There was no more use in running. We were both absolutely soaking wet.

'So where are we going?'

'We're there.' He led me into a cave on our right where the utter darkness and the scent of damp earth greeted us.

'Seriously? This is what you wanted to show me? A cold wet cave?'

He laughed. 'Yes and no. Take off your jumper – it's dripping wet.' He took off his leather jacket, ready to put it around my shoulders.

'No, it's okay.'

'That wasn't a suggestion.'

'Yeah? And what are you gonna do, huh? Take it off me by force?'

'If necessary.' He stretched his hands out towards me.

'Okay, okay, fine!' I turned around and took it off, suddenly realising that I had only my bra underneath.

I stood with my back to him, my heart jackhammering in my chest and my whole being boiled down to listening as I didn't dare face him. I tried to discern anything through the downpour drumming outside, but it was as if Will wasn't there at all.

Finally, he put his jacket around my shoulders. I eased my arms into the sleeves, zipped it up and turned to him, feeling heat pulsating through my body.

He looked me up and down and burst into new laughter. 'You look like a child playing dress-up.'

'Not my fault you're so atrociously tall!'

He tried to hold back his laughter, but he couldn't, and neither could I. If a ball of lightning had flown into the cave, I wouldn't have been able to calm myself down. I couldn't remember the last time I'd felt as free and happy as I did now.

Our eyes met, and our laughter began to fade in unison. My heart thudded and suddenly stopped. I ceased breathing. All my senses focused on him, as if waiting for something that could disturb their daily rhythm and throw them off balance from now on. I froze, but my every nerve was trembling.

Suddenly, the ceiling began to shine. Will looked up, and my laser focus snapped, bringing me back to reality.

Thousands of fern-flower seeds lit up the vast field of long transparent stones that hung from the ceiling like six-sided icicles with sharp ends. They shimmered and twinkled with iridescent radiance, submerging us in a sea of stars. I turned around, unable to believe my eyes.

'Welcome to the diamond caves.'

I glanced up at Will and caught his soft gaze on me. While I'd been studying diamonds, he'd been studying me.

'Do you want to see them closer?'

I nodded, and he lifted me up effortlessly – indeed, like I were a small child. My will and common sense fell away, feeling his face so close to mine, and the last shadow of my sanity dissolved in the radiant glow of diamonds and fern-flower seeds. I saw my hands reaching towards him. I was in a dream – a beautiful sweet illusion, in which everything was possible, and fear and doubt simply didn't exist. I was free, like a seagull soaring on the hurtling air currents, wings outstretched, ready to dive into the aquamarine depth of his eyes. I bit my lip, caressing his broad forehead, his high cheekbones. My fingertips gently touched his lips, and they parted for a moment. In this luscious delirium, I was ready to lean towards them...

His sudden hostile glare woke my mind with a deafening thunderclap. I pulled my hands away.

'Why are you looking at me like that?' I whispered without thinking.

'How?' His tone was cold. Unforgiving.

'Like you hate me...'

His lips broke into a sad smile 'I don't think I could hate you, Lilly White.'

He put me back on the ground. 'It's stopped raining. I think you can find your way back home.'

His raven transformed into his wings, and in a blink of an eye he flew away. I was left standing and marvelling at how stupid I had been.

CHAPTER 9
ENGAGEMENT

I BARELY SLEPT that night, trying to figure out what had happened. Yesterday, everything inside me had turned upside down. My sober mind had clouded as if from drinking wine, and I'd been unable to control myself. His gaze had been a flame melting my sanity, his voice an angel's song soothing my soul and enrapturing my mind. No one had ever had so much power over me. Why was I so drawn to him? I'd met handsome and powerful men before, and my eyes had been inevitably drawn to them. But had I felt a fraction of what I felt for Will? Not even close.

Although, in the thick mist of euphoria that filled my mind in his presence was a tiny but bright and quiet light, like Sirius shining in the sky. This light was a memory – non-existent and yet so real. It was as if my soul had known his for a thousand years. While my heart was galloping wildly in ecstasy beside him, my soul was resting in serenity, like a traveller who, after wandering through oceans and forests, deserts and jungles, had finally returned home.

But that was no excuse to assume he felt the same way. I'd never been particularly popular with the opposite sex, and Will was worthy of someone equal in both appearance and experience. Yes, he looked young, but he was actually eighty-eight. I had absolutely nothing to offer him. I just couldn't interest his experienced mind. And my behaviour yesterday had been so low, frivolous and unworthy that now, thinking about everything, I wasn't surprised by his glare when I'd dared to touch his lips.

'Urgh...'

I owed him an apology, and I had to give him back his jacket, but it was still too early to go to Sodalitas. I couldn't sleep anymore, so I started reading *The Origins of Spirits* to distract my heavy thoughts.

> Spirits, like people, have souls and are mortal. However, not all spirits are characterised by physical manifestation, and those who have flesh are able to dematerialise—

But when I'd taken his hand, he'd squeezed mine back, and he'd been a little nervous. Why? What had made him nervous?

Stop! Focus on the book!

> A good example would be the tree spirits, which can live in symbiosis with trees, dissolving into them, but are also able to separate, taking a physical form of their own—

But the way he'd looked at me in Sodalitas Square and when I'd studied the diamonds—

Stop it! Read the book!

After death, the souls of spirits also pass through the Border World, which is well documented in *Life After Death* by the renowned researcher Fabius Melis.

I glanced at the pile of books on my table, went through all of them and smiled. I didn't have Melis's *Life After Death* book, which gave me a valid excuse to visit the library in Sodalitas. I put on my yellow raincoat, took Will's jacket and tiptoed to the door. Hairito was snoozing on the bed, and I didn't wake her up.

Before leaving, I sneaked into the bathroom, brushed my teeth and studied myself in the mirror. My wavy hair was standing out in all directions as usual. I reached for the comb and brushed it. Assessing my raincoat zipped up to my chin, I unzipped it, revealing my once white T-shirt and sighed. Aisha was right – the appropriate place for this rag was in the rubbish. Should I have changed? Perhaps. But I had nothing better to wear, so I left the house as I was.

My feet were moving as quickly as my heart. I was almost running to Sodalitas, not expecting anything, just craving the sight of him again. I was going mad, but it was sweet madness I didn't want to resist. It reminded me of the times at the orphanage when I'd run away from lessons to the woods and whiled away hours thinking about the Spirit World. It was wrong, but mischief had overtaken me. Just like now.

Once in Sodalitas, I floated up to the second floor and was about to open the door to the library when I heard Christopher say my name in a room nearby. He had never come back to me about my parents.

I walked towards it and leaned my head against the door.

'No. It's impossible!' Gabrielle's voice.

Silence.

'Are you certain?' she half-whispered.

'Ninety-nine point nine per cent,' Christopher said.

Again, silence.

'How – how long have you known?'

'Since the day she arrived.'

'And you were silent all this time? Why?'

'I had my reasons.'

'Now you'll tell them to me.'

'Gabrielle, calm down.'

'I said explain yourself.'

'I can't.'

'What do you mean you can't? Do you understand the danger you've put all of us in?'

'There's no danger.'

'How can you be so blind? She'll lead noxes directly to us!'

'She doesn't even know who she is.'

'But they surely do. She must leave Faivendei right now.'

'Don't overreact.'

'She's leaving today, or you are.'

'Give her one more day here at least. Let her enjoy the ball.'

'I'm not going to risk my guardians' lives even for another second. And you will pay for your silence. Mark my words!'

'I thought you'd say that.' He sighed. 'I'm sorry we can't come to an agreement. We both remember that you owe me a favour, Gabrielle. I agree – she must leave the Spirit World, but please, do it tomorrow. Let her stay here one more day.'

'Why?'

'I can't explain why… I'm afraid you won't understand.' He paused. 'One more day. That's all I ask.'

'Yes, I owe you a favour. But are you sure this is how you want to waste it? Putting everything we're fighting for at risk?'

'One day.'

'She'll become our undoing, and it'll be your fault.'

Her quick steps approached the door, and I ducked into the library. I dashed to the window and leaned on the sill, peering into the fir branches, as if I were daydreaming, when I was actually scrambling to find some explanation for what I'd heard. They swayed in the wind, so serene...

Was it true? Did I really have to leave Faivendei?

I turned my back to the window and stared at the crimson carpet with its yellow ornaments. Could I have misheard? Could they have been talking about another Lilly? No. Of course they were talking about me.

I recalled Christopher's startled gaze when we'd first met, his words: *You remind me of somebody... pray for me to be wrong... it will destroy your life once and forever...* He had known who I was since the day I'd arrived. But what was it? If only I'd showed up at Sodalitas a few moments earlier.

She'll lead noxes directly to us...

What had Gabrielle meant by that?

My memory showed me the dream in which a nox had squeezed my throat over a gaping chasm, calling me to become the darkness – become the omen of light. Why had he come to me in that dream? What if he'd infected me with his darkness while I'd been dreaming? Gabrielle's words echoed in my mind. *She'll be our undoing.*

No.

I'd rather die than betray the guardians. Moreover, Vesta could see human auras, and she'd have surely told me if my soul was filled with darkness. Instead, she kept telling me about my compassion. Could noxes be compassionate? Maybe they could...

But what about Will? After all, he had a highly developed intuition.

But what if my darkness was hidden? What if it was asleep or just lurking somewhere in the depths of my subconscious? What if it had made me seek out the Spirit World in order to destroy it?

Stop it!

I took a firm hold of my thoughts and headed from the library to find Christopher and ask him directly what he knew. But when I opened the door, I bumped into Will and reeled back. His eyes and lips were smiling, but that soft expression soon disappeared behind a mask of furrowed brows. His eyes darted around my face as if he was trying to see through me.

'What's wrong? Thomas?'

'No. No, it's not—' I lowered my eyes and noticed his jacket, still in my hands. I handed it to him. 'Here. Thank you.'

He took a step towards me; I pulled away. I was afraid if he touched me, he would sense what he hadn't noticed before – something dark, something dangerous inside me. Or maybe he'd known from the very beginning that something was wrong with me. Maybe his raven was only watching me because he'd sensed the danger hidden somewhere in the depths of my soul. Maybe he'd come to me yesterday just to get to know me better. Keep your friends close and your enemies even closer.

'Lilly, what's bothering you?'

I just shook my head, unable to summon the power to speak or look into his eyes.

'The way I left you yesterday... it was stupid. I'm sorry.'

If he'd told me this half an hour ago, I'd have been over the moon. But now, it meant he didn't know the truth about me.

He didn't know that tomorrow I'd have to leave Faivendei. I looked away, fighting the tears that had welled up in my eyes.

He lifted my chin towards him. 'Please – tell me what's on your mind.'

I had just drawn breath to speak when the door opened and Gabrielle entered the library. A deathly horror froze her face as she saw us standing so close to each other. Will lowered his hand from my chin, and I stood still, like a field mouse spotted by a snake. She clenched her jaw. I thought she would reveal whatever secret only she and Christopher knew, and Will would never look at me with the same warmth again.

But instead she straightened her shoulders. 'William, what are you doing here? Your fiancée will arrive at any moment.'

A deafening silence permeated the room. I held my breath, waiting for a denial, but Will didn't say a word. My whole gut wanted me to glance up at him, to read in his eyes what Gabrielle's words meant, but I couldn't move. Maybe a second passed, maybe a fraction of a second, but it was an eternity for me.

Then a gelid fire rose from the depths of my soul, awakening some sleeping darkness within me. I walked out of the library trembling from head to toe.

I seemed to be moving towards Aisha's house but wasn't really aware how. He had a wedding planned and he hadn't said a word to me. How did he have the nerve to act like that if he was engaged? He – the keeper of law and order, the bulwark of honesty and nobility? At least Thomas had made his intentions clear to me. How could he look at me with such affection, hold my hand as if his heart was free?

All his valiant and majestic qualities disintegrated into ashes, which were carried away by the hectic whirlwind of my clouded mind. A fire was burning in my chest, devouring my self-control, when suddenly a thought flew through my mind like a gust of squally wind. Everything went quiet for a moment.

Had I asked him if he was in a relationship? No. So why would he tell me if he was or not? Who was I to him? All his looks and touches could have been nothing more than a way of supporting me after what had happened with Thomas. My ego blamed Will, called him a liar, but had he promised me anything? Had he given me any hope, led me on? Not at all. He'd just been trying to make up for being rude in the beginning. That was all it was. The rest had been blown up by my rich but unhealthy imagination. So who was the liar? I'd deceived myself and had no right to be angry at him for that.

Christopher!

How could I forget about him? Wasn't what I'd overheard this morning more important than Will's engagement? What the hell was going on with me? I glanced back, thinking to return, but my mind and heart agreed it was a bad idea.

When I reached the redwood, I rushed up the stairs and opened the door. Aisha was standing in the corridor in front of the mirror, wearing a long white dress made of white flowing silk that accentuated her sophisticated silhouette. Her long red curls were pulled away from her face and pinned at the back of her head with a barrette set with finely cut, sparkling stones.

The ball! I'd completely forgotten.

'Oh, Lilly! How do I look?'

'You look... mesmerising.'

She smiled but shortly noticed what I couldn't find the strength to hide. 'Everything okay?'

'Yes. I just— I'm going to take a bath.' I strode into the bathroom and locked the door behind me.

'Lilly.' She knocked on the door. 'What happened?'

I wanted to explain, but I just couldn't talk to anybody right then. 'Please. I'll tell you later, okay?'

She was silent for a moment. 'Okay… Anyway. There's a surprise waiting for you in your room. I need to leave now, but we'll meet on the Sodalitas Square tonight.'

'I'm sorry, Aisha. I can't go.'

'What? Why?'

'I just can't.'

'But, Lilly!'

'I'm sorry.' I turned on the taps. The sound of water splashing into the bathtub drowned out anything from outside the room.

I undressed and sat in the bathtub, wrapping my arms around my legs. The pine-scented water was rising, bubbling and foaming, and plunging my body into a relaxing warmth. The black hole in my chest didn't recede. But in this tiny room, in the warm water that filled the air with a healing fragrance, I felt safe for a moment, and tears rolled from my eyes, freeing my body from the tension that was also binding my spirit and my mind.

Replaying in my memory my most foolish, unworthy, reckless and evil actions – everything I had ever done out of stupidity or simple ignorance – I tried to assess how fallen my soul was. I wasn't an angel, that was for sure. But a demon? No. An ordinary person, like millions of others. So there was something wrong with my family… It was as hard to believe they were traitors as it was to believe I was a nox. And was there any point in wasting my mental energy on guesswork? Tomorrow all the secrets would be revealed.

But one thing was certain: I had to leave the Spirit World – leave the home I had searched for all these years.

So be it.

ENGAGEMENT

Vesta had said when I'd crossed the border of the two worlds, I'd opened my special vision and now I could see noxes in the Human World. Which meant I could still be a guardian, no matter where I lived. After all, I'd come here to find my purpose. I'd wanted to find my parents, uncover the secrets of my past and become a guardian – to protect people from evil. Falling head over heels for a man hadn't been part of the plan.

It seemed reasonable, but my heart wasn't buying it. It was bleeding knowing that tomorrow I'd have to leave what I'd fought so hard to find. Faivendei, Will, Aisha, Ophelia, Vesta, even Hairito. Here she was well-suited, and I'd have never asked her to leave with me. Without Will, without friends, without home, I would continue to drag my way through my miserable existence until one day noxes laid my useless body to rest.

I noticed my reflection in the shower screen and stopped crying; my pathetic look seemed to cool me off a bit. I felt ashamed for not being able to keep these emotions to myself. The comfort and hospitality of Faivendei had spoiled me, and at some point I'd started to believe this world had become my new home. My bad. And if Gabrielle thought my presence here could endanger guardians' lives, then, well, I had to think about others, not only about myself. I should have trusted and submitted to fate, instead of letting my whims bend my will. I had to be grateful for everything this forest had given to me. Moreover, I still had a few hours of blissful ignorance before tomorrow, when the secrets of my past would be revealed.

Maybe I should go to the ball after all?

I closed my eyes, just for a moment, but when I opened them again, twilight was falling over the forest outside. I got out of the bathtub and headed to my room. And froze.

On my wardrobe hung a long, high-necked, sleeveless dress, shimmering as if it was studded with diamond powder. There was something ethereal about this glitter, something I'd never seen before.

I stepped closer. The white fabric was incredibly thin, yet opaque, and I couldn't make out a single seam or thread, or weave, or any other relief – it was as smooth as a lake's surface. I passed my hand over it. So soft… Fresh lily of the valley flowers decorated its hem, and next to the dress, on the table, was a pair of elbow-length gloves made of the same fabric.

'It's spider silk.'

Ophelia's clear voice rang out behind me. She stood in the doorway with Hairito and Tarry. 'When Tarry heard you had nothing to wear to the ball, he decided to make you a gift. He's been spinning every day for over a month to finish this dress on time.'

My mouth dropped open. 'You mean all of this is Tarry's work?'

She nodded.

'Oh my goodness! Thank you, Tarry. Thank you so much!' I walked over to him and kneeled to stroke his belly. He rustled his pincers in reply.

Ophelia sighed dramatically. 'Such a pity his work was in vain.'

'Why do you say that?'

'You're not going to the ball, are you?'

I smiled at Tarry. 'Well, now, when I have such mind-blowing attire, I have to go, don't I?'

'Excellent.' She grinned, as if she'd expected nothing less. 'Put the dress on, then call me.'

I closed the door and carefully lifted the dress from the hanger, afraid of damaging it.

'Spider silk only looks fragile,' she said from outside the door, as if reading my mind. 'In fact, you can hardly find a stronger fabric.'

The weightless, shimmering, lily-decorated dress fit perfectly. It wasn't loose anywhere, nor did it pinch, and I felt almost naked – I'd never worn anything so light before. I put on the gloves and studied my fingers. The fabric shone in the light of fern-flower seeds like freshly fallen snow on a sunlit winter day. Exquisite. I glanced at myself in the mirror and blushed.

That was somebody else in the reflection, not me. This unknown creature had thin, elegant hands and arms. Her ballerina waist was so narrow I wondered how she could lift a sword without breaking in two. I followed the line of her – my – silhouette. No, I couldn't go out like this.

Or could I? Wasn't it the best way to say farewell? In a spider-silk dress at the ball. I decided to enjoy these few hours no matter what.

I opened the door, and Ophelia, Tarry and Hairito gaped at me.

'It looks amazing!' Ophelia clapped her hands. 'Now sit down. I need to remove the traces of tears from your face.'

'Ophelia, how old are you?'

'I'm seven, but that doesn't matter. I spend a lot of time with Aisha – she teaches me about life. She's afraid something might happen to her and she won't have time to teach me later, just like our mother didn't have time to teach her— Lilly, don't look at me like that.' She giggled. 'Our parents passed away when I was barely two. I don't remember them at all. Now sit down. Do you hear the music playing? It's time to go to the ball, and you're not ready.'

I smiled and sat down on the chair. There was a neat, thin wreath of lilies of the valley on the table, and Ophelia placed it on my head. Then she opened Aisha's make-up bag, took out foundation, concealer, eyeshadows, mascara and lip gloss and told me to close my eyes and get ready for my astonishing transformation.

I thought after having had make-up applied by a seven-year-old, my reflection would show someone who looked like they were wearing Mayan war paint, but it was quite the opposite. She'd just made me look a bit brighter and fresher. I thanked Ophelia and Tarry and headed outside with Hairito, wearing the white shoes Aisha had left for me on the threshold.

The sun had already set, but it was as bright as day in the forest. Thousands of shining fern seeds were floating in the air, warming with their ardour and bringing peace and humility to everyone who turned their gaze to them. And yet even this wasn't enough to keep my enthusiasm from flagging. I knew that as soon as I saw Will with his fiancée, my fragile composure would shatter like an icicle falling from a roof.

CHAPTER 10
WALTZ

I SNEAKED TOWARDS the square like a thief, trying to avoid any-one's eyes, but too many guardians were heading through the woods to the ball just like me. All of them without exception stared at my dress and as a consequence at me. It seemed their gazes drained me of my energy until I had almost nothing left. Thinking what was waiting for me in the square – in the middle of a huge crowd, thank you – I was ready to turn around and go back home when I noticed Aisha, rushing eagerly towards me.

'Lilly! You have no idea how happy I am to see you!' She held me at arm's length and looked me up and down. 'This dress looks so much better on you than on a hanger. You're dazzling! Your dance card is going to be full all evening!'

She always knew how to make me smile. 'Thank you.'

'I just wanted to make sure you were coming.' She winked at me. 'Let's go.'

We continued to the ball together and I stopped noticing the looks of passers-by, for she completely captured my atten-tion, telling me with her usual fervour about how many couples met at the seasonal balls, and about her hopes to find a partner one day, maybe even today.

'Just before you arrived in Faivendei, my close friend Kelly married a shaman from Machtdemberg.'

'Where's Machtdemberg?' I almost managed to pronounce that right, I think.

'It's another enchanted forest with the main portal in the Black Forest, near Baiersbronn, Germany. I heard we're expecting some special guests from there tonight. Kelly wrote that Freya Wolf is coming, with her brother Frey!' She spoke as if the fate of humanity depended on the two of them.

'I'm sorry, but who are they?'

'They're the children of Torsten Wolf – the supreme leader of Machtdemberg. But that's not important. They say Freya is as beautiful as a daoshee.'

I remembered reading that daoshee were the kings and queens of the mountain spirits and had a flawless, unearthly beauty like nothing ever found in humans.

'And,' she continued, 'I've heard she's getting married to Will! Can you imagine?'

I halted. As cheerful as Aisha was, these words sounded like a death sentence.

She stopped as well. 'Everything all right?'

I glanced back.

'Lilly?'

'It's okay. I just thought I forgot something at home.'

She paled. 'This morning – tell me it wasn't about Will.'

'It wasn't.'

'Lilly, he's a Raven.' She lifted her eyebrows at me as if stating the obvious. 'You know you can't be together.'

'It wasn't about him.'

'What was it about then?'

'My parents.'

She froze, as if she'd had a hunch about the tragic fate that had befallen my family all along, but she'd never dared to voice it. 'Did you... find anything out?'

'Not yet. But I overheard Christopher saying he'd found something. I think I'll learn what it is tomorrow.'

She tried to smile. 'Something good, yes?'

'I'm... not sure about that.'

'But you can't know until you talk to Christopher, right?'

I nodded.

'So tonight you must forget about it and enjoy the ball.'

I smiled. 'Sure.'

We continued along the shore of the Domus lake, and I gasped at the sight of decorations in the marble square that shone like rippling water under the moonlight. Girls in long white dresses were tiny stars sparkling in the midnight sky of black tuxedos. A cloud of shining fern-flower seeds hovered over the square, immersing the elegant guests in a warm light, and climbing roses with blush-swollen buds blanketed the grey walls of Sodalitas. I could have sworn they weren't there this morning.

The closer we got, the louder the solemn music of the instrumental orchestra sounded, and sudden nausea gripped my stomach: so different this atmosphere was from the dim of my soul. *Let her enjoy the ball*, Christopher said. It seemed this celebration was the funeral ceremony of my dreams and aspirations, of my plans and hopes.

'Wow, Lilly! I didn't recognise you. You look great!'

A familiar voice brought me back to reality. I glanced up: it was Daniel – a warrior whom I knew slightly. I blushed. 'Thank you.'

A girl I'd never met before ran up to us. Her face was so anxious and her shoulders were so bent forward with fatigue that even her exquisite dress couldn't give her an air of lightness.

'Aisha, I need your help. More guardians are turning up than was initially planned.'

'What? How?'

The girl stalked off, and Aisha began to follow her but suddenly remembered about me. 'Lilly, sorry, I have to go.'

'Of course. Don't worry about me.'

I reached the square, and an intoxicating rose fragrance filled my lungs, quivering above my hammering heart. The hum of the crowd, the laughter and the appraising glances mingled together, clouding my mind. My eyes darted from side to side. My pulse was beating so fast I could barely breathe.

But when I saw *him*, the veil obscuring my vision evaporated as if it had never existed at all.

Proud and handsome, he towered over the crowd on the opposite side of the square like Michelangelo's David. Even if I wanted to, I couldn't look away. His black tuxedo suited him as if he had been born to wear it. The only thing missing from this ensemble was the crown on his head. Like royalty, he kept himself aloof, his cool and impenetrable gaze wandering wearily through the crowd.

He's engaged, he's engaged, he is engaged. I kept repeating that to myself, but it was all in vain.

Our eyes met. He brightened and bowed his head slightly to me. The hair on the back of my neck stood up. Where was my pride? Where was my wounded ego? My eyes fled his gaze, like a vole that scuttles into its burrow at the sight of an eagle's sharp eyes and claws.

He is engaged.

I ignored his greeting, hurrying to the far edge of the square. Hairito followed me.

Making my way through the crowd of appraising eyes, I was secretly reluctant to accept compliments and questions about how I managed to get a dress made of spider silk. I always answered briefly, politely and glancing unwillingly at him.

His gaze never left me. Why? If he was engaged, and if he didn't care about me, why was he watching me so intently? Maybe it was the dress? Everyone admired Tarry's work. I stole another glance at *him*.

No, it wasn't the dress.

Suddenly the chatter died down and the crowd parted, creating room for someone to pass through. Two people, followed by two white wolves, came up to the square.

I thought the statuesque dark-haired man in the black tailcoat must be Frey Wolf. Walking alongside him was a slender brunette with thick, glossy hair flowing smoothly over her perfect shoulders and graceful arms. Her skin glowed in the warm light of the decorations. She was wearing an ivory silk dress cut very, *very* low at her back and moved like a cat... calmly and confidently, as if she knew how attractive she was and wouldn't hesitate to take advantage of it. Without doubt she was Freya Wolf – Will's fiancée. As she glided over to him, he greeted her yet kept his distance.

Freya turned to the throng, and venomous bile rose in my throat, for she was the most beautiful girl I'd had ever seen. She didn't have a single flaw in her face or body. Slender and graceful, she stood with her balletic shoulders squared, not at all shy about the attractive shape of her generous breasts. Her features were uncannily regular, her fox-like eyes were shining, and her full lips were smiling with such patronisation that she looked like she thought the ball was just for her. And the rest of the crowd beheld her as if they had all gathered here to have a lucky glimpse of her. She was the epitome of poise and beauty. As was Will.

I turned to the lake. How could I compete with that? As if there ever was a competition. Why had I let my impossible dreams go so far? I even forgot about leaving Faivendei tomorrow. There was only him in my head. Will, Will, Will. That was enough.

I was heading away when I noticed Thomas walking towards me. Damn. I stopped mid-stride.

There was nowhere to go, and he was only a few feet away from me. But a raven flew right in front of his face, forcing him to back away. The nearby guests turned to him in surprise.

I froze, glancing at where Will had just been, as if no amount of common sense could ever kill my hope.

And he was gone.

'May I have this dance with you?' a dense velvet voice said behind me.

Holding my breath, I turned around. Will held out his hand to me. Was I imagining this?

'Lilly?' he pressed. 'May I?'

His fiancée glowered at me. I had to say no to him. But I didn't. If I was to leave tomorrow, I had the right to at least this dance.

I took his hand, and he led me through the parting crowd into the centre of the square. The boiling anxiety made me feel half-sedated and frantic at the same time. He stopped, placing his hand gently on my waist. A simple touch that sent a searing wave through my body. I instantly forgot about Thomas and Freya, Christopher and Gabrielle. I forgot about everything and everyone, putting my hesitant hand on his broad shoulder. Was this actually happening or was this one of my dreams?

The music changed, and we took the first step of the dance.

I wanted more than anything to look up at him, and yet I turned away, unable to withstand the pressure of his piercing aquamarine eyes. His spirit was like the radiance of the sun, something that gave light and warmth but at the same time could easily blind with its dazzling glow. What had happened yesterday in the diamond cave was still at the forefront of my mind, and I couldn't afford a similar mistake here – in front of a huge crowd. He had a power over me. A power I couldn't resist.

I glanced at the crowd. No one was dancing; all eyes were on us. There was curiosity and confusion on some faces and outright condemnation on others, as if Will and I were committing all seven deadly sins in broad daylight. Gabrielle seemed ready to quarter me for daring to dance with her son. And only Christopher appeared to be happy for us – he was watching us with an almost paternal affection.

'Don't look away,' Will purred. 'Let me see your eyes.'

'What's going on?'

'We're waltzing.'

'No... Why aren't you dancing with your fiancée?'

A shadow of ire blazed in his aquamarine eyes. 'She is *not* my fiancée.'

Of course she wasn't. Despite all the logical arguments, despite Freya's beauty, despite Gabrielle having called her his fiancée, somewhere in the back of my mind I'd felt it wasn't true. He wouldn't have acted like he did yesterday, and he wouldn't have asked me to dance.

Yet I didn't let my guard down. 'But your mother—'

'She wants us to be together. She thinks saying it often enough will make it true.'

'And you...' I half-whispered. 'What do *you* want?'

Heavens knew where I found the strength to ask this. As I waited for his answer, seconds became hours and the world around us melted, dissolving into nothingness, leaving only his insistent aquamarine eyes.

He said nothing, just pulled me closer to him and waltzed resolutely and sensually, controlling my body as if it were as light as a feather. He said nothing, and yet I heard his answer. I surrendered to his power, diving into the abyss of his overwhelming energy. If he asked me now, I could give him my life.

Why? Why did he have so much power over me?

Trying to steady myself, I glanced away at the instruments, which seemed to be playing by themselves; at the magnificent castle, decorated with blooming roses that hadn't been there a few hours ago; at the thousands of glittering fern-flower seeds floating in the air; and at Hairito, sitting with a raven on a spruce branch nearby.

Was there any magic spell that could freeze time? That could let me live in this moment forever.

I was greedily soaking up the sense of peace and security I felt next to Will, the bright colours of the ceremonial procession, the aura of magic that reigned in the atmosphere. If I had a choice, if I had the slightest hope of staying here, of being with him, I would give everything for it. But my inner voice whispered that these were my last moments with him, that I would never again feel the warmth of his impulsive heart.

'Lilly?'

An electric jolt made my pulse race even faster. I looked up at him. The blood was rushing to his cheeks, and some hidden heat was sparkling in his eyes. His lips parted as if he was trying to say something, and I held my breath. But suddenly he stopped dancing. My heart faltered – I didn't know what had made him stop, but a second later I realised the music was over.

He exhaled as if some tension released his senses, kissed my hand and didn't say a word.

I could have stayed in a daze forever if Aisha hadn't grabbed me by my elbow. 'May I have a word with you?'

It wasn't a question. She pulled me down the steps to the lake where it was less noisy.

'What do you think you're doing?' She glared at me, as if I'd committed an unforgivable crime.

'Aisha, it was just a dance.'

'Just a dance? I thought I knew you. How could you be so selfish?'

'What?' I drew back, replaying the events of the last few minutes, trying to work out what I'd done. 'What do you mean?'

'Don't play dumb! You know Will can't commit to anyone outside the Simtri clan: Ravens, Wolfs or Lynxes.'

'What are you talking about?'

She scanned my face to see if I was bluffing, and her anger dissolved before my eyes. 'Erm... I thought... Wasn't there anything about this in the books I gave you?'

'No.'

She blushed. 'I'm such a fool. I should have warned you. But I never imagined you'd fall for Will. He never— He was always indifferent to other girls here...'

'Warn me about what?'

'Lilly, members of the Simtri clan can only commit to each other, otherwise they lose their gift. In other words, they lose about two hundred years of their lives. And no more wings, no more intuition, no connection to their animal. Pursue Will and you'll turn him into an ordinary man. Gabrielle would never let that happen, and she always gets her way. She'll find any possible reason to get rid of you – and me as well. It's a losing scenario for both of us.'

I was about to scream but suppressed it with an effort of will. I couldn't let my emotions run wild here. But they were all charging at me like a cavalry flank, ready to trample on what little self-control I had left.

'Is it serious between you two?'

'No. Freya is his fiancée, and... Look, I'm tired. I better go home, and you go back to the ball, okay?'

'I should've warned you, but I didn't think—'

'Aisha...' I willed myself to smile. 'Never mind. It's fine.'

I turned away and rushed towards the house. Hairito flew after me, grunting, as if trying to talk, but all I wanted was to lock myself in my room, crawl into my wardrobe and sit there until my mind found peace again. I reached home and had just closed the front door behind me when somebody knocked.

I opened and numbed on the threshold at the sight of Will. His sublime black wings were still visible behind him, his bow tie undone, his top dress-shirt studs unbuttoned. He stood still, his neck muscles straining.

'Did I do something wrong?' he snapped.

It seemed he was accusing me. 'What?'

'Why did you run away?'

I glanced back and noticed Ophelia and Hairito standing in the hallway, listening. I closed the door, shutting myself outside.

'You didn't do anything wrong. I'm just tired.'

'Lilly,' he warned in a low voice, 'Ravens have highly developed intuition. I don't like when people lie to me.'

'I'm—'

'The truth.'

I blinked, not knowing what to start with, but somebody's heavy footsteps distracted us. I flinched when Thomas appeared on the terrace, staggering.

'What are you doing here?' Will barked.

A drunken stupor seemed to freeze Thomas's mind. His wild, bleary eyes darted from me to Will, and he chuckled, shaking his head. 'So… I wasn't good enough for you?'

The tone of his voice sent a shiver down my back. 'Thomas, you need to go. Now.'

'Yeah, I got it! Your Highness won't stoop to be with a common warrior.'

Will glanced at me. 'Is there something I don't know? What actually happened between you two?'

'Oh, don't worry, nothing terrible. Yet.' Thomas narrowed his small eyes. 'One day, when she's alone, I'll take what's rightfully mine.'

His words echoed amidst the majestic redwoods, and for a moment silence fell. Only the muffled hum of music and the crowd came from Sodalitas Square. Thomas bared his teeth in a hideous, bloodthirsty smile, obviously meant to set Will off. And it worked. Will's body stiffened with rage; his ebony wings were slowly spreading behind his back, making him resemble an angel of death.

'Will, he's not worth it. Don't.'

I might as well be talking to a wall. Like a predator on the hunt, he focused his entire attention on his prey.

'*I'm not looking for a relationship*, she said. And then I saw you dancing together. She was eying you like a bitch in heat. I'll send her back to the Human World in a wheelch—'

Will's fist snapped out and caught Thomas full in the mouth. Thomas stumbled back, spitting blood. He shook his head once, then pulled out a metal hilt that sprouted a blade.

Will yanked the plume from his pendant; it instantly transformed into a black sword. The two clashed.

Will's eyes glowed with a lethal wrath, and yet his movements were calculated and tactical, as if he wasn't allowing his feelings to affect his body, which seemed to have fallen into a military trance. Thomas, by contrast, moved like an enraged boar – no precision in his jerky movements. But I was afraid his frantic fury could give him the strength to break through Will's precise defences.

'Please, stop it!'

With every passing moment, Will pushed Thomas closer to the edge of the terrace. The veins in his forehead swelled, and his face took on such an animal, inhuman frenzy I thought he could kill right now. Then, with a twist of the wrist I couldn't see properly, Will sent Thomas's blade flying and hit him across the face with the pommel of his own sword. Thomas reeled.

Will dropped his own weapon, grabbed Thomas by the throat, and bent him backwards over the rail.

I grabbed his shoulder. 'Will, please don't!'

Suddenly the door opened. Thomas glanced there and smiled spitefully, revealing teeth covered in blood. Ophelia was peeking through the half-open door. I ran to shut her back inside.

'Come on, you damned bastard!' Will roared. 'Not so chatty now?'

He squeezed his brutal deadly hand, and Thomas started to choke.

I didn't recognise him. It seemed he wasn't just strangling Thomas but also his own pain, taking out his tension and hidden rage on Thomas. I tugged on his shoulder, and for a moment he looked away from Thomas, his eyes – full of crimson ire – sliding to me. With every cell of my body, I tried to take over his pain, to ease the burden he carried. I wanted to help him. I knew I could but didn't know how. It wasn't him – it was his anguish that was suffocating Thomas.

'Enough,' I purred as softly as I could. 'Let him go.'

He blinked, darkness slowly receding from his eyes, and tossed Thomas back onto the terrace, as if against his own will. 'Get the hell out of Faivendei! If I ever see your face again, you're dead.'

Thomas jolted upright and hobbled towards the stairs, muttering, 'You have no idea what you've done. I'll make you pay for it.'

Will started towards him. Thomas fled down the steps.

Bolting to the edge of the terrace, Will stood there until Thomas was out of sight. His shoulders heaved under the pressure of air racing in and out of his lungs. It seemed to cost him a tremendous effort to leave Thomas alive. I wondered if he'd ever killed a man... Of course he had. They had been at war with noxes for a century.

'Don't you ever intervene when I deal with others,' Will gritted out.

'You were about to kill him.'

'He had to be killed.'

Suddenly a raven landed on the terrace rail, cawing. It wasn't Ray – Will still had his wings behind him.

'I have to go back to the ball.' Will's eyes drifted from the raven to me. 'You should join me.'

'No.' I was trembling and couldn't even think about going back to the ball.

He studied my face. 'Did I scare you?'

I wanted to say no but then remembered his intuition. 'A little.'

A sigh. 'You're too frail for this world.'

'You don't know me if you think so.'

Stepping closer, he tucked a lock of my hair behind my ear. 'I do, but... Lilly, you should return to the Human World. It'll be better for both of us.'

'Well, it's your lucky day. Your wish will be granted before long.'

His eyes flared and he erased any distance between us, clasping me in his arms. 'Don't you dare leave now.' A whisper. An order. And a plea.

The warmth of his muscled body made me dizzy. He was squeezing me as if trying to merge us together. I could feel blood pulsing in his veins in unison with mine. *Members of the Simtri clan can only commit to each other.* I had to stop him, but if I did, it could destroy me – it could simply tear my body and soul apart.

He lifted my chin, still pressing me against him. 'You look breathtaking, my delicate white lily.'

Here he was: holding me close as if I was his... lifting my chin and scanning my eyes, my mouth. So direct. So bold. But it wasn't arrogance. It was confidence. He knew exactly what I felt for him. My consciousness was drifting away, but the memory of Aisha's warning still rang in my mind. *Members of the Simtri clan can only commit to each other.*

'Will, I'm really tired. And you should get back to the ball. Let's talk tomorrow. Privately.' My eyes slid to the raven sitting on the railing, watching us.

'All right.' His wings split into many feathers. 'In the meantime, Ray will look after you.'

'There's no—'

'Ray will look after you.' He articulated each word in a tone that allowed no argument. 'Good night, Lilly. Until tomorrow.' He kissed my hand and left.

CHAPTER 11
REVELATION

I DON'T KNOW if I slept that night. My mind surfed waves of anxiety and excitement, and even when I had no strength left, I couldn't fall into a deep sleep. No matter how desperately my spirit protested, I decided not to resist when Christopher and Gabrielle asked me to leave. I figured this bad news would come with an explanation of where my family was and, well, who I was. So strange. A couple of months ago, I would have given my soul for this information, but now... I had gained a new family in my friends, gained meaning for my life, gained hope... and fallen madly in love with someone I couldn't possibly be with.

Did I dare to dream of him now that I knew what it would take for him to connect his life to mine? No. I had to leave Faivendei. He'd said yesterday it would be better for both of us if I left, and now I agreed with him. Moreover, I didn't know what Thomas would do to avenge himself. I could still see the image of his bloodthirsty gaze and sardonic smile when Ophelia had opened the door. I couldn't put my loved ones in such danger. So I had to leave. My feelings confronted this decision like a rushing mountain river, foaming and thundering and swamping all other sounds with its roar. But I blocked it up with a dam of logic and common sense. I made up my mind and willed myself to stop thinking about it.

I gave up on sleep at about four in the morning. Without thinking twice, I got dressed and went to Vesta, knowing the shamans always woke up at 4.45 a.m. I didn't want to disrupt her morning meditation, but I had to see her before I left. I descended the spiral stairs with Hairito and glanced up. Ray was sitting on the cedar nearby. Such a beautiful bird. Maybe he could visit me in the Human World?

No.

I shook my head and continued to Vesta's house. The forest was steeped in morning mist, and the frosty freshness of the air cheered me – it was exactly what I needed.

I reached Vesta's house and she opened the door, as usual, without waiting for me to knock.

'Everything okay, early bird?' She scanned me up and down.

'I just can't sleep.'

'Well, good morning then.' She let me in, giving me a meaningful look.

Did she know about the dance?

I walked inside her dark, cosy house, catching a bright, spicy scent of cinnamon and ginger. Vesta handed me a cup of tea, and we both sat down.

I took a sip. 'How was your raid yesterday?'

'Let me think. I neutralised one Cruelty Spirit and only just stopped myself exterminating the scum who created it. Then I saved a young girl from a marok.'

'Marok?'

'Yeah. A spirit who feeds on fear. They come at night while people are sleeping, sit on their chest and strangle them. They're nasty: people experience exactly the same feeling as they do before actual death. Maroks drain their fear but normally leave the victim alive. However, they can kill someone with a weak heart.'

'You mean it actually strangles people at night? But... people wake up when they feel it, no?'

'Maroks exude a psychotropic scent that makes the victim think they're dreaming. It is actually happening though.'

'That's horrible. One girl I knew from the orphanage told me she had dreams like that. I guess she was a marok victim.'

'Yeah. Anyway... how was your day yesterday? I heard you went to the ball after all.'

'So you already know?'

She chuckled. 'Of course, Lilly. In this village, rumours spread quickly, especially when it comes to William Raven himself.' As she said his name, she raised her voice, as if to emphasise how absurd all of this senseless gossip was.

'What do they say?'

'They say Will is either mad or you bewitched him, if he prefers you to Freya Wolf. And to be honest, this does kind of shake up my opinion of him.' She thought for a moment. 'It's all right if you don't want to answer, but... what is going on between you two?'

'I don't know.' I took another sip of tea. 'Nothing. Nothing, I think.'

'You think?'

She was watching me expectantly. Usually, she didn't push when she saw I was in no mood to bare my soul, but this time her curiosity seemed way too strong. She didn't ask any more questions, but one look into her bright, piercing eyes was enough for me to break and start talking.

'Fine! I like him!' I smiled. 'Actually, I more than just like him. But it's all meaningless now.'

'Why?'

I drew a breath to tell her about my decision to leave, but everything inside me, my every nerve, resisted it as if my body was rebelling against me.

She went still, her eyes scanning my face. 'Lilly? What's happening in there? Why is it meaningless now?'

'Erm... I found out that if he tied himself to me, he'd lose his power.'

She sagged her shoulders. 'Oh no! He will have to become – horrors! – an ordinary man. No more fancy wings; and growing old, just like everybody else. I wouldn't wish such a fate on anyone. Has it occurred to you that he's an adult and can make his own decisions? Let's forget the whole noble-sacrifice thing for a second. How *exactly* do you feel about him?'

'I'm—' I remembered our waltz. 'All right, I'm head over heels. You know, the day before I arrived in Faivendei, I had a glass of water and when I looked into it afterwards, it was exactly how I felt – empty and hollow. I was searching for my parents and a parallel world that I'd only dreamed about, hoping to fill that void. I thought when I understood who I was, it'd get easier for me. Well, I'm still clueless about who I am, but I feel better. Just thinking about him makes me happier and more complete. Don't get me wrong – I know he's not an angel.'

'No, he's definitely not.'

'He can be as cold as an iceberg and at the same time boil with passion. He's blunt and direct, but kind. And his inner strength... it draws me like a magnet. He's intelligent... protective... noble—'

'One question,' Vesta cut in. 'How did you manage to keep quiet about this for two months?'

'I didn't want to admit it, even to myself. I thought it was pathetic and shallow.'

'Do you know how he feels about you?'

I shook my head.

'Have you kissed yet?'

'No. And we won't.'

'Why? You like him. He definitely likes you. If you're afraid for his gift, one kiss won't destroy it. It takes something more, if you know what I mean.'

'If I encourage him, he won't stop until he gets to you-know-what-I-mean. So, for his own good, I'd better stay away from him.'

'This is the biggest pile of bullshit I've ever heard. Why do you make life so complicated? Live and enjoy! Honestly, sometimes I think you're from another planet. A bit of normal selfishness won't hurt you.'

'Vesta, I'm sure deep down you agree with me.'

'Believe me, I don't.' She rose from her chair. 'Anyway, that's up to you. I left my jacket at Equilibrium yesterday. Will you come with me to get it?'

'Of course.'

Hearing this, Hairito rose from the black meditation rug, where she always slept while we were here, stretched and followed us.

The morning mist had cleared. As we walked, Vesta continued her lecture on the benefits of common-sense selfishness. I listened to her with a sad smile, thinking that I would miss her too.

Suddenly, a tall, bulky figure appeared in front of us. It was Constance. The very Constance the Bull who'd given me my first beatdown in Belator.

She approached me with her usual scowl. 'Hi. Do you know where Thomas is?'

'No,' I said, feeling my pulse palpitating. 'Why?'

'Nobody's seen him since last night. If you run into him, tell him to go straight to Bogdan,' she ordered before continuing on her way.

I stood where I was, staring down at my feet – it seemed the ground had started to slide underneath them.

'Okay,' Vesta called me back to reality, 'what do you know?'

I told her about yesterday's fight between Will and Thomas, and his parting threat.

'I'm glad he's gone,' Vesta admitted. 'I hope he never comes back.'

'Lilly!' a wild cry sliced through the morning air.

We both looked around and saw Aisha pelting towards us. 'Ophelia is gone!'

Panic slithered in my gut. Thomas.

'Hairito, please go and find her!' Aisha begged.

She nodded, taking to the skies towards our house in Exilis.

'Maybe she's at school?' I suggested.

'It's closed today.'

'Could she have gone out with her friends?' Vesta suggested.

'No, she never leaves the house without asking me. Never!' Aisha's voice cracked and she began to sob.

'Please don't worry. She must be somewhere in Faivendei; we'll find her,' I tried to soothe her and at the same time convince myself. It wasn't working. I glanced at the lake.

'I'm going to ask the Ravens to look for her in the woods,' Vesta proposed.

'I have a better idea,' I said. 'Let's ask Omnia. She's the heart of Faivendei – she should know where Ophelia is.'

Aisha nodded.

We dashed over and she put her hand on the trunk. 'Omnia the Great, I seek your generous help,' she pleaded through streaming tears. 'You see everything... please tell me where my sister is.'

No answer.

'Please! Please help me find Ophelia!'

We held our breath, but nothing happened.

'Omnia—'

A high-pitched screech, like the cry of a humongous bat, came from behind us. We turned around – Hairito was hurtling towards us, cutting the air with a whistle. She braked in a flurry of wings, then hovered before us in mid-air, making an unusual noise that sounded like speech.

'Holy Universe!' Aisha rushed headlong towards the forest.

'What happened?' Vesta shouted after her.

'Ophelia just crossed the wall!'

Vesta paled, swearing under her breath and running after Aisha.

I was about to follow when I heard Omnia's mellow voice echoing behind me. *Lilly, your journey begins...*

I glanced at the tree and, a moment later, raced after them. Ray took off from a nearby birch and flew swiftly towards Sodalitas.

The three of us followed Hairito. I'd never been near the wall. After my experience with Vandorfort and its subits, I didn't intend to break any of Faivendei's rules. I remembered that people who crossed the wall could end up in any one of the worlds, with no guarantee of a welcome and no possibility of getting back to Faivendei without a guide. Why had Ophelia crossed that wall? Had Thomas made her?

No. Everything was fine. It had to be.

We ran for an eternity until at last I saw a line of identical pines on the horizon, standing at arm's length from each other. I stopped, almost out of breath. Hairito reached a gap between trunks and pointed at it with her long, clawed toe. We sprinted towards it and were almost there when Will landed and blocked our way.

'You can't cross the wall!' It was a bark.

'Ophelia is through there!' Aisha was banging her fists on his chest, trying to push him aside.

He didn't budge. 'It's dangerous. You have no idea where you're going or what's waiting for you there.'

'That's why we have to go after Ophelia,' I pushed on.

'No. Rushing off unprepared will only make things worse. We must return, report this incident to the Leaders' Council and decide together what to do.'

Vesta stared at the three of us as if at a loss for words.

'Let me through, you self-righteous bastard!' Aisha was relentlessly pounding at Will, but he seemed to barely feel her blows.

'Will, please,' I urged. 'We don't have time to wait for the Council's decision. Look at us: a witch, a shaman, a warrior and you – a guide and a Raven. Together we can handle anything. We have to try at least.'

'You don't understand. There could be anything through there. What if we end up at the North Pole? Or the bottom of the ocean, in the sirens' waters? Crossing the wall without preparation is madness.'

'And sometimes the mad thing is the right thing to do.' I put my hand on his shoulder. 'Please…'

He looked at me, at Aisha, and his shoulders dropped as he shut his eyes. 'Oh for fairy's sake. Take a deep breath in case we end up under water.'

He turned, stepped through the opening and disappeared at once. Aisha followed, then Vesta and Hairito. Finally, I crossed the threshold.

The sensation of free fall paralysed my feelings for a moment. When it stopped, I scanned the surroundings. We weren't under water or at the North Pole. We stood on the edge of some forest, on top of a low hill covered with vibrant greenery, and the entire horizon was lined with majestic, snowcapped mountains. It reminded me of Switzerland maybe. It was much colder here than in Faivendei, but a dazzling sun was shining, making the plants look poisonously bright. We were looking from side to side, trying to figure out where Ophelia might be.

Suddenly, the greenery in front of us faded. Slender blades of grass turned brown, then black, and one after another fell lifeless on the ground.

'Damn…' Vesta whispered.

There was no fire, but the grass crumbled to ash. Out of this dark patch of earth flowed a black oily mass, thickening and taking on human shapes: three figures appeared clothed in darkness, and a smaller one hovered in front of them. The black mass covered their faces, then suddenly it dissolved into their bodies. I gasped.

Thomas.

He was in the middle of the three. Except it wasn't him anymore. He wore an inky cloak, and coal tattoos writhed along his neck and cheekbones like hellish serpents. His infernal eyes, with wide ebony irises, were focused on me. He was a nox, and he wasn't alone.

The body levitating in front of the noxes was still covered in an eerie black mass, and thick tar-like drops dripped onto the scorched earth, seeping into it.

Oh no...

I glanced at Aisha. She stood motionless. The black mass liquified, dropped away and sank through the earth, revealing Ophelia's body floating in the air.

'No!'

Aisha ran to her, but another tall nox aimed his thin hands in her direction. Light shot out of them and hit Aisha's legs, instantly shackling her in steel, shocking me, Will and Vesta into momentary silence.

'Please,' Aisha pleaded, 'take me instead; don't touch her! I'm begging you!'

'Do not worry,' Thomas drawled. 'We do not need Ophelia anymore. She already played her part.'

Another nox, short but stocky, remained silent and watched us closely, as if appraising what was going on.

'What do you want?' Will spat.

'You have to be careful when choosing your enemies,' Thomas said with a lethal calm. 'Thomas has been on *our* side for the past couple of years. We caught him once, and he was so scared of becoming a nox that he offered to rat out other guardians to save himself. Quite a few of Faivendei's guardians have become noxes thanks to him. But yesterday he came to us with an unusual request. He was so angry with you, William, that he decided to finally become a nox. He wanted to make you watch her die.' Thomas's eyes drifted to me for a moment before his gaze returned to Will. 'At first, he wanted to kill you too but then decided that two hundred years of mourning would be the best punishment. *We* promised to fulfil his request, and *we* always keep our word.'

I hadn't seen Will draw his sword – it was too quick for my eyes. Every cell of my body was trembling, but I didn't let my fear paralyse my will. I held out the metal hilt that I carried with me, and my sword appeared. It was shaking in my hand, but I tried to keep calm.

Vesta waved her hand and a long energy whip flew out of it – she swung it and freed Aisha from her shackles.

Will launched, pouncing on the tall, skinny nox, which disappeared and instantly reappeared behind his back. Light shot from the nox's palms at Will's wings, encasing them in steel; Will fell, unable to bear the colossal weight on his back.

I ceased breathing.

Vesta swung her whip, trying to wrap it around the nox, but he shifted faster than sight again and shot light at her hands, encasing them in steel.

The stocky nox walked up to Will, studied him and pointed a palm in his direction: thick darkness flowed out of it like tentacles, creeping towards Will's chest.

I jumped at the nox, trying to protect Will, but he threw me to the tall, skinny nox with a single flick of his hand. 'Kill her!'

I fell at his feet but sprang up and adopted a fighting stance. From the corner of my eye, I saw Hairito backing away and hiding behind an oak. She peered at her claw, and sunlight glinted off the old bent ring she always wore.

The skinny nox shot light at my sword and I dropped it to the ground. He grabbed me by the throat, lifting me up. I was floundering in his iron grip, struggling to free myself. The world was slowly sinking into a pinprick of darkness.

'Bastard!' Will's roar reverberated through the air. 'Let her go!'

I looked into the eyes of death – the nox's black irises grew even darker; now even the whites were swirling tar. He scrutinised me, and a thousand chilling voices broke out of his mouth. 'A human, just a human...' It was Noxohit himself. He squeezed my throat tighter, and I couldn't breathe anymore.

'Let her go!' Will gritted out again.

'Just a human...'

Suddenly Hairito slammed into my back and fell to one side, her legs bound with bands of steel. Why had she...

A soothing warmth flooded me with relief. I no longer felt the nox's iron grip on my throat, squeezing my neck and draining my life away. There was no more pain. No more fear.

Only light.

It was as if I'd lived all my life with a veil over my eyes, and only now I saw the light. The mountains grew taller, their snow-capped peaks shining in the sunlight as if adorned with diamonds. Green fields and trees grew even brighter, but it didn't hurt my eyes. It was soothing, placid and relaxing. All other colours intensified, blending together and turning into energy. I was witnessing the birth of the most beautiful aurora. It was like heaven, but I didn't die... I'd never been so alive before. I wanted to lose myself in this feeling, in this energy.

But I had to do what I was born for.

It seemed inside my body was a powerful tool – like a mechanical clock that hadn't been started in a long time. This clockwork had been waiting for the day when it would finally come back into action. It was perfect, and the gears shone like new, but it had lacked the crown that needed to be turned several times to set in motion its dormant power. It had lacked the touch of this *old bent ring*.

The nox stared in confusion, watching the ring that Hairito had managed to slip onto my finger emit a silver light that surrounded my body, sinking into it, all the colours creating a bright energy glow turned into silver light that came from absolutely everything. It seemed that, before, I'd dragged through my purposeless existence at the dark and cold bottom of the Mariana Trench. On my neck and arms and legs were leaden weights of anxiety and fear, worry and doubt. But the light emanating from the ring shattered these shackles. The weights fell to the bottom, swirling the mud, and my body soared up under the force of the colossal but healing pressure. Up and up – towards the light.

I lifted my palm, which exuded a bright light, and guided by instinct pressed it against the nox's chest. The light poured into his body, and I could feel it pour into his heart, his soul. There was no more me and no more nox. There was no Hairito, no Will, no mountains, no forest. I was immersed in infinity, and everything was one. Everything was energy.

In front of me was a cluster of silver energy in the shape of a man with darkness surrounding his spark of life. It flowed along his spine and took up all the space in his head.

I could help him.

A black mass oozed out of the nox's chest. The tarry eyes watched me in horror as he whispered, 'Vandor...' The snakes on his neck faded, his eyes became lighter, and the remnants of the black energy left his body and gathered into a ball in my hand. It shrank into a dark pearl, radiating a rainbow glow, then turned into a white butterfly that fluttered away.

The feeling of oneness disappeared, the leaden weights returned and I dropped to the ground.

Through the thick haze I saw Will and Vesta staring at me. The skinny man I had just... cured?... of Noxohit's energy glared at the remaining noxes and threw beams of light at them. But in an instant, they transformed into a thick black mass and disappeared into the earth, taking Ophelia with them.

The skinny man stared at his palms in glee and laughed loudly. 'Holy Universe, I'm back!' He crouched down beside me. 'Thank you, thank you so much, whoever you are.'

When I didn't answer, his eyebrows rose.

Vesta, Will and Hairito were still bound in steel, while Aisha was sobbing with her head in her hands. And me? I felt like my soul was leaving my body.

'Is she alive?' Will's voice was a faraway echo as my mind drifted to another world.

'I'm not sure,' he said nonchalantly. 'Hold on a second. Looks like she's breathing. More or less.'

His face with its wry smile swam before my eyes.

Will roared like a caged lion, fighting against the weight pinning his wings.

'Erm – I apologise for those.' The former Nox pointed to the shackles that held them. 'They'll disappear soon.'

'Are you Darius Fulman?' Vesta demanded.

The man frowned. 'How did you know?'

'There aren't that many prodigies who can transform light into matter and move at the speed of sound.'

Aisha ran to Darius, howling at him. 'Where did they take her?'

'Don't yell at me! I don't like to be yelled at.' His voice reached me as if I was under water. 'I don't have the foggiest idea where they took her. What, do you think they have a club-house or something? Noxes live under the earth's crust, and it's virtually impossible to find them.'

I drew a breath to apologise to Aisha but couldn't speak. She was gripped by panic and didn't say anything else.

My mind was falling ever faster into a bottomless abyss, but through a foggy veil I could still see Will's shackles as they turned transparent and disappeared. His wings were released, and in a moment, they shattered into feathers before turning into Ray. He flew up onto the branch of a nearby tree and shook his head, as if ridding himself of something. Will rushed over to me and lifted me up, my body sprawled in his arms like a lifeless, withered plant.

'Hold on, Lilly. You'll be home soon.'

The steel shackles binding Vesta's hands faded. She got up, ran to me and pressed the tip of her thin, long finger to the bridge of my nose, closing her eyes. 'She's still with us... She'll be fine.'

He nodded without looking away from me. Unable to hold my eyelids open any more, I was sinking into oblivion, feeling safe in his arms.

'Will,' I heard Vesta's distant voice. 'Is she a vandor?'

He was silent for a moment. 'Yes. The last surviving one.'

'How the hell is that possible?'

'I have no idea...'

His velvet voice echoed in my head as everything went dark.

CHAPTER 12
LUMINIFEROS

ENCHANTING BIRD SONGS and the light breeze brought me out of my dreams. I opened my eyes. The warm wind blew the weightless white curtains – they were floating like ghosts in the air. Next to my bed sat a woman with faded blue eyes, sunken cheeks and silver hair tied back in a bun. Her face seemed familiar to me.

An enigmatic smile flickered across her face. 'Hello, Lilly.'

A jolt went through me like lightning. Everything blurred, and I huddled in the corner of the bed. It was Dr Blake – the psychologist I'd seen back at the orphanage. The one who'd tried so hard to convince me I was mad for believing in the other world. Had she been right? Was I in an asylum, just pulling out of a delusion—

Hairito jumped in my lap and began to purr.

Gradually my breathing returned to normal. My pulse slowed down. I was still in Faivendei – in Equilibrium ward.

I wasn't insane.

And my old psychologist was still sitting at my bedside.

'What are you doing here?' I asked, still not sure if she was real or a ghost.

'Christopher invited me,' she answered as if she'd known him all her life.

No, she wasn't a ghost.

'Do you know where you are?'

She nodded, smiling, as a parent would smile at a toddler's silly questions. Something began to simmer in my blood.

'You don't look surprised.'

'I'm not. I grew up here.'

My hand slid towards the pocket where I kept the hilt of my sword. 'You're going to want to start explaining. Now.'

'Before I start, I want to say that everything we did was out of love for you.'

'Who's we?'

'Me and...' She paused, as if gathering the strength to speak. 'Your parents.'

I sprang out of bed as if scalded.

'Just listen to me. You'll understand.' She held up her hands. 'You were right all along of course. Your dreams were all real. Your parents protected people from noxes, or demons, as you called them in childhood. They were vandors, and so are you. You were born in the enchanted forest of Etrikshire, the main entrance to which is in Scotland. When you were five, Noxohit attacked our forest, and it was an absolute massacre. He infected all the vandors with his dark energy. All but you.'

'Your mother and I were close friends, and I became your... dare I say it? Your godmother. Once, I saved a daoshee whose curiosity led her into the Human World, where she almost fell victim to men's cruelty. You see, I'm a shaman, Lilly. When I rescued her, she promised to grant me one wish.

Knowing how powerful daoshee are, I didn't rush to choose. I returned to Etrikshire and came to visit your parents.

'You were playing happily with your brother, carefree, oblivious to your parents' worries and the world groaning under Noxohit's yoke. At that moment, I realised what I should ask of the daoshee – protection for you and, if possible, for your family. I spoke to your parents, and they agreed... We knew you would be hunted as all vandors were and asked the daoshee to take your gift and hide it in an object that you could put on if needed, bringing your power back to you.' She walked to me and took my hand. 'This is your mother's wedding ring. Your power has been hidden there for all these years.'

A rolling heat set my heart ablaze. I snatched my hand away.

She seemed undisturbed. 'I requested protection for your entire family, but the daoshee said it was beyond her power. All she could do was take away your gift and wipe any memory of you from other people's heads... make it as if you never existed. Thus Noxohit wouldn't know about you. Your parents and your brother were turned into noxes, and no one knows if they're still alive. But you are! The daoshee took you away from Etrikshire. She left you on the doorstep of Angel's Hope Orphanage, but somehow, she couldn't wipe your memory completely. You were talking too much and too openly about our world. It was only a matter of time before Noxohit heard it through somebody's ears, and that would lead him directly to you. The daoshee restored my memory and I made a difficult decision. I still think it was the right one. I took on the role of a child phycologist to help you if not forget then be ashamed to talk of your dreams of this world. Before you judge me, understand, that saved your life. Ever since, I've looked after you.

'I kept this ring secret, but I was afraid you subconsciously sensed its power, and that's why you had those dreams about your past. I travelled to France and hid the ring in the wall of Saint-Ouen Abbey in Rouen, but unfortunately it didn't help; your dreams continued. But I was sure you wouldn't find the ring.'

She glanced at Hairito, who was sitting on the next bed, listening intently. 'This creature must have sensed the power emanating from the ring and found its owner. I think it was hard for her to part with the warming light of the ring – that's why she didn't give it to you. Perhaps the light of the ring gave her the power to turn good, I don't know. But in your moment of crisis, she made the right choice and put it on your finger. It saved your life.'

Fury was still throbbing inside me. I tried, desperately tried, to contain it. I believed that she'd done all this to save my life, but it was still such a fundamental betrayal.

'When you moved to France, I lost track of you, I was so worried. I hoped it was because you'd managed to enter the Spirit World and not because you'd become a nox. Yesterday, Christopher showed up in Etrikshire and told me about you. I arrived here this morning, and while you were unconscious, he told me what happened. Lilly, please don't look at me like that. In my place, you would have done the same.'

'The hell I would! You lied to me! You did everything you could to convince me I was mentally ill, even while I was desperate to find my parents. And all that time you knew the truth! You watched me getting more and more desperate, more and more unbalanced, and you knew the truth!'

Her eyes watered. 'I was trying to protect you.'

My rage burned my sympathy to ashes. 'Protect me? Because of you I've lived a life teetering on the edge of sanity until

I finally found the Spirit World. Because of you, I questioned my every word, every action, thinking at the back of my head that I could actually be insane. I avoided people, afraid that sooner or later they would notice the signs of my delusions and that would confirm my fears. Do you understand how scary it is to live not knowing who you are, with quicksand under your feet? Questioning your sanity every single day? How could you do that to me?'

'I wanted you to just live safely and quietly.'

'I tried to live that quiet life you wanted for me, but the Universe pushed me off that path. And here I am – in the Spirit World, where I had to be from the beginning. But thanks to your efforts, I went through years of loneliness and uncertainty. Sometimes I thought you were right and my parents had abandoned me...' I closed my eyes. 'How could you try to convince me they never loved me when you knew the truth?'

'But despite everything, I kept believing in them, and in this world – I couldn't help it. That was the only thing that gave me the strength to live. And yet, every day I doubted myself because of people like you who tried to convince me that it was impossible! That I was insane!'

'Lilly—'

'Get out. Go back to Etrikshire. I don't want to look at you.'

'You're a vandor, Lilly. The Leaders' Council knows this, as does Noxohit now. While you're here, they're in danger. Gabrielle is one of the most ardent defenders of law and order in the guardians' lands. After the tragedy of Vandorfort... she won't let you stay.'

'I know.'

'Noxohit will turn the Spirit and Human Worlds upside down to find you. I can try... I'm not sure if they'll listen to me, but I can ask the daoshee to shelter you in their lands. He will never find you there.'

'You're my godmother, you even pretended to be my psychologist, but you don't know me at all. I'd rather die than hide from him.' I walked to the door, Hairito following me.

She was right on my heels. 'Do you want to confront him? Noxohit is invincible! All the other vandors are already noxes. Not even the strongest shamans can transform his dark energy into light. And you really think one girl can make a difference?'

'No. But at least I'll try. I've lived a safe and meaningless life for far too long. Partly thanks to you.'

I left the room without looking back and bumped into Vesta in the corridor.

'Thank the Universe you're awake. Come – quick.'

'Where?'

'To Sodalitas. The Leaders' Council meeting's just started. They want to throw you out of Faivendei.'

I nodded and followed Vesta, recalling all the times when Dr Blake had tried to convince me my ideas were the delusions of a disturbed child who didn't want to accept that she'd been abandoned. I thought about my parents...

My mind had hidden in a far corner the memories of those few seconds I'd spent in Vandorfort, but now the images flowed back into my head. I remembered the horror, the unbearable pain that had torn apart the ethereal bodies of the subits. But it was just a shadow of what the vandors and the other guardians infected by Noxohit's poison experienced every day. Imprisoned in the dungeons of their own minds, deprived of the right to control their bodies, they weren't alive and couldn't die. My father, my brother... my mother. If only I could find them, I would heal them all.

'Are you okay?' Vesta was looking at me out of the corner of her eye.

'I'm fine. Will, Aisha, Ophelia? Are they all right?'

'Will and Aisha, yes.'

'And Ophelia?'

'We don't know. The noxes took her.'

I remembered now how they'd disappeared with her. 'Damn… It's all my fault.'

'Are you serious? If anything, we should be grateful to you it turned out this well. We've suspected for a while there was a rat in Faivendei, but we couldn't find him. Now we know who it was.'

'How did Omnia allow this to happen? I mean she sees through everyone, right?'

'Her vision places a great responsibility on her. Sometimes good begets evil, and evil begets good. We can't see everything as she does, so we can only trust her wisdom and intuition. Of course she knew about Thomas, but it would probably have hurt us more than helped us if she'd told us the truth.'

'But we lost Ophelia because of that. I'll find her. It's my fault, and I'll never stop until I find her.'

'Lilly, it isn't your fault. How could you have known—'

'When Thomas was fighting Will, Ophelia opened the door and looked out. Thomas glared at her with a look so vile… I should've told Aisha… I should've stayed home to protect Ophelia. I'm so stupid.'

'Lilly, stop. What happened was just terrible luck. It's not your fault.'

I snorted.

'By the way, Will never left your room while you were unconscious. But Ray spotted Darius trying to get into the diamond caves, and he went to stop him from stealing the gems.

What a prick that Darius is! You saved his life, and this is how he thanks you.'

'Who's Darius?'

'The man you cured of dark energy. Remember?'

His image surfaced in my mind. 'Does he know where to find Ophelia?'

'No. The noxes transform into a black mass and disappear into the ground. Many people have tried to search for their loved ones after they were infected with dark energy. To be honest, I... I don't think we'll ever see Ophelia again.'

'I'll find her.'

'Well I hope you do, but...'

I didn't say anything, but I vowed I'd return Ophelia to Aisha at any cost.

As we walked, the shadows cast by the trees grew longer – the sun was sinking below the horizon. Soon we were in Sodalitas in front of the door to the Council meeting room. Vesta was about to knock but paused when we heard Will's voice from inside the room.

'She's part of our family. You can't drive her out. Live for the prosperity of all living beings, isn't that our rule? If you banish Lilly from Faivendei, you'll doom her to certain death.'

'We have no choice,' came Gabrielle's voice. 'Are you willing to put hundreds of guardians at risk for one person? Come to your senses, William!'

'She's not just one person. She's the last living vandor.'

'And how will one vandor help when their entire kind has already been wiped out?'

'Omnia protects us,' he countered, 'and we don't use the portal more than once in any place. Noxohit has no chance of finding us.'

'Ideas like that are why Vandorfort is teeming with subits. Darkness can find a key to any door. Do you need more proof? Then tell the Council how Omnia reacted to Lilly's arrival in Faivendei. She must leave, and you, more than anybody, know that.'

Silence. Apparently Will didn't want to mention the horror on Omnia's face... or how she'd tried to convince me to return to the Human World. Now it was easy to guess what she was afraid of – another Noxohit attack on Faivendei.

'What's more,' Gabrielle continued, 'she deprived Noxohit of one of his trump cards – Darius Fulman. Now he'll come after her and take hundreds of innocent lives along the way. Will, your father died in Vandorfort, protecting vandors. Her presence in Faivendei can only lead to new tragedies. Are you ready to take on that responsibility?'

'Then I'll leave with her.'

'What?'

I pushed into the room. 'Stop this. I will leave. Alone.'

Around the table sat members of the Leaders' Council: Gabrielle and Christopher, General Fairfax, the witch Felicia Viridis and the shaman Azrael Blumstein.

'I will leave,' I said calmly. 'I'd like to thank you for everything you've done for me—'

The lump growing in my throat prevented me from thanking them for bringing my mind to peace. Now I knew I wasn't crazy. Sirens, fairies, daoshee, dryads and thousands of other spirits lived in a world where nature was alive and forests had souls. It wasn't just a figment of my imagination. Thanks to them, I'd met people who used their mystic powers for the protection and prosperity of all living beings. Thanks to them, I'd found friends and for the first time tasted the sweet and heady fruit of love. I'd spent two whole months of my life in the enchanted forest, surrounded by love and support, care and understanding. Could I dare to dream of more?

I cleared my throat. 'Thank you for letting me stay here. I'll pack my stuff and leave right now.'

'Where will you go?' Christopher asked.

'I'm going to search for Ophelia.'

'*We* are going to search for Ophelia,' Will corrected.

'No. First, you're a prosecutor and a guide, and Faivendei needs you. Second, everyone close to me is in danger now. Third—' I wanted to say that I wasn't from the Simtri clan but didn't.

'Did I ask for your permission?'

'There is another solution,' Christopher said.

Everyone's eyes drifted to him.

'What solution?' Gabrielle pushed on.

Christopher paused for a moment, as if deciding whether to say it. He looked me in the eye and murmured, 'Luminiferos.'

General Fairfax scoffed, Azrael shook his head and Felicia rolled her eyes.

'Christopher, that's a fairy tale, supposed to keep up guardian morale,' Gabrielle snapped.

I stared at them, trying to work out what they were talking about.

'It's not though,' said Azrael. 'Not entirely. Luminiferos exists, but it's impossible to get it.'

Christopher shrugged. 'Just because nobody's done it before doesn't mean it's impossible.'

'Even if it does exist,' Felicia said, 'what do you suggest?'

'I'm suggesting Lilly go find it.'

I drew breath to ask a question, but Azrael didn't let me. 'Are you out of your mind? Not even the strongest shamans can get Luminiferos. How do you think some girl will do it? Vandor or not, it's impossible.'

'I think she has a chance precisely because she is a vandor. Remember Taliesin's prophecy? *The vandors will rid humanity of the dark energy that came from the forbidden part of the Universe.*'

Gabrielle raised her eyebrows. 'I think everyone in this room knows the prophecy fell flat.'

'What if we just misinterpreted it? What if it wasn't about an army of vandors but one single vandor? The spirits won't help us, and without them we'll never overcome Noxohit. Luminiferos is our last hope.'

'Then there is no hope,' Felicia cut in. 'Everyone who ever tried to find Luminiferos died in the search. And they were the strongest guardians. Christopher, are you ready to send this girl to her certain death? Let her go to the Human World, and if she lives there quietly, without using her power, maybe Noxohit will never find her.'

The more they talked about it, the more confused I felt.

'Yes, the risk is high, but I believe in her,' Christopher said. 'She can handle it.'

Gabrielle scrutinised him. 'Where do you get this faith from?'

He didn't answer.

'Can I jump in here?' I managed to say. 'What is Luminiferos?'

'Look, this won't hurt anyone in Faivendei, right?' Christopher breathed. 'And that's what you're worried about. I propose we tell her about Luminiferos and she can decide for herself.'

Felicia shook her head. 'This is pointless.'

'Let her decide.'

'I agree. It won't hurt us.' Gabrielle nodded. 'Do what you think is best.'

'Luminiferos or Ophelia, I'm still going with her,' Will said. Not a question.

I scowled at him. 'No.'

'I'll go and tell Aisha,' Vesta said to me. 'She has a right to know.'

I nodded, and she left.

Christopher turned to Azrael. 'I think it will be more appropriate if you tell Lilly about Luminiferos. It's your area of expertise.'

He shook his head. 'I agree with Felicia. This plan is doomed. But... I'm afraid the girl is doomed too anyway. Noxohit will never stop until he finds her.'

He sighed heavily. 'Okay, Luminiferos. In 1940, in Transylvania, there was a meeting of twenty-one of the strongest shamans from all over the world. For three days and three nights they prayed to the Universe, asking it to send them aid in the fight against Noxohit. At the end of this time, the earth beneath them shook, and the sky was lit up by silver lightning. A bolt shot towards the centre of the circle but was stopped by powerful red energy erupting from the earth. The two energies collided. Between the red energy bursting out of the ground and the silver flying out of space, an orange energy sphere appeared, then above it an identical yellow one, then a green one, followed by blue and finally purple. The red and silver energy streams gradually turned spherical, and the seven spheres shrank to the size of pearls.

'One shaman approached this column of seven energies and tried to touch them, but an unseen force threw him across the field. The same happened with another shaman. Each of them took turns trying their powers, but it was all in vain. The energies all scattered in different directions, and a piece of parchment appeared, containing a chain with a long pendant comprising seven empty rings. On the parchment was written: "*The union of seven will banish darkness from the human soul.*"

'The Universe had sent a weapon to defeat Noxohit, but none of the shamans were strong enough or pure enough or something to use it. They thought those energies were the emanations of light and called them Luminiferos, which came from luminiferous aether – a medium for the propagation of light.'

I swallowed. 'The strongest shamans couldn't touch Luminiferos?'

Azrael nodded. 'You see the problem. And many others searched for it after them, but no one could collect more than the first three emanations. The search killed them.'

Sudden weakness made me look around for a chair, but I got a grip on myself, taking a deep breath.

Christopher gave me a chance to steady myself. 'It's dangerous, Lilly, and your chances aren't great. But this is the only way you can avoid the fate Noxohit has in store for you. And if you succeed, you might save not only yourself, Ophelia and your family but all of humanity.'

Felicia and Azrael were right: I was, indeed, doomed. Spelling it out like that made it more real. But what choice did I have?

'Okay. What should I do?'

'First, you must find a pendant for the emanations,' Azrael said.

I nodded. 'Where?'

'Come, I'll show you in the library.' Christopher got up from the table.

'The meeting is over,' Gabrielle stated. 'Will, can I talk to you for a minute?'

They strode into an adjoining room, closing the door behind them.

Christopher and I went to the library. He settled in a chair next to the fireplace, and I sat in front of him.

That sunny smile brightened his face. 'About thirty years ago, I attended a seasonal ball. I was just over a hundred, but I swear I looked much younger.' He laughed. 'She was only eighteen, and yet she was wiser and stronger than I. Such a gentle and kind creature... I fell in love with her at first sight.' He studied dreamily the flames dancing in the hearth.

I listened, trying to understand what this had to do with the pendant of Luminiferos.

'You may have noticed that in Faivendei, most Ravens are single. You might think we're so aloof that we prefer to be alone rather than condescend to live with anyone.' He let out a low chuckle. 'But the truth is, it's extremely rare for a Raven to fall in love, and if it does happen, it's impossible to confuse the feeling with anything else. It's our damned intuition. It tells us we're going to fall in love even before we see the person. It knocks you down and drags you into the sky, where it feels as if you're lighting up the Earth with your radiance, like a second sun.' He stopped for a second, as if realising he'd gone too far. 'I loved my Jane. But she wasn't from the Simtri clan.'

He looked at me pointedly, and, finally, I realised this story wasn't about Luminiferos at all.

'My mother tried every possible way to protect me, just as Gabrielle is trying to protect Will from you. Jane loved me but rejected me, because she thought it would be selfish not to. She decided for me, and it broke my heart. I still love her and always will.' His eyes became cool and serious. 'Maybe somebody in your past made decisions that brought you more harm than good too?'

I didn't have to dig deep into my memory to agree with that and nodded.

'Then don't decide for others until you're sure it won't hurt them.'

I stared thoughtfully into the fire. 'It will rob him of everything that makes him himself and make him die young.'

'And yet, there are worse things.'

I said nothing.

Christopher got up from his chair and went over to the shelves, taking out a heavy book. He put it carefully on the table and opened it. I walked over to him. He flipped through the pages and came to a chapter called 'Luminiferos'. I saw a drawing of a necklace with a column of seven empty rings.

'This is what the pendant looks like.'

Suddenly, Will burst into the library and loomed over me like a sinister cloud. 'I'm going with you.'

It sounded more like a threat than an offer of help.

My eyes slid to Christopher, then back to Will. 'If this is really what you want.'

Vesta and Aisha entered the room. It was hard to tell whether Aisha was alive or a ghost – her skin was so pale, her gaze so lifeless.

'So what have you decided?' Vesta asked me.

'Will and I are going to search for Luminiferos.'

'Good. I'm coming with you.'

'Don't. It's dangerous and we have almost no chance—'

'With me, you have a slightly better chance. Not to brag.'

'You'll be taking a huge risk, Vesta. Do you really need this?'

She rolled her eyes at me. 'Oh please. It's not because of you. All my life I've wondered if there's any point to what I'm doing. Our mentors teach us from childhood that the Universe is in absolute harmony. If this is true, then Noxohit is a part of that, isn't he? Maybe he's meant to exterminate humanity? Maybe the Universe's experiment with us went wrong, and after all we did, we're meant to disappear from the face of the Earth? It was humans who killed my parents – in a horrible, painful way. And I'm still here, trying to protect humans. If we find Luminiferos, then what I'm doing is right. If not... well, then it was all a waste and I'm an absolute idiot.'

That sounded reasonable to me. What's more, she was a strong shaman and... she was my friend. I'd never ask her to join me, but if she wanted it for herself, I couldn't deny her.

'If you're sure,' I said.

'We are,' Aisha whispered.

I didn't dare ask her not to.

'We won't be looking just for Luminiferos but Ophelia too,' I reassured her.

Suddenly, a lanky man entered the room. Darius. Without a cloak, he seemed even more slender. He was wearing a hideous tartan suite of poisonous green with a polka-dot bow tie. Being almost as tall as Will and having weightless fuzzy hair, he resembled a dandelion puff.

'Did someone die? Why the long faces? If I lived in a forest with diamond caves, nothing would get me down – ever.' His frantic eyes drifted to me. 'Oh, you.' He took my hand and kissed it before I realised what was happening. 'Thank you for bringing me back to life.'

His smirking lips were way too big for his narrow face, making him resemble a mad clown, and his shining eyes were childish and wild, as if he was in a natural state of constant awe.

I snatched my hand back. 'You're welcome.'

'No, that won't do. You saved my life after all. Hmm...' He looked down at the brooch pinned to his waistcoat; it was made up of three beautiful flowers, studded with small shining stones. 'No, maybe not that – I like it too much. How can I thank you?'

'Don't try to kill me again and don't try to steal any diamonds. That'll do.'

'Even if I wanted to, I couldn't.'

'What?'

'I mean steal the diamonds. Omnia won't let me.' He hung his head dramatically, and his eyes froze at the image of the pendant in the book. 'Oh. I saw that thing once, you know.'

Christopher inched towards him. 'Where?'

'At the castle of Octavian Allegrain. Have you heard of him? Five-hundred-year-old vampire. Marvellous art collector.'

I swallowed. 'Vampires are real?'

'Vampires are just evil spirits who long ago drank human blood as a delicacy,' Christopher explained. 'For that they were condemned to be immortal but stay only in one body with no possibility to dematerialise, and with only one type of food to... drink.'

He turned back to Darius. 'When exactly did you see this pendant?'

'About a year ago.' Darius narrowed his eyes. 'Why? What is it?'

Christopher gave me a look, and I immediately got the hint.

'Take us to this vampire, and help get us the pendant. Then we're even,' I said.

'Yeah, sure.' He crossed his arms. 'But first, tell me what it is.'

He glanced back at the book, spotted the title of the chapter and his mouth gaped open.

'You must be kidding me...' He gave us his clownish grin. 'Deal!'

CHAPTER 13
OFFER

DURING THE SHORT moments when I drowsed last night, I had nightmares full of misery, suffering and an infinite desire to vanish – just disappear from the face of the Earth. I saw Ophelia trapped in black goo. I saw my parents and noxes drawing life out of them. Gasping for air like a fish thrown on dry land, I tossed and turned, trying to calm my mind and get some sleep. Eventually I jumped out of bed and started to pack my backpack. I didn't know where the search for Luminiferos would lead us, and for how long I would survive, so I packed less than half the things I'd arrived with.

I glanced at the clock. It was six in the morning, and we planned to leave at noon. I had plenty of time but didn't want to spend a minute longer in my room; it seemed the walls were closing in. Leaving Hairito at home, I set out.

I reached the spot that reminded me of the place where I'd been born. Golden maple leaves were falling ever slowly from the branches onto the forest floor to the accompaniment of a roaring mountain river. The air was so pure and fresh it seemed one deep breath of this life-giving coolness could dissolve my worries and calm my mind. But I remained indifferent, as if the forest had lost the spark it once had. Even the grey clouds floating low across the sky couldn't bring peace to my soul.

I lay down on the ground, studying my mother's ring on my finger. Vandor. The last hope of humanity. I grinned sadly. All my life I'd been trying to understand who I was and now the answer was right in front of me, but I'd never been so far from realising my true essence. My words at yesterday's meeting had been daring, my self-control surprising even me. But more than ever, now I didn't want to die. I had finally been admitted into the joys of life. I felt for the first time the power of love and friendship, and I had chills at the thought that, having just started living, I was going to die.

What if searching for Luminiferos meant I'd completely lose myself? The Universe had given me a chance, had given me the opportunity to show my best qualities, but did I have any? Was I ready to sacrifice my life for the sake of others? Not in words, not in the rush of feelings, but in full awareness of what I was doing?

The truth was… I didn't know.

I glanced at my palms, remembering how silver light had poured out of them. At that moment it had seemed all the cards had been exposed and I'd seen, felt, joined the providence of the Universe. How much I would give to regain that feeling of peace and trust in life, that feeling of the Universe being my loving father, and the Earth being my caring mother. I placed my hands on my solar plexus and closed my eyes.

Time passed, but nothing happened.

When it was almost noon, I had to go back to the house. I collected my backpack with Hairito and met the others on Sodalitas Square. As we walked along the floating path to the centre of the forest, I didn't let myself look back, hiding from the others that leaving Faivendei made my heart cry bloody tears.

We reached the island where the divine spirit, Omnia, was already waiting for us. Approaching her, we bowed.

'William,' she purred, keeping her eyes on me. 'You can call Nairin now.'

He went to the shore, gesturing for Darius, Aisha and Vesta to follow him.

'Already leaving?' Omnia asked me in a mellow voice.

I nodded. 'Maybe you were right. Maybe I should have left Faivendei when I had a chance.'

Her face softened as she smiled. 'You are much stronger than you think, Lilly.'

I looked at the ground, not quite believing what she'd said. After all, she saw through me and knew better than anyone all my fears and doubts.

Have faith... The echo of my mother's voice sent shivers down my spine.

Omnia dispersed into thousands of ethereal flowers that were hastened away by a sudden gust of wind. I stood motionless, staring into nothingness and thinking of my mother's voice. I imagined that; I must have. My head was reeling and I wasn't sure of anything now.

The others were already waiting for me in Nairin's boat. It was time to go. I allowed myself a last glance at the forest, whispering, 'Farewell.'

I joined the others, and my heart seemed to swell with fire, pounding against my ribcage, ready to combust and scorch me to ash. I was leaving behind not only this enchanted forest but also myself as I used to be. I couldn't imagine what was waiting for me ahead, but I was sure of one thing: my life would never be the same again.

I closed my eyes and opened them only when we reached the Human World. A grey bleak world. I was coughing like a teenager smoking her first cigarette. Although we were standing in the middle of the woods, the air was so polluted that it seemed I could see its suffocating thickness. It was unusually warm for the beginning of November, but I couldn't hear as many bird songs as in Faivendei, and I began to understand what Vesta meant when she talked about auras. This whole world had the aura of death.

More than that. It was like a teenager being ruined by a disease in the prime of his life. The Spirit World was his twin brother, who by a lucky chance fell into another family – into caring hands that protected him and valued him if not more then as much as themselves. The Human World was in the middle of an apocalypse, but it wasn't people's fault – they were just a tool that Noxohit so masterfully controlled to bring about the sixth extinction.

It drilled a hole in my chest from which, as if from the mouth of a volcano, scorching lava was bursting out, ravaging all doubt and fear in its way. How could I worry about my small insignificant life? How could I weigh myself against a dying world?

Thankfully, nobody was aware of my inner struggle as we walked through the Loire Valley towards the Château de la Mothe-Chandeniers, where Octavian Allegrain lived.

Vesta scrutinised Darius. 'You move at the speed of sound – why don't you go and get the pendant alone?'

'Ask your Raven.'

'No,' Will bit out. 'We'll get as close as possible. The gargoyle will hide us under her protective dome. The three of you will stay nearby, and Darius, Hairito and I will go inside as soon as the ball begins. Hopefully, the music and the noise from the crowd will help us slip through unnoticed.'

I couldn't stomach the idea of Will in a castle full of vampires.

'Are you sure he's organising a ball tonight?' Vesta asked.

'Octavian is known for his love of entertainment,' Darius explained. 'He holds a ball the first day of every month.'

'I still don't understand why you need to go with him,' I said to Will.

'Because I don't trust him.'

'Which is offensive, by the way,' Darius said with a silken venom.

'That's your problem.'

Darius rolled his eyes, but a smile was tugging up his big mouth.

A couple of hours later, we were at the edge of the forest in front of a majestic limestone castle that stood in the middle of a lake. Warm light emitted by many chandeliers streamed from the tall windows and reflected from the dark water. There was only one path across the lake, leading to the main entrance, and the guests, all with dead-white skin and wine-red eyes, walked gracefully along.

I moved closer to Will. 'This is a terrible idea.'

'Don't worry, everything will be fine. The gargoyle will hide us and no one will notice.'

'If they find you, Darius at least has a chance of escaping, but you don't. Why don't we just reason with Octavian? I'm sure he wants Noxohit gone as much as we do. At the end of the day, they need humans. We're little lunch bags on feet.'

Darius chuckled. 'Of course! Perhaps we should ask for an invitation to the ball too? He's a vampire, not one of your guardians. He doesn't care about the good of all living beings.

Plus, he's an art collector, and they never willingly part with rare and valuable items.'

'I agree with Lilly,' Vesta said. 'What if the pendant is protected?'

Darius let out a dramatic sigh. 'Octavian doesn't need that. He has a keen ear and knows perfectly well that no one in their right mind would dare to steal from him.'

'You're just guessing though,' Vesta hissed.

Darius removed his brooch and pinned it to the inside of his jacket. 'No, I know from experience. This won't be the first time I've borrowed jewellery from him.'

'But no one in their right mind would dare to steal from Octavian,' I quoted him.

'Ah, but surely you see the loophole there.' He gave me his clownish smile.

The sound of instrumental music reached us from the castle, something formal and rhythmic with a harpsichord underlying the strings.

'It's begun.' Will's eyes slid to Darius. 'Ready?'

'Always.'

'Hairito, can you hide us?' Will asked.

She nodded, flew up and landed on Darius's shoulders. Her little horn started to glow.

Darius watched the expanding dome of purple-black energy like a child watching a magic trick. 'Wicked!'

Will turned to me. 'Stay where you are, don't go anywhere and, whatever happens, don't enter the castle. Do you understand?'

No. I couldn't promise that.

'Do you understand?' It was an order.

Vesta nodded. 'We'll stay here.'

'Lilly?' He lifted his eyebrow at me.

My pulse quickened as he was disappearing under the dome. 'Please, just, be careful.'

He turned to Vesta. 'I'm counting on you.'

They vanished.

Time began to pass ever so slowly. Vesta didn't move an inch after they left, focusing all her attention on the castle, while Aisha sat against a tree, as if trying to hypnotise the ground. The music was still playing, giving me hope that everything was fine.

I squatted next to Aisha. 'Don't worry, we'll find Ophelia.'

'Really?' She lifted her red eyes, glossy with tears. 'And how do you think we'll do that?'

'I don't know yet...'

She smiled bitterly, but suddenly her gaze turned pale and distant – she was using not hers but an animal's sight. In a flash, she jumped up to her feet. 'Someone's coming.'

I don't know how the metal hilt got into my hand, but my sword was already drawn. Vesta readied her energy whip. We stood with our backs to each other, peering into the darkness of the forest, trying to make anything out. Suddenly, a figure in a tailcoat landed on the ground in front of us. A young man with marble-white skin and crimson eyes. A vampire.

'What do you want?' Vesta barked.

'How rude.' His deep voice was slow and heavy. 'I'm the one you failed to steal from.'

So this was Octavian. And despite being five hundred years old, he didn't look to be more than thirty.

'Please...' I said. 'I can explain. They're only here because of me.'

'That's a lie,' Vesta countered.

His eyes drifted leisurely to the side. 'I'm holding a ball to-night, and I don't want to spoil my mood with retribution...

but justice must prevail. Otherwise others will get the idea that stealing from me is acceptable. I cannot allow that. Oh no, I can't.'

'I'm sorry. We weren't supposed to do that.'

'Then maybe you can give me one reason why I should let you live.'

'We're looking for Luminiferos,' I tried.

'Really?' He flew up to me and ran his icy finger across my face. 'Who's *we*?'

I went still, becoming aware of each breath I took. 'Me and my friends.'

'Hmm... You need the pendant, I suppose. And why do you think you can get the weapon of light?' he murmured in my ear, pressing his frosty lips against my neck.

'Because I'm a vandor, and Noxohit knows it. If I don't find Luminiferos, I'm as good as dead.'

He drew back from my neck, and it seemed his marble skin blenched even further. 'A vandor? You?'

I nodded.

He studied me silently. 'Prove it.'

'How?'

'Heal my soul, and I will forgive you and your friends for intruding.'

'Her gift only just manifested,' Vesta tried to ward him off, 'and last time she healed a nox of dark energy she almost died.'

'I'm no saint, but I'd like to think I'm better than a nox.'

'I'm not sure healing a vampire's soul is any easier,' she snarled.

'Listen. Your choice is simple,' he uttered with a deathly calm. 'Either you heal my soul and get the pendant, or you and your friends will be the main course this evening.'

'But... I don't know how.'

'I'll show you.' He took my hand and placed it on his solar plexus. 'Close your eyes and listen.'

I did as he said, but nothing happened. What if I couldn't do it? What if I'd spent all my supernatural power on Darius?

'Listen with your heart,' he murmured. 'Separate from your thoughts, from your emotions, from your body. Focus on me – dissolve into my soul.'

I tried to focus on him... on anything but my feverish pulse. Useless. That calmness and inner peace that I'd had when I'd healed Darius's soul had vanished without a trace, and realising that the fate of my friends depended on my broken power made me feel helpless.

'I'm sorry, I can't do it.' I opened my eyes. 'Take me but, please, release my friends.'

He smiled at me. A genuine smile. 'I'm not going to harm you or your friends. But I would be very grateful if you could help me. Long life leaves scars on one's soul.' His crimson eyes slid to the ground, as if something had brought back the memories of his past.

'Do you promise not to hurt them?'

'I do.' He nodded slightly. 'Do you promise to try again?'

He looked at me... almost friendly this time. Although I couldn't find the strength to trust him, his promise gave me hope.

I placed my hand on his chest and took a deep breath. With the exhalation, the accumulated tension seemed to leave my body. My shoulders sagged, and for a moment I ceased breathing. My thoughts stopped their Brownian motion. My blood slowed down, submerging me in an ocean of everlasting peace. I closed my eyes.

'Take your time,' he said as gently as a loving father would to his daughter.

Suddenly, a small wisp of silver energy floated before my closed eyelids. I stopped feeling my body... it seemed I stopped existing at all. There was nothing but this light. Slowly it expanded, illuminating everything around. Before long there was nothing left but light.

'Dissolve into my soul.'

Octavian's distant whisper reached my ears as music, and suddenly I noticed some kind of disruption in the endless stream of silver light, as if in a divine orchestra consisting of billions of instruments, I'd managed to catch one out of tune. It was an energy cluster in human shape with some smokiness at its core – so different from the oily sediment Darius had had. It didn't extend along his spine but was located in his chest, creating some sort of opacity. My whole existence focused on it, and it flew inside my body, like a thin stream of liquid nitrogen. It rushed into my hand, flowed up my forearm and burned my heart with its cold. I flinched.

'Yes... Don't let the darkness paralyse you. You're a vandor. Focus on the light.'

It was stinging my heart like hundreds of angry bees trying to protect their violated hive, and the more I focused on this pain, the faster the bees transformed into giant hornets. The light dimmed – everything was plunging into darkness. My knees buckled and I almost fell, but cold hands caught me in time. I was about to open my eyes—

Focus on the light...

Light. I couldn't see it anymore. But I remembered it was everywhere – it was all there was. Through the force of will, I took a deep breath, and the air, warm as fresh milk, soothed my stinging heart. A lightning of silver energy split the darkness. I took another breath and let the light fill my soul... my mind. And again it was everywhere. No more pain. No more suffering. No more darkness. Just light and love; just peace and joy. For a moment I indulged myself, plunging into this infinity and just being. I didn't want to come back to reality. After this, reality seemed so sorrowful, meaningless and hollow... I wanted to dissolve in this serenity.

But I found the strength to yank myself back to Earth, and the light flowed from my chest through my arm to my hand and into the vampire's body. The remnants of Octavian's opacity dissolved into light.

I opened my eyes. He was studying the surrounding forest, the sky, his own castle with such a rapture in his gaze, as if the Earth was once again bathed in the sun after a long eclipse. I smiled. Everything seemed right and meaningful at that moment.

'What's your name?' he asked me softly.

'Lilly... Lilly White.'

'Come with me, Lilly White. I want to introduce you to my guests. Gift me one dance, and the pendant will be yours.' His eyes slid to Aisha and Vesta. 'Of course, you're invited too. Don't worry about dresses. In the whole of France you won't find a better selection than in my wardrobe.'

Vesta inclined her head to the side. 'I wonder where those dresses came from?'

'I'm an art collector, not a killer. I've never killed a single person in my life. Yes, there are vampires who drink every drop of a human's blood, but there are also humans who kill for fun, aren't there?'

Vesta said nothing, but I thought she knew better than anyone else what he was talking about.

'Well, let's not dwell on depressing matters. Shall we?' He gestured for us to follow him.

'I'm not going,' Aisha snapped.

The remnants of my inner peace were gone. 'We won't stay long. We need the pendant.'

'I don't care. I won't dance while my sister is suffering.'

'What happened to her sister?' Octavian asked.

I bit my lip. 'She was kidnapped by noxes.'

'Oh well. You can't save her now, can you?' Octavian spread his hands to the sky. 'Calm down and enjoy yourself.'

'Calm down? Enjoy?' Aisha hissed and walked away.

'Where can we find you?' I called after her.

'I'll be waiting for you nearby,' she snarled without looking back at me. 'I'll find you.'

We stared after her, and Octavian shook his head. 'Nothing will help her live a long life if she won't learn humility. Hmm... Right! Follow me, ladies.'

We passed through the main door into a spacious hall strewn with ruby orchids. For a moment, I thought they were painted in blood. To our left was the ballroom, where the gentle buzz of a chattering crowd filtered through Schubert's *Serenade*. We walked up along the spiral staircase to the second floor.

I looked at him. 'Mr Allegrain—'

'Please – call me Octavian.'

'Octavian. I hope our friends are safe?'

'Thanks to you, they will be. They've already changed and are waiting for us.'

'Aisha's right – we don't have time to dance,' Vesta grunted. 'Noxes are looking for Lilly and might be here any second. This puts you at risk as well.'

'Then such is our fate.' Octavian smiled. 'I would be delighted to die today, since my soul is pure again.'

'I'm glad for you, but you've lived twenty times more than us, and we aren't ready to be murdered today.'

'I won't keep you long.'

When we entered the dressing room, Will and Darius stood in tuxedos, looking simultaneously festive and miserable, with four vampires behind them. Hairito ran up to me and hugged my legs.

This room resembled an exhibition of haute couture, with many mannequins in evening gowns. I glanced left then right and could barely see either wall. Hundreds of mannequins spread out into the distance to either side.

'Off you go,' Octavian ordered the other vampires, and they obeyed.

'You're lucky today, my friends!' he addressed Will and Darius. 'If it weren't for Lilly, you'd have to pay for your impertinence with blood.'

Will frowned, his aquamarine eyes lingering on the door. 'Where's Aisha?'

'She's—'

'I found one special gown, but I haven't tried it on any of my… guests yet.' Octavian glanced at me, approaching a mannequin with an elegant emerald dress in the centre of the room.

I still wasn't in the mood to party. 'Erm…'

'No excuses!' His eyes shifted to Vesta. 'And you… let me think. You have very beautiful eyes, my dear. Powerful, but vulnerable… Oh! This will be perfect.' He pointed to a silver silk dress.

Vesta flared her nostrils. 'Why do I get the feeling you're playing with us like dolls?'

'The beauty of the evening gowns warms my soul. Besides, I can't allow you to appear among my guests in inappropriate attire. It would offend them.'

Octavian swiftly took the dresses from the mannequins, and handed them to me and Vesta. 'There's a screen. You can change behind it. Oh, and you'll find shoes there as well.

'Gentlemen!' Octavian told Darius and Will as we left to change. 'Please don't deny yourself the company of my guests, but I must warn you, we hypnotise people with extraordinary ease, as you are probably already aware. If you don't want to become a vampire's dinner, please be careful.'

Vesta swapped a glance with me and we began to change. I couldn't understand why he was putting us at risk after I'd healed his soul. But then I remembered that, before he'd become a vampire, he'd been arrogant enough to drink blood as a luxury. Apparently being free from evil didn't turn you into a saint.

'What are your names?' Octavian asked.

'William Raven.'

'Darius Fulman.'

'William Raven... Are you related to Dorian Raven?'

'He's my grandfather.'

'Of course he is. I can see the resemblance now,' Octavian mused. 'He was a jolly fellow before that accident. Very sad. Darius, this isn't your first time here, is it?'

'Oh no. I've often been to France, but mostly the south.'

'I'm talking about my castle.'

Octavian's tone now was as frosty as his skin. Vesta and I both stopped our dressing to listen.

'Unfortunately, I haven't had the privilege of attending one of your balls before. But I promise, I will enjoy it tonight.'

Vesta went back to buttoning the green satin up my back as quietly as she could.

'Darius, you're only alive now because of Lilly,' Octavian warned. 'That state of affairs could change.'

Nobody spoke.

'I want my brooch back.'

Darius snorted. 'Don't know what you're talking about.'

A deafening silence followed. I peered around the screen.

'Fine, fine!' Darius removed the brooch from the inside of his black jacket and handed it to Octavian. 'I'm curious. How did you know I had it?'

Octavian took the brooch carefully and glanced at Darius as if he was a silly schoolboy. 'You have no idea what this is, do you?' He hid the brooch in his pocket.

Vesta finished buttoning my dress, and I looked down at the folds of the hem gathered around my feet. Ridiculous! This dress had been designed for a model, not for somebody as short as I was, and I'd have to wear high heels. I took the first pair that looked like my size from the rack against the wall and put them on. They were very uncomfortable, but at least I was sure I wouldn't trip over the hem of my dress. Vesta was luckier – she was taller, and her dress wasn't as long, so she didn't bother to put on heels – she just wore her trainers. We were ready and emerged from behind the screen.

Octavian gave us a measuring look, clapping his hands. '*Magnifique!*'

I unquestioningly followed his orders disguised as polite requests just because I knew what was at stake, but inside me blazed a fire that could burn this dress into flames. Although it began to fade under Will's unblinking gaze as he scanned me up and down.

'Unbelievable...' Octavian uttered, his eyes darting from Will to me. 'William, would you allow me a dance with Lilly?'

Will's attention cut to him, his hand sliding towards the feather hanging from his necklace, as if he was about to unfold his sword.

'I promise I won't hurt her,' Octavian reassured warmly.

I nodded once and Will agreed – he also knew what was at stake.

We descended to the alabaster ballroom. Crystal chandeliers hung from the ornamental ceiling, their gems scattering drops of coloured light among the guests. The scarlet curtains with pelmets, descending in lush folds from the eight towering windows, seemed to echo the vampires' eyes, which shone against the background of ivory walls like ripe cherries in whipped cream. They turned their sights on us, and I fought a sudden urge to visit a powder room.

'Ladies and gentlemen!' Octavian addressed his guests. 'Please don't get me wrong. This is *not* the aperitif.'

The crowd broke into gentle laughter.

'But I make sure your glasses are always full, don't I?'

The guests raised their delicate cups filled with blood in approval. My stomach turned.

'This beautiful young lady is a rare kind of human.' He pointed at me. 'She is, my dear friends...' He paused for a moment, scanning the throng, as if to ensure all attention was focused on him. 'She is a vandor!'

A short silence was followed by exclamations from the crowd, and a roomful of hungry crimson eyes studied me. He was showing me off like a rare item from his collection, one he was ready to sell to the highest bidder. And I felt like a chunk of meat thrown in a cage with hungry hyenas. I had no choice – I had to trust him. But something told me he could easily duck out of his promise and share me with his guests like a bottle of forty-year-old Talisker.

'Yes, you heard that right! She is the last vandor on Earth not yet infected with Noxohit's darkness!'

'What is he doing?' Vesta hissed.

Will was tense as a bow string. His eyes flashed around the room as if he was trying to assess the situation and devise a plan in case something went wrong. Hairito also guarded me closely, while Darius cast fawning looks at some of the vampires.

Octavian held out his hand to me. I glanced at Will and followed the vampire.

We started to dance, and he smiled. 'So, you set off in search of Luminiferos. May I ask, why are you doing this? I'm well aware you don't relish the prospect of becoming a nox, but are there any other reasons? And don't waste my time. Answer honestly, or I'll force you to tell the truth.'

'You promised not to hurt me.'

'And I always keep my promises. Hypnosis does not hurt.'

I said nothing.

'So? What are your motives?'

'Noxohit is annihilating human civilisation. Anyone would do the same in my place.'

Octavian laughed, revealing his sharp fangs. 'It's nice to know there are still those who believe in that.'

'You don't think Noxohit should be defeated?'

'I think there are those who think he shouldn't be defeated, and I'm not sure I disagree. Noxohit is a logical consequence of people's actions over centuries. I'm not laughing at your zeal to change the world; I respect it. But I've seen too much to doubt that the spread of darkness is irreversible. It has penetrated everything. Noxes live among people, feeding on their energy, and every day there are more of them. Witches and shamans leave seclusion in the Spirit World to join Noxohit. They serve him because they're afraid that if they resist, he'll turn them into noxes. And you can scorn animal fear, but it's a powerful motive and can override more noble desires. How long have you lived with the guardians?'

'Two months.'

'That's why you're still so naïve. Lilly, I'm not saying this to scare you or dissuade you. I simply want to offer you a different choice.' He smiled. 'You don't have to seek Luminiferos if you become a vampire. You're a human, not a spirit, so you won't become immortal. You'll just lose your vandor's gift forever and change your diet a little bit. Noxohit will no longer care about you, and you'll be safe. I can see what might hold you back...' He glanced at Will. 'But it would also be beneficial for him, as you're not one of the Simtri clan.'

'No, it's not just that.'

'Hmm... I had a friend named Azmeral Crow, a powerful shaman, who had a wife and daughter he loved to distraction. One day Noxohit took them both. Azmeral went in search of Luminiferos. He found the first emanation, and it soon destroyed him. Shortly before his death, he told me that Luminiferos is not a weapon of light but a creature of darkness. That these emanations will reveal your dark side, which will destroy you if you make a wrong choice. You didn't really understand what you were signing up for. Take your time and think it over. And if your decision remains the same, I'll give you the pendant.'

'Thank you for being so thoughtful, but I've already made my decision.'

'You're inexperienced and young. That can get you into trouble.'

'Perhaps. But if I think it over for a day or two, I'll still be inexperienced and young. I know I'm doing the right thing, and that's enough for me.'

'Words. They often hide the truth, but the heart never lies. I can hear it right now trying to break its way through your ribcage. Ostentatious bravery, but inside only fear.'

'Of course I'm afraid. But I made a decision and I'll stick to it. I kept my side of the bargain; now please keep yours.' I stopped dancing. 'I'll truly appreciate it if you give me the pendant right now.'

'It wouldn't be fair to deprive my dear guests of your company, would it? They may never see such a rare... human... again.'

'Octavian, thank you very much for your hospitality and your kind offer, but my friend is right – we're putting you and ourselves in danger by being here, especially now that you've announced who I am. I would be grateful if you'd allow us to leave now. Along with the pendant.'

He sighed, but a soft smile tugged at his lips. 'Very well then. Follow me.'

Imperceptibly, I sagged. Will, Vesta, Ray and Hairito were watching us closely as we walked towards them.

'Oh, my dear friend,' Octavian said to Will. 'She's a veritable treasure.'

Will didn't reply, just took my hand and pulled me, a bit forcefully, closer to him and further from the vampire.

'Come with me. I'll give you what you came for.' Octavian headed down the corridor.

I glanced back at the crowd. 'Where's Darius?'

'Having fun,' Will snapped with obvious disgust.

'We don't need him anymore,' Vesta added.

Leaving Darius alone with dozens of vampires didn't seem like a good idea, but at the same time, he was very gifted and hopefully could protect himself.

We entered a dim room with ominous red corduroy walls. The only lights were under the panes of glass covering thousands of sparkling, colourful stones. Tiaras and pendants, earrings and necklaces, rings and bracelets – every kind of human adornment was kept here in a museum-quality presentation. In the middle stood a small square pillar. On top of it sat a nondescript silver chain and a pendant comprising seven soldered rings.

I released Will's hand and walked towards the column.

'The pendant of Luminiferos,' Octavian confirmed my guess. 'My friend Azmeral told me that emanations are not simply a collection of seven energies. He believed they are alive and choose when to appear, and for whom. They can be anywhere and don't appear on any map.'

Vesta crossed her arms. 'That sounds promising.'

'By putting the pendant on, Lilly will sign a contract with the Universe.' Octavian was talking to Will. 'She won't find peace until she gathers together all seven emanations.'

'What if she doesn't wear the pendant, but we still search for Luminiferos?' he asked.

'Not a single emanation will reveal itself. The necklace, and the bond between it and her, will serve as proof of her commitment to the chosen path. This is a mandatory step, her signature on the contract with the Universe. She will have to commit to this. Completely.'

Noxohit was destroying the Earth, draining people's energy. He'd kidnapped Ophelia and transformed my family and hundreds of thousands of other guardians. They suffered daily, devoid of will, watching Noxohit use their hands to destroy everything they held dear. If Luminiferos was the last hope for them, if my gift could help me gather all the emanations... I had to at least try, even if it meant almost certain death.

'I'm in,' I said. 'Open it up.'

Octavian smiled and lifted the glass cover, taking the pendant from the stand and handing it to Will.

I frowned. 'But—'

'Quiet!'

Octavian froze, listening to something. Hairito pricked up her ears and glanced warily towards the door.

'I'm sorry. You were right...' he whispered. 'Noxes have arrived.'

CHAPTER 14
MISSION

'FOLLOW ME. I've got a hidden passageway that can lead you back, directly into the forest.' He flew across the room and opened the door to the library.

'What about Darius?' I asked.

'There's no one in the castle but us,' Octavian said. 'The others escaped in time.'

'I warned you,' Vesta snarled.

'I know.' Octavian reached towards a shelf and pulled one of the books. The wall swung open, revealing the passage. He took a torch from the wall and handed it to Will. 'Go down the stairs, then straight through the tunnel, and you'll be a hundred metres or so back in the forest.'

'Won't you come with us?' I asked.

'No, I'll distract them.'

'They'll kill you.'

He glanced back. 'You have to leave. Now!'

'But—'

He smiled at me. 'It's all right. Everything's going according to the plan.'

His crimson eyes shone with such a frightening childish joy. What was he up to?

Will put his arm around me, pulling me along. I went reluctantly, looking back at Octavian, who disappeared behind the closing wall.

Why had he done that? Why had he stayed? He could have gone with us. He was a vampire – he could have easily run away. I recalled his earlier words: *I would be delighted to die today.* I shook my head as if trying to rid it of these thoughts. He would surely save himself at the last moment. Could a vampire become a nox?

I nearly tripped when one of my heels caught on the metal stairs. I took them off and we continued down the spiral staircase.

'Do you want me to carry you?' Will proposed, looking at my bare feet.

'No, I'm fine,' I said automatically.

When we reached the tunnel, we halted. The stale air reeked of mildew and moist dirt, and only water drops splashing onto the concrete floor disturbed the eerie silence. Will pointed the torch ahead, but we couldn't see where the tunnel ended.

Something bolted a few inches from my bare feet, and I jumped, nearly screaming. But it was only a rat. Will lifted me up – this time without asking for permission. I didn't resist.

'Vesta, can you hold this?' He handed her a torch.

I couldn't wait to get out of this tunnel, hoping that somehow Octavian would let us know he was safe.

'I can walk,' I said to Will when we reached another spiral staircase that led up, but he ignored me.

At the top we found a wooden door. Will put me back on my feet and pushed it open.

'Hairito, hide us.'

She flew up, landed on his shoulders and radiated purple-black energy, hiding us under her dome before we went outside. The door was hidden in the roots of an old hollow oak. We walked round it to see the castle—

No!

Six noxes stood on the second-floor balcony with Thomas in the centre. Tarry tentacles sprouted from his palms, wrapping around Octavian's body and holding him in the air above the lake. I stepped forward, but Will pulled me back.

'One last chance, Lilly White!' Thomas shouted. 'Your life for his. Come out, and he will be safe.'

I glanced at Will, but he lowered his gaze, drawing me closer to him.

'Well, well. Ophelia, Octavian, who will you sacrifice next to save your pathetic life? Will? Vesta? Or maybe the gargoyle that's hiding you from me right now? You can't hide forever, Lilly. The sooner you surrender, the fewer people will die. Find the courage to come out and save the ones you love.'

'Do I have to tell you,' Will whispered, 'that he's just trying to manipulate you.'

'So what now? We watch Octavian die?'

'We don't have other options,' Vesta said. 'Otherwise Nox-ohit will kill not only him but all of us. We have a mission, Lilly, and we can't give up the first time it gets hard. He made his choice.'

Suddenly Octavian cackled. 'The greatest evil humanity has witnessed, and you're that stupid? You're doing me a favour!'

The ebony tentacles gripped Octavian's body tighter. The dull snapping of breaking bones was followed by a piercing wail that shrilled through the night. I shuddered, grabbing at Will's sleeve. He buried my face in his shoulder.

They were killing him because of me. I was witnessing a murder for the first time in my life… and I could save him. All I had to do was just come out, and his life would be spared. It was a moment where I could prove to myself that I was willing to sacrifice myself for others… that I was strong enough.

I just stood there paralysed.

'You're doing me a favour!' Octavian howled from his crushed lungs. 'She healed my soul… today… Today is the best… day… to die.'

'If you insist.' Thomas's venomous bite warned that he was eager to oblige. 'I'm counting to three, Lilly, and if I don't see you, his blood will be on your hands. One!'

His voice reverberated through my shaking limbs.

'Two!'

I forced myself to look up.

'Three!'

The oily tentacles pierced Octavian's body. In the blink of an eye, nothing was left of him but ash, which fell as a grey haze to the surface of the tranquil lake. Thomas withdrew his tentacles, and Octavian's empty suit dropped into the water. The noxes suddenly blurred into shapeless dark masses, sliding down the walls, as if the castle had started to bleed onyx blood. They vanished one by one until only Thomas was left.

'Isn't it mesmerising to watch the moonlight glittering in these motes of ash? One could almost call it fairy dust. Look. Admire. Memorise. Soon your family, Ophelia, Will and everyone you hold so dear will sparkle in the same way.' A lethal smirk contorted his face. 'Sleep tight, Lilly White.'

A deafening clatter filled my ears. In a blink of an eye he'd murdered a man – turned him to ashes, and he'd enjoyed every minute of it.

Fairy. Freaking. Dust.

I pulled away from Will.

'They found us so quickly...' Vesta muttered.

Her words echoed in my mind. Suddenly the dark colours of the forest and the castle mixed together in a delirious whirl-wind.

'Octavian announced to everyone that Lilly is a vandor,' Will said. 'Surely some of the vampires were on Noxohit's side.'

I fell to my knees, unable to focus, fighting to stay con-scious. Will tried to pull me up—

'It's okay... I'm fine.'

'We have to go,' Vesta urged. 'It's too dangerous to stay here.'

'Okay.' I tried to get up quickly, but my head was still spin-ning, and I almost fell. Will caught me in time.

'I'm fine.'

'Whatever,' he said. 'We need to find another lake. It'll be safer to spend the night in the Spirit World, and we can't use this one.'

'We can't go back to Faivendei,' Vesta countered.

'No, we can't. We'll ask Nairin to take us some other place safe for guardians.'

'With her attitude, she might send us where spirits live.'

'No. She isn't brave enough to risk our already tenuous al-liance.'

'If you say so.'

'Where's Aisha by the way?'

'She didn't want to go to the ball,' Vesta explained. 'She said she'd wait for us here.'

Ray took off and flew out of the protective dome into the wood.

'He'll find her,' Will said.

We walked in silence through the forest, wrapped in night-time mist. Against my will, I kept replaying the scene of the infernal tentacles plunging into Octavian's body and ripping his life away. Yes, he was a vampire who fed on human blood... but I could still hear him saying he'd killed no one in his entire life. What's more, he'd saved us. I hadn't even started to search for Luminiferos yet, but one person had been burned to ashes and another kidnapped because of me. I had no right to put Will, Vesta and Aisha at such high risk. I had to take the pendant from Will and continue on my own. It might reduce my chances of survival to zero, but it would also prevent them from sharing Octavian's fate.

Hiding behind excuses was useless. I hadn't tried to save Octavian not because I had a mission or anything like that. I was scared. That was all. And I had no guarantee that I could find the courage to save my friends if their lives were at stake.

Eyes... eyes... A faint echo came from somewhere deep in a thicket.

We stopped at once, listening.

Eyes...

Suddenly, the fog split in a burst of air that almost knocked us off our feet. The electrified mist crackled, and blinding light illuminated the forest for a moment.

And as the glow dimmed, there was Darius.

'Hey, guys? You there?'

'Shut up!' Vesta hissed.

'Ah, here you are!' Darius scanned the surroundings. 'Erm... Where exactly are you?'

Will grabbed his arm, pulling him into the protective dome, then recoiled at the sight of two red wounds on Darius's neck and bloodstains on the collar of his white shirt. 'What the hell happened to you?'

'It's a long story.' He winked at Will. 'But the moral of it is, never mess with a vampire.'

It seemed Will was ready to slap him so hard that Darius's grandfather would feel it.

'Why the long faces?' Darius said. 'What happened?'

'Noxes killed Octavian,' Vesta snapped at him.

'And why on Earth does it bother you?'

'He sacrificed himself to save us,' I breathed in a quiet reprimand.

'Horse shit! Vampires move almost as fast as me – he could easily run away. But he didn't. Why? Because he's lived for over five hundred years, and I bet he had a hard time of it. All those dresses, jewellery and balls were nothing but an attempt to numb the pain of an inner void.' He pointed at me. 'You, as I understand it, cured his soul, which will provide him a smooth passage to the Border World. He didn't sacrifice himself for your sake. He committed suicide with noxes' help.' His eyes shifted to Will and Vesta. 'Do *you* at least understand that?'

'Why where you looking for us?' Will demanded.

'Did you get the pendant?'

'That's none of your business.'

'Listen, the castle is empty now, so if not, it'll be easy to take it.'

'We have the pendant,' Vesta told him.

'Really? Erm… then I can go get our clothes back.'

'No,' Will bit out.

'Why?'

'I don't trust you.'

'Again, why?'

'You helped us find the pendant. Thanks. This is where we part.'

'Once more, why?' Darius seemed to be trying to set Will off.

'Because you're not the first person I've known who was cured of Noxohit's poison. But you're the first who recovered so quickly. People take weeks, months, some even years to recover their sanity. You didn't take a second. And I think it's because your true nature is as depraved as the darkness of Noxohit. Besides, you're reckless and unreliable.'

'Look, Raven, I can transform light into matter and move at the speed of sound. These are handy talents. You know you need me.'

'I also know that I have no guarantee you won't betray us. Maybe it was because of you the noxes came and killed Octavian.'

'You have powerful intuition. Use it. I will not betray you, and I want to help. Now tell me honestly, do you think I'm lying to you?'

Will scrutinised him. 'Why?'

'I have my reasons, but you don't need to know them. I suppose my gift might be enough to let me join you.'

I couldn't help but notice he'd changed. His wild eyes, which normally didn't rest on one object for more than a second, had calmed down. They'd acquired a healthy shine and such unexpected insight that it seemed a completely different person was standing in front of us. Perhaps this was his true self.

'I think he's telling the truth,' I said.

'I can't believe I'm saying this' – Vesta lifted her eyebrow – 'but on this particular matter I trust him too. He wants to help us.'

Will clenched his jaw, glaring at Darius. 'I'll be keeping an eye on you.'

'Always welcome to try, but I'll warn you up front, you're not really my type.' He gave Will his clownish smile and disappeared at once, returning to the castle for our clothes.

Soon we found a small lake. Will dipped his hand below the surface, whispering, '*Iternovus.*' The ship rose from the depths in the middle of the lake. A moment passed, and I spotted Nairin's predatory eyes, scanning the shore intently.

'Dear Nairin,' Will called her. 'We need your help.'

'Where do you want to go now? You know how hard it is to carry so many people! And I don't want to!' She disappeared under the water.

Vesta sighed. 'Here we go.'

'Nairin, please,' Will murmured. 'You've always been very kind to me.'

She completely ignored him.

Suddenly Darius appeared, giving us our clothes and backpacks. He glanced at the boat. 'Where's Nairin?'

She surfaced again, practically purring. 'You remembered my name.'

'Of course, sugar. I could never forget you.'

She laughed, lowering her head in mock embarrassment. Vesta gave me a meaningful look and rolled her eyes.

'Nairin... your beauty is absolute and needs no adornment, and yet I dared to bring you a gift.' Darius smiled. 'It's a small thing, but I hope you will accept it. When I saw it, I immediately thought of your sublime green hair. It's a comb studded with diamonds and emeralds—'

He hadn't finished, but a levitating ramp had already appeared. Darius headed to the ship, nodding at us to follow.

'What about Aisha?' I asked.

'I'm here,' she replied, appearing out of nowhere.

'Where have you been?' Will made sure she was unharmed, then scrutinised every inch of her face, as though trying to see through her.

'Nearby. I saw noxes and... I wanted to confront them, but that would be stupid. I couldn't fight them alone, so I walked away from the castle.' She lowered her gaze.

Ray flew over and landed on Will's shoulder, then we all climbed into the boat, and Nairin carried us back to the Spirit World.

We were at the edge of a lake in a night-time forest almost identical to the one we'd just left, but it was much warmer here. There was a path leading deep into the woods, and as soon as we landed, Will sent Ray to make sure it was safe. Vesta and I went behind the trees to change into our clothes.

Vesta looked at me. 'Are you okay?'

'I am. But Octavian isn't. Nor is Ophelia.'

She let out an irritated huff. 'Lilly, it's time to thicken up your skin. Things will only get worse, and you have to prepare for that. We aren't on a school trip, you know. We have a tough mission and, believe me, we all went into it knowing the risk we're taking.'

'I don't think so. I won't allow someone else to die because of me.'

'You think we're doing this for you? Take off your crown. We're risking our lives for the whole human race. I know what's happening in your head right now – you're planning to leave. Do that and you'll rob the planet of its last chance. You need us

and we need you. We aren't your bodyguards; we're your part-
ners. None of us is counting on returning home anyway.'

She walked off to the others, and I watched her go, feeling
as if she had poured a bucket of ice-cold water over my head.
My worries disgusted her. There was no softness or compassion
in her gaze, only strength of spirit and firmness of heart.
Against this background, I clearly saw my own worthlessness
and cowardice.

Maybe she was right. Maybe we had a chance. Maybe I
could find the courage to become stronger.

Ray returned with good news – the forest was safe and
empty. We walked into an abandoned village full of ruined
houses overgrown with trees and shrubs.

'What happened here?' I mused.

'Perhaps some time ago it was like Faivendei,' Will said.
'Then the guardians left it, or Noxohit destroyed them. Still, we
should be able to find a place to sleep.'

'Don't tell me you mean these creepy houses?' Darius
yelped.

'Do you have a better option?'

'Of course. It's warm as the tropics here. You can do
whatever you want, but I'm sleeping outside.'

'I agree,' Vesta said. 'There's still a lot of dark energy here.'

Will shrugged. We walked away and found what had once
been a theatre – a modest wooden stage, starting to sag at one
corner, and benches circled around it. Darius picked up a bench
and lay down, placing his jacket under his head. He reached
into his waistcoat pocket and pulled out that familiar three-
flower brooch, delicately studded with diamonds. The one that
had belonged to Octavian.

It seemed the play of moonlight in the sparkling stones reflected in Darius's eyes, giving them such a calming radiance

that for a moment I forgot about everything in the world, dissolving into their soothing silence. He glanced at me as if feeling my gaze and smiled, but it wasn't his usual clownish grin. He looked at me as if we shared a common secret.

'I knew you didn't go back to the castle for our clothes,' Vesta snapped. 'They were just an excuse.'

'Oh please,' Darius breathed. 'Octavian's definitely not going to use it.'

'Jerk.'

'I've been called worse.'

Vesta dropped her backpack, closed her eyes and started casting spells, moving her hands through the air as if controlling it.

'What are you doing?' Will asked.

'Trying to contact Azmeral Crow. He found the first emanation. Maybe he can help us.'

Will nodded in approval. Aisha walked towards the lake and I followed her.

'Let her be.' He took my hand, trying to stop me.

'No, I have to talk to her.'

Aisha went to the edge of the lake and sat down on the ground, hugging her knees. I sat beside her.

'I haven't apologised to you yet—'

She was silent.

'I'm sorry about Ophelia. It's my fault, and I'll do everything to—'

'No, you won't.'

'You don't believe me?'

'Lilly, you came in search of Luminiferos, and that's your top priority now. We're not looking for Ophelia; we're looking for emanations of light. It might take a lifetime...' Her voice faltered. 'Meanwhile, she's alone... But I understand. You're a vandor and perhaps our last chance to banish Noxohit. The fate of humanity is more important than... than the life of some little girl.'

'They're connected. Finding Luminiferos will let us save Ophelia.'

'I know you believe that, Lilly. But unfortunately, faith alone isn't enough. I also believed Omnia would save my parents from noxes. Then I thought I could protect Ophelia and be a mother to her. None of that happened, however much I wanted it. Listen—' She sighed. 'I don't blame you. I only blame myself. If anybody should ask for forgiveness, it's me.'

'What are you talking about? You have nothing to apologise for.'

She let out a bitter chuckle and rose from the ground. 'Come on, we need to rest.'

When we returned, Will was sitting on the stage, and Vesta was still trying to summon the spirit of Azmeral Crow.

Darius propped himself up on one elbow. 'For fairy's sake! If you're going to mumble like that all night, I'd rather go sleep in one of those creepy houses.'

'Vesta, an hour in the morning is worth two in the evening,' Will said. 'Let's get some sleep and try again tomorrow.'

Vesta nodded reluctantly and went to a bench. Aisha lay down. I met Will's gaze. Knowing he understood everything I felt at that moment only made it worse. I didn't want to look weak in his eyes, and I surely didn't deserve his compassion.

Settling on one of the benches, I pretended to sleep, Hairito sprawled beside me on the ground.

Will sat on the stage for a while, and then I heard him lie down. My eyes were closed, but I was wide awake. Maybe an hour had passed, maybe two, and my patience broke. I got up from the bench and tiptoed to the lake shore.

Just as I sat down, I saw Will coming over to me. He glanced at me warily, as if I were a wild bird that might flutter up and fly away at any moment. But I was glad he was also awake. He sat down, pulling me closer to him.

'Will?'

'Hmm?'

'Why didn't I listen to Omnia?'

'Because you're stubborn and headstrong.'

'I should have gone back to the Human World when I had a chance. Ophelia, Octavian... it's all my fault.'

'Lilly, you have so many conflicting emotions even I can't figure them out sometimes.'

I smiled faintly. 'I want to be honest with you.'

'Good. It's hard to lie to me, and I rarely forgive those who try.'

'I wanted to continue the search alone after you gave me the pendant.'

'Of course you did.' He shook his head. 'Do you still?'

'I don't know. Vesta tried to make me believe that together we might have a chance to succeed, that we can actually save humanity. Do you believe that?'

He was silent, looking out in the darkness of the night.

I nodded. 'Exactly. It's obvious to everybody.'

His eyes slid to me. 'What is?'

'That I'm going to die or become a nox very soon. Maybe Thomas is right – maybe I'd better give myself to Noxohit before you all get murdered.'

'You need to learn to abstract from other people's opinions. They will always underestimate you, at least now, while you're at such a vulnerable age.'

'You don't look much older than me.'

He lifted his eyebrow at me.

'Well, give or take a few decades.'

'My body might look young, but experience is always re-flected in the eyes. I can't do anything about the things I've seen; I can't erase the memories from my head. But your eyes reflect a person who might cry if they accidentally stepped on a snail.'

'So I look like a gullible sheep?'

'No.' He smiled. 'You look like a delicate lily on a thin fra-gile stem. Too kind, probably, for this world.'

'I let Octavian die because I was scared. How is that kind?'

'No, Lilly. You weren't scared. You were overwhelmed by helplessness. And that was only because of your kindness and compassion. Not many people would care for a vampire's life. But Noxohit knew that you would. He knew you would blame yourself. He knows all your weaknesses and believe me... this was just foreplay.'

'Yes, Octavian also said I was naïve. He made me realise I don't have what it takes to find Luminiferos, and quite frankly, I agree with him.'

'He judged you by the cover, and I confess, I did too. But he'd have changed his mind if he'd watched your every step for two months.' He smiled. 'He'd have looked closer and seen this lily is made out of steel. He would have seen how she exhausts herself in Belator, not showing a single sign of tiredness to oth-ers but crying silently from fatigue when she gets home. He would have seen how she runs up hills with such frightening resolution in her eyes. She doesn't see obstacles, only her goal. And he would have seen how those runs end in Equilibrium, where nurses heal her bloody blisters. Every. Single. Day. In my eighty-eight years I've never seen a human who had such a strong spirit in such a seemingly weak body. When you choose so, your determination is unsurpassed – it seems only death can stop you. So to answer your question if I believe we can save humanity... I believe you can do it if you choose to, if you open your eyes and see how strong your true self really is. But if you let Noxohit drown you in fear, then, yes, we're all doomed.'

For a long time I sat without saying a word, thinking about everything he'd said. There was truth in his words. Paradoxically, before my vandor nature revealed itself, I was more confident. Maybe the zeal that Will admired so much was actually madness, born by a sensual frenzy and the arrogance of an inexperienced heart. It was easy to steer my fate and take risks when my eyes hadn't seen death, when I had no friends, no family – when I had nothing to lose.

'What Thomas did to Octavian...' I said. 'Can they kill anybody just as easily?'

'Thomas became a bearer of the dark spirit. They are stronger and able to create new noxes.'

'I don't understand... Why doesn't Noxohit destroy humankind all at once then?'

'Because he enjoys pain. There is no pain, no suffering after death. He prefers to slowly break human souls, watching people destroy themselves.'

'I want him to pay for everything he's done. I want him to suffer.'

'Well, then, Noxohit's already won.'

'What?'

'There are only two fundamental feelings – love and fear. Everything else is just the manifestation of one or the other. Tell me, what did you feel when you healed Darius's soul? Was there even a slightest shadow of fear in your heart?'

'No. That feeling was encompassing; it was reviving and so pure.'

'It was pure consciousness – it was love. Absolute and unconditional. As a vandor, you have a power to unite with the Universe while still in a human body. You can tap the infinite source of love and use it to heal people's souls. But if your heart is filled with fear, you won't be able to use your power, and Noxohit will easily destroy you.'

'I'm not afraid of him.'

'You aren't listening to me. There are only two true feelings – love and fear. Your anger and desire to wipe him off the face of Earth is nothing but the fear of losing your attachments. I guess you didn't have many attachments in the Human World. Now you have Ophelia, Aisha, Vesta, Hairito—'

'You.'

He smiled. 'Me.'

'But isn't attachment a manifestation of love?'

'Attachment is a manifestation of ego, the polar opposite of love. Just think. If one of us dies, our souls will be united with the Universe. And you know better than anyone else how wonderful that feeling is – ordinary people, not vandors, can't experience it while still in a physical shell. Here we grow above ourselves, improve, strengthen our spirit. There, we are only at peace. So is there any point in mourning those who rest in serenity? No, Lilly, at such moments you are afraid not for us, but for yourself, because it will be hard for you if one of us dies. You're afraid of being alone again.'

'Don't you have any attachments?'

'Of course I do. I might be a Raven, but I'm still a human. Lilly, I'm not telling you to overcome or fight attachments – just be aware. A simple awareness will already help you to transform your fear into love.'

Was he right? Were all my fears selfish?

It seemed I'd just been caught in a crime I didn't even know I'd committed. My whole gut was trying to find arguments that could justify my wounded pride, which burned with a bright, blistering flame in my chest. But suddenly I saw what was happening inside me as if from outside.

'Pride,' I asked, 'is it also a fear?'

'Pride, vanity, greed are nothing but the fear of being worse than others, fear of being rejected. Fornication and gluttony are the fear of the ephemerality of being; an unbridled desire to sweeten one's passions before physical death. Despondency and sadness are also the fear of dissatisfaction of one's passions and attachments. Love and fear, Lilly. It's as simple as that. If you feel good, you heart is full of love; if you feel bad, then you're afraid of something. Does your anger make you feel genuinely good?'

I shook my head.

'You'll only be able to defeat Noxohit with a heart free of rage. This is when your compassion isn't really in hand. He'll continue to exploit it to destroy your moral defences. Don't allow him to manipulate you. Be compassionate – it's a quality of love, but get rid of this unnecessary guilt over Ophelia, Octavian or anybody else, because, when not controlled wisely, the guilt is a quality of fear.'

'How can I get rid of guilt?'

'You have to realise who you are, what your purpose is, and always keep it in mind. Until you can do that, you'll be an easy target not only for Noxohit, but for anybody who'd like to manipulate you.'

'Do you know who you are?'

'I know who I'm not. It's the same thing.'

'And you know what your purpose is?'

'I do. Well… at least I used to.'

'And you never feel guilty?'

'Sometimes, but it doesn't overpower my senses. And I don't give it any credence.'

I paused. 'I understand what you mean, but I can't stop seeing Octavian's face. I can't believe that a moment ago he was alive, and now he's just ash. I just can't stop thinking about it.'

'Lilly, as much as I hate to admit Darius was right, I agree that Octavian was glad to die. Trust me – I know how he felt. I've seen this before… You remember when you'd just arrived in Faivendei? The day before, I'd gone out into the Human World with General Fairfax and Azrael. We hunted for two bearers who'd been chasing the guardians of Faivendei and converting them to noxes. Omnia doesn't tolerate murder, even if it's noxes, but we'd decided to get rid of them.

'One of our witches acted as a decoy. They followed her, and we followed them. She entered a church, they tried to follow, but we blocked their way. One nox ran away when she saw us. Azrael seized the other with his whip, and Bogdan plunged a knife into her heart. Noxohit's dark energy flowed down the blade and left the woman's chest. She fell to the ground, living out her last seconds as herself, finally. She looked at me with such… gratitude. This is why, the next day, when you arrived in Faivendei, you found a downpour and fog – the forest was mourning. And despite what I just said to you, despite knowing that woman was grateful, I blamed myself and felt just like you do – overwhelmed with wild anger at myself and at Noxohit.'

It seemed the night silence was broken by elegiac lilts of the organ melody he had performed in that church. *The Aria of Death* I'd thought back then. If only I'd known how close I was to reality. He'd been playing it just after they'd killed that nox.

'That piece you played on the organ… was it yours?'

'No. But I'm flattered you think I could write something like that.' He smiled. 'It's Bach. In his thirties, he spent a month with a local princeling at the summer palace. When he left, his wife Maria Barbara was in perfect health, but when Bach arrived home, literally when he arrived on his doorstep, he learned that while he was gone, she had died and already been buried. It's believed that he wrote that fantasia in response. One of my favourite pieces.'

'Yes, it explains a lot. When I was listening to it, it seemed I felt his grief. I felt *your* grief. What helped you to get over it?'

'Statistics.'

I blinked.

'In the past two months, none of us have been infected. I was born to live for the sake of justice among the guardians, to protect them. That's why I have these wings, my longevity and my intuition. Some will die – it's inevitable. But as long as I'm true to myself and my mission, my conscience is clear.

'You're a vandor, Lilly. You can heal human souls, and this gift brings responsibility with it. You must help people – it's the only thing that matters. Not your friends, not Ophelia… not even me.'

He took the Luminiferos pendant from his pocket, studying its glow in the moonlight. 'With your arrival in Faivendei, my purpose has changed. I lived to protect guardians. Now I live to protect you. And I will do everything to make your mission succeed. But the question is… are you ready for it?'

I swallowed. 'Do it. I'm ready.'

Slowly, he placed the pendant around my neck. Once it touched my skin, I felt an energy stream pass through my veins, radiating out and disturbing the peace of the sleeping lake.

'So…' He drew me closer to him. 'The contract has been signed.'

CHAPTER 15
PEACE

Darius's snoring woke me just as the rays of morning sun hit my eyes. I glanced to the side: Will was already gone. Sitting up on the edge of the stage, I stretched my back. My entire body was numb after spending the night on the wooden floor. Memories of yesterday flashed through my mind: noxes, Octavian, the necklace, Will...

When we'd walked back from the shore of the lake, he'd been holding my hand. He hadn't let it go even when we lay down together on the dilapidated wooden floor of the stage. He'd pulled me close, kissed me gently on the back of my neck and wished me good night. My pulse couldn't return to normal. In fact, I'd resisted sleep, not wanting to miss a single minute while Will was so close to me. But the reverent silence and the stars wheeling in the coal-dark sky had dragged my conscious-ness into the world of dreams.

Revelling in the memories, I touched my neck and flinched at the wave of goosebumps running from my head to my toes. It seemed millions of my nerve endings were so disturbed by the touch of his lips that, even now, they were still gripped in tension. I shook my head, snorting at my hopelessness and willing myself back to reality.

Vesta was casting incantations again, trying to contact Azmeral Crow; Aisha was lying on the bench, watching passing clouds; and Darius was snoring as loud as a giant goblin.

I stretched again and walked towards the woods, noticing Will in the distance. He was standing next to a birch tree, and in the quiet of the forest, I heard him whispering in that language that was as soft as the cream of tiramisu, with many L and R sounds fondling the air. I crept up quietly, trying not to disturb him, but halted at a lordly eye cast over me – Ray was perching on the branch of an oak on my right.

Will placed his hand on the tree trunk and bowed, then turned to me. 'Sneaking around?'

'I didn't mean to intrude. Were you speaking Albor?'

'Yes. I sent a message to my mother.'

'Will, how did she let you go?'

'She didn't. But I made my choice. When my father died, I decided to never leave Faivendei, to support her. It was seventy-seven years ago – I was eleven. But now the situation has changed. I felt it and she felt it too, no matter how firmly she tried to deny it.'

'I imagine it wasn't easy for her to accept.'

'She didn't take it well.'

'Of course. If you don't mind me asking... I overheard your father died during the battle at Vandorfort.'

'He was murdered by noxes. Before he died, he gave me this.' He showed me the portal key on his wrist. 'His parents left Faivendei not long after, dedicating themselves to searching for old, forgotten enchanted worlds. They hoped they could find a place safe for guardians, where noxes cannot pass through. With them gone, my mother had no other choice but to become the supreme leader of Faivendei. It wasn't easy for her: to cope with the death of a beloved husband, raise a son alone and govern the whole forest. But she's always been responsible and had a very strong sense of justice. She devoted her entire life to the service of the guardians. That's why she's so protective of me and others. My mother may seem harsh, but she's a fair and principled ruler.'

'I never doubted that. And... I'm sorry about your father.'

He inclined his head to the side, a mask of gentle indifference lingering on his face. 'It was a very long time ago. I barely remember his face now. But... thank you.' His eyes drifted to the side. 'So how is your progress with Albor? Have you started to learn it yet?'

'Not really. I've been focused on the history of the Spirit World.'

'I'm surprised. With your devotion to trees, I thought Albor would be the first thing you'd try.'

'I thought so too, but Aisha and I decided it was more important for me to understand the history and the rules of the world I was going to live in.'

'Sensible.' He glanced at the birch. 'Anyway. Do you want to say anything to the tree?'

I grinned. 'You have to ask?'

He let out a chuckle. 'Come here.'

I walked over to him, and he stepped behind me.

'Place your right palm on the tree and whisper...' he said enthusiastically but suddenly paused.

And stayed paused. Time passed, but he remained silent.

'What should I whisper?'

I heard him gulp. '*El...*'

The murmur of his dense velvet voice poured into my ear. His arm wrapped around my waist, slowly drawing me closer to his body. I froze, but the temperature of my pulsating blood rose at the pace of a comet firing its way into the Earth's atmosphere. Trying to steady my fast and shallow panting, I repeated the word.

'*Riomi*,' he purred, drawing me ever – *ever* – closer to him, his warm breath caressing my shoulder.

I gulped, repeating it.

Pressing me against his muscled body, he kissed my neck just below my ear, whispering, '*Laro.*'

My heartbeat echoed through my core, raising my hair on end. As I spoke the last word, a gentle wind set the nearby trees in motion, rustling the sparse leaves of a late-autumn birch and, for a moment, clearing my mind.

I beamed. 'What did I say?'

He released me in the blink of an eye. 'It was a standard greeting.'

I turned to him. 'But what do those words mean exactly?'

His aquamarine eyes became cold and motionless. It seemed my simple question had dropped an infinite, glacial wall between us.

'It means…' He stalled. His pinkie twitched slightly.

I went still. *El. Riomi. Laro.* Three words. I knew.

'It means *I love you.*'

I reeled, but his gaze still kept the same indifference, unfreezing my mind at once. I swallowed to relieve the dryness of my mouth. 'And what did the birch say?'

'She said she loves you too. Wouldn't it be something if people, instead of saying *Hi* or *Hello*, would say *I love you*? I think the Human World would only benefit from that.' He grinned. 'Come on. Mother sent us a lutin with breakfast. We need to eat.'

He didn't look at me while we walked over to the stage, and it was driving me crazy. What did he want from me? What was on his mind? And those three words... it was just a standard greeting, I knew that. Yet I replayed them over and over again, as if trying to imprint their luscious sound forever on my memory.

We reached the stage, where silver trays full of freshly baked pastries, tea and coffee already waited for us. There was also a plate of oatmeal cookies, and the familiar sweet scent woke Hairito.

'Oh, that smells wonderful! I'm so hungry I could eat a horse.' Darius rose from the bench, yawning, and walked over to the trays of food. He took a golden croissant and wolfed the whole thing down in one bite.

'Leave something for the girls,' Will warned.

'Well, they better hurry up. You snooze, you lose.' He munched on a second croissant. Two bites this time.

'Aisha, go eat something,' Will called.

'I'm not hungry.'

'I didn't ask you if you were hungry. Go eat. We all need strength.'

Aisha got up from the bench, trudging towards us.

'We should call Vesta...' I said. 'How long has she been trying to contact Azmeral?'

'For a while,' Will answered.

'It seems your Vesta isn't up to much,' Darius mumbled between bites of his third croissant. 'Maybe we should go back to Faivendei and ask for someone stronger.'

'You know, sometimes it's best to keep your opinions to yourself,' I said and reached for the coffee pot. I filled a cup and handed it to Will.

'Thank you, Lilly.'

His lips broke into a playful crooked smile – my favourite – releasing all my tension. He was back. As if the invisible chains that had shackled his senses after I'd asked that question were unleashed, and whatever there was between us was back to normal.

Vesta came over to the stage. 'I don't know why, but I can't contact him.'

'Maybe he's already reunited with the Universe?' Will tried.

'No, I can sense him. But I get the feeling he either doesn't want to or can't answer me.'

'So now what?' Darius asked.

Suddenly I heard a dulcet male whisper, reaching me from... the pendant. I almost jumped.

'What is it?' Will asked.

'I just... I thought I heard a voice. Well... I did hear a voice.'

Vesta leaned towards me. 'What did it say?'

'Border World.'

'Hmm... Yes, that might help,' Darius mused, 'but to get in there we have to die.'

Aisha looked up from the ground. 'Today is the second of November.'

'Holy Universe!' Vesta smiled. 'You're right.'

'And what's that got to do with anything?' I asked.

'Today is the day of all souls. The gate to the Border World is open, and theoretically we can pass through.'

My eyebrows rose against my will. You could actually visit the Border World before your death?

'Where is the nearest gate?' Will asked.

'In Mont-Saint-Michel.'

When we finished our breakfast, we returned to the lake and Will called Nairin. Despite all his entreaties, the capricious

siren returned us near Octavian's castle – three hundred kilometres from Mont-Saint-Michel. When he'd asked her if she
could take us straight to the Border World, the siren had
thought he was joking, but once she realised he was serious,
she'd wailed, '*Absolutely not.*'

We walked to the nearest town and were lucky enough to
catch a bus just about to leave. Darius wished us good luck, saying he would reach the fortress in a quarter of an hour. For us
it took a little longer than that...

The bus was half empty and we moved to the back, where
we could talk without awkward eavesdroppers. I looked out the
window at the passing landscapes under leaden rain clouds,
thinking that today the air here no longer seemed so polluted.
Maybe my lungs had adapted to the local environment. Maybe
people had also adapted to life under the yoke of Noxohit – a
life in chaos, chronic fatigue and constant fear. Maybe if he had
openly declared himself and his plan to suppress the will and
destroy humanity, people wouldn't have cooperated in creating
such deplorable and seemingly hopeless circumstances. Maybe
they would have rebelled and started fighting the tragic fate he
had in store for them.

All these wide fields and sparse forests that flashed by the
window – they were all destined to die, to be consumed by an
unquenchable human thirst. An unnatural, imposed thirst that
people used as a drug to cure the pain and emptiness that Noxohit so skilfully sowed in their minds. If only it were possible to
heal all their souls at once, to open their eyes and help them see
the truth – see the light... if only it were possible to pull them
out of the vicious circle of ignorance Noxohit was putting them
in...

I sighed.

'Lilly?' Will grinned at me. 'Where is your mind flying to?'

'I'm just thinking about Noxohit and this dying world.'

'Don't think about how it's dying. Think about how you're going to save it.'

I smiled, glancing back out the window. What had I done to deserve such generosity from the Universe? I was in danger of death or worse – becoming a nox. But I wasn't alone. My friends were with me and... Will. I didn't know what was on his mind, but he wasn't indifferent to me. Why? What on Earth did he see in me? How was it that fate had so lavishly rewarded me? Maybe it was to make up for the past years of loneliness. I took his hand, feeling my heart smiling with gratitude.

When we arrived at Mont-Saint-Michel, it was already getting dark, and the main entrance was closed. I'd never been here before, and this medieval city perched on an islet under the shade of the ancient abbey that crowned the rocky mount could already sweep me off my feet. But that wasn't why I was in awe. The narrow roads of the fortress crowded amongst clustered buildings shone, emitting a silver light into the sky like glowing brooks streaming into the sea.

When we drew closer, I saw these shining streams were nothing but the souls of the dead meandering along the streets among the tourists. Of course, they were nothing like the frenzied and vicious subits of Vandorfort. But I still stayed close to Will, veering cautiously from side to side to avoid them.

'Amazing, isn't it?' Vesta was shining like the lights on a Christmas tree.

'That's one way to put it,' I replied.

'They're harmless, Lilly,' Will said. 'When you crossed the border between two worlds, you opened your so-called third eye; so now you can see them.'

'Great.'

Will and Vesta chuckled.

'Why are they leaving the fortress anyway?'

'They're going to meet their loved ones,' Vesta explained. 'After death, human souls go to the Border World. They stay there for a while, then disappear. But before that, the soul can return to the Human World.'

'Where do they disappear to?'

'We think they eventually reunite with the Universe.'

'Darius!' Will suddenly shouted. 'What the hell?'

I glanced around. Darius was standing near the wall in a yellow sweatshirt with *J'aime Mont-Saint-Michel* on it, holding a massive camera. He looked like a seasoned professional, adjusting the lens and taking pictures of the setting sun painting the horizon with its fiery light.

'Oh, guys! I thought you were hanging out back there and forgot the plan. What took you so long?'

'Where did you get the camera?' Will snapped.

'I borrowed it from a tourist.' He glanced at the elderly couple a few metres from us.

'Are you out of your mind? Give it back. Now!'

'Of course I was going to give it back. I just got bored, waiting for you.' He shrugged, took a selfie with his tongue sticking out and flew away.

The elderly woman was scolding her husband, and he was hanging his head like a grey-haired dog with his tail between his legs. Darius disappeared in a blur, and the man's camera case gave a jerk. By the time the old man opened the bag, Darius was standing next to us again. The man's face lit up with a joyful smile. The woman glanced at the camera and gave him a playful slap on the back of his head. She continued to the exit, and the old man followed her, gripping the camera tightly in his hands.

I shook my head at Darius's smug smirk and glanced at the others. 'So what's the plan?'

'We follow those souls that return to the abbey and, if we're lucky enough, they'll lead us directly to the portal,' Vesta said.

'Let's say we get *in* there,' Will said. 'Do you know how to get out?'

'That's why it's good this is November the second – the portal is open all day and night, so we shouldn't have any problem.'

'Good. Hairito, hide us please,' Will said when there were no passers-by.

She hid us, and we slipped through the exit into the fortress. It was much quieter inside, and I only saw the occasional living person... The wet cobblestoned streets of Mont-Saint-Michel, reflecting the yellow light of ancient lanterns, were filled with souls, which the last few tourists were oblivious to. We followed them through the narrow streets, climbing higher and higher towards the abbey that towered over the islet. When we got there, I saw the souls passing through the main entrance and disappearing inside the empty shrine.

'This is a portal?' Will asked.

'You're right,' Vesta said. 'Looks too simple.'

'One way to find out.' Darius stepped over the threshold. He was still in the Human World.

Vesta stopped in the middle of the church and closed her eyes, casting incantations. I tilted my head back, gaping at the immense walls that seemed to be trying to reach the heavens, as if this place was built by titans and not by mere men. The nave was lined on either side by a row of large, circular arches, behind which ascended a line of stained-glass windows with warm light streaming through. Similar windows with ornately carved, peaked apexes surrounded the altar ledge and all those countless casements filled the cold stone shrine with the faint pastel light of the setting sun. I couldn't hold back my smile, thinking that somewhere here was a portal to the Border World – the world for the souls of the dead to rest. This was the perfect place for it.

Vesta came out of her trance. 'The portal is open but not to the living. I can't find it.'

Darius shrugged. 'I told you you'd chosen the wrong shaman.'

'Shut up, will you?'

'What now?' Aisha lifted her eyes to Vesta's.

'I don't know…'

'Does the portal create fluctuations in the magnetic field?' Will asked.

'Certainly. But how does that help us— Of course! Ray can see it, can't he?'

Will nodded.

Ray took off from his shoulder and flew away. We headed out into the small garden that nestled in the middle of the cloister gallery. Three expansive arches gave a view of the boundless sea under the plumed scarlet sky. We reached them and stared into the distance. We didn't speak because no words were necessary. I glanced at the others from the corner of my eye – they seemed so calm, yet I couldn't shake the feeling they were watching the setting sun as if in a final farewell.

'He's got it,' Will said and strode back inside.

We were almost running, trying to keep up with him as he hurried along the cloister then turned away from the church.

'Where are you going?' Vesta called after him.

'The portal isn't in there.'

'Where then?'

He turned to one of the narrowest streets I had ever passed through and stopped in front of a secluded archway leading underground. My hair stood on end. There was something dark... something lethal within its shadowy depths. A sudden flapping of wings and a bird's cawing broke the oppressive silence making me shudder. Ray. Will took from his pocket a small glass tube filled with brown seeds and shook them. Slowly they illuminated, emitting a mesmerising yellow glow.

Darius stared like a toddler. 'Beautiful devils, those fern-flower seeds.'

'Let's go,' Will called.

When the narrow, damp stone passage led us to an immense hall with massive ancient columns holding the high ceiling, I halted, surprised by the scale of the room... I hadn't expected to find something like this underground. But the rest of our path was less spectacular – less cathedral and more dungeon. Soon we stopped at the top of a flight of stairs leading down to a hefty wooden door.

Vesta backed away. 'Don't tell me it's there.'

'Yes, I feel it too.' Will clenched his jaw. 'But that's where the portal is.'

'It's no better than Vandorfort down there. This place is crawling with subits.'

'Things are finally livening up.' Darius smiled at Aisha, but she didn't even look at him.

'How many?' Will asked, staring into nothingness – making decisions, devising a plan.

'Enough to kill us all.'

'But what are subits doing here?' I asked, trying not to tremble.

'Even this sacred place has seen human cruelty,' Vesta said. 'Many have suffered within those walls; some have died in terrible agony. During the French revolution, the cells in this basement were used to imprison people. No light, no water, no food… I've heard some cells were so tiny it was literally impossible to turn around. It's painful to even think what those prisoners went through.'

I shivered at the picture in my head… and at the thought of meeting subits again.

'There must be some other way in. Could there be another passage leading to the portal?' Aisha asked.

'I don't know,' Will replied. 'Ray only sees this one. Vesta, how dangerous are those subits?'

'It's hard to say. Of course, over the years, the monks' prayers have eased their thirst for revenge, but I wouldn't risk it. I bet they're guarding the portal.'

'Oh come on! It'll be fine.' Darius hurried down the stairs, waving his long, thin arms as if they were detached from his body.

'Don't you dare!' Will called out.

'Look, the choice is simple. Either you go down there or you return to Faivendei empty-handed and wait to die.'

I shook my head. 'I should go alone.'

Vesta rolled her eyes at me.

'Do you think you can protect us from them?' Will asked her.

'From one or two, yes, maybe even three. But there are a lot of them.'

'The portal isn't that far away…'

Vesta thought for a moment and nodded.

As soon as I took a step towards the door that separated us from the subits, my knees shook and my chest burned, as I remembered how the infernal tiny snakes had stippled both my body and my soul in Vandorfort. But I glanced at the others and shoved my fear down as deep as I could.

We went down to the door, and Will tried to open it, but it wouldn't budge.

'Well, that's not a problem when you can create matter from light,' Darius said smugly.

He took a metal cigarette lighter out of his pocket, flicked his thumb on the wheel and it instantly shot out sparks. The wick lit. Darius moved his fingers around it, and the faster he did so, the faster the light spilled out, turning into a wide silver funnel of glowing energy. The flame went out. He slowly reached towards the keyhole, and a gleaming vortex flew inside, the energy transforming into a metal key. Darius turned it, and the ancient lock mechanism unlatched with a loud creak that echoed through the tunnels.

He flung the door open, bowing. 'You're welcome.'

'I'll go first,' Will said. 'Lilly, you're coming with me. Then Aisha and Vesta, and Darius at the rear.'

'Oh, I see! If you need to sacrifice somebody, it'll be me.'

'Didn't you want to have fun?'

'Fine. If the subits attack us, it'll be easier for me to run away.' He smiled, but Will ignored him.

Vesta glanced in both directions. 'It's clear for now. But they're nearby.'

All my instincts blared at me to run away, but I trotted ahead, ignoring my buckled knees.

As we entered a dim passage with crumbled walls, an indistinct, eerie whisper reached us from all sides. Will gripped my hand and strode forward. So much for our hopes of passing through unnoticed.

Get out! a long wail resonated through the walls. *Get out!*

'They're behind us!' Vesta cried.

'We're close.' Will broke into a run.

'Quick!' She readied her whip.

We reached a locked, barred iron door.

'Open it!' Will said to Darius.

But it was too late.

Dozens of subits pounced on us, their eyes glowing blood red in the gloom of the dungeon. Vesta swung her whip at them, and they scattered but after a fraction of a second re-appeared again.

My eyes were darting in all directions, when a legless subit crawled up to me infernally quick and seized my feet, knocking me down and dragging me away along the frigid ground.

'Get off!' I kicked at him, but my foot went right through him.

Will and Hairito rushed to help me, but another subit set upon them, knocking them down as if they were two frail seed-ling pines. Will sprang up, struggling to fight back, but his hands passed through the ethereal subit's body without causing it the slightest bit of harm. A waste of energy. Hairito squirmed out of the other subit's iron grip and jetted over to help me, digging her claws and teeth into its ghostly flesh. The fiend shrieked, throwing Hairito away as if she was as light as a robin. She hit the wall and slid to the floor.

'Hairito!' I cried.

Darius finished the key and opened the door: he and Aisha managed to run through. The subit dragged me further and further away from them, and the world started to spin before my eyes. Vesta lashed her whip at him, and the subit dissipated for a moment, just long enough for me to run for the door. I picked up Hairito on the way and rushed into the room beyond.

Hairito awoke and gave her head a shake. Vesta was trying to help Will, but three more subits were attacking her. She held them back, cracking her whip while Will was being strangled. The raven pecked ferociously at the subit – he bellowed but didn't let go.

I dashed towards him, but Darius shoved me back then lit his lighter and disappeared in a flash. Suddenly, a thin metal wall formed between the subit and Will. The wraith vanished. Darius grabbed Will's arm, helping him into the room, then flew back to Vesta and carried her in at the speed of sound. The enraged subits tried to follow us, howling like banshees, but they couldn't cross the threshold.

I grabbed his face. 'Will, are you okay?'

He got to his feet, helping me to stand as well. 'Yes… all right. You?'

I nodded.

'We're… safe here.' Vesta was catching her breath.

Darius leaned out the doorway. 'That's what I'm talking about! Screw you, ghouls!'

'Thank you for saving me,' I said to Vesta.

'I think we should all thank Darius,' she replied, coughing. 'Without him… none of us would have survived.'

'Well, finally I get the recognition I deserve. I repeat: you are always welcome.'

The subits disappeared into the gloom of the stone cellar, and silence finally returned. My shoulders sagged, but I was still shaking all over. That was far too close.

I glanced around – we were in a compact square room with a huge arched passage leading off, pitch-black inside. Large luminous snowflakes flew out of it. Vesta stretched out her hand, and one snowflake fell onto it. It didn't melt…

'Warm snow.' She smiled at the darkness beyond the arch. 'It's the portal.'

I held Will's hand, and we all passed through it.

Stepping over the threshold, I plunged into absolute darkness, and for a split second it seemed my body had dispersed into trillions of pieces... as if I were dissolving into the Universe. But it didn't scare me – it was like returning home.

The light gradually grew in front of me, and the first thing I noticed was the honeyed air. Its sweetness was watering my mouth. Then an islet appeared in the middle of an ocean, covered by shining snow with crystal snowdrops breaking through its surface. It was soothingly warm and infinitely lulling.

The islet resembled Mont-Saint-Michel but had a single modest church on the very top of a mountain. There was no sun, but it was bright – luminous white snowflakes, like tiny stars, were falling from the sky, and one after another, souls rose from the ground and flew towards the church. Others floated from the church into the ocean, dissolving in the water and making the coast glow with myriad lights. Adorned in shiny white robes, the souls were magnificent. Just by looking at them I felt my mind filling with peace.

Suddenly, Will came up out of the snow. Then the others. They were as luminous and translucent as the souls. I looked down at my arms.

'Are we dead?' I asked.

'Not yet, but we better not stay here too long.' Vesta glanced at the church, where several giants were standing armed with spears. 'See them? Those are the guardians of peace, and if we break the harmony of this place, we'll be in trouble. Don't touch anything here. She looked around and spotted a small hillock. 'Let's hide before they spot us.'

We went behind it, and Vesta fell back into her trance, whispering incantations and trying to summon Azmeral Crow.

'Do you feel it?' Aisha was peering at the sky.

'The snow?' Will asked.

She nodded.

'I feel it too.' Luminous snowflakes permeated my insubstantial body, bringing even more peace and warmth into my soul.

'This place has always scared me,' Aisha mused. 'When you live in the material world, no matter how many wonders surround you, you always question whether there's anything after death. It's nice to know that my parents really are at peace.'

Her calm and measured tone warmed my heart. It seemed for a moment she'd woken from her grief, becoming again that sunny and joyful Aisha I knew.

'Interesting.' Darius was sitting on the ground, playing with the snow.

I walked over. 'What are you doing?'

'There's a question that's always tormented me. Can I create a human out of light? I've tried to recreate my brother so many times... I managed to build his body, but before long it disappeared.' A sad smile tugged slightly at the corners of his wide lips. 'It's kind of masochistic, creating his lifeless body and watching him disappear over and over again.'

'You had a brother?'

'I think it's because I'm just a mortal,' he went on, as if he hadn't heard my question. 'I can transform, but I can't create. However if I try to transform this light – the light of human souls... can I make a person out of it?'

He was gazing at the shining snow in his hands when suddenly a navy glow glittered next to us. Darius put the snow back on the ground, dusted off his hands and got to his feet. The radiance came from the ghost of an aged, withered man.

Vesta snapped out of her trance at once. 'Mr Crow.'

He stared at the pendant, as if it were cursed. 'I know what you want, but I can't help you.'

'Mr Crow, we've come a long way to talk to you,' I said.

'Commendable bravery. Though pointless.'

'You're one of the few who obtained the first emanation of light,' Vesta pushed on. 'Please tell us how you did it.'

'I got what?'

'The emanation—'

'My dear, if I had actually acquired it, I'd still be alive. It's one thing to find it, but quite another to secure it. My advice to you is to go back where you came from and forget about Luminiferos.' He turned his back on us.

It was Aisha who called out to him. 'The noxes kidnapped my seven-year-old sister. They killed all my relatives.'

'They also seized my parents and brother,' I added. 'There isn't a single guardian who hasn't suffered because of Noxohit. We *must* find Luminiferos to exile him from Earth.'

'I see you've found some noble motives to hide your true, more prosaic ones,' he said. 'But since that thing is already around your neck, I suppose there's no going back.' His eyes slid to the pendant. 'The first emanation wants to identify your genuine self. It wants to discover if you're worthy of the weapon of light. Do you know who you truly are?'

I had nothing to answer.

'I didn't. I would have preferred not to know that. But you don't have a choice anymore. Luminiferos will force you to find an answer. And while you're trying to find it, Noxohit will be continuously messing with your mind. My search ended up here… after little more than a month.' He indicated the church. 'Your journey may end just as quickly, or even before it begins.'

I looked at him breathlessly, when the voice from the pendant floated to my ears. *Save the ones you love…*

He glided towards me. 'Yes, I hear it too. *Save the ones you love.* Easier said than done.'

'But what does it mean?'

'You'll understand when the time comes.' He turned away again.

'Do you know where I can find the first emanation?'

He stopped and, without turning back, said, 'You'll find it in Broseliand, and the pendant is your key to that forest.'

He soared, disappearing into the sky.

'That makes no sense,' Vesta mused. 'Broseliand doesn't exist.'

'Actually, it does.' Will frowned, staring at the ground. 'And I know who can help us get in there.'

'Who?' I asked.

'My grandfather, Dorian Raven.'

'I thought Broseliand was a myth,' Vesta said.

Suddenly they all froze, focusing their gazes at something behind my back. I swirled around and flinched at the sight of Octavian's soul.

CHAPTER 16

INFATUATION

BUT WAS IT really him? It seemed an angel was standing in front of me, shining with absolute peace. Yes, he looked exactly like Octavian, but it was still hard to believe my eyes.

'Lilly White...' He shook his head. 'To be honest, I didn't think you'd die quite that soon.'

'Erm... I'm not dead. We came here to talk to Azmeral Crow.'

'He's still here? Can't wait to meet my old friend.' He smiled. 'I'm glad you're alive. So it wasn't all in vain?'

'I'm sorry, Octavian,' Vesta said, 'but we have to go back.'

'Of course. Lilly, please don't even think to blame yourself for my death. I was tired. I've been waiting for it for a long time, and thanks to you, my journey to the Border World was quick and painless.'

'I... I really wanted to save you.'

'You don't understand. You did.' He put his hand on my shoulder. 'Good luck, Lilly. If I can, I'll help you from this side.'

When he touched me, somehow an image of his five hundred years flashed through my mind. What an incomparable worldview he had – he, who'd watched how people driven by an inexhaustible desire to understand the origins of their nature and the essence of being had replaced one philosophy with another, how the dawn of science and art had gradually overshadowed brute force and fanaticism. How in moments of despair people had forgotten about the priceless knowledge and lessons of history – how they'd allowed themselves to be led by their atavistic past, which woke up from the depths of their sleeping genes, like an enraged monkey, compelling them to conquer and dominate as the only way to survive. So many victories and defeats, so much pain and glee... Five hundred years. Silent tears rolled down my cheeks, but it wasn't remorse – it was joy, for I saw and felt that he was genuinely happy to finally finish his journey.

'Thank you, Octavian. May you rest in peace...'

'I will. I am.'

Serenity blessed his smile as he vanished. Will took my hand. I wiped my cheeks and we headed to the shore of the ocean, where the souls of the dead were dissolving, returning to the Human World. Octavian's journey had come to an end, but ours had just begun.

We sank under the water, following the souls, but nothing happened.

'Vesta, why are we still here?' Will demanded.

'It should have worked...' She glanced back at the entrance of the church. 'The guardians have gone. Something's wrong.'

Will rolled up his sleeve, revealing his portal key. 'We can't enter the Border World with the sirens, but maybe they can help get us out of here.'

He whispered, '*Interterra,*' immersing his hand in the effervescing water. I thought Nairin would come, but instead of the white boat with the seahorse bow drowned in little treasures of the sea, my eyes met a crystal wonder with the finest patterns engraved on its surface. Water flowed down them, shimmering like a rainbow in the radiance of falling snow. Vesta glanced at Will for an explanation – apparently, I wasn't the only one who was seeing this boat for the first time.

A blonde siren slowly surfaced, studying us one after another. She resembled an exquisite porcelain doll, dressed in a white corset with airy sleeves; a high tiara made of spiked shells, pearls and jewels crowned her small head. Her feline eyes reminded me of Nairin, but her direct gaze and regal posture revealed not just haughtiness but a certain grandeur.

'We are pleased to greet you.' Will bowed to her, and we copied him.

'You're not dead. What are you doing here?'

I blinked. Did all the sirens have such ravishing beauty and such a blunt demeanour?

'We needed to talk to someone who was already dead,' Will murmured.

'Why?'

'We're looking for Luminiferos,' I said.

The siren turned her predatory gaze on me. 'Noxohit is your problem, not mine. Why should I help you?'

'You don't have to—'

'I know I don't. I am Anaxel Dor – the Princess of Sericaterra. I don't owe anyone anything.'

'Dear Princess Anaxel,' Will purred, 'we rely on your aid. And to thank you, let us present you with—'

'I'm not interested in musical mirrors.'

'Maybe you'll change your mind when you see it. I leave a part of my soul in every one I create.'

His lips broke into a crooked, tender smile and… I couldn't believe it… his cheeks tinged with pink. The voice of logic telling me he was having her on to get us back suddenly fell quiet. It seemed my heart was spreading venomous roots that entangled every organ of my body, squeezing the life out of them.

The corners of her lips curled up slightly and she lowered her chin, melting under the spell of his charm.

'Well, show me then,' she challenged him with a playful smile.

Will pulled a mirror out of his pocket, and the Princess of Sericaterra concentrated her laser focus on the little thing, which was decorated with a white lily. He glanced at the mirror and hurried to put it away, taking out another one, this time inlaid with blooming purple fuchsia and a delicate humming-bird.

'No,' the siren countered. 'I want that mirror. The one with the white lily.'

'Believe me, there is nothing remarkable in that. But this one is decorated with diamonds, and the melody being played—'

'Either you give me that mirror or you stay here forever.'

Will's mask of servility and obedience suddenly dissolved into a rage that hardened the even features of his face. 'No.' It was a growl.

'Well, good luck then.'

The ship started to sink. The soft pink hue of his cheeks turned to marble as he cast a leaden glare upon the siren. What kind of secret could be hidden in the mirror to make him act like this?

He took it out of his pocket and gave it to the siren. 'Now take us to the Human World.'

'First, I want to see what you were trying to—'

'Run!' Darius's sudden cry broke the serene silence.

The giants flew over from the other side of the island, spears at the ready.

'Quick, quick, quick!' Darius appeared out of nowhere, already in the ship.

'Get in. Now!' The siren closed the mirror, and we jumped in in a blink of an eye.

I curled up in a ball when the giants were just an arm's length from us, but the boat sank down and disappeared under the water.

The excruciating feeling of free fall was followed by pitch-darkness, and once my eyes adjusted, I saw the fortress of Mont-Saint-Michel. A levitating white ladder stretched from the boat to the shore.

We were halfway along it when something grabbed Will's hand. He almost fell into the water but regained his balance in time. Princess Anaxel put the mirror into his hand, giving me an impish smile before fleeing into the dark depths of the ocean. Once we were ashore, the ship disappeared.

I glanced at the mirror. What was in it? Why had the siren given it back? Why had she looked at me so strangely?

Darkness filled Vesta's eyes as she glowered at Darius. 'What happened there?'

He just shrugged. 'Nothing.'

'Uh-huh. What did you do?'

'Nothing! Scout's honour.' He barely held back his grin.

Vesta's hand started to glow; her whip was ready to burst out. 'Darius... don't make me do this.'

'Oh please! You aren't fast enough to catch me.'

Vesta's whip was out. 'You've got to stand still sometime.'

'All right, all right.' He reached into his pocket and pulled out a crystal sprig of snowdrops from the Border World. It still radiated a bewitching silver glow.

'You stupid bastard! Do you realise that if it weren't for that siren, we would never have been released from that world? You could have got us all killed!'

'Actually, I'm the only reason you're all alive, as you said yourself. You should be grateful.'

Vesta clenched her hands, and her light-grey eyes lit with crimson rage. We all froze, but she took a deep breath, and on the exhale her whip disappeared.

'I warn you, Darius,' she uttered with that chilling calm. 'You do something like this again and I'll incinerate you. Your gift might be useful, but I'm not sure it's worth the risk.'

He stopped grinning, tucked the sprig of snowdrops in his pocket and turned away.

Vesta's attention cut to Will. 'Where does your grandfather live? Just please tell me he's still alive.'

'He was last time I checked. He lives near Paimpont – just about a hundred kilometres from here. But... don't expect a warm reception.'

We took a bus, and Will, Darius, Vesta, Hairito and even Ray fell asleep as soon as they sat in their seats. Aisha stayed awake. As did I.

She peered through the window. 'Being there was like taking a warm bath. Here, all my real feelings came back. Although... I wonder whether "real feelings" is the right term. Are they?' She looked at me. 'What if the peace and harmony of the Border World are real, and the fear and suffering of this world are just... illusions? How easy life would be without grief or loss. You know, for a moment I went soft and thought I'd be happy to stay there – in the Border World. Release all the pain and... just be.'

'Aisha, I can try to heal your soul—'

'No. I deserve to feel what I feel.'

'You don't.' If anyone did, it was me.

'I'm tired.' She closed her eyes, pretending to sleep.

Where was the active and wilful Aisha I'd first met? She had vanished in the course of just a few days. How long would it be until someone else suffered the same fate? Darius had joined us voluntarily, but he was pursuing personal interests. Vesta and Will, on the other hand, were in this situation only because of me. They both had tried to convince me otherwise, but if it wasn't for me, they would have never gone in search of Luminiferos. No, it had all happened because I'd come to Faivendei. Omnia had cried upon seeing my future. How could I be so arrogant as to think I knew best what to do? And now they could lose everything because of my wrong choice. Not just their lives but their souls. Such an unjustified risk and for what?

I grinned sadly. Well, the last hope of humanity…

How could I withstand the greatest evil in the Universe if I couldn't even protect myself from a single legless subit in the dungeon of Mont-Saint-Michel? I wouldn't live a day without my friends. The way they'd looked at the horizon in the cloister of the abbey… they had already accepted the worst outcome of this mission, and yet nobody had panicked. I wished I were as strong and brave as they were. *Save the ones you love…* The voice from the pendant was ringing in my head. I just… How? How could I do it?

Lost in my thoughts, I didn't notice that we'd arrived in Paimpont until the bus stopped. We got off, and Will fixed me with one of his searching gazes, which seemed to penetrate into my soul, piercing through to all my worries. He shook his head and pushed past me, heading towards the wood.

We followed him through dense, overgrown wilds, with no signs of human life. Soon we found a small wooden cottage with sagging walls and a ramshackle roof. Dim light streamed out through the tiny casement windows. We reached the rotten door and Will knocked.

'Who the hell's that?' A raspy growl.

The door opened, and a grey-haired, withered old man in ragged clothes with a long beard and discoloured blue eyes glowered at Will.

'What do you need? And why did you bring all this lot here? How many times do I have to tell you? I will not return to Faivendei!'

'Hello to you too, Grandfather,' Will murmured calmly.

'If I said no, it means no!'

'That's not what I came for.' He used again that tone that made his dense velvet voice sound utterly hypnotising.

Dorian narrowed his bleak eyes. 'What then?'

'Can we come in? It's late and we have nowhere to stay.'

The old man looked around Will to shoot a murderous glare at me and the others. 'I don't have room for all of you.'

'We'll sleep on the floor. Please let us stay the night.'

He snorted like a disgruntled bulldog but let us in. Hairito ran through the house, sniffing around. The old man scowled at her but remained silent.

Despite the fire in the grate, it was cold inside, and the scent of burning wood mixed with dry herbs and dust. Bookshelves and glass jars, covered in cobwebs, lined the walls, and the only source of light apart from the fireplace were three candles, resting in the holder buried in congealed wax.

Ray flew over to another raven with faded plumage who sat on one of the shelves. That raven's eyes were as pale as Dorian's, and his temper was just as cold – Ray jumped around him, while he only pecked and cawed bitterly.

'I don't know how you all propose to fit in here,' Dorian snapped.

'It doesn't matter.' Will sat down in a chair without breaking eye contact with his grandfather. 'We came here for your help.'

Darius went to the fireplace to warm his hands.

'What do you need?' Dorian barked.

'To get into Broseliand.' Still the same calm and composed tone.

The old man let out a nervous laugh, but when he saw his grandson's serious face, he shook his head. 'Are you out of your mind? What are you asking for?'

Will didn't even flinch. 'I'm asking for your help.'

'You must be kidding me!'

'Grandfather—'

'It's impossible!'

'No, it's not.'

'If it weren't, I would be there already! I'd have been there long ago...'

The door of the house was tightly locked, the windows closed, but sudden frosty wind caressed my skin, and the hair on my arms stood up. It wasn't a stream of air but a chill blowing from a frozen, lonely soul. I forgot about everything in the world, and only this cold remained. It seemed the body of this man who had lived for over two hundred years was an icy prison for his soul, which, like a naked, defenceless toddler, was trembling with chills in a place as dark as coal. It was unnatural. So wrong...

I walked over to Dorian and, without a second thought, put my hand on his solar plexus. Our eyes met for just a moment, but it was enough for us to understand each other. He felt who I was and mutely asked for help, and I knew if I helped him, I would save not only his soul but maybe also mine.

I closed my eyes and shuddered at the ghostly cold that filled the shack, and yet I threw aside my inner shield and let the frost creep under my skin. I trembled all over, mentally clinging to the light – to that warm, pulsating energy that permeated the world. I still couldn't see it, but I remembered that it was all there was.

Suddenly, I felt a faint glow floating before my eyes, and I gasped with anticipation of that pure, infinite, omnipresent energy that slowly filled the space around us.

When I'd first used my gift, I'd hardly been aware of what was going on. The second time I'd listened to Octavian, trying to learn how to use it deliberately. But now I was revelling in what was happening, savouring every moment. This life-giving, healing light blurred the boundaries between people and objects, gradually connecting everything – absolutely everything – into a single whole. This great force released my tension without the slightest effort, penetrated into every cell of my body and spread the melody of divine peace through my mind.

Tears were swelling behind my closed eyelids. I was so grateful for this possibility to feel – to see – this crystal-clear, endless stream of sparkling light. How could I describe it in one word? Peace? Love? No... those words were too weak to express the power of the light.

With a force of will, I descended from the seventh cloud and focused on a radiant cluster in the shape of a human body standing in front of me. There was a pollution inside – a bottomless funnel, devouring all light. I focused on this gloom, took a deep breath and drew it out through my palm. It froze my heart at once. I inhaled deeply the healing energy, and slowly the ice started to melt. I took a few more breaths, and it melted in flames, transforming into a luminous force that passed through my hand and into the body of the old man.

I opened my eyes.

'I forgot... I forgot how sweet the taste of hope is,' Dorian whispered through his tears. 'What is your name, my dear?'

I saw his raven straightening up, his eyes brightening. He snuggled up to Ray.

'Lilly.' I smiled at him, feeling myself much lighter, as if I'd just got over a long fever.

'You're a vandor, aren't you, Lilly?'

I nodded. 'We're looking for Luminiferos, and we know the first emanation is in Broseliand. We need to get in there.'

He sighed. 'If only it were that simple. I've been trying to enter that forest for ten years. You can only get to Broseliand if you already have an artefact from that place. What's more, the artefact can only be used once.'

I pointed to the pendant on my neck. 'This is the key to Broseliand.'

'What— Are you sure?'

'Unless the man from the Border World was lying, then yes, I'm sure.'

Will moved closer to him, putting a hand on his shoulder. 'Do you understand what this means?'

Dorian nodded. 'I... I just can't believe it... I hope you're right.' He bustled to the kitchen corner. 'You must be tired from the road. Would you like some tea?'

'Yes please,' I replied, and the old man began sorting through his jars of herbs.

Aisha and Vesta joined Darius in front of the fireplace.

Will glanced at me, grinning. 'Feeling better?'

I nodded.

'You're a vandor, Lilly. You need to follow your purpose, then your soul will be at peace. Instead, you allow your fears and doubts to take control of your will.' He sighed. 'What am I going to do with you?'

'I don't know.'

His foxy eyes studied my lips. 'I think I do.'

Aisha took a black-and-white photo of a woman from the shelf. 'Is this your wife?'

Dorian nodded. 'Abigail... We travelled a lot together, looking for the hidden worlds of the past. The last one was Broseliand. Getting there wasn't easy – as I said before, it requires a special artefact. After studying various materials, we found that the medallion of the Lady of the Lake was one of them. Many years of searching it took for us to find it. We knew that the ten-thousand-year-old Ponthus beech – a beast of over a thousand feet tall – was the portal to Broseliand. But the problem was, this tree is in the Spirit World, in the territory of spirits, not guardians. Those lands are dangerous. Several times we tried to reach the Ponthus beech, but only on the seventh attempt did we succeed. We were in Broseliand and grew absorbed in its tropical gardens. We thought the medallion was our key to leaving the forest, but after half an hour, the portal began to close. Our ravens turned into our wings; we flew back as fast as we could. I thought she was just behind me, but... I made it out, and she didn't. If I'd known, I would have stayed there with her forever. Instead, I returned to this world alone.'

Dorian paused and only the crackle of the fire broke the silence.

'I promised myself I wouldn't stop until I rescued her. Ten years passed, and now here you are. Tomorrow night will be a full moon – only then will we be able to enter Broseliand. But for now, please have some tea.' He handed out the mugs and went to the cupboard, from which he took some damp old blankets.

'It's not much, but it's better than nothing.' He put them on the floor and turned to the others. 'What are your names? And who is this cute little thing?' He patted Hairito, and she purred in reply.

'She's a gargoyle,' I replied, taking a sip of fragrant chamomile tea.

'I thought so, but I've never met a tame gargoyle before.'

'She's unique.'

'And so are you, my dear.' He smiled at me, making me blush.

We finished our tea and put out the candles. Whether it was the effect of the chamomile or the strain of an emotional day, I quickly dived into the world of dreams.

WHEN I WOKE up, it was still dark outside, and the others were still asleep. Unable to keep my eyes closed anymore, I got up and went into the forest. Breathing the cool morning air in big gulps, I looked for a place amongst the almost-bare trees to take a moment, just to immerse myself in nature. I climbed a mighty oak and sat on one of its majestic branches.

'I hope you don't mind,' I whispered to the tree. I didn't think it did.

The soft chirping of sparrows was lulling me back to sleep, when suddenly I heard footsteps approaching. I opened my eyes. It was Darius.

Glancing from side to side and making sure nobody was around, he took the sprig of snowdrops out of his pocket – so gently, so carefully, as if his life depended on it. He stared at the snowdrops as if mesmerised, and suddenly I felt a warm wave emanating from him... Goosebumps rose on my neck. I'd felt this before, when he was looking at the diamond brooch.

'What is it you see there?'

He started but, seeing me, relaxed. 'What do you mean?'

'Something happens to you when you look at the snowdrop. I can feel it.'

He grinned. 'I see light.'

'That didn't really answer my question.'

'When I run at the speed of sound or create matter from light, out of the corner of my eye I see the energy that permeates everything. It's an encompassing feeling. But you know it yourself, don't you?'

I nodded.

'Come here. I'll show you what I see in it.'

I climbed down from the oak.

'Give me your hand.'

'Why?'

'Come on, I won't bite you.' He pressed my hand to his chest. 'Now close your eyes and just feel.'

My eyes stayed wide open.

'Trust me. Really.'

I sighed and closed my eyes. Focusing my attention on my hand, slowly I started to see the world in the form of energy and gasped. The cluster of light in front of me was *not* in human shape – it was broken, contorted. And the place where its heart should have been was empty. There was no darkness; it was just... hollow. Darius looked at the crystal flowers in his hand, and they were so bright, it almost blinded my vandor's vision. I turned my eyes back to him and watched the radiant energy fill the hole in his chest, making him more complete... more alive.

He put the snowdrops aside, and in an instant the cavity emptied out again. I opened my eyes.

'But... I healed your soul.'

'From the darkness of Noxohit, sure. But not from the rest.'

'I can try to heal you again.'

'No.'

'Darius, your soul is so... damaged. What happened to you? I can help. You don't need to live with that.'

My words seemed to ignite his blood, for rage instantly swept the last hints of a smile from his wide lips, which tightened in a white slash.

'Help me? Help yourself first. Do you really think your own soul looks any better than mine? You can fool the others, pretending you want to save the world, but I know your true motives, you lonely, pathetic orphan. You're ready to die for others just to prove to yourself you deserve to be loved. A needy beggar of approval. At least I don't lie to myself. I know who I am. And you're nothing without them, just a zero, a waste of space. So go fix yourself first, Lilly.'

He left me standing there with my mouth hanging open as I tried to digest everything he'd said. Way too much of it felt true.

'Lilly.' I heard a dense velvet voice behind me.

I turned to Will, my pulse throbbing in my temples. 'Did you hear that?'

He nodded.

'What if he's right? What if I agreed to this suicide mission only to prove that I deserve to be... loved? I don't think I'm doing the right thing. Actually, I think all this is a huge mistake. I don't know who I am... I'm so afraid. Will, I'm so confused...'

He smiled, as if all my worries were childish babble. 'I'm glad I found you like this.'

'What?'

'You give too much power to your emotions, deluding yourself into thinking they determine your true self. Emotions and thoughts... they just come and go. Be aware of them, watch them as if from a distance. But don't let them to determine who you are.'

'You don't understand.' I turned to leave.

He grabbed my hand. 'Let me prove my point, and I'll show you that I understand you better than you do.'

'Just let me go. I just... I want to be alone right now.'

'Please, Lilly, do it for me. I can't watch you hurting yourself over and over again.' He pulled me closer to him, wrapping his arms around my waist. 'Please...'

I tilted my head back and looked through the blur of my tears into his aquamarine eyes. 'Okay.'

'I know how hard it can be to understand your real motives. But at the end of the day, what really matters is the choice you make.'

'How can I know if I'm making the right choice?'

'Easy. Stop listening to your fears, start listening to your heart.' He smiled. 'Close your eyes.'

'What?'

'Your senses often distract you from your true vision. Especially eyesight. Close your eyes. Good. Now focus on your heart.'

He tucked a strand of my hair behind my ear and lifted my chin towards him. I felt him leaning towards my face.

'Breathe. Forget about me and the world around you. Focus on your heart.'

I inhaled deeply, trying to calm my mind and focus on my quivering heart. Still, I flinched when his lips touched my cheek. My focus was lost, but I kept my eyes closed. He kissed my other cheek, getting closer and closer to my lips. How could I focus on my heart, when my whole mind was entranced, savouring every touch of his lips on my skin? I forgot about Darius, I forgot about everything at that moment, craving for his lips to meet mine. I'd been waiting for this for so long—

'Heart, Lilly.'

His lips, soft as velvet, pressed gently against mine. I brushed my hands through his satin hair, pulling him closer to me.

'Stop.' He removed my hands from his neck.

I opened my eyes.

'Look how easy that was. In a matter of seconds, I shook your emotional balance. So tell me, who are you now? Before, when Darius voiced all your fears, you were a coward ready to give up your mission. Now, after a few seconds, you transformed into an infatuated girl, longing for a kiss. Which one is the real you?'

'You played me...' I could feel my face whitening. I struggled to get out of his grasp, but he held me tightly. 'Let me go!'

'What am I to you, huh?'

I stopped moving. 'You know exactly how I feel about you.'

'No, actually I don't. Am I just a juvenile infatuation? A pretty guy who's driven your teenage hormones mad?'

I gulped. 'Why are you saying this?'

'I want proof that I wasn't mistaken in you. I want to awaken within you that resolute and headstrong girl I first met. Show me the truth, show me that I can rely on you if my life depends on it. Because we both know it will.'

'Of course you can rely on—'

'Show me.'

'How?'

'Close your eyes. Forget about me. Listen to your heart. Only with a still mind will you be able to overcome evil.'

I was beginning to hate how right he was. I took a deep breath and closed my eyes.

My inner state resembled a rotten, leaking boat, dragged into the middle of a furious ocean by the squally wind of my unbridled feelings. Leaden waves were hitting its sides, deafening me with their roar. They threatened to break the boat into splinters and spread the remains to the four corners of the globe. How to subdue an ocean? It was impossible.

Don't overcome or fight it – just be aware of it.

Will's words echoed in my memory. I looked at the foaming waves, carefully examining their soot-black colour and their movement, when suddenly they simmered down. The deep-blue shade of the sky was getting lighter; a single ray of sun broke through the clouds.

'I believe in you,' I heard Will whispering.

He kissed my neck. A rampant gust of wind returned the clouds and carried the boat even further from the sanctuary of the shore shimmering on the horizon. I took a deep breath. Was he right? Was what I felt for him just raging teenage hormones? I didn't know. In any case, we weren't meant to be together – I wasn't one of the Simtri clan. But did it really matter? Wasn't the mere realisation that he was alive and well enough for me? If I wanted to protect him and the others from Noxohit, I had to still my mind – I had to stop thinking about myself and start thinking about others.

A sudden warm and mighty breeze carried me away from the storm towards an island, illuminated by the sun. It seemed to be a corner of clarity and peace.

Will kissed the corner of my lips, awakening lightning that seemed to cut the ocean in two with its deafening thunderclap.

But as strange as it was, this raving storm was behind me, somewhere far in the distance. I was a bystander, watching what was happening in my mind.

The sky cleared; the waves calmed. He kissed the other corner of my lips, and his touch felt like young willow leaves caressing my skin under a gentle breeze. My heartbeat was steady; the ocean was tranquil. I opened my eyes. His were shining, his lips stretched in a blissful smile.

'What?' I asked.

'I think I've just got my answer.'

CHAPTER 17
CALATHEA

THAT DAY, I almost didn't talk to anyone, investing every free minute in the practice of inner peace, detachment, and awareness of my emotions and thoughts. It reminded me of the state I entered when I healed people's souls. Discovering that it was readily available was like finding an oasis when you were dying of thirst. I just couldn't stop training my mind. Seconds smoothly passed into minutes, minutes into hours, and quite imperceptibly day turned to night. Will finally called me home – we had to leave in a few hours.

I might have overloaded my brain muscle, for as much as I wanted, I couldn't fall asleep. I tossed and turned, I counted sheep, I tried to follow an imaginary clock hand, counting seconds, but all was in vain. My tired mind wouldn't let my body have the sleep it so desperately needed. Eventually I gave up and just peered at the ceiling. I didn't know how long I stared at it, but at some point, the line between dreams and reality blurred. I was slowly falling into slumber when something jolted me awake.

Someone's gaze fell on me with a crushing weight. I glanced at the open window – an ebony thing was creeping inside the house.

It was not human.

I opened my mouth but couldn't make a sound. I tried to jump up but couldn't even move. Was I dreaming?

The thing crawled towards me with sharp, erratic movements on all fours, its arms and legs splayed unnaturally, its long hair dangling in twisted knots. Suddenly it stopped and glared in Vesta's direction.

A second passed, then the thing continued to crawl towards me. It stood up to its full height. I couldn't see its face but knew that once it touched me, I would die – just dissolve into space.

And it wasn't a nightmare. I was wide awake.

I struggled to scream to wake the others, but to no avail.

It bent down, sniffing my face and plunging me into a fetid cloud that smelled of decaying flesh and rotten eggs. I gathered all my strength and managed to let out a dull moan.

Vesta removed her blanket increasingly slowly, getting up and readying her whip.

The thing lifted its leg and placed a foot on my chest, forcing me deeper into the sofa. I gasped for air, feeling my eyes rolling back. It climbed onto my chest, squatted down and stretched its abnormally long neck towards my face.

Air... I couldn't breathe.

Vesta stood behind him.

It reached out its icy, bony hands and grabbed my neck.

Finally, I howled.

Will woke at once, springing at the thing. Vesta cracked her whip, trying to catch it, but it flew out of the window in a flash, disappearing into the darkness of the night.

I jumped off the sofa, gasping.

'For fairy's sake, Will!' Vesta hissed. 'I almost had it!'

The others were awake now.

'What...' I coughed, massaging my neck. 'What was that?'

'That was a marok,' Will said.

'What was it doing in the wild?' Aisha asked, her eyes wide.

'It didn't come here by accident,' Vesta replied. 'Noxohit's henchmen are looking for Lilly. We have to leave. Now. Noxes will be here any moment.'

I threw on my jacket, took my backpack and, waiting at the door, watched as if through a broken kaleidoscope as Dorian put out the fire and the others fussed, readying themselves to leave. I was standing straight and not moving, but it seemed my body was swinging from side to side, like a pendulum in a clock. My consciousness was floating somewhere in the clouds.

'Dorian, do you mind if I take these nuts?' Darius asked, making everyone stop what they were doing and focus their attention on him.

He stood in the kitchen with some almonds in old, faded packaging.

Dorian blinked. 'Erm... sure. But I wouldn't eat them if I were you. They're probably as old as I am.'

'Thanks.' Darius put the bag in his pocket, flashing his clownish smile.

Our eyes met and, in a heartbeat, his playful gaze turned hostile.

'Where's the nearest lake?' Will asked as we left the house.

'We won't need it,' Dorian said.

'How do we get into the Spirit World then?'

'I'll show you.'

He hurried around the back of the house, through the dense bushes, and we followed him. A few minutes later, we stopped in front of three towering dolmens that shone silver in the light of full moon. They were arranged in a triangle among the trees, and across their tops lay a giant slab.

Dorian approached one of the stones and put his hand on it, uttering, '*Permiterre.*' He went to the second one, calling out, '*Adire,*' and finally to the third one, whispering, '*Introrsum.*' A blinding warm glare poured out of the fourth stone, which loomed above our heads, bathing the trees and the dolmens and us in dazzling light. Second later we were in the Spirit World.

We left our shelter of three dolmens, which were absolutely identical to those standing near Dorian's house in the Human World.

It was cold but windless... and frighteningly quiet. The air was filled with a rich scent of moist earth. Looking around, I saw gnarled, bent and twisted trees looming between endless boulders of all possible sizes. A cadaverous blue mist shrouded the woods. Lichens, ferns and shaggy growths colonised every twig, every trunk, every stone just like marine life that thrived on sunken ships.

'Remember this place and these words: *permiterre, adire, introrsum.*' Dorian looked each of us in the eye. 'They'll help you get out of here if anything happens to me. Will, your key won't work here. Even sirens avoid this land. It's hard to find a place with a higher density of spirits, hence danger. Everything here's alive – every shrub and every tree has its own spirit. They'll watch your every move. They're watching you even now.'

I glanced at the nearest mossy but leafless tree. Its trunk was twisted in such an odd shape that it looked painful. And its bark... was that a human face screaming in anguish? I reeled back. It seemed the tree could stir at any moment, releasing the enraged spirit captured within.

'This forest is a home for both evil and benign spirits. But don't fool yourself. None of them are happy to see humans in their lands. They will play tricks on you. Follow me and don't stop, no matter what you see, hear or feel. Do you understand?'

We nodded.

Dorian climbed ahead among the trees, and we followed him, avoiding the many writhing roots that interlaced between the boulders. The forest was motionless, as if frozen in space and time, and yet it seemed to me the branches of the trees were swaying without a single breath of wind, like seaweed waving under water. Every cell in my body rang with uneasy anticipation as I kept looking back over my shoulder, not knowing what I was trying to find.

We circled around thorny scrub covered with ample cobwebs jewelled with droplets of dew, and the path brought us to a long, narrow lake of inky water. I peered into its charming depths and my legs suddenly turned leaden. My whole gut resisted moving forward. It seemed a thousand tiny strings were pulling my body towards the lake. As soon as I dived, this water would heal me – I just knew it. I knew it would melt my worry away...

Dorian glanced back at me. 'Stop looking at it. All you'll find in that water is your death.'

His words helped me to break eye contact with the lake, and that brought me back to reality. I sighed. 'Thank you.'

We continued on our way, skirting and not even touching the branches of the largest trees, afraid to wake them. Suddenly, the air grew warmer and more humid, as if the blue fog had turned into steam in a rapidly heating sauna. I gasped for the thinning air, trying to breathe, but my lungs weren't even half filled. It seemed the forest was trying to suffocate us, and there was nowhere to run, nowhere to hide from the choking wilds.

Will took my hand, making me flinch.

'Lilly, whatever it is, it's not real. Focus.'

His grip on my hand changed the focus of my attention, and instantly the air turned cool and fresh. I rubbed my eyes and glanced at the others, trying to find any signs of worry or distress, but their faces were still as stone, their movements intense but steady. I was the weakest, letting the forest play tricks on me. My pride tried to find an excuse such as the marok attack or a total lack of sleep, but did it matter? We were moments away from finding the emanation, and I had to get a grip.

Suddenly Ray cawed. Will stopped dead and turned back. I followed his gaze and saw Aisha disappearing into the thick fog shrouding the forest.

'Darius, stop her!'

At the speed of sound, Darius flew towards the swirling mist where Aisha had disappeared. He vanished as well. Time passed. There was no sign of them.

'Will?' I urged.

'Let's go.' He set off after Darius.

'We mustn't go off the path!' Dorian warned.

'We're not leaving them.' He headed deeper into the fog.

Hairito, Vesta and I went after him. Dorian swore under his breath but followed us anyway.

I was trying to make out anything as we plodded through the thick sea of mist, when suddenly the haze cleared, revealing a small lake with five girls sitting on its bank. They rested on broad tree roots that were covered with moss, and their long golden hair spread out over them, streaming down into the water. Darius lay in the lap of one of them. She stroked his face, singing in a clear voice that seemed to pacify the air and the trees. Another girl swam like a siren, dragging Aisha's unconscious body out into the middle of the lake.

When they noticed us, inhuman rage disfigured their angelic faces. They screeched, ripping away the silence that enveloped the woods. Ray soared over Will and broke into many feathers, becoming his wings at once. Will flew towards Aisha, who was now awake, but the red-eyed fiend grabbed her with both hands, not ready to let go of her prey. Will drew his sword, waving it near her throat. The fury hissed, revealing a row of sharp teeth, but released Aisha and dove into the depths. Their cries brought Darius back to reality. He jumped to his feet and in an instant was next to us.

'Quick!' Dorian led us in a run away from the lake.

'What were they?' I asked Vesta, panting.

'Korrigans. Human flesh is their favourite delicacy.' She turned to Aisha. 'Why the hell did you wander off the trail?'

'I heard Ophelia's voice…'

'Seriously? After Dorian warned us, you still fell into that trap? You were lucky we got there in time.'

'Lucky?' Dorian barked. 'That cry woke up the entire forest. Now we can only pray we get out of here alive!'

Will glanced at him. 'We're still sticking to the plan, no? We have to get to Broseliand.'

'No. We're going back to the Human World.'

'What if noxes are waiting for us there?' I asked.

'At least there we have a chance of surviving. You have no idea how dangerous this forest is for humans.'

Suddenly, I spotted movement out of the corner of my eye. A shiver ran down my spine at the sight of tall spirits with bark instead of skin and hair made of crooked branches protruding from their heads. One of them glared at me, shrieking. His eyes glowed a frozen green.

'Spriggans on the left!' Vesta cracked her whip.

But they weren't just on the left. More appeared in front of us, bringing us to a halt. We had violated the sacred peace of the forest, and spriggans surrounded us like angry wasps from all sides. They outnumbered us at least three to one.

Dorian lifted his hands. 'We won't hurt you. We come in peace.'

One of the spriggans opened his bark-lipped mouth, letting out a sepulchral laugh. 'Your kind doesn't know what peace is.'

'We aren't ordinary people. We're guardians, and we come to take from Broseliand what belongs to us, nothing more.' Dorian stood as if rooted to the ground, talking slowly, weighing every word.

'You are nobody in this world and own nothing here,' the spriggan said. 'But you can be of some use for these trees, for our children... Your decaying bodies will become a nursery for a new growth. The fewer of your kind, the better for the planet.'

They lunged towards us all at once. I pulled the metal hilt out of my pocket – a thin sword appeared in my shaking hand. One spriggan jumped at me, and I was ready to apply my fencing lessons in a real fight for the first time, but Will leaped between me and the spriggan, spreading his wide inky wings in front of my face.

'Will, let me help!' I tried to step around his protection.

'Stay where you are!' he shouted over the roaring battle.

Hearing stomping footsteps charging at me, I whirled around, and my heart leaped into my throat as I watched another spriggan closing in on me. Suddenly, the idea of fighting an eight-foot-tall spirit seemed like a fatal mistake, but I readied my sword anyway.

Will swung at him, sending the spirit flying off to the side. 'Thank you...'

He was too busy fighting to respond.

Hairito was digging her sharp claws and teeth into the wooden skin of one spriggan. Another creature bumped into Dorian. He dodged and pulled out his black sword, striking the hand of the spriggan that had tried to punch him. The spriggan struggled to hit him with his other hand, but Dorian parried the blow with his steel-hard wings. Another fiend ran towards Vesta, but she lashed out and wrapped her whip around his neck, sending him crashing to the ground. Hairito soared into the air and pounced on a spriggan who was trying to get close to me from behind.

I darted from one to the other, trying to find a way to help when suddenly I realised that Darius, with his gift, could shackle all these spriggans in a heartbeat.

I looked around. He was leaning against a tree, holding that bag of almonds and popping one into his mouth. He chewed a little, grimaced as if he'd eaten a lemon and spat it out, hiding the bag back in his pocket. Finally, he seemed to notice the battle unfolding before his eyes. He clapped his hands and disappeared at once. Spriggans started falling to the ground, their legs imprisoned by steel. We jumped back to a safe distance then Darius turned up in front of us.

Will breathed heavily. 'Couldn't you have done that a little sooner?'

Darius gave his signature smile. 'You know, my friend, you have serious problems expressing gratitude.'

'We don't have time for this!' Dorian called, running away.

Literally everything was now in motion. Even the boulders were spinning around their axes under our feet. The ferns came to life. I noticed some movement behind their leaves and, looking closely, I made out tiny creatures, no larger than my palm, with human-looking faces and bodies, but some had spiral horns and hooves; others had sharp long ears and mother-of-pearl wings or long feelers set on their foreheads. But all of them had black eyes, like small buttons, that were surveying us. I didn't notice any rage or anger in their gazes, just curiosity... and probably some fear.

Suddenly, a strange hum rose in the forest, like the buzz of thousands of drones. I spun around. The air was full of blue flying creatures – they looked like insects but were the size of sparrows. Their bodies were covered with thorns and armour, and their sharp stingers, the length of toothpicks, were all aimed at us.

Vesta glanced back over her shoulder. 'Oh shit! Racosects behind us!'

I remembered reading about them. One sting could paralyse forever; two stings could kill a man. There were a lot of them.

We sprinted ahead until we found ourselves in the middle of an empty patch of land surrounded by pines. Aisha suddenly stopped and dashed away from us. Darius noticed it and vanished as well.

'Watch out!' Will called and covered me with his body, crouching down.

A cage of shining white bars descended over us.

'Great!' Vesta flared her nostrils. 'Don't touch the bars – they're poisonous spider-silk.'

At once Will's wings split into feathers, reforming into Ray. We straightened up. The pine trunks stirred and opened, unleashing lanky humanoid creatures with green skin, match-like limbs and ebony eyes. I'd already encountered one of their kind. Dryads.

'Well, well...' said the tallest dryad, who wore a crown made from branches twisted into a braid. 'Dorian Raven! You know you're in the spirits' territory. A deal is a deal. We allow you to live in the Spirit World on the condition that you and the rest of your species do not enter our lands. Ever.'

Dorian turned to us, whispering, 'Let me do the talking.' His eyes shifted to the dryad. 'Marselas, we just need to get to Broseliand. We didn't mean to trouble you.'

'Once again, a deal is a deal.' He cast his eyes over all of us. His penetrating gaze stopped; he tilted his head, staring at me. 'I see another Raven and a shaman, but you... I see but can't believe.'

'She's just a human,' Dorian said.

Marselas turned his predatory gaze on him without blinking. 'You come to my home, you disturb my peace and you dare to lie to me? Ah, but from your kind I'd expect nothing less. Humans... deceitful, malicious and devious creatures. I thank the Universe every day for sending us a saviour. Finally, Noxohit will erase your kind from the face of the Earth, and life will blossom again on the planet. And we will be able to breathe again.'

I tried to keep my mouth shut, but it was getting harder by the second. His words, uttered with such undisguised satisfaction, inflamed my blood, making my heart rocket. His visibly sincere belief that the pain, suffering and extermination of some could bring benefit, peace and salvation to others was absurd, short-sighted and just idiotically stupid. He was a spirit after all. Didn't he see that everything was one?

Maybe he felt the anger simmering in my body, for his sight now was focused only on me, and I couldn't help but return his glare.

'I can't wait to see your kind extinct,' he gritted out to me.

'Do you *actually* believe you wouldn't die right after us?'

'Lilly…' Dorian muttered as if trying to calm me before I dug us a deeper grave.

'Why would I believe that?' Marselas charged at me, approaching the cage. 'You think Noxohit is evil? He's a long-awaited cure. You're nothing but a delusional little girl believing in fairy tales, believing in a world without pain and loss and death. *His* coming to the Earth is no attack… it is a blessing.'

'If we don't stop him, he'll exterminate everything on this planet. Not just humanity.'

'No, he's just after the humans. Blind, greedy humans who are destroying other life like overpopulated, insatiable pests.'

'You're wrong.'

'The pattern was clear long before Noxohit arrived. At the beginning of time, all races lived together. We guarded the forests, sirens guarded the waters, daoshee the mountains and men the earth. Like the four elements, we were inseparable, and our union was key to the welfare of the planet. Now, your kind, the weakest of the four but the most insatiable, have forced us into another world. The Universe has given you everything you need to live and prosper, but it will never be enough for you. You are never satisfied.'

I moved closer to the bars of the cage. Will tried to stop me, but I didn't even look at him. 'You only see one side of the coin. Many humans care about the world and put others before themselves. Shamans, witches, the Simtri clan… all of them were created by the Universe to heal people and guide them on the right path. Don't you see? The Universe sent Luminiferos to help us protect ourselves from the Dark Spirit because it believes in humans. And so should you. With your help, it would be a thousand times easier to defeat Noxohit.' I paused to catch my breath. 'Fight with us.'

Marselas was penetrating me with his predatory ebony eyes.

'Vandors. You were born to protect humanity, so I can't blame you for taking your job seriously. But if you opened your eyes, you would see the ugly truth about those you want to save. Thousands of years speak for themselves. We've been waiting for help for a long time. And although people like yourself will also fall victim to the Dark Spirit, we will offer no resistance because this sacrifice is necessary to save the Earth.'

He turned to the other dryad. 'Move their cage into the village. Keep them there until I decide what to do with them.'

'Please let us go,' Vesta said. 'Noxohit is looking for us. He could appear at any moment.'

'Then I will give you to him,' Marselas stated with no hesitation. 'My enemy's enemy is my friend.'

I tried once more to break through his wall. 'The Dark Spirit isn't anyone's friend. He craves only destruction, and he'll stop at nothing. Once he's destroyed our civilisation, he'll cast his eye on you, and you know it.'

Marselas ignored me and walked away. Four dryads grabbed the spider-silk, which was harmless to them, and dragged the cage through the forest to their village.

Adrenaline was still pumping through my veins, and I stared unseeingly around, trying to process what had just happened. I didn't know where I'd found the courage to speak in such a tone to the leader of the dryads. And I was sorry it hadn't worked.

The dryads carried the cage to a vat that reeked of rot and was surrounded by a swarm of flies. They left us behind a massive redwood and shuffled away.

'Where are Aisha and Darius?' Vesta asked quietly when we were alone.

'They hid just in time,' I said.

Darkness boiled in Will's aquamarine eyes as he glared at the dryads. 'Cowardly bastards!'

'And yet,' Vesta breathed, 'I can see their point.'

'Can you now? Then why are you helping us?'

'Will, I want to believe that humanity is worth saving, but every day I fight evil spirits created by human actions. I want to believe in people. I keep asking the Universe to give me some power to love and understand them, but I can't ignore facts. And the fact is, the more I fight evil spirits, the more of them there are.'

'The Human World may not be perfect, but it doesn't deserve this fate,' I cut in. 'Vesta, you of all people know how much they suffer. They're blindfolded and live in ignorance, ruled by fears that shackle their minds in a perpetual fog. I don't look the other way from the evil they do, but only light can dispel the darkness. And Noxohit is not the light.'

She said nothing. We were standing there in silence, when suddenly I heard footsteps approaching the cage. It was a dryad I recognised at once.

'You!'

She flinched, putting a finger to her lips – calling for silence. 'I want to help.'

Stretching out her hand to the cage, her fingers grew into long green branches, thickly overgrown with leaves. They wrapped around the spider-silk bars, which melted before our eyes, leaving us free. Hairito passed by the dryad, growling at her.

'Why are you helping us?' I asked quietly.

'Later. We need to hurry.'

She led us through the forest away from the village, making sure no one was following us. When we were out of earshot, I repeated my question.

'A couple of months ago you were trying to kill me, and now you want to help?'

'I never wanted to kill you, Lilly White. I always wanted to help.' The dryad smiled at me warmly. 'My name is Calathea.'

'Help?'

She looked at Hairito and shrugged. 'I was trying to protect you from the gargoyle. I agree with everything you said to Marselas. Even though the Human World is dangerous for us, I still choose to live there. I protect humans from evil spirits. About two months ago, I saw a gargoyle sitting on a tree observing a sleeping girl – you – and wanted to help. When you went to the lake, I was watching you, and I wasn't alone – the gargoyle was somewhere nearby. She showed up, and I was about to reveal myself when I spotted her eating cookies. That surprised me, to say the least. So I kept watching, wondering what this strange gargoyle wanted from you, and when she tried to attack you, I rushed to help. But she hid you from my sight.'

'She didn't want to attack me.' I shook my head, remembering how Hairito had taken on an aggressive stance, trying to prove she could look menacing.

'Well, that's how it looked. The next day I searched all over the country for you. We can see from any tree in this world, and I found you in the woods of Brittany. I was there in a moment, emerging from a trunk. But he met you.' She looked at Will. 'So I left, knowing he could protect you from the gargoyle. After that, I tried to keep track of you in Faivendei, but I couldn't because Omnia the Great guards that forest. When you were back in the Human World, I realised the gargoyle had become a friend and was no longer a threat to you. I overheard you saying you were searching for Luminiferos, and that finally cleared away my doubts. Before that, I'd still thought my brothers might be right about people. But you inspired me. So... yes, I want to help.'

I didn't know what to say.

Calathea glanced towards the dryad village. 'We have to hurry. I'll take you on a safe path to the Broseliand portal.'

'Wait,' Vesta called. 'Shouldn't we find Aisha and Darius first?'

'No time. When my brothers and sisters realise that you're gone, they'll head for the portal too. First, we get the emanation, then we search for them.'

Her eyes drifted to Will and Dorian; they nodded in approval.

'Let's go.' She strode ahead.

'Thank you for saving us,' I said.

'You're welcome.' She smiled. 'I'm sorry if I scared you back then.'

'No, it's fine...'

'I'm glad you managed to get into Faivendei so soon after you lost your room in Paris.'

'Why?'

'After I spotted the gargoyle, I started to watch you and... I noticed unusual activity around you. It was as if you attracted all kinds of spirits, evil and benign. I knew that in Faivendei you'd be safe. It's good that you found your new home there.'

'It wasn't for long.'

'Don't worry. Soon they'll realise they made a mistake and call you back.'

'Even if they do, I can't go.'

'Why?'

'I'm a vandor. I'd be a danger to the entire forest—'

'That's not true. After the first time noxes attacked Faivendei, Omnia reinforced its defences. Do you know why she's almost never seen in public? She spends every moment checking the areas around the portals, which are always moving. I could neither see nor hear nor feel what was happening to you, and I'm a benign spirit. I think only daoshee lands are safer than Faivendei. So the guardians there have nothing to fear.'

'I don't know… Darkness can find a key to any door.'

Her ebony eyes fixed on the ground. 'Still, it's nice to know that you have a home – a place to go back to.'

Home… Would I ever go back there? No, probably not. I lifted my eyes to Calathea's. 'And where is your home?'

'It's with the people I protect. Now, it's with you.'

She was smiling, but that smile didn't reach her eyes. She was going against the will of the other spirits, believing in something they considered an idealist's utopia. And because of this belief, she had no home and no support from her own kind. Alone, without gratitude or recognition, she lived to protect people who didn't even know she existed. She was a spirit, but she acted like a guardian.

'Well…' I smiled. 'You're with us now. And I'm glad.'

Calathea grinned back.

'By the way, what did you mean when you said I attracted other spirits?'

'Yes, I was confused about that at first too. But when I found out you were a vandor, the answer was clear. Evil spirits are attracted by your energy because unconsciously they want to be healed. And benign ones are drawn to you because they charge from your light. Even before your power unveiled itself, that light was flowing through your veins.'

'This light... I didn't feel it. Even now, I only feel it when I heal others. My head is full of doubts and fear from morning to night.'

'Only mad people live with no fear, Lilly. But people like you – those who tremble but move forward, who fall but get up – they inspire others.'

I was thinking that over, but my train of thought was disrupted when I spotted a giant tree on the horizon. It towered like a colossus over the forest. The ten-thousand-year-old Ponthus beech – the portal to Broseliand.

When we reached it, my mouth dropped open. Never had I seen such a magnificent and strange tree. The Eiffel Tower was a toy compared to this titan. Its roots, overgrown with moss, ferns and lichens rose a few metres above the surface of the soil. They seemed to be as wide as subway tunnels. And its trunk was so twisted it looked as if someone was trying to wring the life out of it.

'Hurry, Lilly!' Dorian urged.

I closed my mouth and ran up to the trunk, taking off the pendant.

'Touch it to the tree and say, "*Permiterre adire introrsum.*" Loud and clear.'

Pressing the pendant to the trunk, I took a deep breath and spoke the words. A thundering crack shuddered the earth, and the trunk twisted, slowly unwinding.

'It worked!' Dorian's relief brightened his face.

The tree twisted around until the lines on its trunk were vertical, and a stream of light appeared up the middle, passing through it. Then the line widened, opening the portal and revealing a new world.

CHAPTER 18
SACRIFICE

A DEAFENING ROAR reached us from the other side, but I couldn't make out the source behind the curtain of steam flowing out towards us. It was like we'd opened the door to an unbearably warm greenhouse with a raging thunderstorm inside.

'Quick! We only have thirty minutes!' Dorian called and dove into the steam.

'I'll stay here,' Calathea said. 'I'll try to keep the portal open as long as I can. But hurry – you'd better get back in time.'

Taking a cautious step into the unknown, sultry world, I looked around. We were on a hanging bridge. It started from a portal that hovered in the air in the middle of a rumbling cacophony and ended at the slope of one of those evergreen hills towering menacingly all around us. The source of the roar revealed itself – a giant two-level waterfall that rushed down the mountain into a foaming pool. Our bridge hung just above it amongst the clouds of spray and lather.

Shrouded in a blanket of stormy clouds, these hills were thickly covered with a cloak of lush, impenetrable jungle. I inhaled deeply the warm and humid tropical air. The world swirled in my head, and I unzipped my raincoat, trying to cool myself down. I couldn't stand the heat, but the reason for this dizziness wasn't the temperature. *Save the ones you love...* I heard the whisper from the pendant again.

'Will, I'll look for Abigail.' Dorian soared up and into the forest on the summit of the hill.

We crossed the bridge. A path unspooled in front of us, and in the distance, a tiny scarlet glow flickered, like a lantern from a faraway lighthouse.

'Is it...?' My eyes slid to Will.

'Let's go.' He took my hand and the three of us rushed towards it with Ray and Hairito flying overhead.

The closer we got, the better I saw a sphere floating in the air, emitting a misty red glow. The sight seemed to send a warm sunlit stream through my body, dissolving my tension and giving me strength. We'd found it, and it was much easier than I'd expected.

The emanation was just a few metres from my reach when a sudden seismic jolt knocked us to our knees. We jumped up, trying to stay steady despite the quaking earth's surface.

'What the hell is going on?' Vesta struggled to regain her balance.

An ebony jet gushed from the ground like searing lava from a volcano's mouth, forcing us to back away. The mass thickened, taking on a human shape. Ray transformed into Will's wings, and he shielded me behind him. But when I saw who emerged from the darkness, I stepped out into the open.

'Aisha, what are you doing?' I asked.

'I'm sorry...'

'Sorry? Sorry for—'

Thomas stepped out of the darkness and stood next to her.

As I watched, slack-jawed, a dozen other noxes appeared, and in front of them floated the unconscious body of Ophelia. I looked at her chest. She was breathing. But Aisha...

'What's going on?'

She didn't reply to me nor raise her eyes from the ground.

Will and Vesta were scowling at her, but I knew there was some explanation. She couldn't betray us. Noxohit had made her do it.

Thomas smirked. 'Lilly, why are you looking at me like that?'

'You destroy people's lives, you drain their energy, wreak chaos in our world, kill the guardians who live to help others. Do you want me to keep going?' I hissed in a voice I barely recognised.

The whites of Thomas's eyes had darkened, becoming two infinite pools of oil. He straightened up, relaxed his shoulders and stretched his neck, as if adjusting to a new body.

'All true, and I do not deny it.' A thousand echoing voices reverberated from his mouth. 'But if I am here, there must be a reason for it. Is that not what everyone is telling you?'

Noxohit.

Cold sweat ran down my back, even as the air grew more stifling. 'You're a mistake that needs to be corrected, a problem that must be resolved. I *will* find the seven emanations, whatever it takes, and I *will* send you back where you belong.'

He let out a low, grave chuckle. 'You know, Lilly, I actually like you. I also believe the Universe makes mistakes – creates defective people for instance, who store darkness and spread it over your planet. My noxes are the wolves, forest orderlies who clear your planet of filth. I do not touch those who live in harmony with the Universe, because I am a part of it.'

'You turn guardians. You turned Thomas, whose body you're in.'

'Thomas volunteered. He had a darkness in him long before I got involved.'

'You exploited and magnified it. There's light and darkness in everybody and if you turn people towards darkness, then we – guardians – will fight to the last for light, because that's our purpose. And if we're here, there must be a reason for that as well.'

'Oh, I have been making good use of the guardians so far, Lilly. And you will be one of my wolves, whether you want to or not. So why waste time? Why fight? Your entire family is with me. Join them.' He said this as if he were completely in control, utterly confident of his power.

I already knew that my parents and my brother were noxes. So why, when Noxohit said the words, did this truth become a withering poison burning my body from the inside? It seemed the air had turned into a toxic gas, and with each breath, my mind was clouding more and more while my blood turned to napalm. I was no longer able to restrain this incendiary mixture, and my hand instinctively reached for the hilt of my sword.

Will stopped me. His eyes asked me to remember everything he'd taught me. I closed my eyes for a moment, taking a deep breath. This wasn't me. It was Noxohit's doing.

'I'm already with my family,' I said calmly.

A hellish laugh escaped his lips. 'Family? You mean like Aisha, for example? She betrayed you to save her sister. She gave you away when you were in the vampire's castle. And now, when the dryads trapped you, she returned to the Human World, told us about your plans and showed us the way to Broseliand. She knew what it meant to you, but her sister was more important to her, because she, unlike you, understands the real meaning of the word *family*. But even Aisha's treachery pales before that of your beloved William…'

My eyes shifted to Will, but he looked as confused as I felt.

'Yes…' Noxohit savoured. 'When I said your family is with me, I meant your father and brother. Sorry to break it to you like this, but your mother is already dead.' He smirked at Will. 'Murdered, in fact.'

I stopped breathing, feeling the echo of my pulse in my throat. The last time I'd seen my mother in a dream was before Hairito had given me the golden tube with an invitation to Faivendei. In that dream, she'd left me suddenly, and the nox had said she was dead. Somewhere in the back of my mind, I'd known it was true, but I hadn't been ready to accept it. I'd clung to the hope of meeting her again like a shipwrecked sailor clinging to a stump of mast drifting in the open ocean. But Noxohit's words, so bloodthirsty and triumphant, were a storm wave looming over my head and threatening to crush me in the blink of an eye.

'The leader of Faivendei's warriors, the so-called General Fairfax, recently killed your mother on the sacred grounds of the church. And he…' He pointed to Will, drawing out the moment. 'He watched her die.'

I hunched, fighting back those traitorous tears that were welling up in my eyes.

'Do you remember, the day you arrived in Faivendei? There was a downpour and the forest was drowning in fog? Omnia was mourning your mother, who was murdered by those you so treacherously call your family.'

'No…' I reeled back, staring at Will, almost begging him to tell me it was a lie, but his distorted face only proved Noxohit was telling the truth.

'Lilly, I swear, I didn't know that woman was your mother.'

There were no shots fired over my head and no grenades exploding, but a deafening roar tore at my ears, blurring my vision. Pictures flashed through my mind – painfully vivid memories... The dried blood beneath Fairfax's cracked fingernails. That blood... that blood belonged to my mother. My stomach clenched as if trying to get rid of its contents. For thirteen years, my mother had lived in the torments of hell as a nox, only to be stabbed by her brothers – guardians – like a pig for slaughter.

The sounds of that funeral melody Will had played on the organ sounded in my head and I could no longer hold back my tears. *The Aria of Death*. The one whom all my dreams were about, the one whom I'd fallen in love with, had watched the killing of the purest being in the world.

I heard my mother's laughter in my mind, shimmering like a nightingale's song; I saw her eyes: seraphic, soft, sincere. Good God... How could a human being radiate so much kindness and love? No, she wasn't a human – she was my guardian angel, who'd given her life, her freedom so I could live.

I'd spent most of my life looking for the Spirit World, hoping to find her. But I was too late. Maybe I could still meet my father and brother, but I was never destined to see her eyes, to hear her laughter again. Fairfax had stabbed her in the chest, and Will... he'd watched her die. I wanted to screech at the top of my lungs, to hurtle away, but where could I run away from the truth?

I glared at Will, feeling myself drenched in molten iron. His wings were folded; guilt filled his eyes. Vesta was staring at me as if I were a werewolf that could, at any moment, transform into a monster. Then I saw Noxohit looking out from Thomas's body. He had kidnapped Ophelia, killed Octavian, transformed my family and hundreds of thousands of other guardians into noxes.

And right now, he was winning a new victory.

His gaze was full of sadistic pleasure and savage triumph. I suddenly remembered Will's words. *He sees the world in the form of vibrations and frequencies. All your worries, hopes and fears are just wavelengths to him. What are you afraid of, Lilly? Losing your mother? So he won't have to say anything. He'll just affect you with wavelengths that you won't see, hear or feel, but every cell in your body will shudder, knowing that your mother is dying and there's nothing you can do.*

Noxohit was playing with my mind like it was a toy. Had Will rejoiced in the killing of that nox? He hadn't known it was my mother; he hadn't even known me at that moment – we'd first met a few hours after that tragic event. But he'd grieved her; he'd blamed himself. And had there been another choice? That body had belonged to my mother, but she hadn't had power over it. She'd been a bearer, and had been infecting other guardians from Faivendei against her own will, ruled by Noxohit's darkness within. Will had said that in the last moments of her life, she'd looked... grateful.

Octavian. He had been a vampire for five hundred years. He had also been thankful to be finally free.

I felt I was emerging from a dark, narrow tunnel where my own selfish grief had imprisoned me. My mother had been glad to die. It had been a release for her.

I swallowed to relieve the dryness in my mouth. 'You know my weaknesses and you know what levers to pull. But make no mistake, I won't let you cloud my mind.' I walked over to Will, taking his hand. 'I was in Vandorfort, and I know what people infected by your darkness feel. I know their pain. General Fairfax didn't kill my mother. He killed a nox and released my mother's soul from the darkness you're using to poison our world. I can't stand bloodshed, so I'll try to save the souls of the noxes you send after me… But if I fail, we'll free them. Just as General Fairfax freed my mother.'

With every word I spoke, his expression changed, the smile fading from his face.

'I would like to see you do it,' Noxohit blazed. 'Bravery is worthy of respect only when it is not based on idiocy. There are three of you and thirteen of us. Do the math. But I am not as cruel as you think, Lilly White. My only goal is to save your planet, to remove the species that devours everything in its path and threatens the extinction of all life on Earth. You may not understand that yet, but one day you will. For now, let me be generous and offer you a choice.'

Darkness crawled out of his palm like the tentacles of a hellish squid. Ophelia opened her eyes, and when they began to wrap around her body, she screamed, startling the birds from the nearby trees.

'Ophelia, I'm here! I'm here!' Aisha ran to her, but two noxes held her back. 'Let her go! You promised not to hurt her!'

Noxohit didn't even look at her. 'Aisha betrayed you deliberately. Open your eyes, Lilly. She is not your family. Take the emanation, and I will let you and your friends go. But in return, I claim Ophelia's life. It will be a loss for Aisha, but it certainly will not be your fault. Traitors have to pay for their disloyalty.'

The darkness crept around Ophelia's body like an ebony python strangling its prey. It seemed her bones were about to crack. She opened her mouth, but only a muffled moan left her unnaturally cramped lungs.

'No!' Aisha burst into tears, struggling to break free of the noxes' iron grip.

I started towards Ophelia, but Will stopped me.

'I see you are still indifferent to the voice of reason,' Noxohit said slowly. 'Well, in that case, surrender to me and I will
spare these girls and your other friends. If you still believe you
can overcome us, then think twice. You will become a nox anyway. But if you resist, they will all die, because of you.'

Every cell of my body was shaking, but I wasn't afraid. I
knew what had to be done.

'The emanation or Ophelia,' he said, smirking. 'Which is
it?'

'Lilly, don't do anything stupid,' Will said. 'He didn't keep
his promise about Ophelia. He won't let us go even if you're
transformed into a nox.'

'I agree,' Vesta added. 'Take the emanation, then we'll save
Ophelia.'

I shook my head. 'Don't you remember how he killed
Octavian? In an instant. Without Darius, we don't stand a
chance. I can't put you at such risk. What's more, to get the
emanation, I need to save the people I love. Can't you see? I
have to sacrifice myself. Then the emanation will come to me.'

'What if you're wrong?' Will grunted. 'What if you don't
get the emanation, or what if you do and it still doesn't help?
You'll be a nox. You must remember Luminiferos is your top
priority! You're a vandor, Lilly. Our last hope!'

'I'm not, Will. If I become a nox... well. You don't need
me. You'll find Luminiferos on your own. I can't save humanity
if I can't even save the people I love.'

Will froze, as if giving all his energy to seeking a weighty
argument to dissuade me from my decision. But I had no other
choice. He knew it, even if he refused to accept it.

'Lilly,' he gritted through clenched teeth, 'don't do this.'

Vesta put a hand on my shoulder. 'Noxohit is manipulating
you. He'll never let us go. Come to your senses.'

'He wants me, not you. It's the only chance for you to survive.'

She snatched her hand away.

'You will become a nox,' Will said.

'Then you'll find Luminiferos, and it will save me.'

'You don't get it, do you? Anything can happen to you in the meantime. The other guardians might kill you while we search for the weapon of light. How can you... don't you... don't you understand? I—'

'Will.' I grabbed his arm, not letting him finish. Whatever he wanted to say, it might shake my already fragile confidence. 'I'll never forgive myself if Ophelia is killed because of me. My soul will never find peace.'

He dwarfed my hand in his. 'I won't let you go.'

'You must, Will,' I whispered through the lump growing in my throat and pulled away from him.

Anger, confusion, frustration and fear were burning in his eyes; his body shuddered, as if from cold. It seemed before, giving free rein to his feelings, he'd still been calm and collected, but now he couldn't keep it together anymore. For a moment, his eyes froze, as if unable to withstand the mental pain.

But he let me go.

I walked towards Noxohit, and my every step echoed with a sharp pain in my chest. I tried to be strong, but tears gushed from my eyes, releasing the feelings I had been bottling up.

I stopped. 'Let them go.'

'When you come to me,' Noxohit said.

I stepped forward, but Hairito reared on her hind legs, making some articulate sounds. Words? I suddenly remembered she had done the same in Faivendei, when Ophelia had got lost and Aisha... Holy Universe! Of course! Aisha had understood Hairito when she'd told her Ophelia had passed through the wall of trees. How hadn't I noticed it back then? And now, it seemed, Hairito was talking to her again. Aisha listened. Her eyes widened, darting from me to her.

'What's Hairito saying?' Vesta pressed on.

Aisha lowered her head.

'What did she say?' Will demanded.

She wouldn't answer. Hairito growled and hissed at her, pulling me back.

'I have waited too long. One…'

'Don't! I'm coming.'

'Two…'

The black tentacles gripped Ophelia tighter, and she howled again. I broke free of Hairito's grip, bolting to Noxohit.

'I'm here. Let them go.'

He released Aisha and Ophelia, and they ran to the forest, hiding behind the trees.

'Wise decision, girl. You could never overcome me, and I am glad you have realised that. With or without Luminiferos, you never stood a chance.'

'Enough. Do what you must.'

I turned, shooting a look of false confidence at Vesta and Will. Their faces were distorted with helplessness, but this wasn't how I would remember them. I would remember their rare but so charming smiles and radiant eyes; I would remember their strength of spirit and fearlessness – maybe these memories would help me not to lose my mind if I became a nox. They shouldn't have been here. They shouldn't have put themselves at such risk. They had to continue living and protecting people from the dark. My heart was jackhammering from the near-death adrenaline level in my blood, but I didn't doubt my decision, not any longer. I was doing the right thing.

'Let us get started.' Noxohit coiled his tarry tentacles around my body.

His energy flowed from his other palm, and he placed it against my solar plexus. My whole body shrank. I ceased breathing, waiting for that tearing soul-and-body pain. But maybe I still had a chance? I glanced at the emanation. Why wasn't it coming to me? I'd saved the people I loved. Hadn't I?

Noxohit smirked at me, giving an order to his wolves, 'Kill them all.'

A dozen of them advanced on Hairito, Vesta and Will.

He laughed. 'I cannot believe the prophecy claimed that vandors would banish me. You are the most naïve of all people!' His smile disappeared, dissolving into a devilish expression – his true expression, which reflected the personification of all the pain and fear, all the chaos and violence on Earth. 'Now you know the people you love will die because of you, I can finally make you a nox.'

His darkness flooded my body like a fierce river. Every drop of it was a long, sharp knife shredding my insides into scraps. I twitched, clenching my teeth and struggling to hold back the howl trying to escape my chest. But suddenly the physical pain ebbed. The darkness didn't recede; it lurked – quietened down, as if preparing to assail me with a new force. At this false moment of silence, I felt a shadow that, like a gale, came roaring to my mind. It seemed I was falling down an infinite tunnel.

Lilly... The echo of my mother's voice reached me.

I stopped falling and saw her withered, dying body curling up in a ball in the corner of an obscure, empty room.

Lilly... She called me again, her eyes closed, her face distorted with pain.

I dashed to her, but the faster I ran, the further she moved away from me. My strength was leaving me, but I never stopped. It seemed my body was floating in the vacuum of space, but there wasn't a single star that would give light to this endless, all-consuming darkness. The Dark Spirit... No, Noxohit wasn't a spirit – he was an infinity that devoured everything in its path, not leaving a glimmer of hope.

The floor vanished and I collapsed into the abyss again. Screams and moans, howls and cries thundered from all sides. Thousands... hundreds of thousands of other people flashed before my eyes, people who, like my mother, were ever locked in the dungeons of this infinite, frigid tunnel. I saw what guardians experienced when they were imprisoned in a cage of their own bodies, when they transformed into noxes and the darkness poisoned their souls. I was joining them right now. A shiver ran from my head to my toes, bringing me back to reality.

Noxohit was smiling. Like a knacker strangling a helpless puppy – he enjoyed his crashing force and power over me. A new wave of his darkness, sharp as knives, slashed at me and I screamed, unable to contain it.

'No need to cry, my dear. It will all end very soon. Look.' He turned me around.

Will was trying to reach me, but four noxes were attacking him from all sides. Vesta wielded her whip, hitting other noxes, but it only kept them at a distance – a distance that was growing smaller with every blink of an eye. Hairito escaped a nox's grip and leaped into the air, flying towards me, but another one grabbed her by the throat and hurled her into the woods; she hit a tree and, screeching, fell to the ground. Her eyes froze, her chest rising and falling several times a second; she whined but couldn't move.

Tears rolled down my cheeks. What had I done?

No... I couldn't let him kill them.

Gathering my remaining strength, I focused on my breathing. The energy was everywhere – I just needed to inhale it. Azmeral had told me the first emanation wanted to know who I was. Well, I was a vandor. If I could heal others, then I could heal myself. I could heal Thomas. I could save the ones I loved.

I took a deep breath. It seared my body, but I inhaled again. Every expansion of my lungs was shattering my organs, but I kept drawing breath. My heart nearly stopped, but I gasped for air one more time. And again. And again. The light was coming to my body, but my efforts felt like a single candle trying to heat up a Gothic church.

Noxohit chuckled. 'I am a bit disappointed. I expected more from *the last hope of humanity*. I would love to meet a worthy rival, but there is no such thing among your kind, so I have had to settle for a weak little girl. Anyway. Let us proceed.'

One more stream of his dark mass gushed into my body. One more time knives slashed my flesh. There was no more Will. There was no more Vesta. There was nothing but this agony and urge to die just to stop the pain. My mouth was open... Was I screaming? I... Who was I? What was I? There was no me in this body – it didn't belong to me anymore. My soul was floating above my chest, and all I wanted was to break the bond with this poisoned vessel, but overwhelming gravitational pull was dragging me back inside. I couldn't share my life with his darkness. I hoped my heart would stop.

My body stopped moving, but it stayed alive. I watched everything as if from outside. Will roared, struggling to get to me. Vesta was trying to break through the group that had surrounded her. Hairito was bleeding but was now crawling towards me. My head hung limp, and black patterns writhed around my neck like hellish serpents. I was witnessing the birth of a nox in my own body.

Aisha turned to Ophelia. 'Hide in the bushes and close your eyes.'

I heard her as if she was within arm's reach.

Ophelia lifted her tearful eyes to Aisha's and hugged her sister as tightly as her weak, childish arms would allow.

'Let go,' Aisha beseeched. 'Otherwise it will be too late.'

Ophelia released her, bursting into tears.

'I'm sorry for everything, Ophelia. I truly am. Try to become a better person than me. I love you.' Aisha kissed her head, watering her red curls with salty tears.

She ran to Noxohit, pulled out her mother's golden dagger and plunged it to the hilt in his back.

Noxohit's presence vanished, leaving Thomas as the nox he was before. He growled, releasing my lifeless body, which sprawled on the ground. With an animal rage, he tore the blade from his back and plunged it into Aisha's chest.

'No!' Ophelia wailed.

Aisha turned to her sister, staggering, blood oozing from her mouth. 'Run...'

She collapsed next to me, and a sudden shock wave returned me to my body. The pain was gone, but the darkness was still there – I could feel it sliding around inside. I opened my eyes and, as if through mud, saw Aisha.

'Lilly...' she whispered. 'Gargoyle...'

She gasped once, then her eyelids closed, and her face became deathly still.

'Kill the girl!' Thomas snarled, and the two noxes left Vesta and Will, running after Ophelia.

She was rushing towards the path but glanced back and tripped over a tree root, falling to the ground. Horrified, she tried to crawl away on all fours as the two noxes approached her.

I had to save my friends. Maybe if I got to the emanation, it could give me the strength? Slowly, with an impotent shudder, I turned my head. A bright shining emanation, a round ruby, radiating such an attractive glow... It was here – a few steps away from me. All I had to do was find the power to get up. But my body was filled with Noxohit's darkness – as if with lead. It seemed I was chained to the ground.

And the emanation vanished. I'd lost my chance.

I turned back to the battle. Two noxes were following Ophelia as she scrabbled away like a frightened crab. They mocked her attempt at escape, drawing their swords and raising them over her. Ophelia stopped moving, glanced at Aisha's body and closed her eyes, as if wishing to die with pride. The swords came down on her—

But two others parried the blow.

Dorian stood over Ophelia, next to a woman with a shock of curly grey hair – his wife, Abagail. Will saw them and smiled in relief. In an instant, steel shackled the noxes' limbs. Darius appeared out of nowhere.

'Darius!' Vesta couldn't hide her joy.

'Quick! The portal will close in a couple of minutes,' Darius urged. 'Will, grab Lilly. Dorian, take Vesta. Abigail, take the girl; I'll bring Aisha. Hurry up!'

'You won't get away with this!' Thomas hissed.

Darius gave him his clownish grin. 'Yeah? Try to get out of here first.'

A venomous smirk contorted his face. 'You know better than anyone that darkness can find a key to any door.'

Darius ignored him, picked up Aisha's body and disappeared at once. Will lifted me up with Hairito, who moaned in pain. Dorian collected Vesta, and Abigail took Ophelia, rushing to the portal.

I could see it ahead now. The passage was growing narrower with every moment. Darius passed first through the portal with Aisha. Will, Hairito and I were next.

He put us both gently on the ground and bent over me, brushing my hair from my face. 'Lilly, please say something…'

I blinked at him, unable to move.

'Are you with me? Are you still yourself?'

I blinked.

'Oh, Lilly.' He folded me in his arms.

Calathea was struggling to hold open the shrinking portal. It seemed it might break her in half.

Abigail and Ophelia came through next. Ophelia jolted to the motionless body of her sister, who was lying with the dagger still in her chest. Calathea jumped out from the portal. Not even a child could squeeze through the remaining tiny gap in the tree.

Vesta prepared her whip, shouting something to Dorian. The portal had almost vanished, and Abigail clutched her head.

'Now!' Vesta called.

Dorian's wings broke into feathers and turned into his raven, which flew through the portal in an instant. Vesta swung her whip, and it hit the tree, sending a blast of lightning through it. For a moment, the portal widened, and the two of them flew in by inertia. In a heartbeat, the portal closed.

Abigail threw herself into Dorian's arms.

We were safe, but Noxohit's poison was still within me. The shadows of his darkness crept from the corners of my soul, dragging my mind down his infinite tunnel.

CHAPTER 19
FAITH

My eyelids were heavy, as if the weight of the whole world was dragging them down. I closed my eyes and the somnolent buzz in my ears seemed to be a lulling carol, charming and luring me to fall down and down.

Suddenly, everything shuddered as if the Earth was splitting up into bits. What was happening? Was I dying? I felt no pain; I couldn't even sense my own body anymore. This must have been a dream. I'd wake up, and everything would be fine.

'Lilly!' a muffled shout, as if I were under water.

'Lilly, don't close your eyes!'

Why wouldn't he leave me alone? All I had to do was wake up from this nightmare. There – in that bottomless darkness – was boundless peace. Peace...

'Stay with me,' the dense velvet voice called.

Dense velvet voice. It sounded familiar, as if centuries ago I'd known whoever it belonged to. Someone dear, someone I loved.

Suddenly, glowing emerald waves illuminated the darkness, like the Northern Lights, bringing hope. Will...

I opened my eyes. He was holding me, shaking my shoulders, trying to bring me back to consciousness. A green human-like creature loomed above me.

I closed my eyelids. A dream. Just a dream...

'I can help!' the creature said.

She put a hand to my nose, and warm smoke crept into my nostrils. I jittered awake, feeling my nose and mouth filled with acid that set my nerves ablaze. My mind was suddenly clear, and I would have jumped had I been able to move.

I opened my mouth but couldn't make a sound. I looked around: we were still in the Spirit World, in front of the Ponthus beech. Why couldn't I move or speak? Was it over? Had Noxohit's poison possessed me?

'Lilly, it's okay. It's going to be all right.' Will's shaky voice didn't sound convincing.

Vesta ran over to us. 'Let me see her.'

She pressed the tip of her long, thin finger to the bridge of my nose and closed her eyes, although they kept moving underneath her eyelids, as if she were dreaming. I stopped breathing, waiting for her verdict.

She smiled. 'Don't you cry, little baby! You're just in shock. You'll be fine.'

Will let out a sigh of relief. I did as well, but on the inside.

Ophelia's sobbing reached my hazed mind. She was crumpled over Aisha's body.

Vesta rushed to Aisha, pressed a finger on the bridge of her nose and listened.

'She's alive, but...'

Ophelia's eyes widened. 'But?'

A tall grey-haired woman walked over to them. 'There is still hope. They might be able to heal her in Equilibrium.'

Who was... Ah, yes. Abigail – Dorian's wife.

'She won't—' Vesta looked warily at Ophelia. 'Aisha won't make it. Her soul is already on the way to the Border World.'

'I can do it,' Darius said with a shrug. 'If you wouldn't mind, that is.'

Vesta looked at him thoughtfully. 'Yes, I think you could. But you can't enter Faivendei alone.'

'Unless Will gives me his portal key.'

'Never!' It was a growl.

Hairito whined, lying motionless next to us.

'The gargoyle has lost too much blood,' Vesta added. 'She needs to get to Equilibrium too.'

'Raven, be reasonable,' Darius said. 'If you lend me your key, we might save both of them. Otherwise their deaths will be on your hands.'

No, not on his... on mine. I wanted to get up and beg Will to give Darius his key, but I was still imprisoned in my stupor. Though I squeezed his hand as tightly as my slowly returning strength would allow.

He glanced at me. I opened and closed my mouth like a fish stranded on dry land, and only on the third attempt was I able to whisper, 'Please.'

He frowned at me. 'I can't entrust my key to *him*.'

I knew his father had given him the key before he died. But I also knew Darius wouldn't steal it... at least I wanted to believe that. But the lives of Aisha and Hairito were worth the risk.

'Please,' I whispered again.

He sighed, as if knowing himself he didn't have much choice. Putting me on the ground, he rolled up the sleeve of his jacket and held out his hand to Darius, who grabbed it quickly. Will glanced at his key, as if giving it a final farewell and pronounced loudly and clearly, '*Clavidere* Darius.' The lines disappeared from his arm and reappeared on Darius's.

As soon as he had the key, Darius carefully lifted Aisha. Dorian picked up the whimpering Hairito and placed her on Darius's shoulders. She wrapped her arms around his neck. He vanished in a flash.

He would make it. He would save them. He had to.

Desperation had pushed Aisha to betrayal, but she had a noble soul, and she'd proved it. If she hadn't intervened, there would have been nothing left of me.

'We need to get out of here,' Calathea said.

We headed back to the portal, Will carrying me in his arms. Dorian and Abigail were walking in front of us. After ten years of separation, they had finally been reunited. At least there was one positive outcome of this suicide mission...

I glanced at the grey clouds rushing across the leaden sky. When I had given in to Noxohit, I'd thought I could protect Ophelia and the others. As a result, the emanation hadn't come to me, my friends had almost been killed, and Aisha and Hairito were still in mortal danger. I'd been making mistakes one after another, endangering the lives of those I loved. It had to stop. I couldn't let them die because of me. Yes, they believed with a vandor's help they could find Luminiferos. The only problem was... the vandor was me. I had to leave them as soon as possible.

Had I really thought I could stand up to Noxohit? Now it seemed so stupid and presumptuous. My parents had made the right decision leaving me in that orphanage. Why couldn't I just sit still in the Human World? Why wasn't a quiet and safe life enough for me? Why did I always chase after something big? Purpose... I'd found it, but now I was facing a fate worse than death. I was going to become a nox. It was only a matter of time.

His darkness... it wasn't just energy, just a black goo living under the Earth's crust. He was the embodiment of the greatest evil that had ever been. Other guardians were right – humanity's days were numbered. And shamans, witches, the Simtri clan and even spirits would follow them to the grave. He wouldn't stop until he'd absorbed all life on Earth. Now, after I'd been in his infinite tunnel, I didn't doubt that. He was right. With or without Luminiferos, I didn't have a single chance.

We reached the portal without incident, returned to the Human World and went to Dorian's house. Once inside, Will laid me carefully on the bed.

'We can't stay here long.' Vesta bit her lip, looking out the window. 'Noxohit knows where we are. The noxes will be here any minute now.'

'Yes. But without a portal key, we won't get far,' Will countered. 'I'll go ask my mother to send us another guide.' He left the house.

Abigail was scanning the shelves and jars of herbs, looking around with blatant curiosity. 'Is this house yours?' she asked Dorian.

'Yes. I built it right after we parted, and all these years I've been trying to get back into Broseliand.'

She smiled at him softly. Despite her age, she looked young. Her tall and slender body was clad in white silk trousers and blouse, and a long alabaster cloak with an airy spider-silk hood and sleeves. Her hair, despite being grey, shone with strength and health and... sometimes it seemed to me she was literally glowing.

'Abigail... may I ask something?' Vesta said. 'How did you survive there for ten years?'

She smiled. '*Survive?* I was welcome there. Broseliand, like Faivendei, cares about its wards. I lived among the elves, who accepted me as one of their own. They live without fear, for they see everything as a sacred manifestation of the Universe. They avoid excess and flourish in abundance. They study the Universe and find their wisdom in doing so. However, the longer I lived there, the more I wished to come back to Faivendei and the Human World...'

'Wow... I suppose you missed Dorian that much.'

'Yes, absolutely. But I missed the Human World too.'

'Why?'

'I'm a guardian. I want to keep fighting for my beliefs. I want people to live as those elves in Broseliand do.'

'With all due respect,' Vesta said, 'I think you spent too much time among the elves and forgot what the Human World is like.'

Abigail let out a warm chuckle. 'How could I forget? I am a human. I'm full of fear, pride and selfishness, something living with the elves brought into sharp relief. But I also have empathy, humility and love. Every morning I wake up a new person, and every day I make a choice between good and evil, progress and degradation. In Broseliand, peace and prosperity doesn't mean you stagnate. In that world, you exceed yourself daily, and find happiness in doing so. The Human World is ruled by Noxohit. He feeds on humans' energy, sows fear in their minds and robs them of their will, leading them to degradation and eventual annihilation. I'm a guardian, and as long as I'm alive, I want to protect people and help them return to the right path.'

Calathea nodded. 'I agree. Humanity is in a blind fog right now.'

Vesta shrugged. 'When hasn't it been? I agree with you both – we have to help. But there is so much cruelty in human-kind. They revel in it, enjoy the pain and inflict it consciously. I don't know... I hope I'm wrong, but sometimes I think we deserve this fate.'

Will came in the door. 'The guide will be here soon.'

'The sooner the better.' Vesta switched her attention, look-ing out the window again. 'Every second here could be our last one.'

He nodded and walked over to me. 'Still paralysed?'

I moved my pinkie.

'Well... it's better than nothing.'

I glanced at his wrist, now bare of the portal key. Mar-shalling my returning power, I whispered, 'It was... right.'

'I hope so. But if he runs away with my key, you know whose fault it'll be.' He pressed his lips together, raising his eyebrow mockingly at me.

I managed to gather enough energy to smile.

A sudden clap of thunder shook the walls of Dorian's ram-shackle house. I shuddered. Dorian, Abigail, Vesta, Calathea, Will and Ophelia jumped to their feet, staring at each other in dread.

Calathea looked towards the forest. 'Too late...'

Another clap of thunder rang out.

'It's coming from the dolmens,' Dorian said. 'Someone just passed through the portal to our world.'

'Noxes?' Vesta asked.

'Spirits don't use this portal. But even noxes don't have the power to leave Broseliand when the Ponthus beech portal is closed.'

'Unless the elder elves have awakened to open it for them,' Abigail mused. 'They wouldn't let the darkness stay in their land.'

'We need to get out of here,' Calathea called.

Dorian shook his head. 'If it's really noxes, it's too late.'

'We don't know who it is until we check,' Will said. 'Let's go.'

Dorian nodded, and they headed for the exit.

'You and Ophelia should stay here – and don't argue!' he cut off as I opened my mouth. 'In your condition, you can't help and will only be a burden.'

A chill of helplessness made my limbs shake, but I held back my tears by force of will, despite the tightness squeezing my throat. What if it were noxes? What if Will and the others were about to be killed because of me while I was hanging loose here, paralysed with fear? Faint, pathetic, hopeless creature! Will was right – I was a burden to him and the others and had been since the day I'd crossed the border of the two worlds.

'Lilly, don't worry. Try to remember everything I told you.' He smiled.

'Please... be careful,' I breathed, unable to restrain the tears that had welled up in my eyes.

He nodded and left the house. Ophelia clasped her knees together, her hands trembling as she fumbled with her scarf. I beckoned her over, and she sat down next to me. Taking her hand, I lied that everything was going to be all right.

Suddenly, the door creaked open and Thomas entered the house, smirking at me and dragging his sword behind him. All the oxygen seemed to burn out of the air. I tried to get up but couldn't find the strength. I wanted to pull the hilt of my own blade, but my hand wouldn't obey me.

'I promised to pay you back, didn't I?' he drawled. 'You thought your Will was out of control? Oh, Lilly, Lilly… If you'd listened to me, none of this would have happened. If I had my way, I'd just kill you here and now, but unfortunately, Noxohit wants you. And yet, why deny myself the pleasure?'

Starbursts exploded behind my closed eyelids as he slapped me across the face hard enough to throw my still partly paralyzed body to the floor. The thick taste of iron streamed from my nose to my mouth. The pulsating pain quickly spread across my face and plunged the world into a deafening cacophony.

He kicked me in the stomach. Searing agony clenched me into a curled ball as I tried to avoid his continuous blows. Ophelia jumped at him, but he threw her aside. She hit the wall and didn't get up again. I couldn't see anything behind the blur that clouded my mind.

Thomas grabbed my arm and pulled me out of the house.

'We never finished our business earlier,' a thousand chilly voices said. Once again it was Noxohit in Thomas's body. 'But do not worry, we have plenty of time.'

He dragged me along the ground; roots and stones, branches and pine needles peeled my skin away. I tried again to draw my sword, but it was in vain.

Somewhere close, I could hear the clash of swordplay.

'Oh, they are still alive…' he said. 'For the moment. This will not take long.'

He dropped me on the ground, glancing at me indifferently and releasing those black tentacles from his palm. They wrapped around me, lifting me into the air. Silent tears rolled from my eyes.

'There, there. It will be over very soon.'

He turned my motionless body around so I could watch as his noxes murdered those I loved. Will charged towards Noxohit, but another nox slipped under his wing, slicing his leg. He dropped to one knee, roaring, but forced himself up again, limping into the fight once more. Vesta was fighting back against three noxes, her whip shaking in her hands. Dorian and Abigail were struggling to protect themselves from another four, while Calathea was trying to strangle two with her branches. And Will, even wounded, was fighting three other fiends at once. We were outnumbered, and the noxes, all smirking like hyenas, seemed to feel no fatigue.

'See?' Noxohit savoured greedily every moment. 'And just think, this is all your fault, Lilly. You are not the last hope of humanity – you are not even a guardian. You should have left Faivendei when you had a chance. Now everyone you love is going to die. But you will be locked in your body for a while. You will have plenty of time to think about what you have done.'

Maddening panic clouded my mind; my spirit was running amok in my body, frozen by horror. Will and the others were clearly exhausting themselves in the battle.

But between the endless thrust and parry, Will had one brief moment of peace. He relaxed his shoulders, as if the tension had released from his body, and glanced at me, nodding and... smiling – so calmly, so serene. He believed in me; he believed I could save them. Where had he found this confidence? How could he ignore the obvious? I was too weak to even save myself.

I believe you can do it if you choose to, if you open your eyes and see how strong your true self really is. But if you let Noxohit drown you in fear, then, yes, we're all doomed... His words echoed in my memory. He'd told me Noxohit would exploit my compassion to destroy my moral defences; that if my heart was filled with fear, Noxohit would easily destroy me...

I wouldn't let that happen.

I closed my eyes and listened to my feelings, which slammed into my chest like tsunami waves. *Don't try to fight your thoughts and feelings – just be aware of them,* I said to myself. But how could I distinguish anything when the clang of swords was ringing in my ears and the tumult of internal chaos reverberated in my mind? It felt like I had a war going on inside me.

You will always be strong. No matter what obstacles come your way, you'll overcome them all... My mother had said. *You have everything you need... just have faith...*

I took a few deep breaths, trying to calm down or at least ease the inner storm. A wild fear shackled my senses, but what exactly was I afraid of? I was afraid for Will, I was afraid for the others. But if they were to die today, their souls would be reunited with the Universe, where only boundless peace reigned. While I was to be locked up in a Noxohit tunnel with a burning sense of guilt that they'd been killed because of me.

For thirteen years I'd lived alone in the Human World, thinking at the back of my mind that my parents had left me in the orphanage because there was something wrong with me. Now, when I'd found a new family in my friends, in Will... they were all to die because of my weakness, because of my worthlessness, because there was indeed something wrong with me.

It was as if lightning had struck me, and I opened my eyes. My thoughts weren't about Will, about Vesta, or about the others – I was suffering from my own helplessness. I was thinking about... myself.

I remembered Octavian's words. *Separate from your thoughts, from your emotions, from your body. Focus on me – dissolve into my soul.*

I cast off the veil of selfish despair that was obscuring my sight and glanced at Will and the others. There was no hesitation in their movements – they fought as if they'd said goodbye to their lives a long time ago. But now I could feel that each of them was burned by the flames of horror and panic they so skilfully hid inside. How had I not seen it before? Just like me, they were afraid; just like me they were vulnerable. But they kept fighting. They believed in me and were ready to die for their faith, which shone inside them like eternal light.

Even if I wasn't the last hope of humanity, even if I wasn't worthy of the first emanation and the weapon of light, even if I was the most pathetic vandor that ever existed on Earth, it didn't matter. I didn't know what my purpose was or who I was, but I knew who I wasn't. I wasn't a coward ready to give up before the battle began; I wasn't the one who wouldn't even try to fight fearing defeat. If I was destined to become a nox, then I would do it just like Will and Vesta: fighting until my last breath. For those I loved. For light and hope.

I closed my eyes, concentrated and saw the light. At first, it was just tiny flashes flickering around me, but the more I focused on them, the brighter they became, until they filled all the space. Everything was light; everything was one again.

The battle unfolded before my eyes, but instead of people, clusters of light shimmered around, and it was hard to distinguish who were noxes and who were guardians. Noxes' souls were distorted by the darkness of Noxohit, but the souls of the guardians were distorted by angst, and yet the light was shining in each of them, binding us all and making us one.

Light... I wasn't this body. I wasn't even this mind constantly tormented by fear and doubts. I was the light, just like all the people on this planet.

All the people...

Thomas.

I took a deep breath and focused on Noxohit's tentacles, which encircled my body. It seemed this darkness had opened its arms to me and, without resisting, I welcomed them inside my body and fell into the depths of his infinite tunnel.

'Lilly.' I heard my mother's voice but ignored it.

'Thomas,' I called into the dark.

His body, curled into a ball in the corner of the darkness, appeared before my eyes.

'You can't beat him,' he whispered.

'I'm not trying to.' I stepped closer to him. 'I want to help you.'

He snorted, but I kneeled next to him, pressing my palm to his chest. The shock wave knocked me into Thomas's memories.

RAIN. IT's DARK outside. A tiny room. Bed, sink, kitchen, closet. A little boy is writing something in a notebook while his mother makes soup. The key turns in the keyhole. A drunk father falls inside with a drugged, laughing girl in a miniskirt and torn black nylon stockings. He grabs the boy's mother by the hair and throws her into the closet. The boy runs after her. He's learned his lessons – he knows what will happen if he doesn't do it himself. The closet is locked with a key. The mother covers her son's ears, her tears roll down his cheeks.

Obscurity. Time lurches forward.

The boy returns home after school. Opens the door. His mother is lying on the floor in a pool of blood. The TV is blaring at full volume – a snow-white smile, advertising a toothpaste. He falls to his knees. His mother is dead. His father is snoring. The one who'd killed his mother, who'd beaten him since birth, that giant was now asleep, an empty bottle lying by his feet. Slowly and silently, he takes out the longest, sharpest, thinnest knife and creeps up to his father.

Lurch.

Night. The edge of the forest. An underground passage. One flickering lamp. The boy is sitting on the concrete floor, hugging his knees and silently wiping away the tears from his cheeks. Footsteps are approaching. The boy jumps to his feet, backing away. Has his father returned from the dead?

'Don't be afraid. I won't hurt you.' A familiar voice.

The man walks into the light. It's Christopher Raven.

'I can help,' he says to the boy.

Lurch.

Thomas becomes a warrior, but the past follows him. The noxes catch him and offer him a choice. He betrays the guardians, and every time he returns to Faivendei, Omnia meets him but says nothing.

'You know what I'm doing,' he says to her once. 'Why don't you exile me?'

'Balance,' she replies. 'The fall of one soul raises another. Soon she will come. She will be drowning in the mud of your darkness, but as a white lily – as a lotus – she might use it as a nursery to grow, to blossom and thrive. I cannot exile you from Faivendei; you have too important a role to play in her life.'

'Who are you talking about?'

'Soon... she will come.'

A SHOCK WAVE brought me back to the infinite tunnel. Thomas lay in the depths of darkness, twisted into a ball.

'Now you see. I don't need your help. You needed mine.'

'No, Thomas. It shouldn't be like this. I can save you.'

'My salvation was never part of the plan. But at least the fall of my soul can raise yours.' He smiled, his body glowing. 'Don't you see, Lilly? I'm the omen of your light.'

I opened my eyes, returning to reality. Will and the others were still alive.

And they would stay alive.

Taking another deep breath, I absorbed the sweet energy of the forest that surrounded us.

'Nice try,' said Noxohit in Thomas's body, turning me towards him and putting his hand on my chest.

The darkness beheld me through Thomas's eyes. But I was looking through it straight into the depths of his soul. There, I had seen the light. In his large, adult body lived a frightened boy with a crippled psyche and a broken fate. I wanted to help him. And I knew I could.

Suddenly, all other sounds faded. I could no longer hear the clash of swords, the shouts of my friends, the noxes, or even the rustle of the leaves... Not a single sound. Silence. I inhaled, absorbing the healing energy of nature. The vile smirk slowly slipped from Noxohit's face. His darkness burst into my body with the power of water falling down in a cascade.

The earth quaked, and everyone stopped fighting, trying to keep their balance. A stream of irrepressible ruby energy erupted out of the ground, wrapping around my body and continuing onwards into the sky.

It burned Noxohit's hand; he wailed but didn't let me go. He kept injecting me with darkness, struggling to finish what he had begun.

The red stream of energy curled back down from the sky and dissolved inside me. Its warmth passed through every single cell of my body before collecting in the pendant. I glanced at it: the lowest of the seven rings now had a ruby radiating an unearthly scarlet glow.

The first emanation.

I smiled, stretching out my hand and pressing it against Noxohit's chest. His eyes slowly lightened, revealing the whites – he was leaving Thomas's body, but not without a vile smirk contorting his lips.

'A worthy rival after all,' thousands of voices broke out from his mouth. 'My darkness embodies your soul like a second skin. There is no need to transform you – it will break you from within.'

His tentacles released me, and Thomas tried to escape.

But he couldn't move. My light was holding him still, and he growled and thrashed like a caged lion. Energy dark as oil poured out of his chest, turning into a black ball in my palm. Thomas's eyes turned a celestial colour, the inky snakes crawling over his neck disappeared, the rage contorting his face gave way to shock and bewilderment. The remnants of the dark energy left his body, and he fell to his knees, staring into the unknown.

I held the ebony sphere between my hands, watching it and squeezing, until it shrank to the size of a pearl, then transformed into a silver butterfly. It spread its wings and flew away.

Suddenly, Thomas jumped at me, swinging his sword. I closed my eyes, lifting my hands. The sound of metal plunging into flesh reached me. Mentally checking my body, I opened my eyes.

No!

Will was standing between Thomas and me. A moment passed and I noticed: he was unharmed, however thick red liquid was dripping from his sword. Thomas staggered back, blood spurting from his lips.

'Thank you...' he whispered and fell to the ground, deathly still, with wide, open eyes.

One by one, the noxes melted into a black mass and dissolved into the earth.

I kneeled next to Thomas to close his eyelids as if it would help his soul to rest.

Will stretched his hand to me, lifting me up. 'You can't save everyone, Lilly. But you saved us.' He smiled, pressing me tightly against his chest. 'I knew you could do it.'

Had I? Had I really done it?

My eyes drifted to the pendant, the tiny stone emitting red waves, surging and swaying like an aurora. I must have done it. But I still couldn't believe it.

'Are you all right?' I asked him. 'How's your leg?'

'Don't worry. Fern seeds will deal with this scratch in a matter of minutes.'

Vesta, Calathea, Abigail and Dorian ran over to us.

'Are you okay?' I looked them up and down.

They nodded, smiling.

Vesta's wide eyes were focused on the pendant. 'You got it!'

I picked it up again and studied the ruby glow. No... I still couldn't believe it.

'But how?'

How indeed?

'I think... I think I had to save the people I love. I had to save Ophelia in Broseliand. Otherwise Noxohit would've killed her, and I'd never get the first emanation. But then I almost became a nox. When Thomas tried to transform me, Noxohit himself was in his body, and his power was overwhelming. I was surrounded by his darkness... and I tried to overcome it, thinking I was fighting the most powerful evil in the Universe. But then I saw. All I had to do was to forget about his power, his darkness, and just focus on the light. And it was only thanks to you guys I managed to do it.'

'As simple as that.' Vesta laughed, as if all the tension had drained from her body in one go.

Will grinned at me. Abigail, Dorian and Calathea were also smiling.

'Ophelia!' I said, seeing her walking towards us. 'Are you all right?'

'I'm going to have a bump.' She touched the back of her head but flinched and pulled her hand away. 'But I'm fine.'

Suddenly, I heard footsteps approaching us from the depths of the forest. I braced myself for another fight, but Christopher appeared. He froze in place at the sight of Abigail, as if he was seeing a ghost.

'Mother?'

'Hello, son.'

'Mother!' He folded her into his arms. 'But how?'

'The first emanation was in Broseliand,' Will explained.

He cupped her face in his hands, scanning every inch of it as if trying to ensure his eyes weren't deceiving him. Ten years... almost as long as I had gone without seeing my parents.

'You'll tell me all about it later. We'll have plenty of time to talk.' He smiled at her and turned to Ophelia, who was looking at him with a mixture of hope and fear. 'Aisha is in Equilibrium, and she'll be fine. As will Hairito.'

Tension left her stiffened body, and a smile of relief tugged up the corners of her doll-like lips.

'So you did it after all.' Christopher beamed at me. 'You're going back home – to Faivendei.'

'But I can't—'

'Yes, you can. Surely you won't dare disobey Omnia's direct orders?'

'Does she want me back?'

'More than that. Tomorrow there will be a big celebration in Faivendei.'

'Why?'

Everyone looked at me as if I'd said something very stupid.

'This banquet is in your honour, Lilly,' Christopher explained.

'In... what? Are you sure you didn't misunderstand something?'

He laughed. 'Positive.'

I glanced at the ground, trying to process what I'd heard. I was going back... home. Maybe I was imagining this? Maybe I was in one of my dreams again?

'Are we invited?' Abigail asked Christopher.

'Of course, Mother. Why do you ask?'

'I'm not sure Gabrielle will be glad to see us after how we left.'

'She'll be thrilled to see you both,' Christopher reassured her.

'Not sure about that, but...' Abagail smiled. 'I miss home.'

'Christopher, we need to get back,' Vesta called. 'Noxohit will send his noxes again.'

We went into Dorian's house to collect our belongings and followed Christopher into the woods.

'Happy to go home?' Will asked.

I couldn't contain my grin. Slowly, it was sinking through me. 'I hadn't hoped to go back at all.'

'Lilly,' Calathea called me. 'I have to go. But I'll always be nearby.'

'Where are you going?'

'To protect people,' was all she said.

I looked at Will and Christopher. 'She saved our lives, fought beside us against the noxes. She protects people from evil spirits, and she has no home. In her own world, she's an outcast. She's one of us – a guardian – and we must take her to Omnia.'

Will laughed, shaking his head. 'First you bring a gargoyle to Faivendei, and now you want to scare everyone with a dryad?'

'I don't want to cause any problems,' Calathea said.

'Lilly is absolutely right.' Will gave her a friendly smile. 'Come with us.'

Her face lit up as if in her heart of hearts she'd hoped he'd say that. 'Truly?'

He nodded.

'I've always dreamed of meeting Omnia the Great.'

'Come on then,' I hurried her along. 'You'll like her.'

CHAPTER 20

FAMILY

THE WHITE BOAT decorated with pearls and precious stones brought us back to Faivendei. Nairin, spotting the first emanation of light on my chest, had fallen into a silent awe and had returned us home without any questions or complaints. That alone had been a pleasant surprise.

I checked myself out of habit, still not used to emerging dry from the water, but, as usual, there were only a few drops on my hands. The twilight was gathering over the forest, but it was light thanks to the soaring fern-flower seeds that illuminated the space around.

Home sweet home.

Omnia and Gabrielle stood next to each other on the little island behind the tree branches that hung right into the lake. It was hard to believe my eyes, but the closer we got to the shore, the more clearly I saw Gabrielle smiling. Her eyes were shining with sincere relief at the sight of her son returning home. The floating ladder stretched out from the ship, and Ophelia was the first one to rush down it towards Equilibrium.

'Lilly White,' Omnia murmured when we stepped onto the shore. 'You did get the first emanation.'

My eyes shifted to Will and Vesta. 'They did. I'm just wearing a pretty necklace.'

She smiled.

Gabrielle couldn't take her worried eyes off the blood on Will's jeans as he walked over to her.

'It's just a scratch,' he said, folding her slender body into his arms.

She seemed to be trying to restrain herself but soon lost the inner battle and clung to him, her shoulders sagging. For the first time she looked both vulnerable and happy, and a sincere warm feeling for her awoke in my heart. But I turned to Omnia. While she manifested in this body, I could talk to her, and there was something I was looking forward to asking.

'Omnia, I saw something in Thomas's memory. You knew I was coming. You knew who I was from the very beginning, didn't you?'

She nodded.

'Why did you want me to return to the Human World then?'

'Some of the future I had not seen before unveiled when I saw you face to face.'

The future that had made her cry. 'Can you tell me what it was?'

'I already have.' She grinned, leaving me befuddled as she walked over to Calathea. 'Well, well! Is there another forest spirit in our midst?'

'Yes, I...' Calathea stared at the ground. 'It's a great honour to meet you.'

Omnia let out a low chuckle. 'I know what you have done for my wards. For this I grant you shelter in my domain. Faivendei is your home now.'

She staggered back a step and glanced at us, as if making sure she hadn't imagined it. 'You'll let a spirit live among the guardians? After my brothers and sisters showed Noxohit the way to your land?'

'There are many spirits in Faivendei, including myself. I would be pleased if you joined us.'

'I've never had a home of my own. Thank you, Omnia; thank you for your trust. I won't fail you.'

I suddenly felt someone's searching gaze on me – Gabrielle was studying me from her considerable height. What was that on her face? A smile?

'Welcome back,' she said.

Those words, dry as her tone was, were honey to my ears.

She turned to her parents-in-law. 'Mother, Father.'

'You need to rest and prepare for tomorrow,' Omnia said. 'I will expect you all at the banquet. Calathea, stay with me please – I need to ask you a favour.'

Will, Vesta and I were heading to Equilibrium when we saw a man walking in our direction. His face seemed familiar to me. Was he a shaman? I was pretty sure we'd already been introduced to each other, but his name had slipped my mind. He'd been keeping his eyes down but looked up and beamed at me as if we were old friends.

'Lilly, you're back! Hi!'

'Yes... Erm... Hi.'

He smiled understandingly. 'Quentin.'

'Oh, yes, sorry. Hi, Quentin.'

His eyes lingered on the pendant of Luminiferos. 'Is that what I think it is?'

'Yes,' Will almost growled, making me blush.

Quentin flinched, as if he hadn't even noticed Will until now. 'Anyway... welcome back.' He continued on his way.

'You're now a celebrity in Faivendei,' Vesta said. 'I hope fame doesn't go to your head and make you forget your friends.'

Will raised his eyebrow at me. 'Now I'll have to protect you from more than just noxes.'

'They just don't know yet that I wouldn't even have got the pendant on my own. If it wasn't for you guys, I'd never have made it.'

'Hallelujah!' Vesta teased. 'I hope you won't try to push us away anymore. We're a team, Lilly. And you're right, you wouldn't have got far without us.'

I laughed. I just couldn't contain my happiness. It was such a relief to be here and to know that all my friends were safe.

At Equilibrium, we found Aisha and Hairito's room, where Ophelia was already sitting on the edge of the bed holding her sister's hand. She put a finger to her lips for silence, and Vesta, Will and I tiptoed over to them. Hairito was snoring on another bed with her wings bandaged.

'They'll be fine,' Ophelia whispered.

A nurse entered the room and called Will to treat the wound on his leg. Vesta went home to finally sleep in her own bed, and I took a shower, put on the softest bathrobe in the world and fell asleep with Ophelia in the room next door to where Aisha and Hairito slept.

WHEN I WOKE up it took me some time to recall who and where I was. Ophelia's face was hovering over mine. Ophelia... Equilibrium... Aisha...

I started awake and looked at the pendant – the first emanation was still there. It wasn't a dream.

'Finally!' Ophelia whispered. 'They were about to put off the banquet because of you. No one in Faivendei liked that idea, as you might expect.'

'What time is it?'

'Half past five.'

I jumped up. 'What? In the evening?'

'On the evening of the following day. You slept the clock around.'

'But why didn't anyone wake me up?'

'Omnia forbade it. She said you needed to recover. You probably would have slept a few more hours if I hadn't asked the lutins to stop playing the piano. When the music cut off, you woke up. Technically, I didn't wake you, so I didn't disobey Omnia's order.'

I let out an amused huff. 'I'm sure Omnia would see it that way too. Has Aisha come round yet?'

'No, but the nurse said she would wake up in few hours.'

'What about Hairito?'

Ophelia pointed under my bed, and I found the gargoyle curled up, snoring softly. Her wings looked perfectly sound. As if sensing my gaze on her, she woke up and jumped on my bed.

'Are you all right?' I asked, petting her.

She spread her broad wings proudly, making me smile.

'Come on, we have to go. You need to change for the banquet,' Ophelia called.

When we reached our treehouse, she opened the door and Tarry jumped on her, rustling his pincers.

She stroked his hairy belly and laughed. 'You missed me then, sweetie?'

'Hi, Tarry,' I said.

He bobbed up and down and rustled his pincers. I'm pretty sure it was an enthusiastic 'hello'.

'Let's go,' Ophelia ordered me, and we went to Aisha and Ophelia's room.

She opened the wardrobe and began searching through her sister's dresses nonchalantly.

'Ophelia... Was it difficult for you there... with the noxes?'

'No. It's like it didn't happen to me. All I remember is leaving home in Faivendei and waking up in Broseliand.'

She suddenly stopped sorting through the dresses and turned to me. 'Lilly, you saved my life there and I'll never forget it.'

I felt a little uneasy under her gaze. Why was the wisdom of a fading old woman reflected in the eyes of this seven-year-old child? A life surrounded by frequent deaths had forced her to develop beyond her years, which was impressive of course, but a little sad.

I smiled at her. 'No problem.'

'Here we go! This one is just perfect for the occasion.' She stood on tiptoe to take from the rack a scarlet, knee-length chiffon dress.

I glanced at the make-up table. 'You're not going to—'

'Oh, yes, I am. Everyone is going to look at you, and the pillow lines are still imprinted on your face. Don't even argue. Sit down.'

SUMPTUOUS FESTIVE TABLES, laden with culinary delights and adorned with candles and rustic decorations, crowded Sodalitas Square. It seemed all the guardians of Faivendei were there that night. One of the organisers led us to our seats, and as we walked through the square, people rose from their chairs, shaking my hand and looking at the pendant as if it were the eighth wonder of the world. Our seats were in the centre, next to Will, Vesta and Calathea, who were already there. There was also a seat for Darius. But it was empty.

We walked over to the three other chairs. Will smiled when he spotted me. Ophelia quickly settled next to him. I couldn't help but laugh at his displeased expression as I sat next to her. Hairito landed by my side, and a mountain of strawberry-flavoured oatmeal cookies appeared on her plate. Her pupils dilated in an instant, and she licked her lips.

'That dress matches the pendant perfectly,' Will complimented me.

'Of course,' Ophelia replied with an air of importance. 'I did think of that beforehand, you know.'

He and I exchanged looks over her head, giggling silently, when Omnia appeared in the centre of the square.

'My dear family! Yesterday was a significant day.'

Everyone fell silent.

'Yesterday, one person among us proved that humans deserve salvation, and the Universe took a step towards us. Many of you thought Luminiferos was just a myth, but it is real and the proof is in front of you. Let the first triumph of Lilly White be a reminder to us all that light is stronger than darkness, no matter how invincible darkness might seem. We thank you, Lilly, for the inspiration you gave us with your first victory. We thank you for the light you carried with you from the day you were born.' Her eyes drifted away and she smiled at someone.

I followed her gaze and was so glad to see Dr Blake was here. She was sitting next to Christopher. I owed her an apology for that scene I'd made.

'But,' Omnia said, 'before you become an official member of our family, you must take the oath.'

She glanced at me expectantly, and so did the other guests.

'What are you waiting for?' Ophelia hurried me. 'Go!'

Profound silence reigned in the square. I got up and went over to Omnia, trying to ignore the many curious stares that followed me.

'You still remember the oath, don't you?' she asked me quietly as I approached her.

Of course I did. Two months I'd lived in Faivendei, and I'd started every day reading the oath, hoping to become a guardian one day. I hadn't done it the past few days, giving up on the idea of returning to Faivendei or of even staying alive for any length of time, but I couldn't possibly forget it. I nodded.

She stretched out her hand towards the willow, and blossoms flew to her along with fern-flower seeds. They danced around each other, joining in a sparkling blush-coloured wreath. I couldn't believe it. It was the initiation.

I remembered the moment Will had first told me about Noxohit – about the threat looming over humanity. I thought I'd found my life's purpose then. Of course I hadn't dared to dream I could defeat Noxohit. I would have been satisfied with protecting the lives of a couple of dozen people from noxes.

But fate had other plans.

The cost of my life now was seven emanations collected together. If I found Luminiferos, I could save humanity. If not, I'd die... or worse. I wasn't scared, at least not today. It was an honour for me to live for the prosperity of all living beings and the planet as a whole. An honour to officially become a guardian.

But in the back of my mind, I remembered that I still had six emanations to gather.

Omnia raised the wreath above my head and held it there. 'Don't swear to me. Swear to your family.'

I turned to the crowd. How many people were there? Five hundred? A thousand? Myriad eyes were studying me. My attention jumped from one face to another, but I found no traces of condemnation, envy or malevolence. Their eyes shone with the light of renewed hope. The hope that I shared with them. I took a deep breath.

'As a guardian I, Lilly White, do solemnly swear
To use my gift in the service of others,
To protect and heal in the name of love,
To thrive and progress as one with all living beings,
To never yield to darkness,
And to carry my title with dignity here and above.'

I bowed to the crowd, and Omnia placed the wreath on my head. 'Welcome to the new member of our family!'

The guardians shot up from their seats, cheering, whistling and clapping.

'Now, please,' she said, 'let us feast!'

I turned to her. 'Thank you, Omnia. I won't let you down.'

She smiled. 'Now that you're one of us, I have a little gift for you.'

'I thought initiation was the gift.'

'Initiation was the right you earned.' She winked. 'Come with me.'

She walked towards the woods, and I followed her with Will, Hairito and Vesta joining us. As we were making our way through the forest, I couldn't shake the feeling the surroundings were quite familiar. But the path was new. In fact, the path hadn't been here before. I wanted to ask Omnia where exactly we were heading, when I heard familiar voices talking behind us. I looked back: Dr Blake and Christopher were following us as well. Will studied my former 'child psychologist' with a puzzled look.

'I'll explain later,' I said and walked over to Dr Blake. 'I'm so glad to see you. Thank you for coming.'

She smiled. 'I couldn't do otherwise. If only your parents were here. They would be so proud of you, Lilly. I'm sorry for doubting you earlier. I must have forgotten how stubborn you can be.'

I laughed softly. 'Dr Blake, please forgive me for everything I said to you last time. I behaved terribly, and I'm deeply—'

'No need to apologise. I understand.'

'All's well that ends well,' Christopher said, casting an eye towards the emanation.

'I couldn't have done it alone.' My eyes slid to Will and Vesta. 'I was lucky my friends were with me. And we still have six more emanations to collect.'

'And you'll do it,' he said without the slightest hesitation.

'Initially you were the only one who believed I could collect as many as one. Even I didn't.'

He chuckled, and I couldn't help but smile to myself. Next to him I felt as comfortable and calm as under a cashmere blanket in front of a fireplace with a book in my hands and a mug of chamomile tea on a stormy day. There was nothing hidden or false in his words and actions. Good will shone in his eyes and smile. He was diplomatic but not distant, composed but not aloof. I didn't know him that well but felt as if I could trust him with my life. Of course, I was incredibly lucky to be under the auspices of a man like him. But it was still a mystery to me why he'd singled me out to begin with.

'Sorry for asking, but... my parents. How did you know them?'

Dr Blake glanced at him with a sly grin.

'I thought it was obvious,' he mused.

'Not to me.'

He was silent for a moment. 'Remember when I told you that story about me and Jane?'

'Yes, but what does— no. I'm pretty sure that's impossible.'

The others halted, listening to us.

'Jane was your mother, Lilly. As you remember, she decided to save two hundred years of my life. We separated, and sometime later she married your father, Robert. When you came to Faivendei, I couldn't believe my eyes – you look so much like her. And your perseverance, your willpower, your inner light – it seemed her best qualities manifested in you. I knew that if Jane had searched for Luminiferos, she would have succeeded. That's why I believed in you.'

His words stirred up the water from the bottom of the quagmire, and the memories that floated to the surface, though joyful, put a damper on me. I remembered how, as a child, I'd had a nightmare and my mother had lain down in my bed, pressing me to her warm body, which smelled of June roses in full bloom. How she'd sung my favourite Selkies' Lullaby, and how I'd fallen asleep again to the angelic lilt of her voice. During the thirteen years that I'd searched for this world, the memories of her had been an oasis for my barren soul, a glimpse of hope in the ocean of despair. But the way she'd died...

I lowered my gaze. Hairito whined, leaning on my legs and looking up at me. Those two yellow pools of sadness made me smile. No. Today I would cry only for joy.

Christopher put a hand on my shoulder. 'Will told me how she passed away. But now she rests in peace. I don't think there's anything worse than living under the yoke of darkness. She's free now, Lilly.'

I nodded, continuing to walk. 'I just hope I'll meet her one day. Not only in my dreams.'

'And you will. When your time comes.' Dr Blake smiled at me. 'By the way, Christopher showed me the sketch of your parents' house. Tell me, do you still dream about it?'

We stopped in front of an arched bridge. I recognised the place now. On the other side of the river was my secret spot, that reminded me so much of the place where I'd lived with my family for the first five years of my life.

And now, nestled on the far side, was a little castle with a lonely tower. An identical copy of the house from my dreams.

Omnia flew over to me. 'I thought it was time for you to have a home of your own.'

My mouth dropped open. 'Thank you! Thank you, thank you, thank you!'

She grinned and vanished, and Christopher and Dr Blake returned to the banquet. I ran across the arched bridge. Will, Hairito and Vesta followed me.

I entered the house, reached the fireplace, then continued to the kitchen, studied the stained glass with the image of a white lotus and smiled. Every single detail here was just like it had been in my dreams.

I crept back into the corridor, glancing at the door to the master bedroom. I approached it, not daring to turn the doorknob, but Hairito didn't wait for me and opened the door herself. I stepped inside. She jumped onto the bed and began sniffing and rubbing against it as if it were gargoyle catnip.

'What's going on with her?' Will asked.

I shrugged. 'No idea.'

Everything here was as I remembered it. In the centre stood a bed of dark wood inlaid with geometric patterns with an emerald canopy suspended from four spiral-carved posts. A maroon carpet covered the floor, a picture of a coniferous forest hung on the wall and thick closed curtains blocked the light from outside.

But one thing was new. A small object on the nightstand...

So often I'd imagined that I recalled the faces of my parents and brother, but that was just a fiction of my mind. For some reason, the daoshee's magic hadn't worked on me completely, so I remembered them. But their faces had been wiped clean from my memory. My mother's eyes, father's smile and brother's hands: that was all I could remember about their appearance.

But now there was a small framed photo on the nightstand. I swallowed hard, bringing it closer to my eyes.

Four people, one family. My family. Once I saw their faces, the memories came flooding back. My mother was graceful, exquisitely beautiful, and I wondered how Christopher could compare me to her. She had finely drawn facial features and her eyes... well, now I understood why I reminded him of my mother. She was holding a little girl in her hands – baby me. Next to her stood a beaming man whose eyes sparkled with enthusiasm, as if his glass was always half full. Exactly the same playful smile was reflected on the face of the young boy – my brother – whom he was holding in his arms. Seeing them so happy when I knew they had since been transformed into noxes made my stomach roil. Where could my brother and father be now? They were trump cards in Noxohit's hands, and surely he would use them against me.

Vesta sat on the bed in front of me. 'Are you all right?'

Will put his hands on my shoulders.

I nodded, placing the photo frame back on the nightstand.

'Yeah, more or less,' I said. 'I'll have time to enjoy my home, but now we have to return to the banquet or there'll be nothing left. I don't know about you, but I'm as hungry as a wolf.'

We returned to Sodalitas Square. When there was almost no food left and we had satiated our appetites, musical instruments appeared in the centre of the square. The harp leaned back by itself, the violins hung in the air, as did the clarinet, lutes, flutes, accordion, bagpipes and oboes. Everyone jumped from their chairs, gathering into the centre of the square.

'Oh, this is going to be fun!' Will smiled, grabbed my hand and led me into the crowd.

Ophelia beamed, taking Hairito by her paw and following us. Vesta returned to her supper, shaking her head in disapproval of all this unhealthy excitement.

'What's going on?' I asked Will.

'Well, even though we all came to Faivendei from different parts of the world and we can't even say for sure if we're in Brittany, we still try to follow the local traditions.'

'I don't understand.'

The violins and lute started to play, and I immediately recognised the cheerful Breton tunes. Will put his arm around me and circled, jumping up and down. I didn't know what to do, tripped over his feet, couldn't keep up with him and laughed loudly at myself. Other instruments joined the violin and the lute, and all the dancers took each other's hands, leading a fast dance in a circle. There was less free space between us than between sardines in a can, but the atmosphere of joy and unity was so overwhelming that it didn't seem to bother anyone.

'I like this tradition! But I need some water!' I rushed over to the table, panting, when the melody stopped.

Will, Ophelia and Hairito followed me.

'Vesta, why don't you dance? It's so much fun.'

'Not for me,' she said without taking her eyes off her food.

I poured myself a glass of water and drained it quickly.

'Rest up a bit,' Will told me as he took his seat.

I slumped into my chair. 'I made a complete fool of myself out there, but I don't care. We enjoyed ourselves, didn't we?'

I was so ecstatic I didn't seem to notice anything, but when our eyes met, the music and the buzzing of the crowd started to ebb, as if somebody had turned the volume down.

Ophelia stepped between us, breaking our eye contact and grabbing a large glass of water with her small hands. She drank it all in one go and turned to me, squinting. 'I don't sense fear in you anymore.'

I couldn't help but chuckle. 'What do you sense then?'

'I don't know, but I like it. It's very sweet. It's like the scent of briars in bloom. Wait a minute...' Her eyes slowly drifted to Will. 'You have exactly the same scent...' She turned to me again, then to him, back at me, back at him, and closed her eyes, blushing. 'Did I sit in the wrong chair?'

I laughed loudly this time, and Will smiled, getting up from the table in a single fluid motion and stretching out his hand to me. 'Let's go.'

'Where now?'

'You're not the only one who has a secret spot in Faivendei. I've seen yours. Let me show you mine.'

CHAPTER 21

GARGOYLE

I GOT UP FROM my chair and we walked off hand in hand. Well, he walked. I was running trying to keep up with him.

'Will, what are you up to?'

He snickered but didn't answer.

Suddenly a familiar voice came from an oak. 'If someone had told me William Raven actually knows how to have fun, I would never have believed them.'

Darius. He was back. He hadn't run away.

He leaped off the branch he was sitting on and walked over to us. 'Are my eyes deceiving me?'

Will stood still. 'You surprised me, Darius.'

'Did you really think I'd run away with your key?'

'To be honest, that's exactly what I thought.'

'Well.' Darius rolled up his sleeve, revealing his forearm. 'Maybe now you'll start to trust me.'

Will gripped his hand, grinning. 'I don't think so.'

'*Clavidere,* William,' Darius said, giving his signature smile.

The three wavy ink lines disappeared from Darius's forearm and returned to Will's.

'Right!' Darius clapped his hands. 'Now, I'm going to go tell the most beautiful guardians I can find who they actually have to thank for getting the first emanation.' His eyes darted between me and Will. 'Don't worry, I won't keep you. I see you're both itching to hide somewhere secluded.'

'Darius, you're an asshole!' Will rolled his eyes at him, but he was already gone.

I couldn't help but peer at Will with an I-told-you-so expression, and he chuckled, tilting his head to the sky. The moonlight reflected off the muscles in his neck. I averted my gaze and willed myself to stop thinking about covering every inch of it with my kisses.

'So, where are you taking me, William Raven?'

He smiled and stepped close to me – too close – lifting my chin towards his face. I tilted back my head, feeling my heart faltering yet again at how miniscule I was compared to him. My invincible majestic cliff.

His thumb traced gently over my lips. 'If only you knew what effect it has on me when you say my name.'

Oh my...

He set my mouth ablaze with the necessity to graze his lips, to be held in his strong arms. I was afraid of it as much as I craved it. His expression and his body language changed, as if he was using all his Raven's power to read through me and give me all that I lusted for. How would it feel to be his? To submit to this intense ocean knowing that he, with his highly developed intuition, knew exactly what I needed. How would it be for him? To feel how the touch of his lips erased all the boundaries and common sense in my mind, to feel how passion broke free within me, how I savoured his every touch.

I reeled back, taking a deep breath to cool myself down.

I didn't know where he was taking me, but I guessed what was on his mind. The same thing that was on mine. It was too much for me to say no, but I had to. We couldn't be together.

All of a sudden, Ray flew up to him and circled over his head, disintegrating into thousands of feathers that gradually formed silky jet-black wings behind Will's back. My knees weakened. Statuesque, tall and unfairly handsome, he stood in his tuxedo like an angel from heaven, but his gaze, his lips, his powerful wings made him too seductive. He didn't look like a man – he looked like one of Zeus's sons, who'd run from Olympus to Earth in search of temptation. He was silent, as if reading my mind and enjoying my reaction. Beautiful as an angel, he was luring me like a demon from hell.

'Why the wings?' I asked, my voice shaky.

'We have to get to the top of Dormont. Of course we can walk there, but I'm afraid it might take a while.' He looked down at my feet. 'And it might be a little uncomfortable in your heels.'

'Ophelia insisted on them.'

He stepped closer. We were alone in the forest; only trees and gleaming fern flowers witnessed us, and one kiss wouldn't take his power away…

No.

It was useless to look for excuses. We couldn't be together. The moment our relationship began, it was doomed to end. Either he would have come to his senses or I would have broken up with him, shattering my heart into rhinestones at the same time. I had to be wise; I had to be strong for both of us. I backed away.

'Are you afraid of me?'

'No. I'm afraid of myself.'

He took another cautious step, like a tiger stalking its prey, and picked me up in his arms.

And frowned at me. 'Your heart…'

'I'm afraid to fly,' I replied, perhaps too quickly.

'Don't be. I'll be careful.' He smirked slyly, not buying my excuse.

We took to the skies. The higher we soared, the more the picturesque view opened before my eyes, and it helped me to take my mind off of Will's plump lips, which were now so close to mine.

Hovering above the water, three mossy paths thickly decorated with glass candleholders converged at the centre, where Omnia's majestic tree bloomed – the heart of the forest, protecting the land. Fern flowers painted the forest with a golden-scarlet glow, and their seeds lit up all the space around. The spacious marble square of Gothic Sodalitas was filled with a tremendous crowd of guardians, still jumping and laughing, dancing and singing to energetic Breton tunes. I glanced at the witches' cabins that nested in the canopies of mighty redwoods, at the shamans' conical towers in their spiral. Sodalitas, Exilis and Amedas – one castle and two villages that had brought me so much joy…

I'd crossed the portal to the Spirit World looking for my family, for my life's purpose; they weren't what I'd expected, but I'd found them both in Faivendei. I placed my head on Will's shoulder, leaving all the worry behind and just revelling in the moment.

We reached the top of the hill, and he set me on my feet. I walked to the edge of the cliff.

'Faivendei is breathtaking.'

I heard him approaching me. My focus was so sharp that when he put his hands on my waist, I flinched.

'Happy birthday, Lilly,' he murmured in my ear.

A searing current rushed through my veins, making everything pulse, but I stepped away from him. I had to keep my mind clear despite the whirlpool of dizzying sensations that were about to charge at me.

But suddenly, I realised what he'd just said. It was the fifth of November.

'Holy Universe! It's my birthday!' I clapped my hands to my mouth. 'But how do you... ah... the archive.' Aisha had entered my details in the archive on my first day in Faivendei.

He took from his pocket a mirror with a white lily carved on it. The mirror that he hadn't wanted to give Anaxel in the Border World. 'I didn't make it for that siren. I made it for you.'

'Thank you, Will.'

I opened it. A familiar tune played, and out of the white haze appeared an image of Will and me dancing our first waltz at that very first ball. I gasped. He and even I, we were beautiful there – almost perfect together. And the way he looked at me...

I swallowed. 'Will...'

'When you arrived in Faivendei, I felt nothing but hostility towards you. Omnia was clearly afraid of you, and you brought that gargoyle. My mother asked me to keep an eye on you, and I did. But the more I watched you, the more I wanted to get to know you better. At first, I couldn't believe I was seeing the real you. People just aren't that kind, I thought. You're sincere, like an angel. So pure... My white lily.' He gently tucked a strand of my hair behind my ear. 'But most important, your kindness is not a weakness. No, it's the backbone of a strength and courage like I've never seen before.' His lips broke into a crooked smile.

'And your eyes... they hypnotise me. So many times I watched you without taking in anything you said because all my attention was focused on your eyes. I thought you'd bewitched me, because I'd never experienced anything like it before. And trust me, I've met many women in my eighty-eight years. But none of them were like you. You've taken complete control of me. I thought I knew life, but you came and turned my world upside down.

'I tried to fight it. What's the point of entering into a relationship if any of us can die tomorrow? But at the same time, what kind of life is it when you don't live today because you fear tomorrow? I've had my sorrows and I left them behind; I'm ready for a new chapter in my life with you, Lilly. I found you and I'll never let you go.'

He leaned towards me, his lips approaching mine.

It pained me almost physically, but I slipped out of his arms. All I wanted was to be with him, and his confession made obeying common sense absolutely unbearable. 'Will, you can't be with me. I'm not one of the Simtri clan.'

'You're trying to save my hundreds of years, ignoring that without you they'll be years of misery. My heart... how to explain... Imagine a healthy heart beating in the rhythm of life and abundance, a firm and strong heart. Now imagine how the horrors of the past turn this beautiful engine into a slitted, shrunken and barely beating knob of flesh. The longer you look at these numerous bleeding cuts, the more clearly you see the faces of loved ones who are no longer there. You hear their screams, begging for help. You see their faces distorted with pain and ask yourself why they're dead and you're still alive. These memories, like knife wounds, dot my entire heart.

'At the beginning of my life, I didn't see much death; I didn't know its poisonous power. The older I got, the more wounds accumulated, and my heart stopped healing itself. It was beating sluggishly, and every pulse of the decomposing, fetid flesh was a sharp pain in my chest. No human should see so much death in one lifetime.

'Then you entered the church in Dinan. I knew then that our destinies were intertwined. So the voice of intuition told me, but I tried to resist it with all my might. You looked so defenceless, so tender, so vulnerable – absolutely not adapted to the world I lived in. I thought you wouldn't last long... either you'd leave of your own free will, or the noxes would turn you. I just wasn't ready for another blow.

'But the more I watched you, the harder it became to fight against fate. Your zeal to fight Noxohit when you didn't yet know you were a vandor struck me of course, but it wasn't only the power of your spirit that attracted me. As Omnia said, you carry the light with you wherever you go. You agreed to this suicide mission not to prove that you deserve to be loved, as you said once. You agreed to it because you see the best in people, because you believe in humanity. When I gave free rein to my temperament, you patiently watched me, not succumbing to the whims of a wounded ego. Your bright eyes seemed to shatter my shield and look straight into the depths of my soul in search of the reason for my rudeness. The same with Vesta, Aisha and even Thomas. For you, only good people exist to whom bad things have happened. How long have I been looking for one who would unify in herself not only beauty but also inner strength, not only dignity but also kindness. Yes, I'm mad about you, but, Lilly, I've lived long enough to learn how to resist the first impulses of my feelings. I wouldn't go against solid logic if there was another option. There is none.' He stepped towards me. 'I don't want three hundred years if they're spent without you.'

I stepped back, my limbs shaking. 'Don't say that. You don't know what you're talking about.'

'I do.' He continued towards me.

I circled him. 'We have six more emanations to find. You said that was my top priority now. We can come back to this talk afterwards.'

'I've made my decision.' He stepped closer.

I stepped aside, balancing on the edge of the cliff. 'What if it was a hasty decision?'

He moved close to me, spreading his wings. I couldn't run anywhere.

'Will, I just want to protect you...'

The smile vanished from his face in an instant, turning his gaze cold if not hostile. 'Lilly, I made my choice, and I'm asking you to make yours. I can wait as long as you need, but if you've decided to delay until my interest in you fades, then let me warn you, that will never happen. If you're sure you don't want to be with me, then have the courage to tell me right now.' He stepped back, folding his wings and clearing my way. 'I love you, Lilly. But if you don't feel the same, just tell me and I'll carry you back to the banquet.'

I had no other moves to make. It was checkmate. My composure resembled withered aspen leaves, and those three words he'd uttered were a gust of wind, exposing the thin branches of the tree, until there was only one single leaf left. It stubbornly held on to the twig, unwilling to give up.

He loved me...

The wind died down, silencing my mind. As if in a final farewell, the leaf grew still and loosened its grip, floating down like a feather.

He loved me...

My feet were still on earth, but my soul was in the Garden of Eden.

I stepped closer to him, so close that I could feel the warmth of his body. Neither of us was moving or breathing. I tilted my head back so I could look at his face. His expressive aquamarine eyes studied every inch of my face, as if trying to imprint it on his memory or stretch the moment out for eternity, while I was begging inwardly for his lips. A moan escaped my mouth when he clasped me in his arms, as if he'd waited for this all his life. A bit too strong, but if he didn't hold me, I would certainly collapse.

'My angel...' He pressed his lips against mine.

I put my arms around his muscled body and plunged into the warm azure ocean of love. Through the thin fabric of my chiffon dress I felt our hearts throbbing in unison as his lips – as velvet as his voice – greedily savoured mine. He smiled and lifted me up with absolutely no effort.

I examined the softness of his face with the tips of my fingers just like in the diamond cave. The light of the full moon reflected in his aquamarine eyes, sparkling with relief and happiness. No regret or fear or hesitation. Just determination and an insatiable need to feel me... to be sure it wasn't a dream... to be sure I was his. I leaned towards his lips, and goosebumps passed through my passion-inflamed body as they instantly found mine.

May this last forever...

'See? Why run away from your feelings?' He put me down on my feet and kissed me again. 'I know you love me. There's no need to deny it.'

'I don't.' I stood on tiptoe, reaching for his lips again.

'I love you, Lilly,' he whispered into my mouth, looking expectantly at me.

'I love you, Will.'

He smiled with relief as if he'd needed me to put my obvious feelings into these three words – as if he still couldn't believe it despite all his intuition. He leaned down for my lips again. And again. And again. His kisses were growing more ardent, his hands sliding more freely along the thin fabric of my dress, and every cell of my body yearned for more. I couldn't find the strength to stop him. A little more and I would have fallen into his abyss, forgetting everything, even my own name.

But soon he stopped himself, his gaze cutting towards the wind caressing the leaves.

'No. Not now!' he snapped at the air.

It pulled me out of my rapture in an instant. 'What? What's happening?'

'It's all right. I just don't want to let you go.' He smiled, kissing me again. 'Aisha's regained consciousness.'

'Really?' I stepped away from him. 'We have to get to Equilibrium.'

It was as if the Universe was helping us.

He sighed but picked me up and soared into the air.

When we got to Equilibrium, I went straight to Aisha's room. I reached for the door handle, but Will stopped me.

'You two should talk in private.'

He pulled me to him and kissed me again, as if it would never be enough for him. Certainly, it would never be enough for me. But the door opened and Ophelia came out. She blushed as if realising she was once again in the wrong place at the wrong time. We smiled.

'She wants to talk to you,' she said to me and ran away.

'I have to go,' I said, but he drew me towards him and we kissed again. 'Will, I really need to go.'

'I know.' He smiled, pressing his forehead against mine. 'We have a whole life ahead of us.'

I kissed him on the cheek and opened the door to Aisha's room. Casting one more glance at him, I closed the door behind me.

Aisha looked much better, yet her pale face was laden with fatigue.

'Lilly,' she drawled feebly. 'Come here.'

I walked over to her. Hairito was sitting there too.

'Lilly, please… if you can, forgive me. I lost my mind when Ophelia was kidnapped. I got mad at you when you went to the ball and used animal vision to find the noxes. They weren't lying – I called them. When you apologised, you made me feel so ashamed of what I'd done. But my worry for Ophelia was still stronger. I promised my parents I'd protect her. When the spirits attacked us in the woods, near the portal to Broseliand, I realised that I would die fighting them when I could have died for my sister. So I returned to the Human World, and the noxes were already there – they just didn't know how to get through the portal. I offered myself to them in exchange for Ophelia, but they said they'd just kill her if I didn't take them to you. I know that it's hard to forgive, and yet—'

'Aisha, stop. I understand everything. You almost died saving me. If it weren't for you, I'd be a nox by now.'

'It was the least I could do. Please let me continue the search for emanations with you. I want to make amends.'

'Of course. But what about Ophelia?'

'It was her idea.'

'A little wise woman.' I grinned, and Aisha smiled back.

'Do you forgive me?'

'I do. But there's one thing you need to tell me.' I glanced at Hairito. 'She spoke to you in Broseliand, didn't she?'

'I should have told you straight away, but I was afraid if you found out, it would distract you from saving Ophelia.'

'I don't understand.'

'You better sit down.'

I settled next to Hairito. She didn't look up at me.

'I can't read her mind, but I understand her when she talks to me. The first time was when they kidnapped Ophelia, then in Broseliand, and now she's told me her full story. Well, as far as she remembers it,' Aisha sighed. 'I don't know how to say this—'

'Just say it.'

'We've often wondered why Hairito acts so human. Lilly, it's because this gargoyle has your mother's soul.'

I froze. My whole body and my mind went numb. *What did she just say?*

'Erm…' I finally managed to mumble. 'Is this some kind of a joke?'

'No, it's not. Your mother was killed near the church. When she died, the memory of you came completely back to her and she couldn't leave this world without making sure you were all right. Her soul had already left her body, but the power of her love was so strong that she animated the stone gargoyle on the roof of that church. She had unfinished business here and returned to life in the body of Hairito to bring you back your power.'

I remembered my mother's last words in the dream, when she'd left the room and disappeared into the light. *I will always be here for you.* That was the same day Hairito had shown up. I suddenly felt lightheaded.

'That might explain how she found out about the ring that contained my power and why she didn't want to give me the letter at the lake. And her human behaviour. And why she was so glad to see my new home. But…' I turned to Hairito. 'Why haven't you said anything all this time?'

Hairito lowered her head again.

'Lilly, she has your mother's soul, but she isn't your mother. She has a character of her own, a life of her own. Your mother's memories are like dreams for her – very vivid but still dreams. Hairito told me that the only thing that kept your mother sane while she was a nox was mentally repeating your name. The daoshee wiped her memory of you, but she still remembered your name and the feeling associated with it. Repeating it over and over again brought saving wisps of light in the infinite darkness. And sometimes she felt as if you were calling her back too. Even not remembering you, she carried her love through that darkness. That's why Hairito has such a strong bond with you.'

She had been calling me? All these years I'd dreamed about her and my family only because her spirit had called to mine. My eyes burned with swelling tears, and I sobbed. Sobbed for her purity, for her strength, for her love.

Hairito seemed to say something. I looked at Aisha.

'She's asking for your forgiveness,' Aisha said.

I scooped Hairito in my arms like a humongous cat, wrapping my hands around her and feeling warmth streaming through my chest like a ray of sunshine. Yes, my mother was dead, but her spirit was here, with me. Even after physical death, she – my holy guardian angel – had never stopped protecting me.

I LEFT EQUILIBRIUM with Hairito, intent on heading to my new old home. I had no strength left to think about everything that had happened today. The repeated assault of emotions had left me dizzy.

I strode towards home. The voices of celebration coming from the square started to sound like they were under water and at the same time became deafeningly loud. My hands started shaking, my eyes went dark and I halted halfway to the house as if rooted to the spot.

What the hell was going on?

The gloomy shadows of the trees sifted through the murk, and there wasn't a single fern-flower seed that would dispel the darkness. I continued on my way, almost running.

I burst into the house I'd seen so often in my dreams, hoping the familiar setting would save me from the invisible and probably non-existent force that followed me. But when I walked into the living room, my unease gripped me even tighter. The images of the floor cracking and thousands of oily, disfigured hands dragging me down into Noxohit's infinite tunnel surfaced in my memory. I went straight to the master bedroom – my corner of peace and harmony. I took off my dress and lay down under a warm duvet with Hairito, where my tired mind slowly drifted into the world of dreams.

I heard a voice.

My heart palpitated against my ribcage as I heard it again. Sulphurous, infernal, it was as if scraping metal were able to form words. And I didn't need to even hear it, for I felt some alien presence freezing the house.

I removed the blanket and slowly, silently crept into the living room. Every step I took filled my legs with lead until I found myself on all fours in front of the hearth.

The floor itself melted, transforming into a sticky, slimy mass. I looked at my reflection in the ebony goo and shuddered.

My reflection didn't.

It was smirking, narrowing its tar-black eyes, snakes crawling up its neck and face. The darkness was devouring my body like quicksand, slowly but steadily bringing my face closer to that smirking fiend, waiting for me inside the mass. My chin almost touched the goo when suddenly everything stopped. I looked into my reflection's eyes.

A hellish laughter of myriad voices reverberated from its mouth, which contorted in a venomous grin. 'Do not forget, Lilly White. I am still within.'

ACKNOWLEDGEMENTS

A tiny seed needs the warmth of the sun, the freshness of the air, the nutrient soil, water and time – a lot of time – to grow into a tree. And so an idea to transform into a finished book requires a tremendous effort and a team of people working together. If I was to mention every single person who helped me on this journey, my acknowledgement section would be longer than the novel itself.

The idea of this series came to me back in autumn 2018 when I first uncovered the spiritual treasure trove. It felt as if I had found a parallel world full of bliss and meaning. So first, I'd like to thank all those spiritual teachers who live to spread the knowledge of life. Their books and lectures inspired me to write this novel.

I'd like to thank Alla Vieru, my best friend, who was my very first beta reader back in winter 2020. Her love, warmth and patience have always been of monumental importance to me.

Any novel requires a shrewd analysis of professional editors and even more so if it is a debut novel. I can't thank Dave King enough – his support and praise became warmth and water to my seedling of a novel, which at some point started withering in an unforgiving winter of rejections. Also, Laura Kincaid's kindness, professionalism and eagerness to help aided me in each step of this journey, and I am so grateful for it.

And I would like to thank my family and friends, who believed in me when no one else did. I'm so grateful to my dearest friend Alan who is always there to listen my endless chatting and encourage me to pursue my dream.

My father's unconditional love and support has always been a safety blanket I could rely on.

I am lucky enough to have two guardian angels I know of. One is in the sky, but another one is still here – in our world. He is my muse – my wings. He makes me fly. None of this book would be possible – not a single chapter – without his unconditional support, patience and faith in me. I am eternally grateful to my husband, Anton, whose love is like a lighthouse that always guides me towards the sanctuary of the shore even in the darkest nights.

And last but not least, I'd like to thank my mother – the most loving, compassionate and resilient woman I knew. This book is dedicated to her and first published in 2023, on the day she would have turned sixty.

ABOUT THE AUTHOR

A Doctor of Philosophy, Yana spent years as a nano-researcher before diving into exploration of existential mysteries through fictional characters and magical worlds. Her debut series LUMINIFEROS unites contemporary fantasy and romance in a heartfelt journey of self-discovery, compassion and unconditional love. She lives in the urban jungles of London but dreams of lush coniferous forests stretching beneath leaden clouds that almost constantly curtain the sky.

FIND OUT MORE
WWW.YANAMETRO.COM

NOTES

NOTES

NOTES